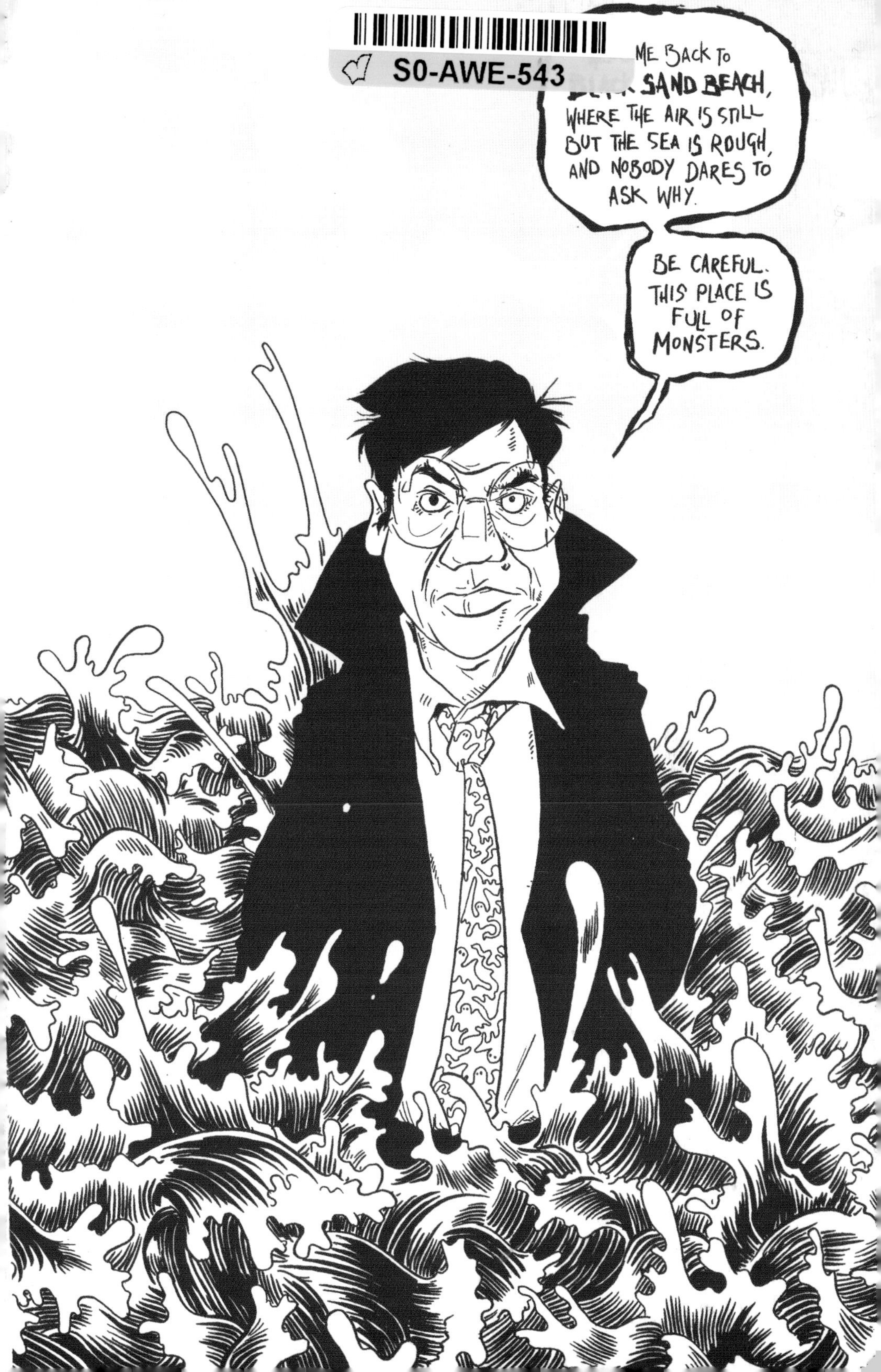
ME BACK TO SAND BEACH, WHERE THE AIR IS STILL BUT THE SEA IS ROUGH, AND NOBODY DARES TO ASK WHY.
BE CAREFUL. THIS PLACE IS FULL OF MONSTERS.

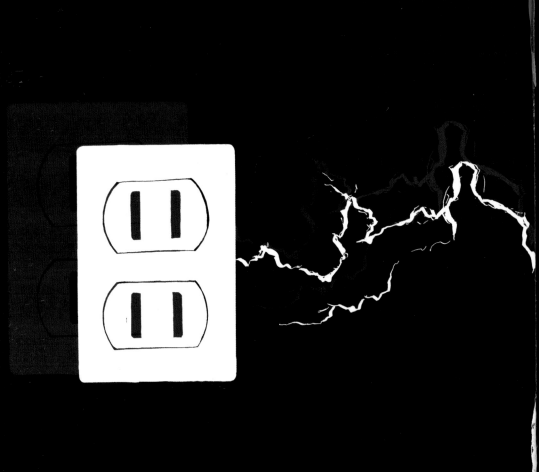

BLACK SAND BEACH

HAVE YOU SEEN THE DARKNESS?

BY RICHARD FAIRGRAY

For Dancer

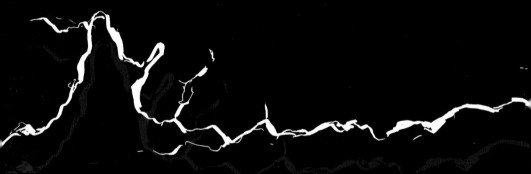

PIXEL INK

Text and Illustrations copyright © 2022 by Richard Fairgray
All rights reserved
Pixel+Ink is a division of TGM Development Corp
Printed and bound in January 2022 at Toppan Leefung, DongGuan, China.
Book design by Richard Fairgray
www.pixelandinkbooks.com

Library of Congress Cataloging-in-Publication Data

Names: Fairgray, Richard, 1985- author.
Title: Have you seen the darkness? / Richard Fairgray.
Description: First edition. | New York : Pixel+Ink, 2022. | Series: Black
Sand Beach ; 3 | Audience: Ages 8-12. | Audience: Grades 4-6. | Summary:
Told in alternating timelines, Dash and his friends try to use the
Darkness to capture the monster they accidentally freed, while in 1994
sisters Mabel and Kasey come face-to-face with the shapeshifting
creature their father is hunting.
Identifiers: LCCN 2021041404 (print) | LCCN 2021041405 (ebook) | ISBN
9781645950912 (hardcover) | ISBN 9781645950929 (paperback) | ISBN
9781645950936 (ebook)
Subjects: CYAC: Graphic novels. | Monsters--Fiction. |
Shapeshifting--Fiction. | LCGFT: Graphic novels.
Classification: LCC PZ7.7.F344 Hav 2022 (print) | LCC PZ7.7.F344 (ebook)
| DDC 741.5/993--dc23/eng/20211003
LC record available at https://lccn.loc.gov/2021041404
LC ebook record available at https://lccn.loc.gov/2021041405

First Edition
1 3 5 7 9 10 8 6 4 2

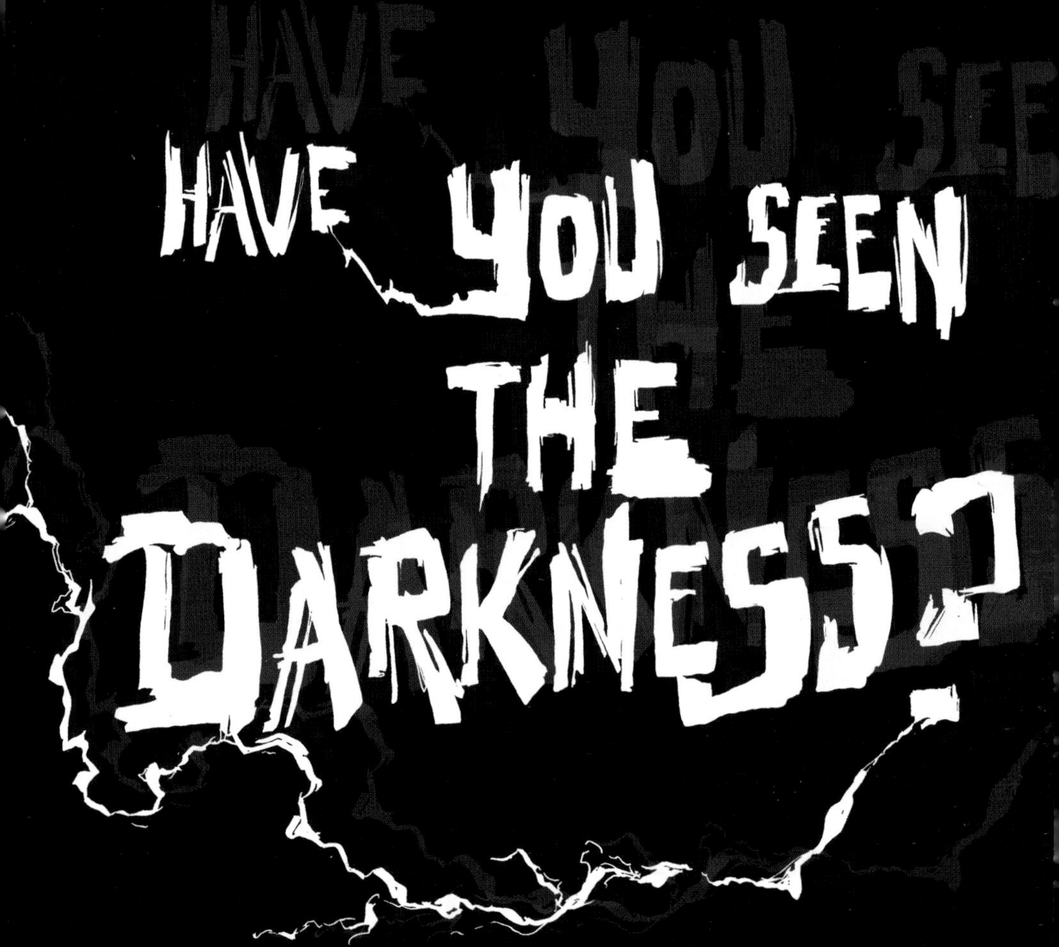
HAVE YOU SEEN THE DARKNESS?

PREVIOUSLY

After discovering his journal from the previous summer at Black Sand Beach, Dash thought he was finally going to be able to piece together the missing patches in his memory and (maybe) find out what it was that made him forget. But then Ramsays, the zombie sheep, grabbed the journal and disappeared into the woods.

The kids followed, picking up chewed fragments of the book along the way and reading parts of the story. It seems Dash had spent the previous summer bonding with his new stepmother and two local girls named Mabel and Kasey.

When they found Ramsays, he was caught in an ancient lock. As Dash read the rest of the journal, the kids debated whether or not to to help the trapped creature.

Mabel and Kasey turned out to be ghosts. They hadn't died, they'd just been near the Darkness for so long that they'd forgotten how to be alive. Dash had helped them, teaching them how to breathe again with the hope it might bring them fully back.

Of course, this is Black Sand Beach and things are never as they seem. Because Ramsays was not simply an unkillable zombie, he was something much, much worse.

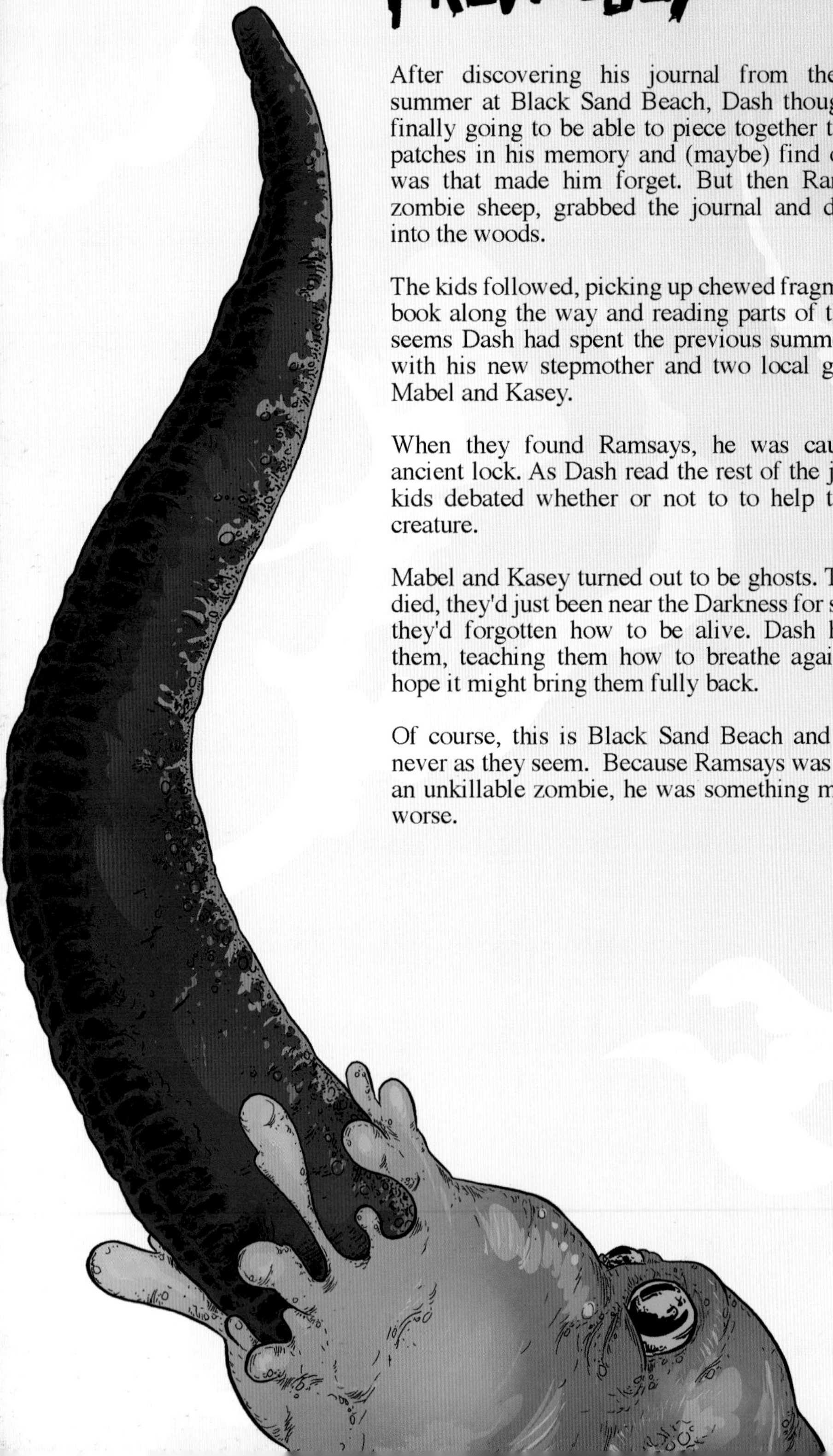

BEFORE THEY WERE

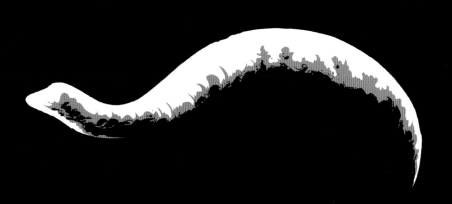

MONSTERS

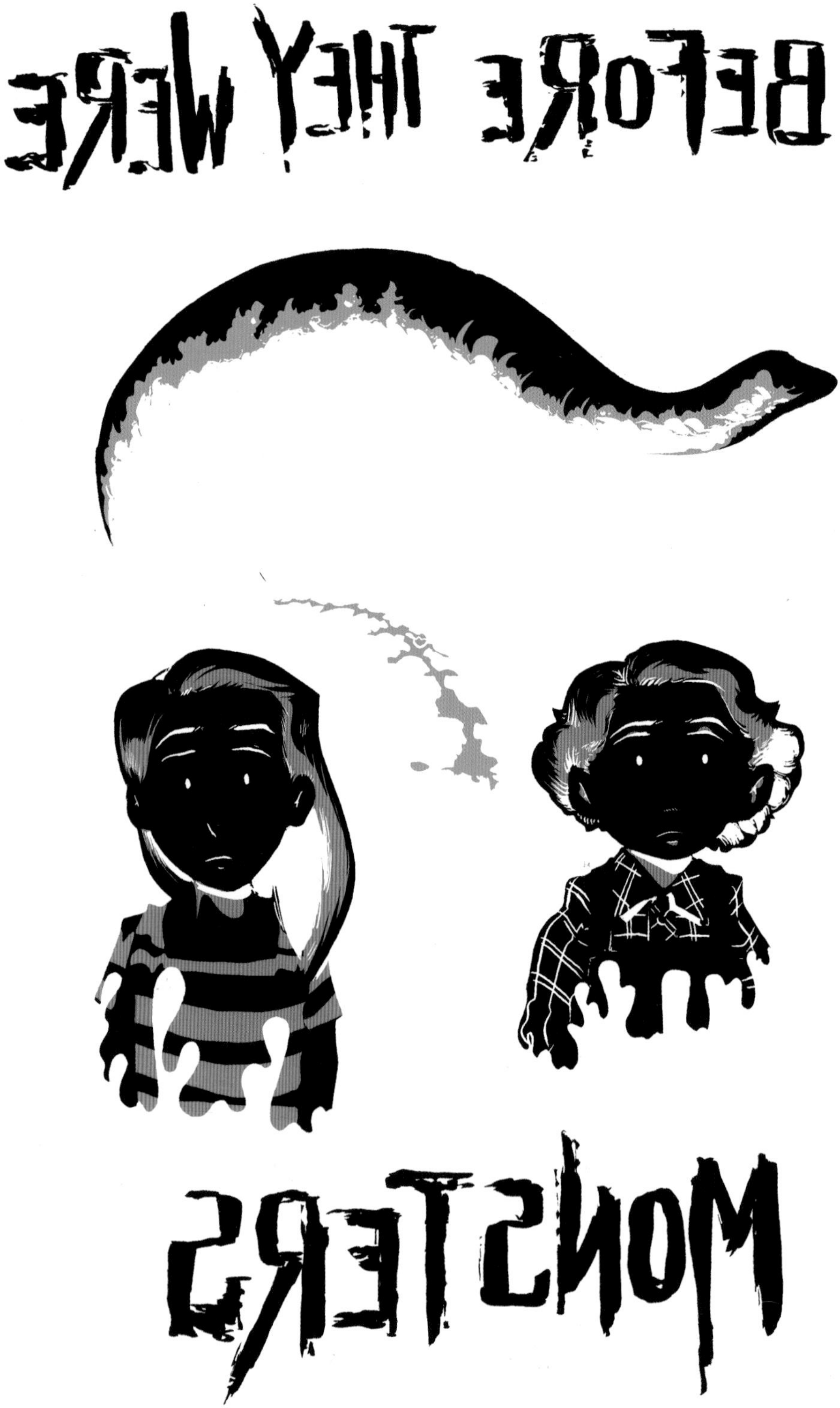
BEFORE THEY WERE
MONSTERS

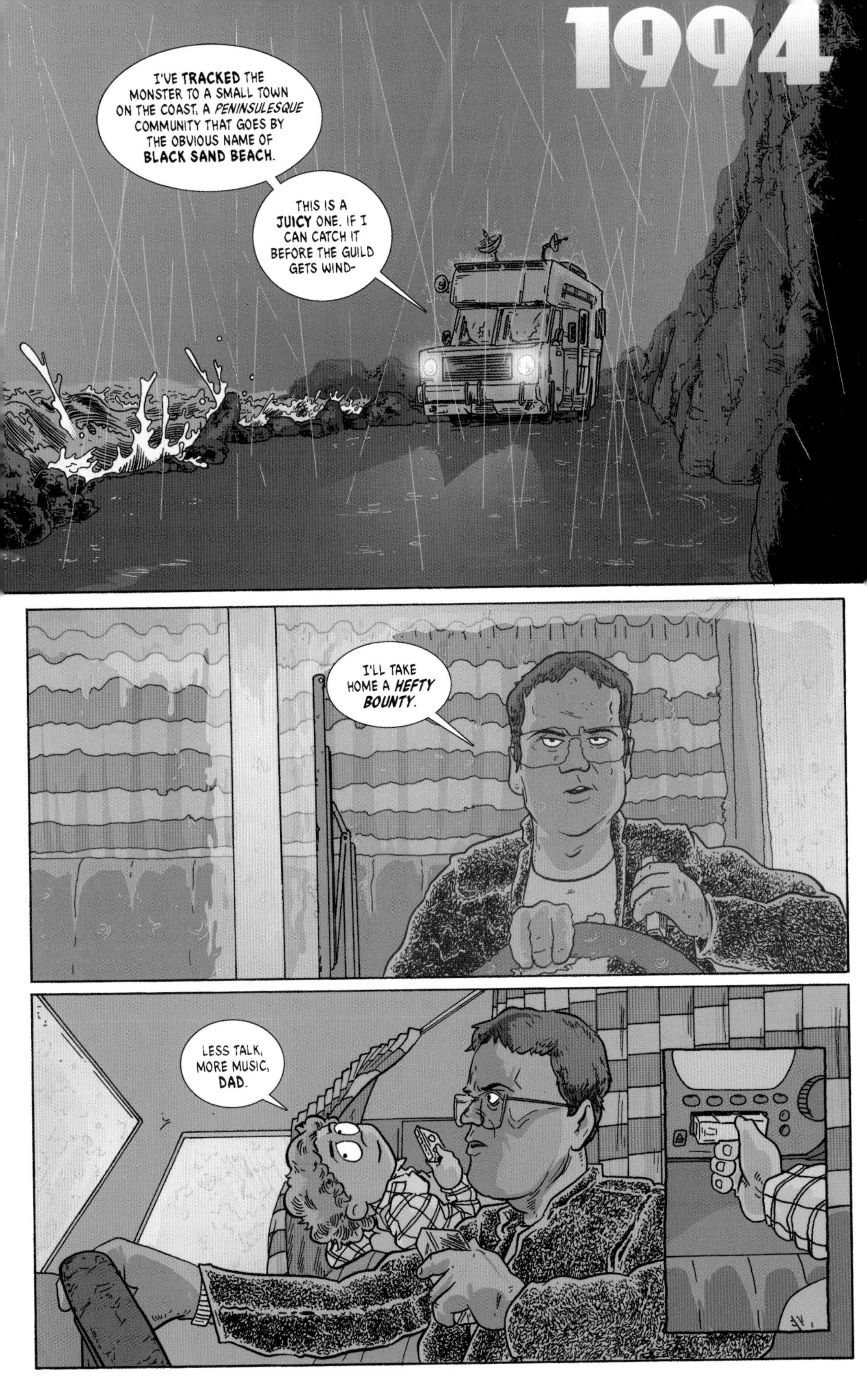
1994
I'VE TRACKED THE MONSTER TO A SMALL TOWN ON THE COAST, A PENINSULESQUE COMMUNITY THAT GOES BY THE OBVIOUS NAME OF BLACK SAND BEACH.
THIS IS A JUICY ONE. IF I CAN CATCH IT BEFORE THE GUILD GETS WIND-
I'LL TAKE HOME A HEFTY BOUNTY.
LESS TALK, MORE MUSIC, DAD.

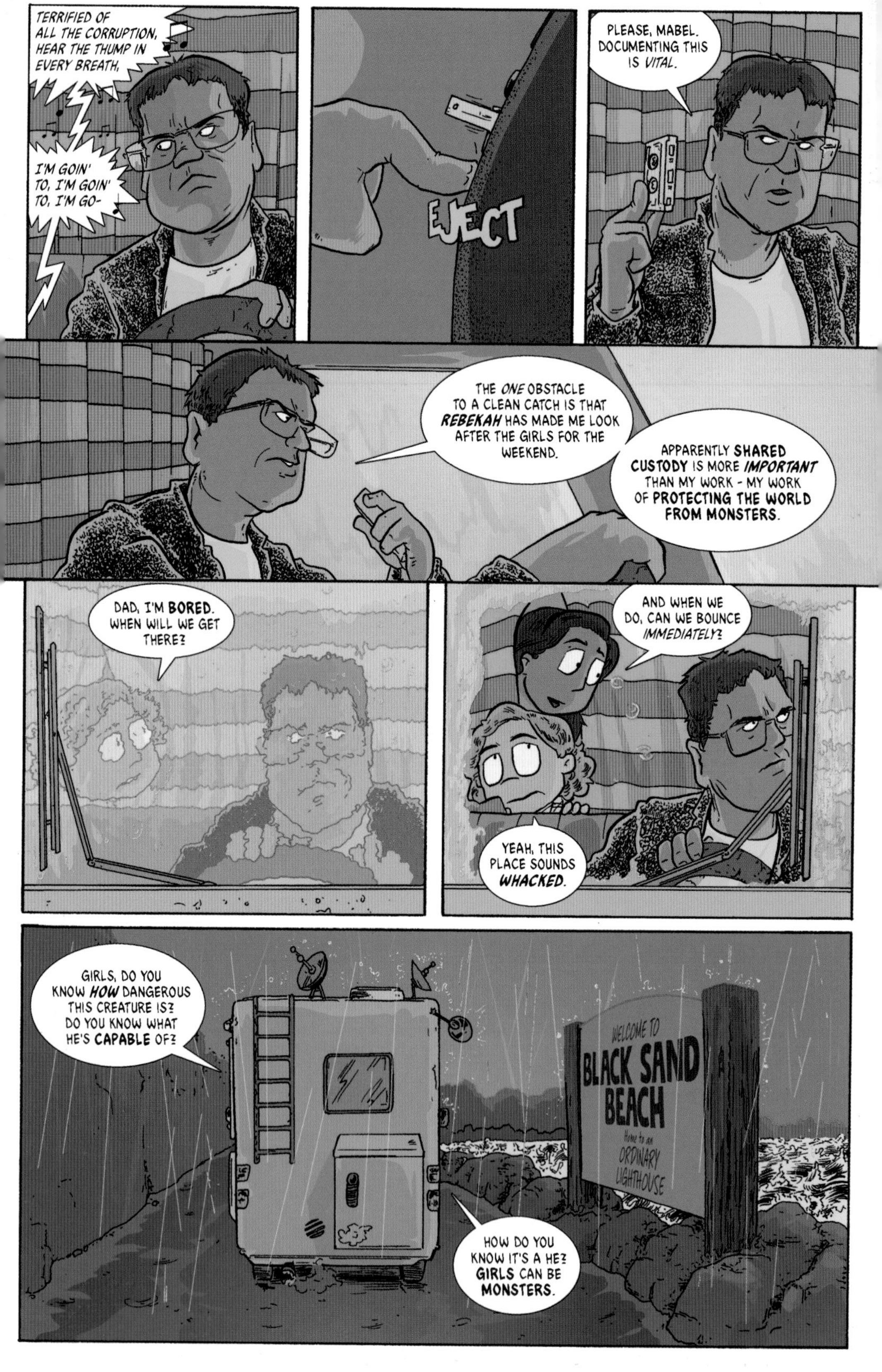
TERRIFIED OF ALL THE CORRUPTION, HEAR THE THUMP IN EVERY BREATH,
I'M GOIN' TO, I'M GOIN' TO, I'M GO-
EJECT
PLEASE, MABEL. DOCUMENTING THIS IS VITAL.
THE ONE OBSTACLE TO A CLEAN CATCH IS THAT REBEKAH HAS MADE ME LOOK AFTER THE GIRLS FOR THE WEEKEND.
APPARENTLY SHARED CUSTODY IS MORE IMPORTANT THAN MY WORK - MY WORK OF PROTECTING THE WORLD FROM MONSTERS.
DAD, I'M BORED. WHEN WILL WE GET THERE?
AND WHEN WE DO, CAN WE BOUNCE IMMEDIATELY?
YEAH, THIS PLACE SOUNDS WHACKED.
GIRLS, DO YOU KNOW HOW DANGEROUS THIS CREATURE IS? DO YOU KNOW WHAT HE'S CAPABLE OF?
WELCOME TO
BLACK SAND BEACH
Home to an
ORDINARY LIGHTHOUSE
HOW DO YOU KNOW IT'S A HE? GIRLS CAN BE MONSTERS.

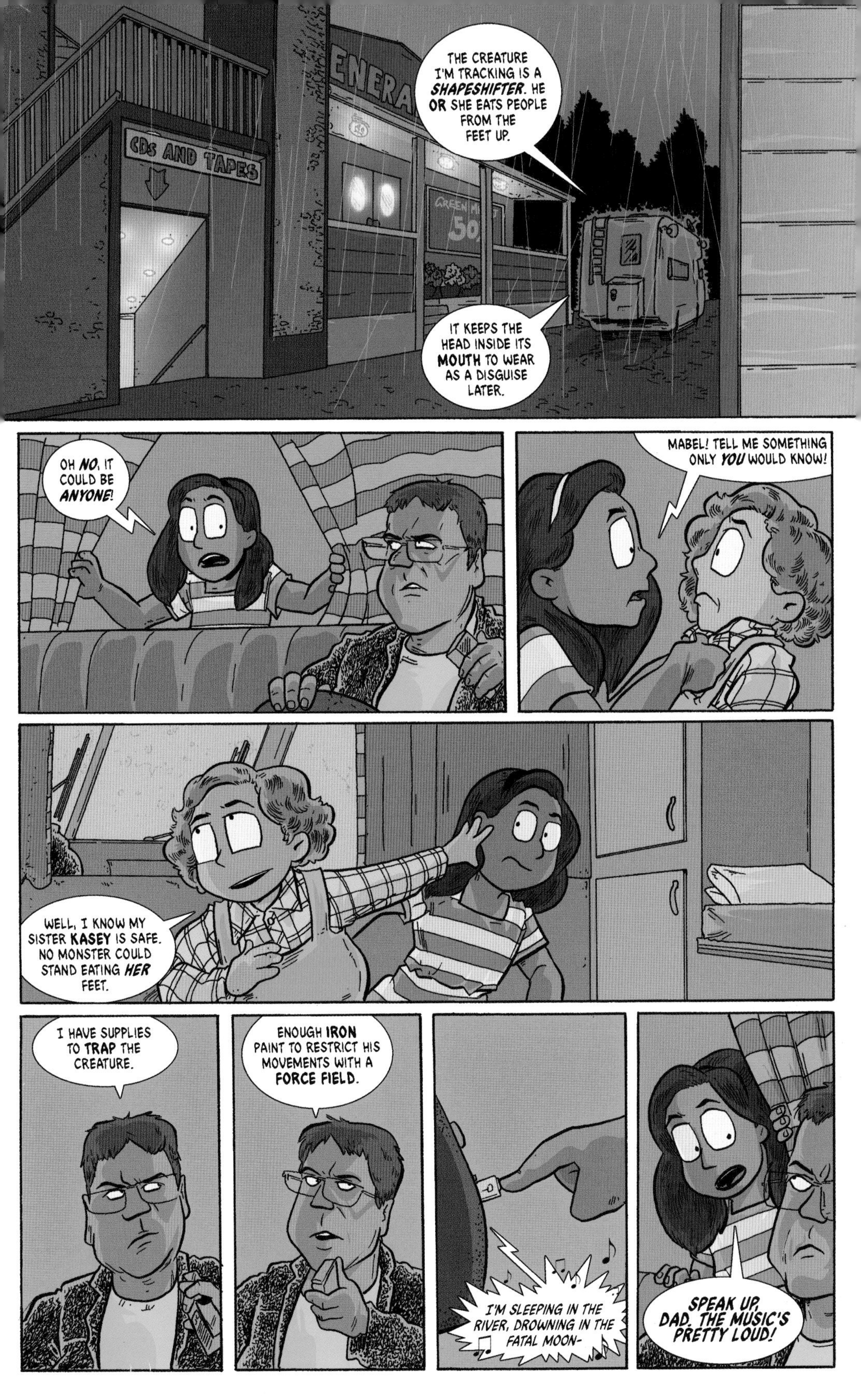
CDs AND TAPES
THE CREATURE I'M TRACKING IS A SHAPESHIFTER. HE OR SHE EATS PEOPLE FROM THE FEET UP.
IT KEEPS THE HEAD INSIDE ITS MOUTH TO WEAR AS A DISGUISE LATER.
OH NO, IT COULD BE ANYONE!
MABEL! TELL ME SOMETHING ONLY YOU WOULD KNOW!
WELL, I KNOW MY SISTER KASEY IS SAFE. NO MONSTER COULD STAND EATING HER FEET.
I HAVE SUPPLIES TO TRAP THE CREATURE.
ENOUGH IRON PAINT TO RESTRICT HIS MOVEMENTS WITH A FORCE FIELD.
I'M SLEEPING IN THE RIVER, DROWNING IN THE FATAL MOON-
SPEAK UP, DAD. THE MUSIC'S PRETTY LOUD!

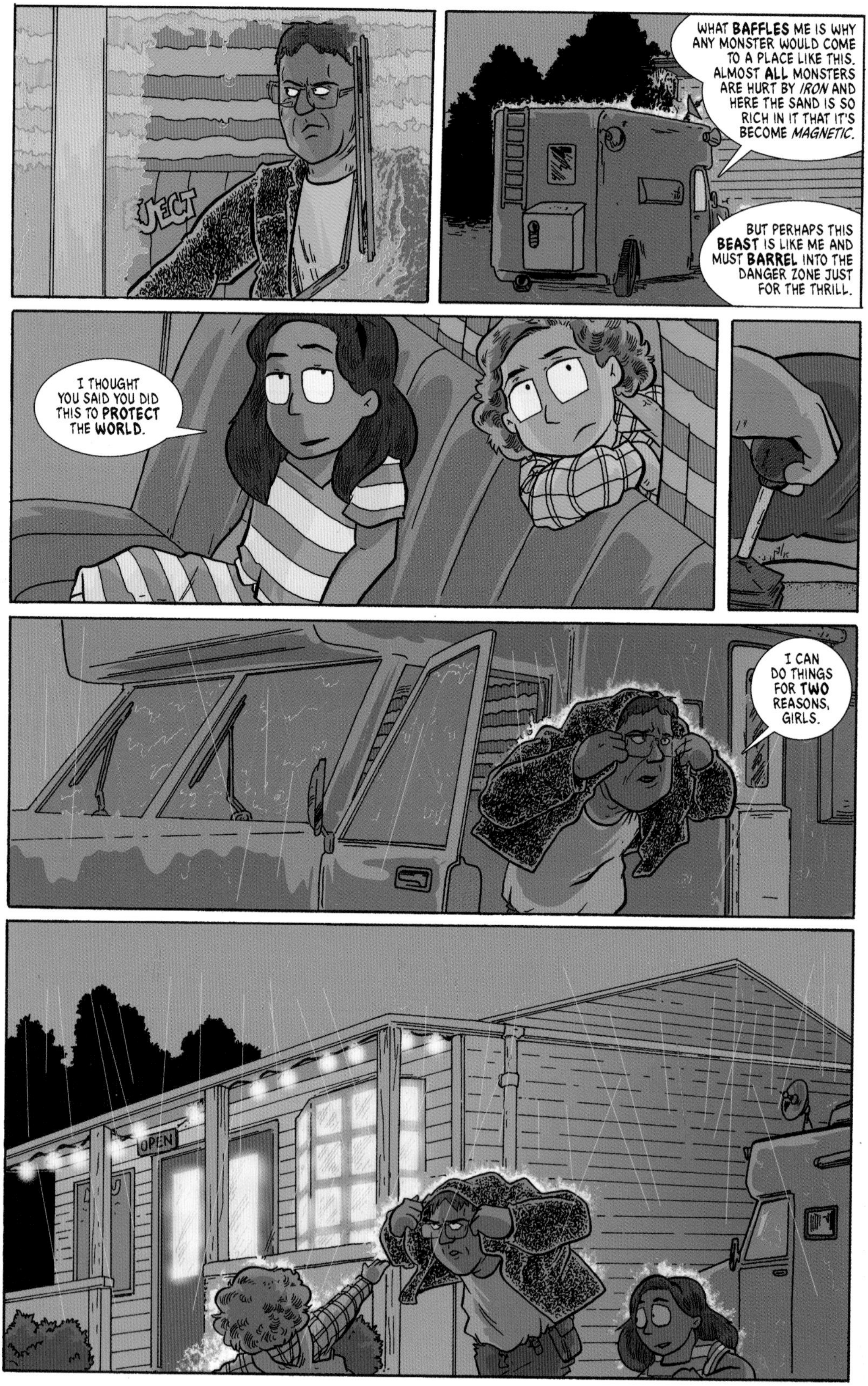

JECT
WHAT BAFFLES ME IS WHY ANY MONSTER WOULD COME TO A PLACE LIKE THIS. ALMOST ALL MONSTERS ARE HURT BY IRON AND HERE THE SAND IS SO RICH IN IT THAT IT'S BECOME MAGNETIC.
BUT PERHAPS THIS BEAST IS LIKE ME AND MUST BARREL INTO THE DANGER ZONE JUST FOR THE THRILL.
I THOUGHT YOU SAID YOU DID THIS TO PROTECT THE WORLD.
I CAN DO THINGS FOR TWO REASONS, GIRLS.
OPEN

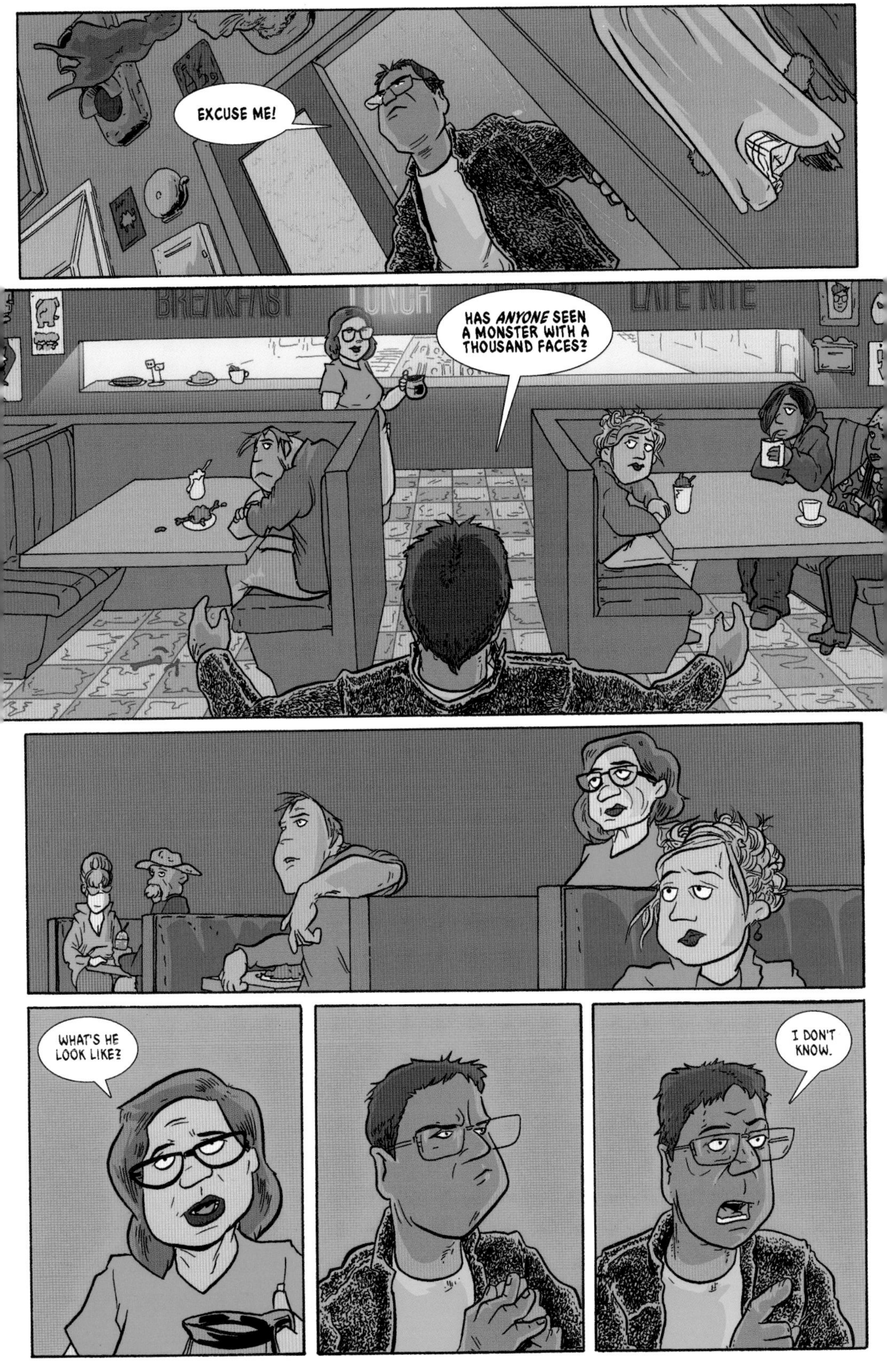
EXCUSE ME!
HAS ANYONE SEEN A MONSTER WITH A THOUSAND FACES?
WHAT'S HE LOOK LIKE?
I DON'T KNOW.

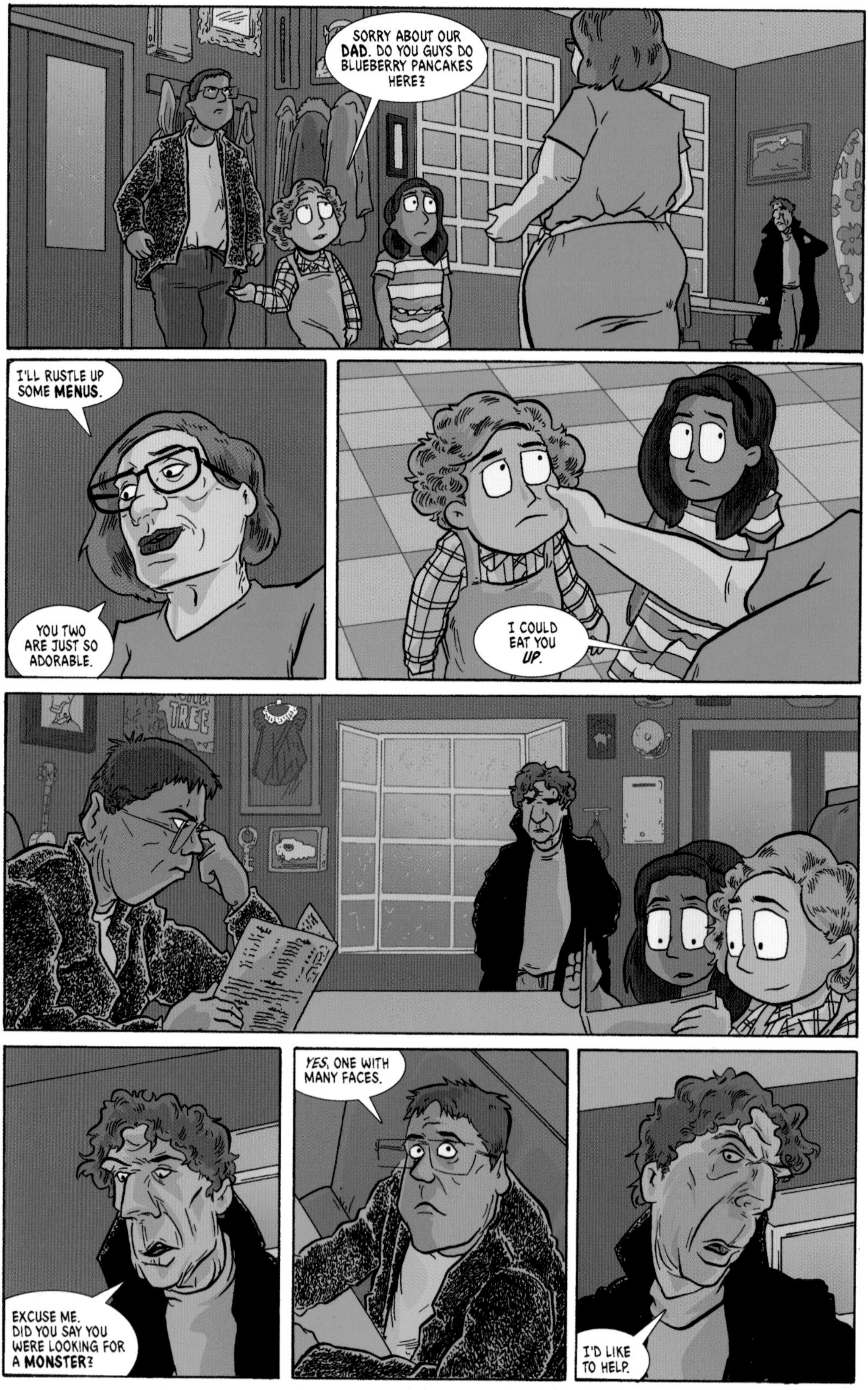
SORRY ABOUT OUR DAD. DO YOU GUYS DO BLUEBERRY PANCAKES HERE?
I'LL RUSTLE UP SOME MENUS.
YOU TWO ARE JUST SO ADORABLE.
I COULD EAT YOU UP.
TREE
EXCUSE ME. DID YOU SAY YOU WERE LOOKING FOR A MONSTER?
YES, ONE WITH MANY FACES.
I'D LIKE TO HELP.

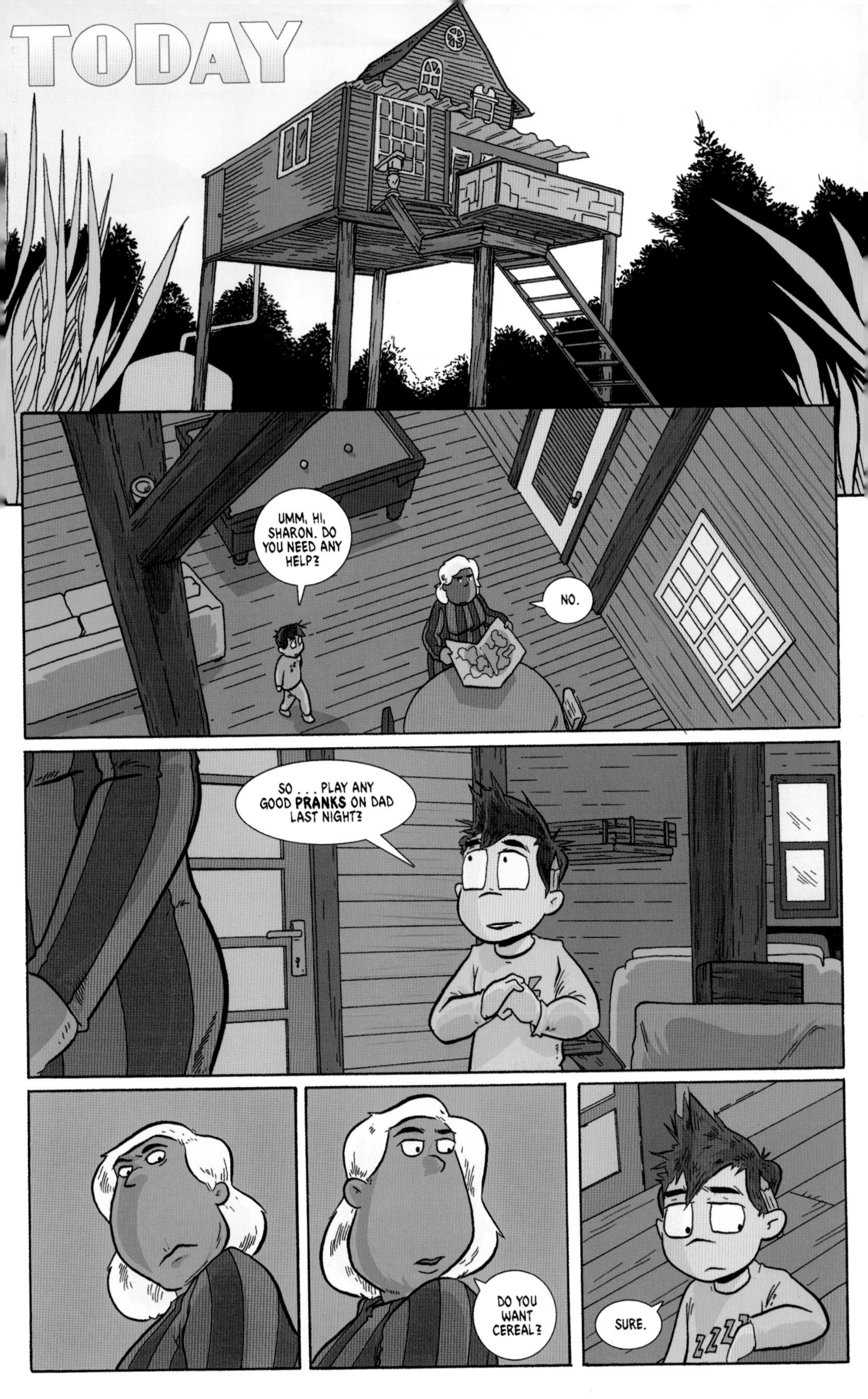
TODAY
UMM, HI, SHARON. DO YOU NEED ANY HELP?
NO.
SO . . . PLAY ANY GOOD **PRANKS** ON DAD LAST NIGHT?
DO YOU WANT CEREAL?
SURE.

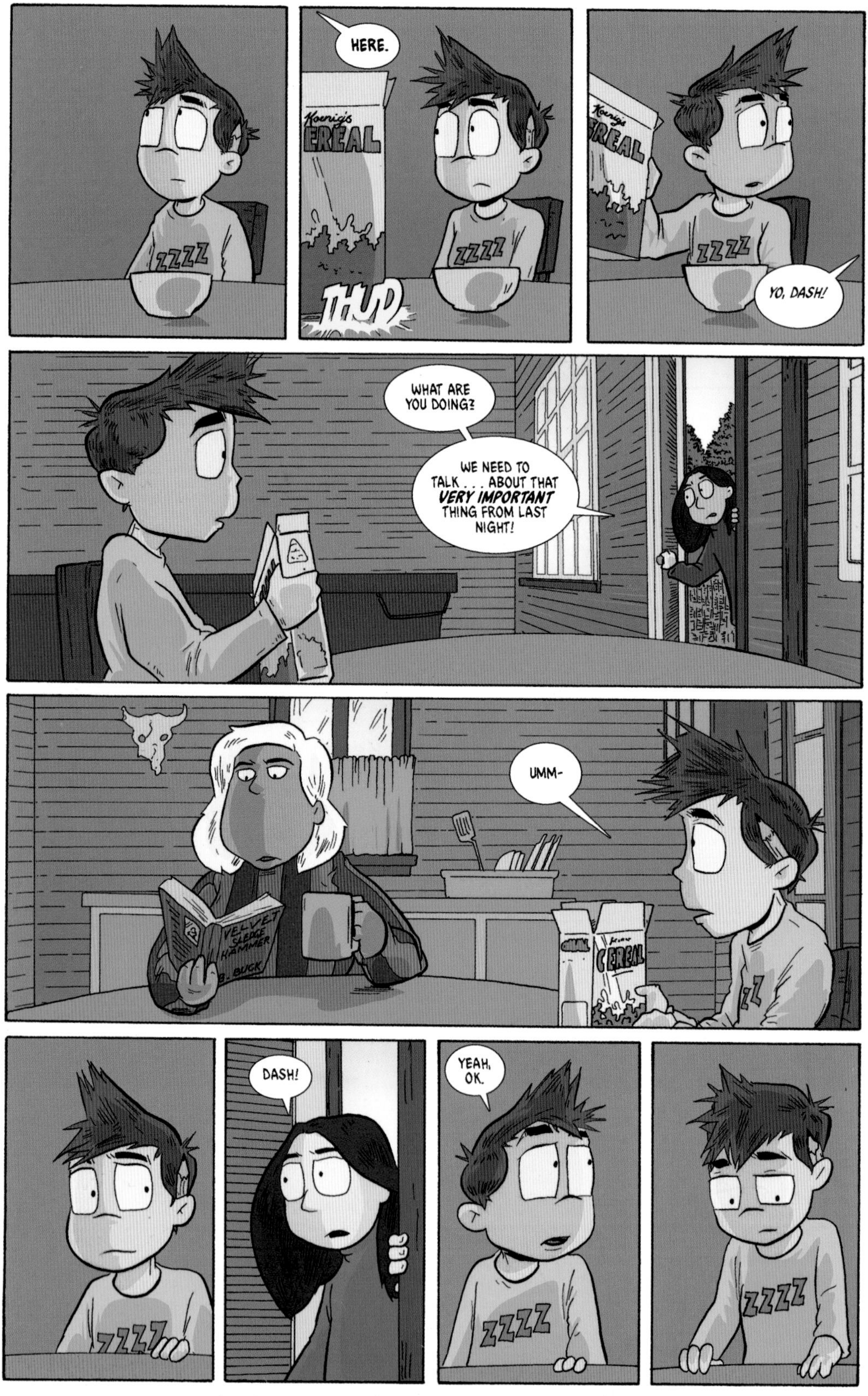
HERE.
Koenig's CEREAL
THUD
YO, DASH!
WHAT ARE YOU DOING?
WE NEED TO TALK . . . ABOUT THAT VERY IMPORTANT THING FROM LAST NIGHT!
VELVET SLEDGE HAMMER
B. BUCK
UMM-
CEREAL
DASH!
YEAH, OK.

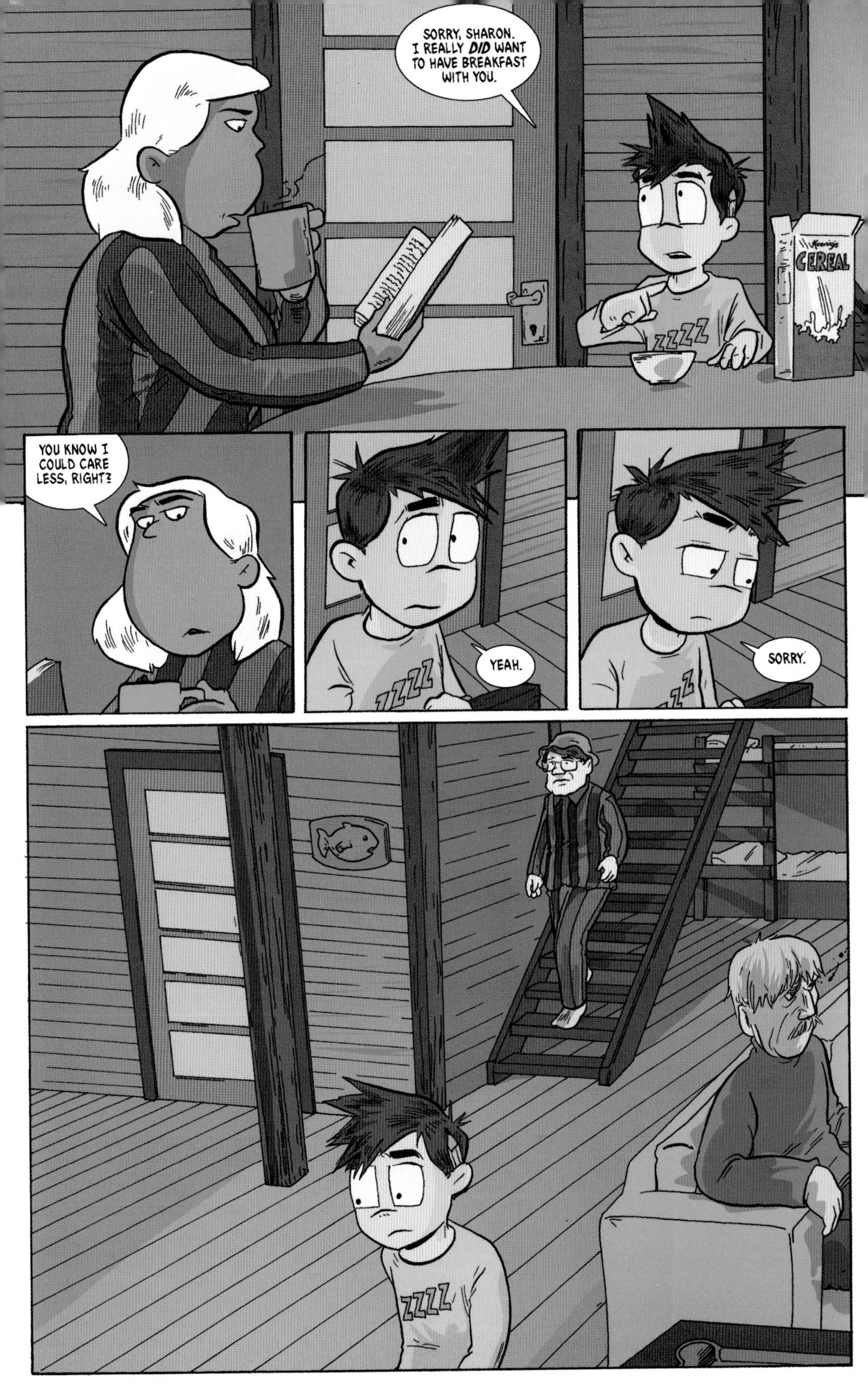
SORRY, SHARON. I REALLY DID WANT TO HAVE BREAKFAST WITH YOU.
CEREAL
ZZZZ
YOU KNOW I COULD CARE LESS, RIGHT?
YEAH.
SORRY.

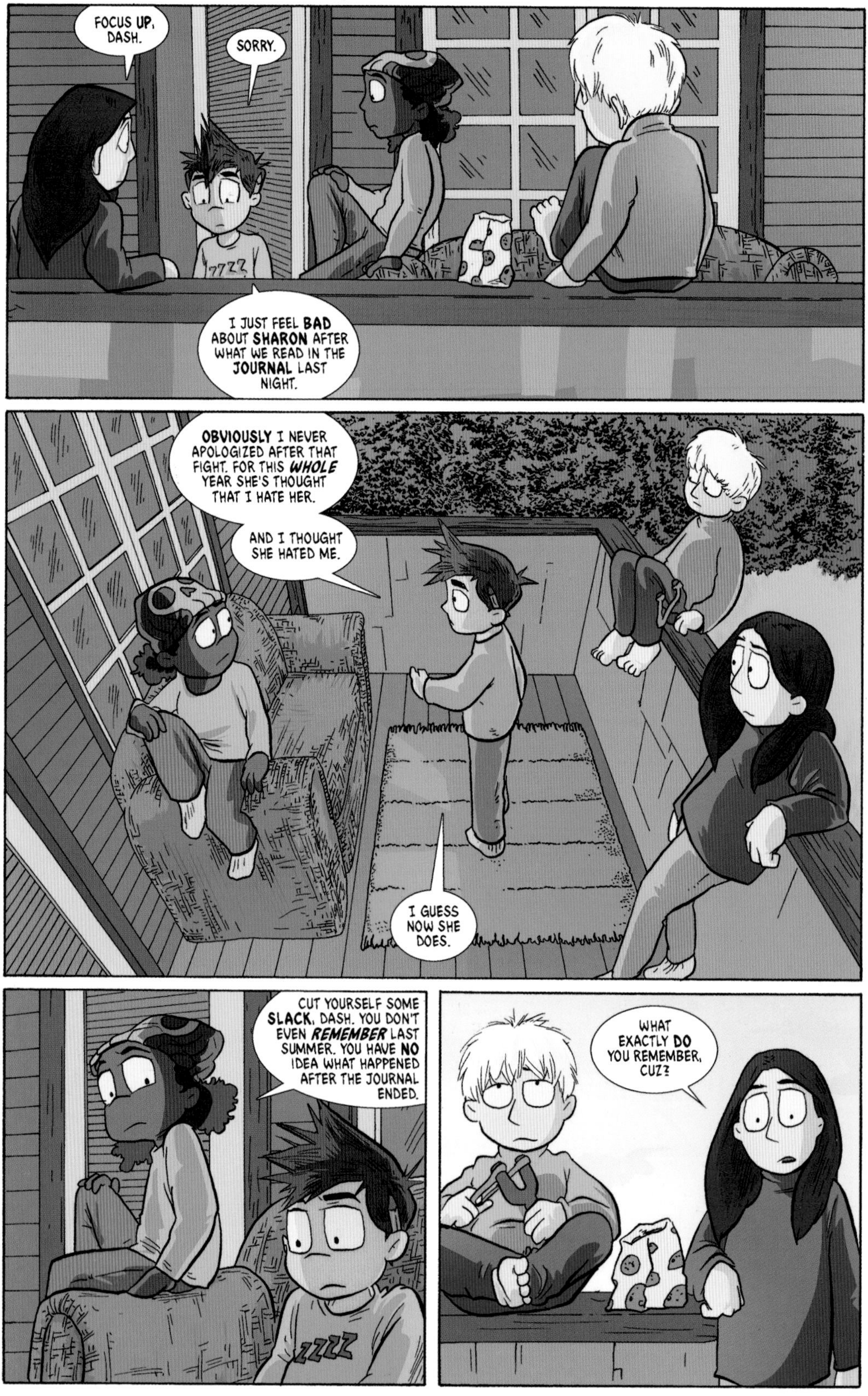
FOCUS UP, DASH.
SORRY.
I JUST FEEL BAD ABOUT SHARON AFTER WHAT WE READ IN THE JOURNAL LAST NIGHT.
OBVIOUSLY I NEVER APOLOGIZED AFTER THAT FIGHT. FOR THIS WHOLE YEAR SHE'S THOUGHT THAT I HATE HER.
AND I THOUGHT SHE HATED ME.
I GUESS NOW SHE DOES.
CUT YOURSELF SOME SLACK, DASH. YOU DON'T EVEN REMEMBER LAST SUMMER. YOU HAVE NO IDEA WHAT HAPPENED AFTER THE JOURNAL ENDED.
WHAT EXACTLY DO YOU REMEMBER, CUZ?

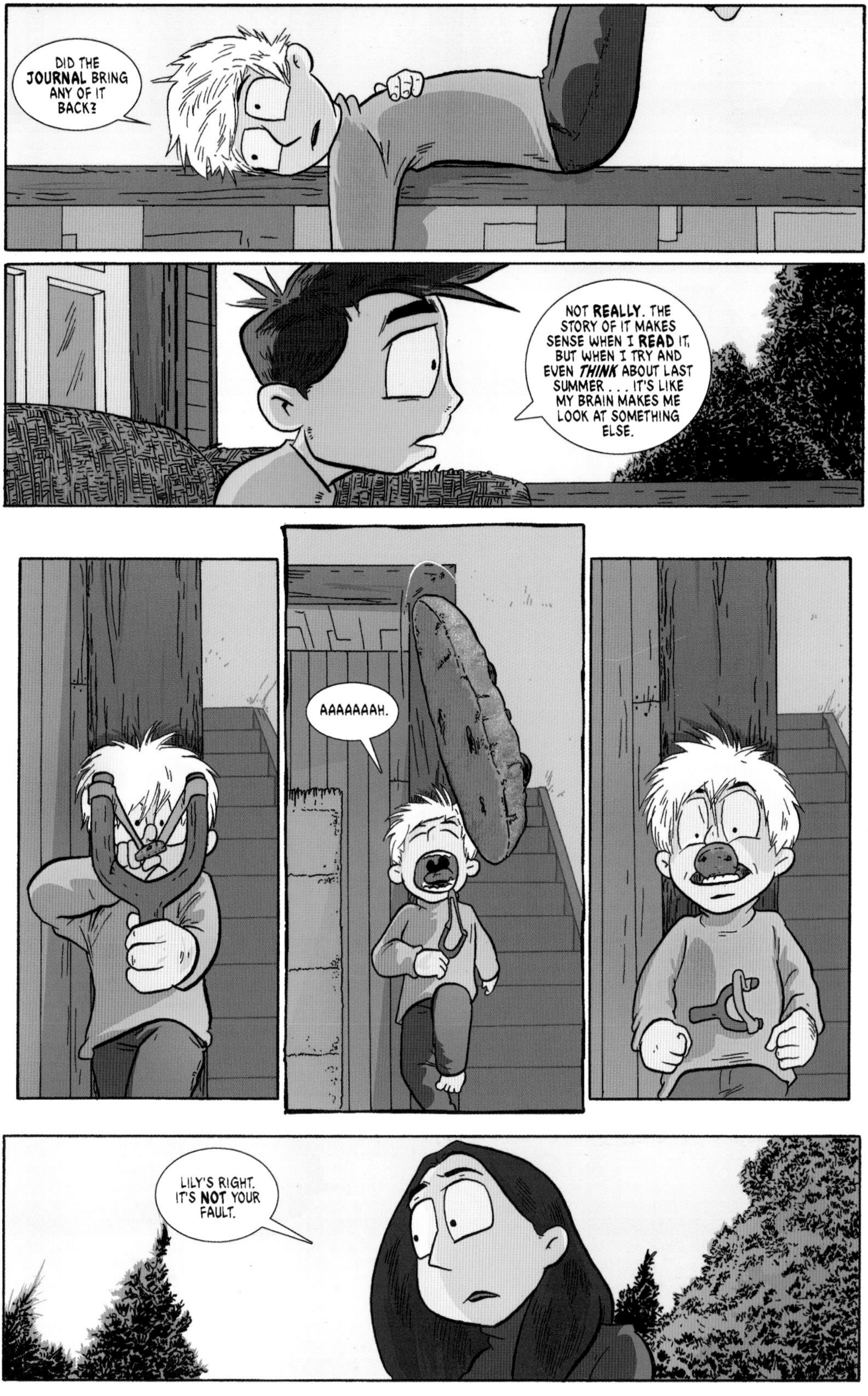
DID THE **JOURNAL** BRING ANY OF IT BACK?
NOT **REALLY**. THE STORY OF IT MAKES SENSE WHEN I **READ** IT, BUT WHEN I TRY AND EVEN ***THINK*** ABOUT LAST SUMMER . . . IT'S LIKE MY BRAIN MAKES ME LOOK AT SOMETHING ELSE.
AAAAAAAH.
LILY'S RIGHT. IT'S **NOT** YOUR FAULT.

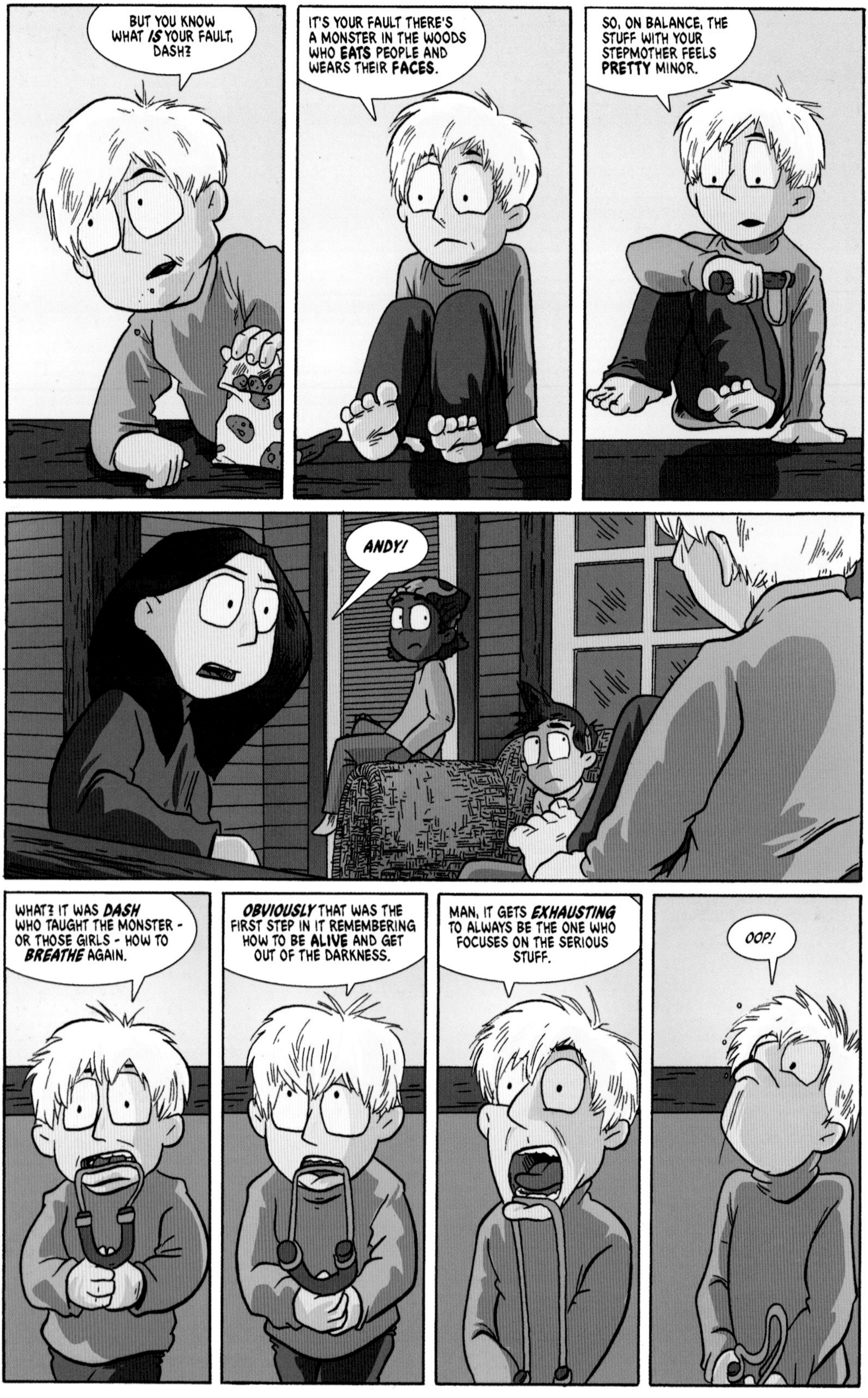
BUT YOU KNOW WHAT *IS* YOUR FAULT, DASH?
IT'S YOUR FAULT THERE'S A MONSTER IN THE WOODS WHO **EATS** PEOPLE AND WEARS THEIR **FACES**.
SO, ON BALANCE, THE STUFF WITH YOUR STEPMOTHER FEELS **PRETTY** MINOR.
ANDY!
WHAT? IT WAS *DASH* WHO TAUGHT THE MONSTER - OR THOSE GIRLS - HOW TO *BREATHE* AGAIN.
OBVIOUSLY THAT WAS THE FIRST STEP IN IT REMEMBERING HOW TO BE **ALIVE** AND GET OUT OF THE DARKNESS.
MAN, IT GETS *EXHAUSTING* TO ALWAYS BE THE ONE WHO FOCUSES ON THE SERIOUS STUFF.
OOP!

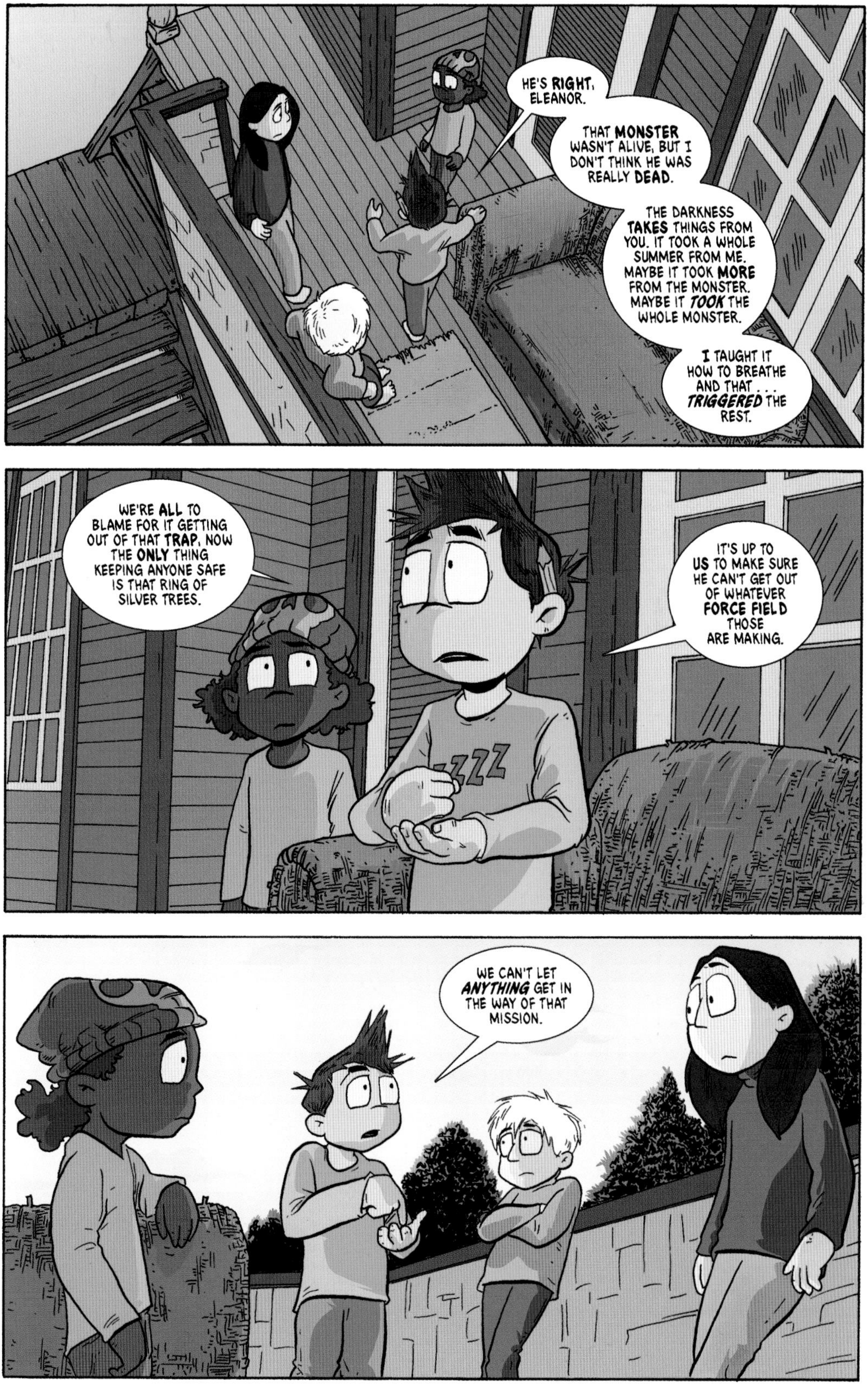
HE'S **RIGHT**, ELEANOR.
THAT **MONSTER** WASN'T ALIVE, BUT I DON'T THINK HE WAS REALLY **DEAD**.
THE DARKNESS **TAKES** THINGS FROM YOU. IT TOOK A WHOLE SUMMER FROM ME. MAYBE IT TOOK **MORE** FROM THE MONSTER. MAYBE IT ***TOOK*** THE WHOLE MONSTER.
I TAUGHT IT HOW TO BREATHE AND THAT . . . ***TRIGGERED*** THE REST.
WE'RE **ALL** TO BLAME FOR IT GETTING OUT OF THAT **TRAP**. NOW THE **ONLY** THING KEEPING ANYONE SAFE IS THAT RING OF SILVER TREES.
IT'S UP TO **US** TO MAKE SURE HE CAN'T GET OUT OF WHATEVER **FORCE FIELD** THOSE ARE MAKING.
WE CAN'T LET ***ANYTHING*** GET IN THE WAY OF THAT MISSION.

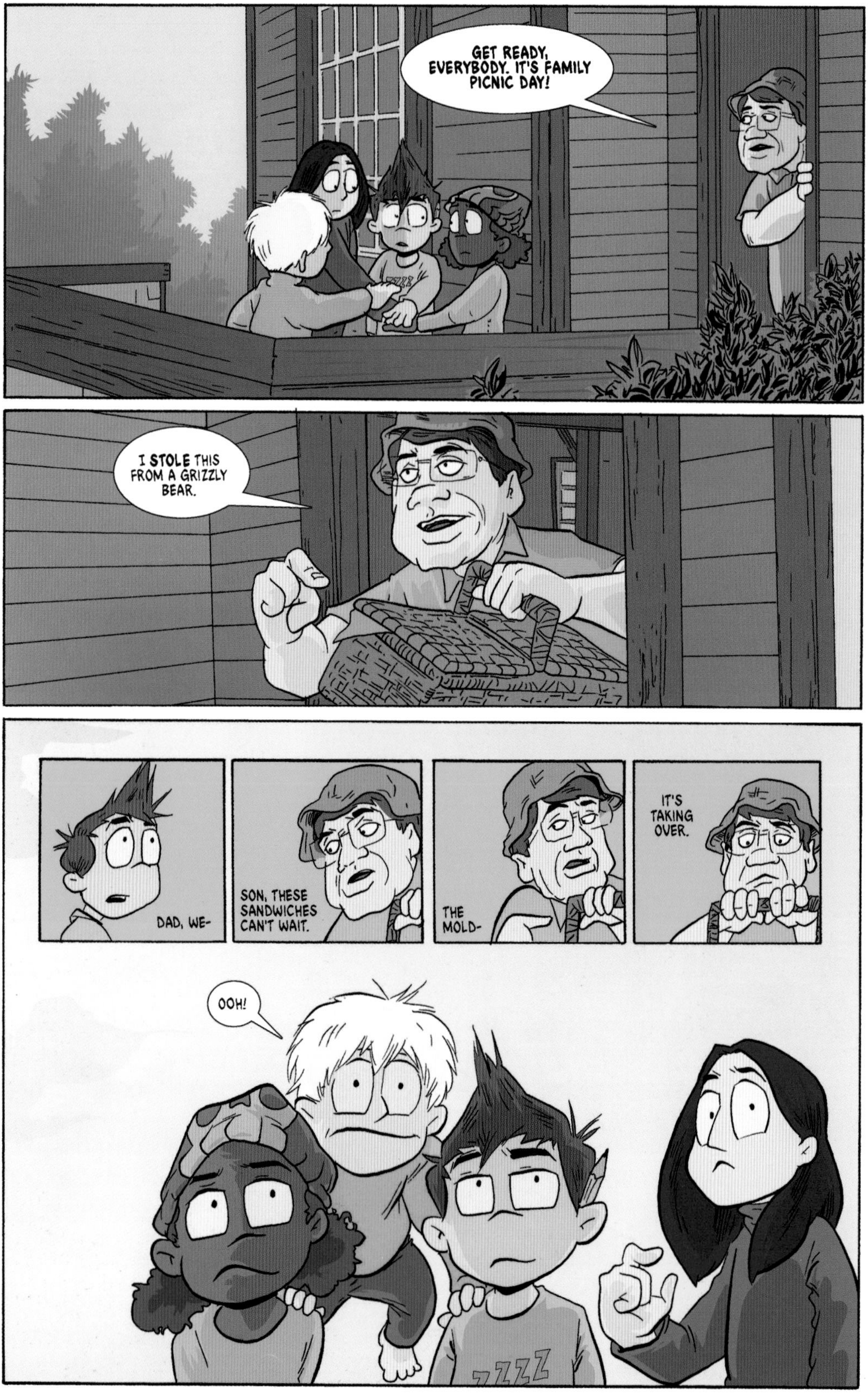
GET READY, EVERYBODY. IT'S FAMILY PICNIC DAY!
I STOLE THIS FROM A GRIZZLY BEAR.
DAD, WE-
SON, THESE SANDWICHES CAN'T WAIT.
THE MOLD-
IT'S TAKING OVER.
OOH!

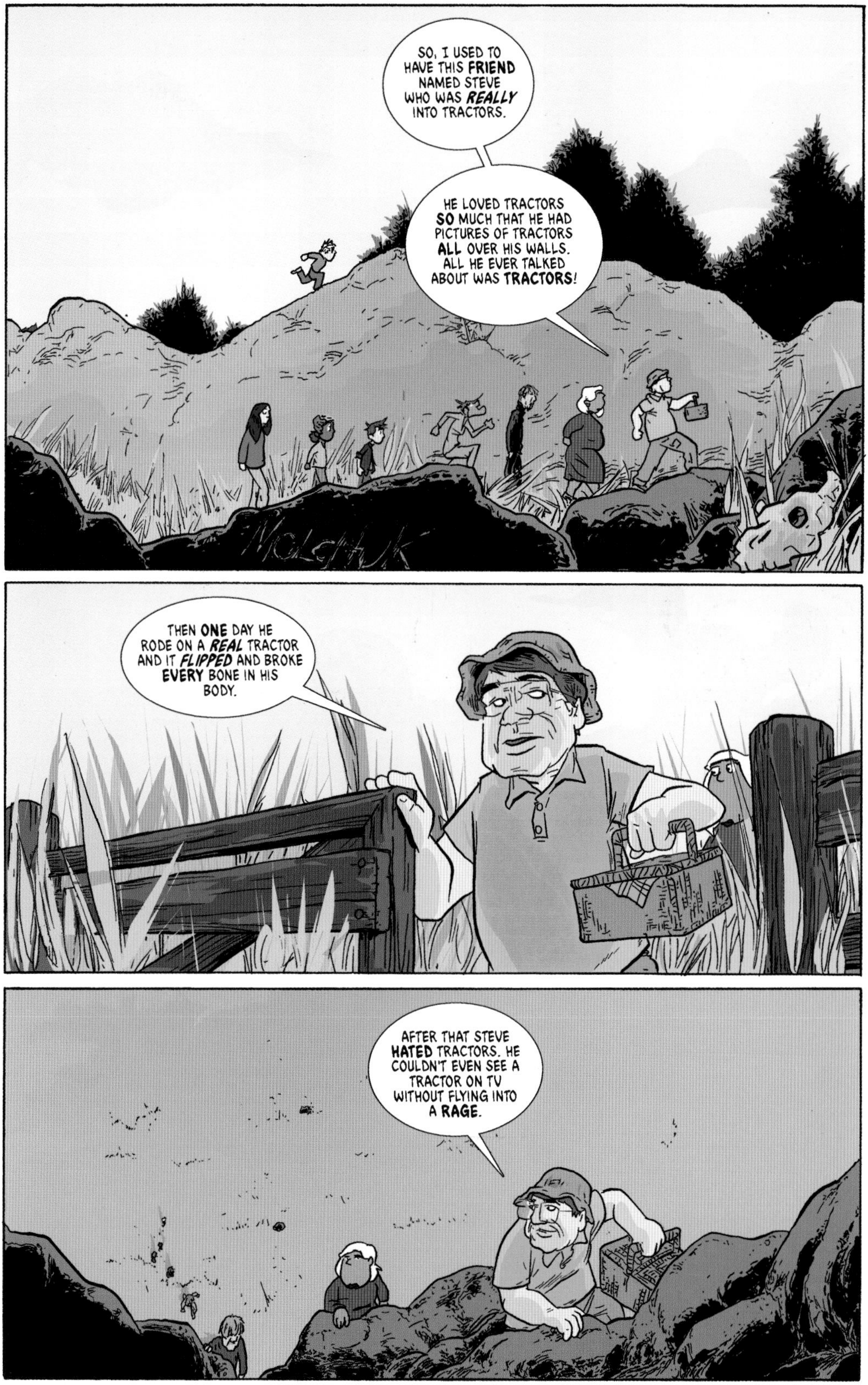
SO, I USED TO HAVE THIS FRIEND NAMED STEVE WHO WAS REALLY INTO TRACTORS.
HE LOVED TRACTORS SO MUCH THAT HE HAD PICTURES OF TRACTORS ALL OVER HIS WALLS. ALL HE EVER TALKED ABOUT WAS TRACTORS!
THEN ONE DAY HE RODE ON A REAL TRACTOR AND IT FLIPPED AND BROKE EVERY BONE IN HIS BODY.
AFTER THAT STEVE HATED TRACTORS. HE COULDN'T EVEN SEE A TRACTOR ON TV WITHOUT FLYING INTO A RAGE.

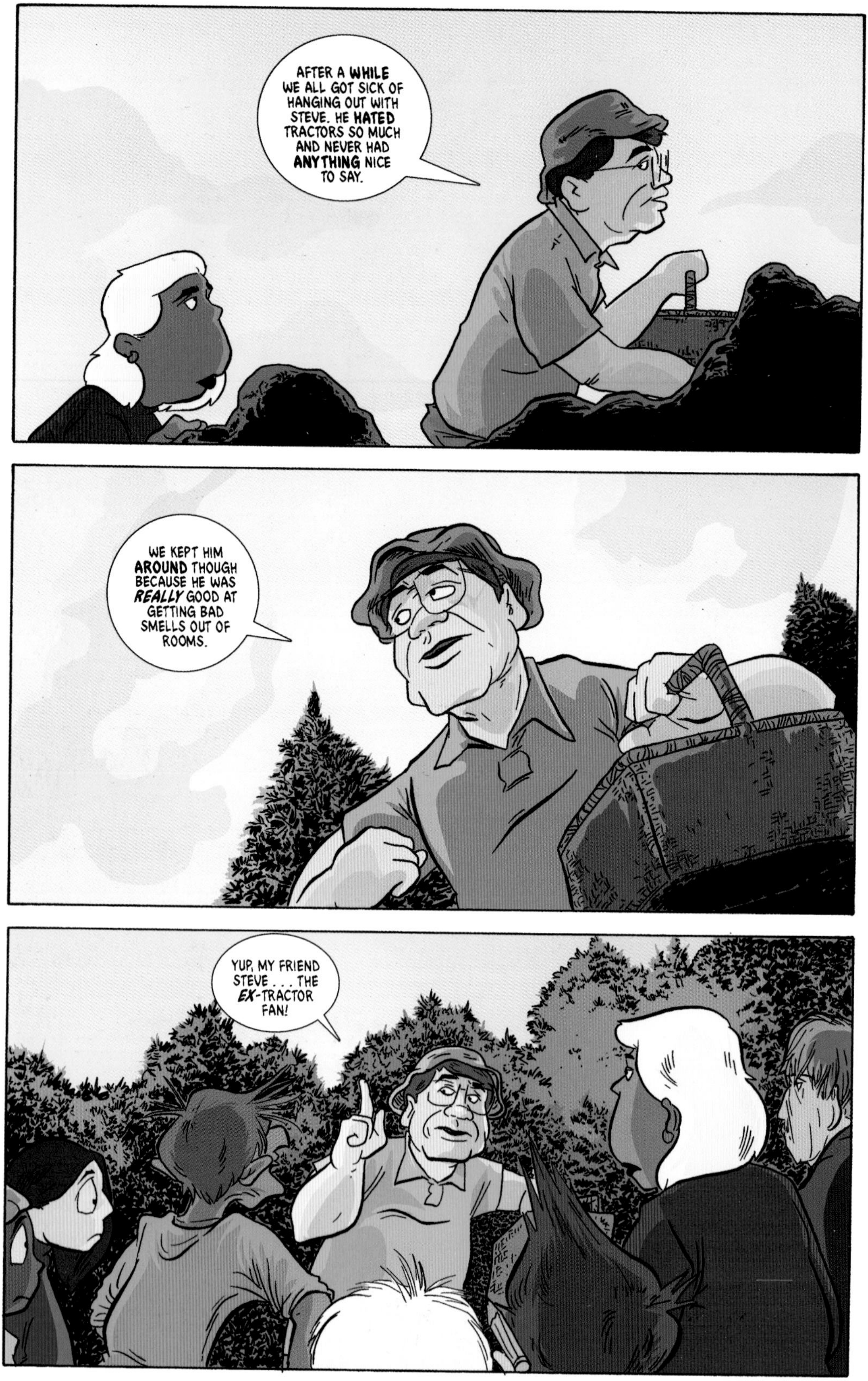
AFTER A WHILE WE ALL GOT SICK OF HANGING OUT WITH STEVE. HE HATED TRACTORS SO MUCH AND NEVER HAD ANYTHING NICE TO SAY.
WE KEPT HIM AROUND THOUGH BECAUSE HE WAS REALLY GOOD AT GETTING BAD SMELLS OUT OF ROOMS.
YUP, MY FRIEND STEVE . . . THE EX-TRACTOR FAN!

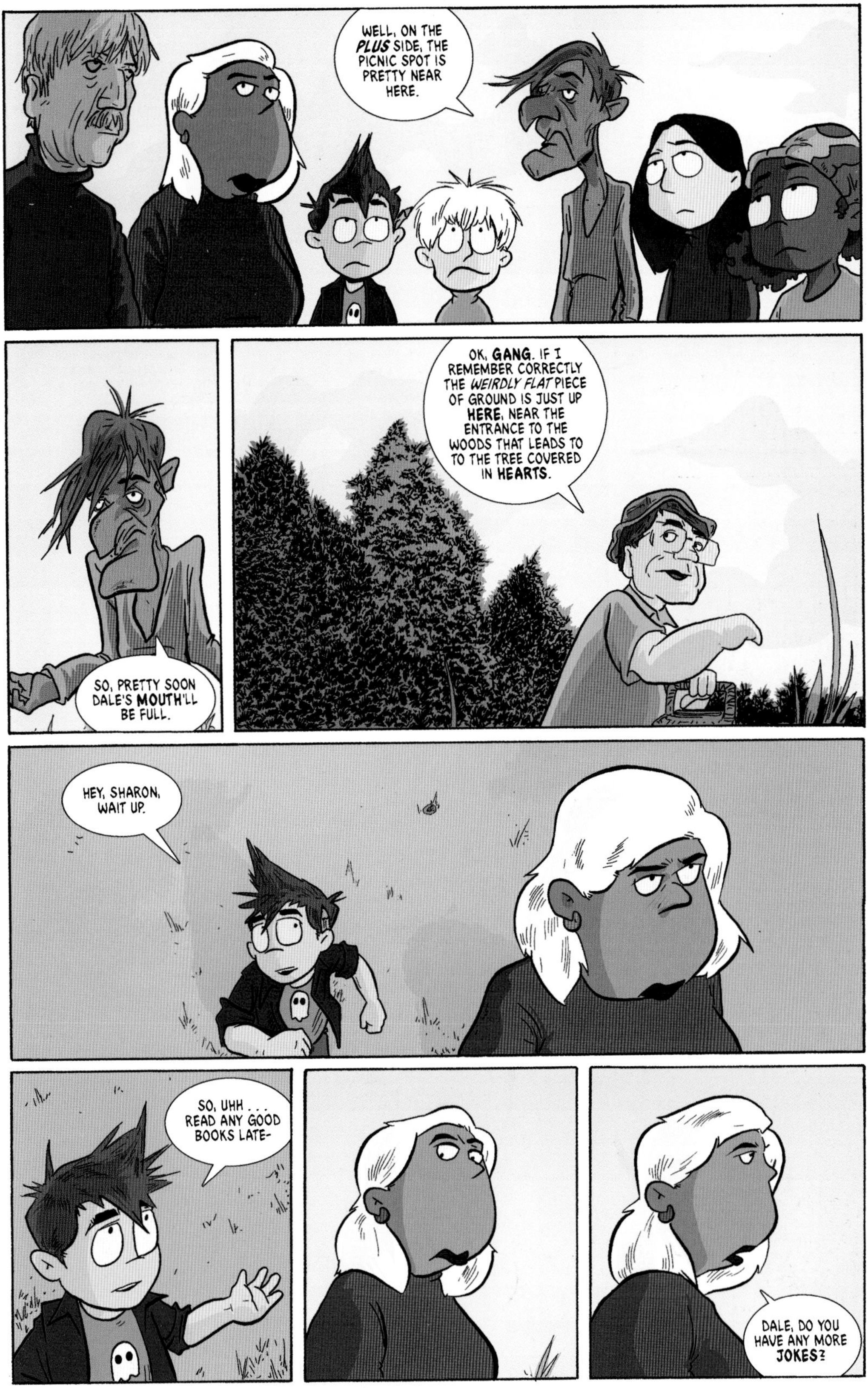
WELL, ON THE PLUS SIDE, THE PICNIC SPOT IS PRETTY NEAR HERE.
SO, PRETTY SOON DALE'S MOUTH'LL BE FULL.
OK, GANG. IF I REMEMBER CORRECTLY THE WEIRDLY FLAT PIECE OF GROUND IS JUST UP HERE, NEAR THE ENTRANCE TO THE WOODS THAT LEADS TO TO THE TREE COVERED IN HEARTS.
HEY, SHARON, WAIT UP.
SO, UHH . . . READ ANY GOOD BOOKS LATE-
DALE, DO YOU HAVE ANY MORE JOKES?

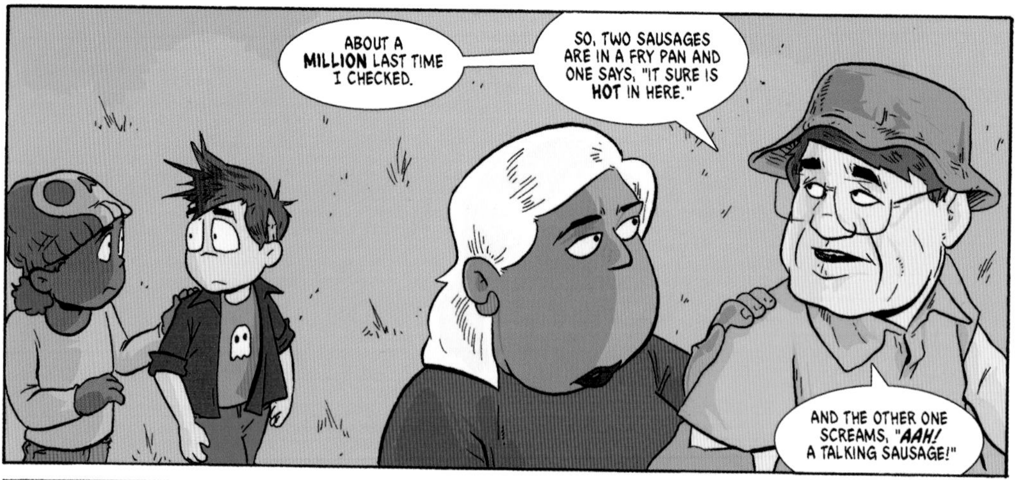
ABOUT A **MILLION** LAST TIME I CHECKED.
SO, TWO SAUSAGES ARE IN A FRY PAN AND ONE SAYS, "IT SURE IS **HOT** IN HERE."
AND THE OTHER ONE SCREAMS, "***AAH!*** A TALKING SAUSAGE!"

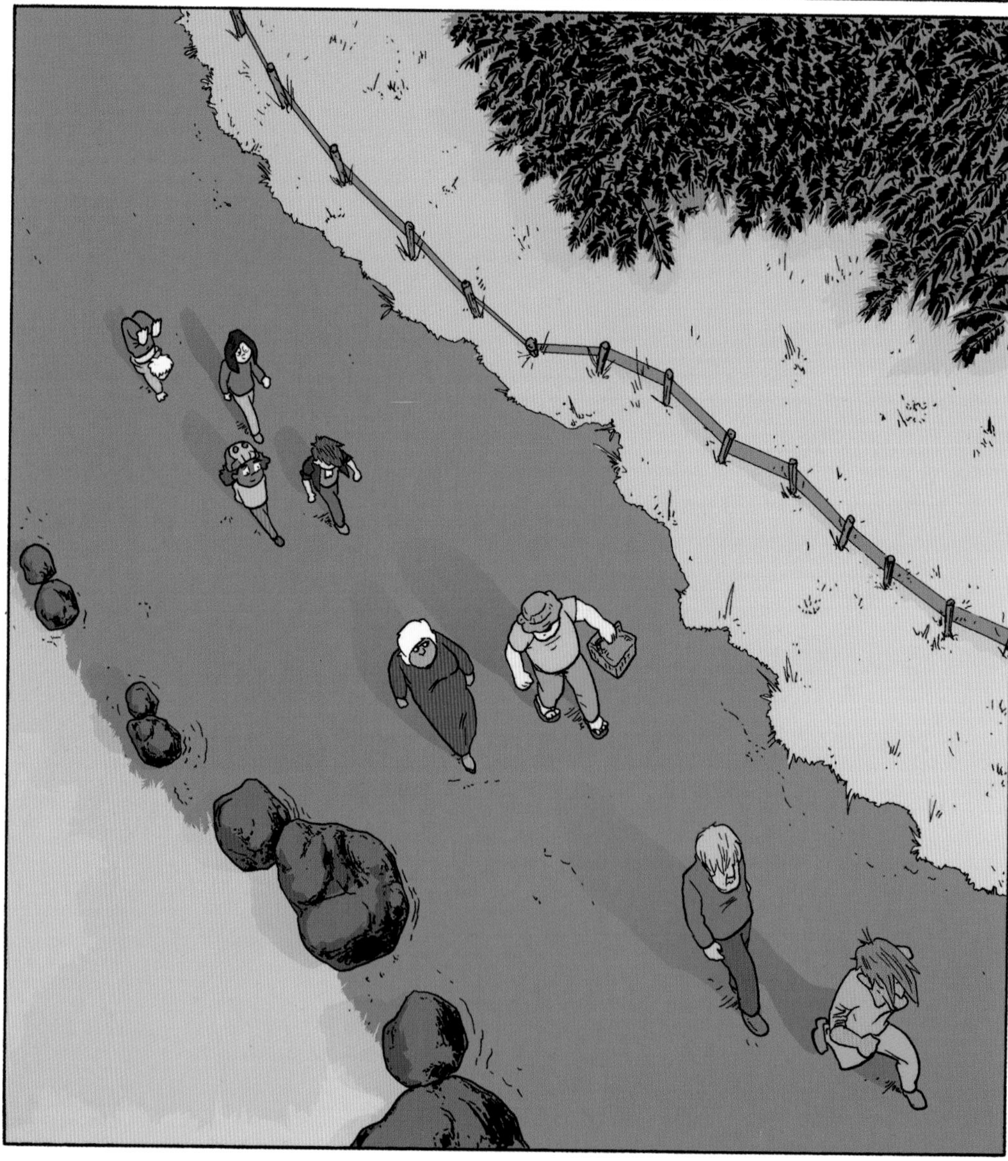

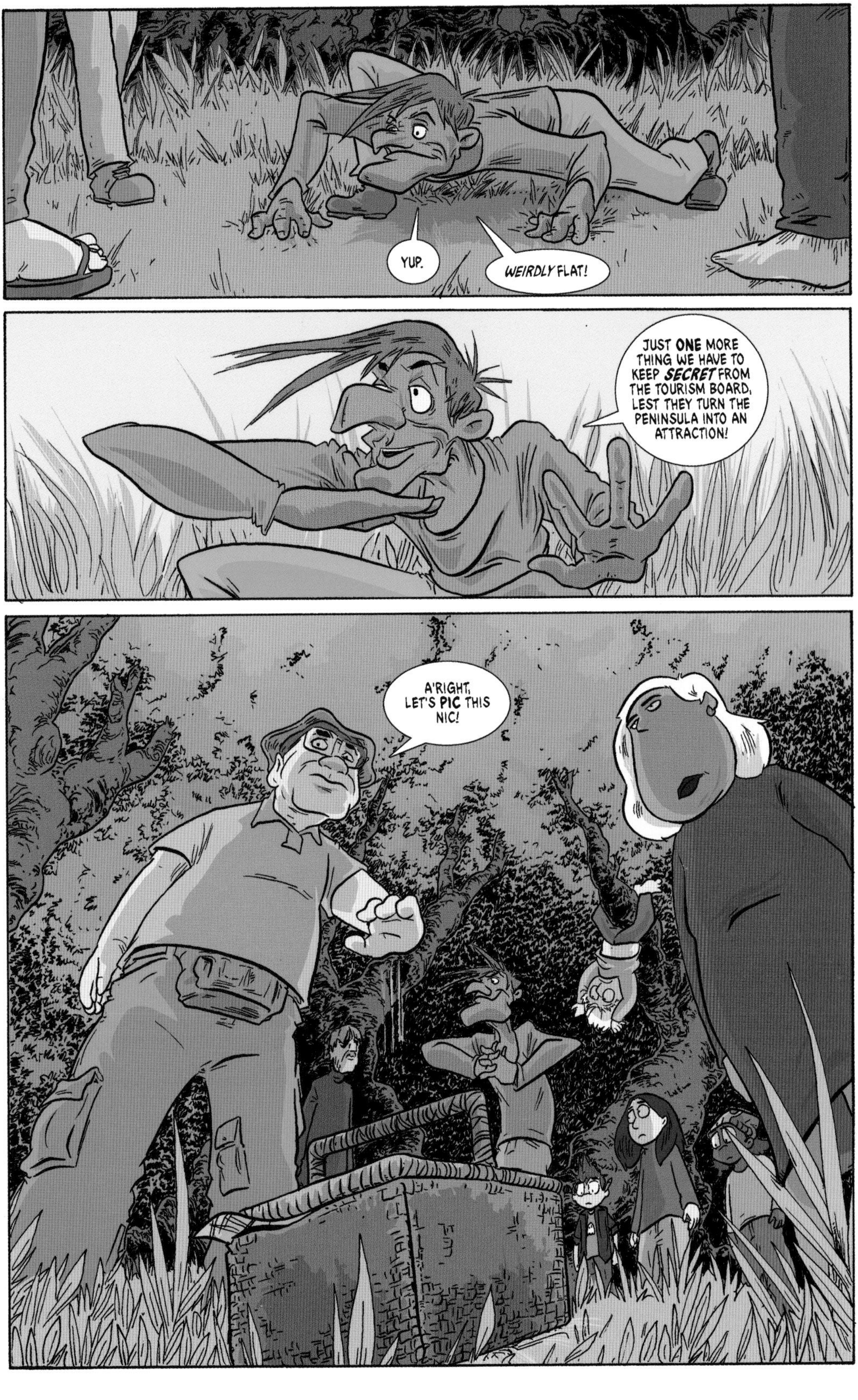
YUP.
WEIRDLY FLAT!
JUST ONE MORE THING WE HAVE TO KEEP SECRET FROM THE TOURISM BOARD, LEST THEY TURN THE PENINSULA INTO AN ATTRACTION!
A'RIGHT, LET'S PIC THIS NIC!

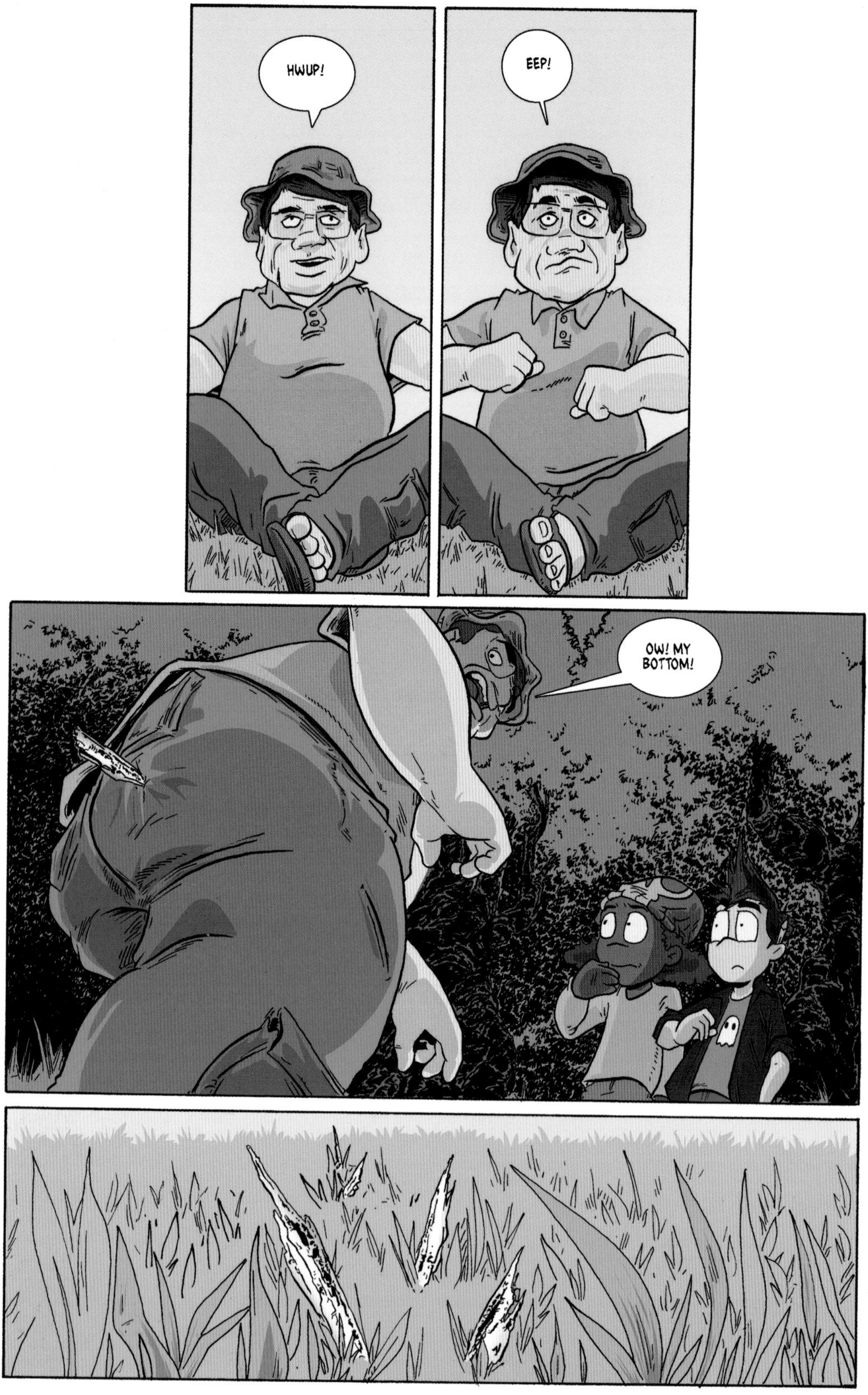
HWUP!
EEP!
OW! MY BOTTOM!

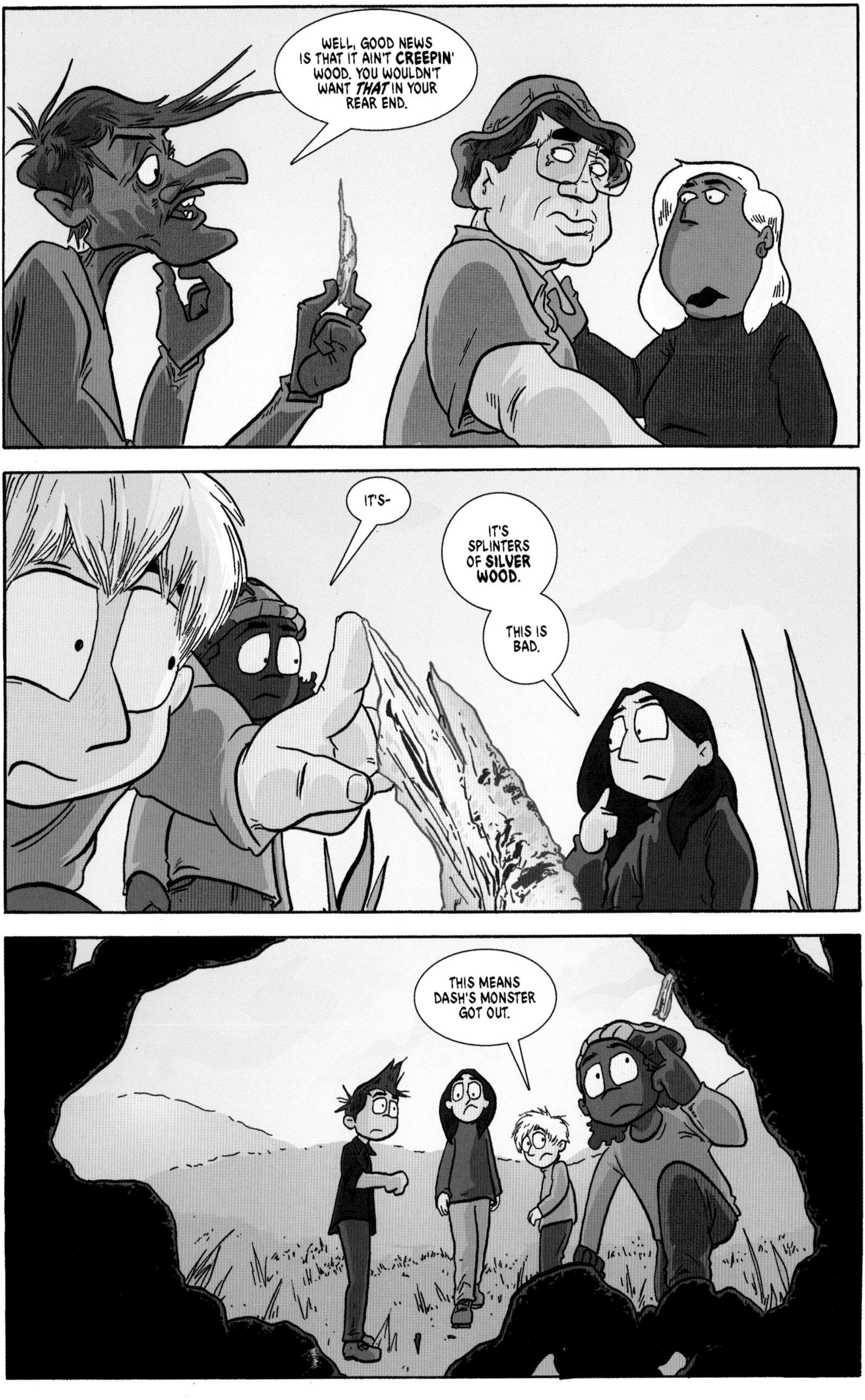
WELL, GOOD NEWS IS THAT IT AIN'T **CREEPIN'** WOOD. YOU WOULDN'T WANT ***THAT*** IN YOUR REAR END.
IT'S-
IT'S SPLINTERS OF **SILVER WOOD.**
THIS IS BAD.
THIS MEANS DASH'S MONSTER GOT OUT.

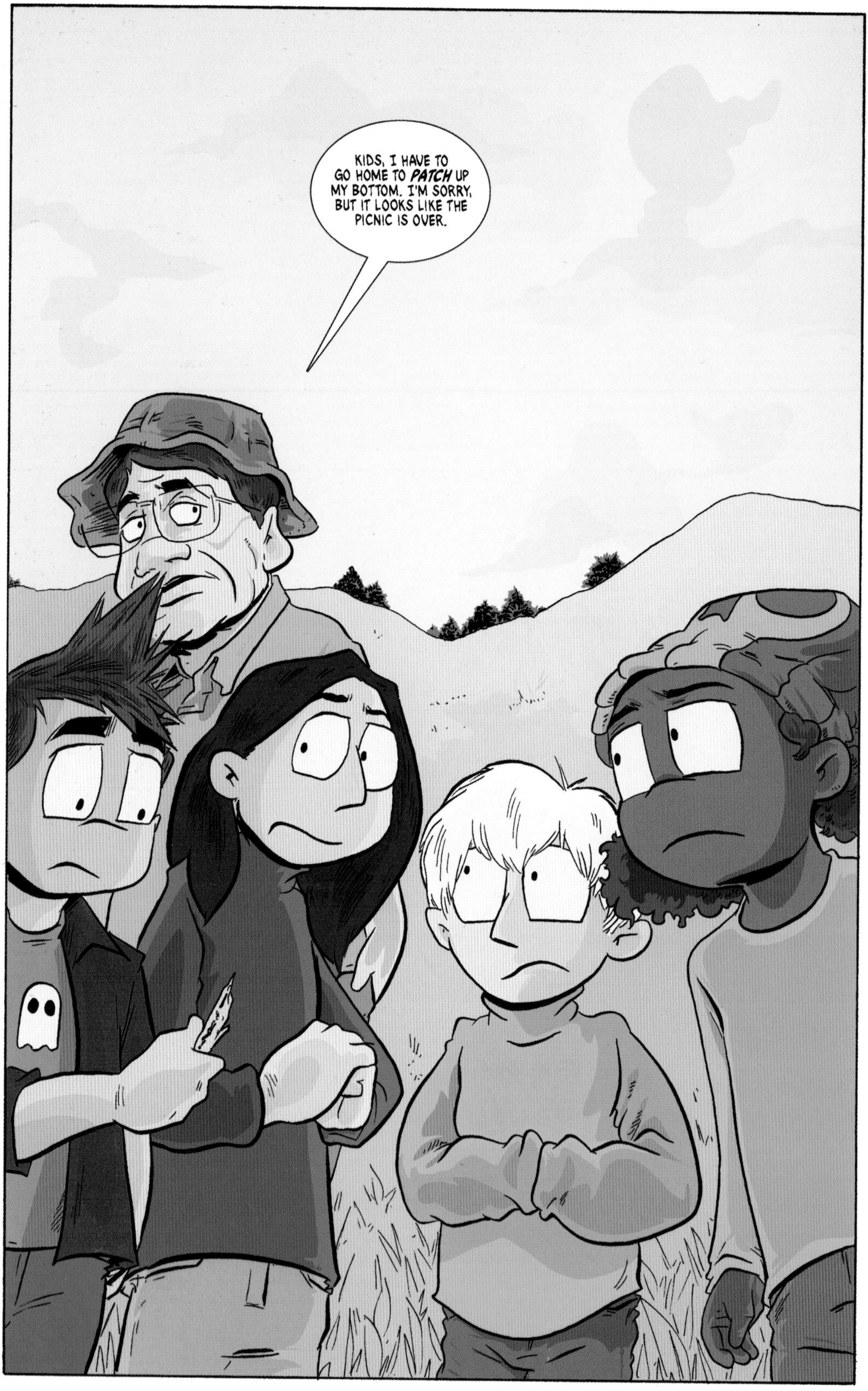
KIDS, I HAVE TO GO HOME TO *PATCH* UP MY BOTTOM. I'M SORRY, BUT IT LOOKS LIKE THE PICNIC IS OVER.

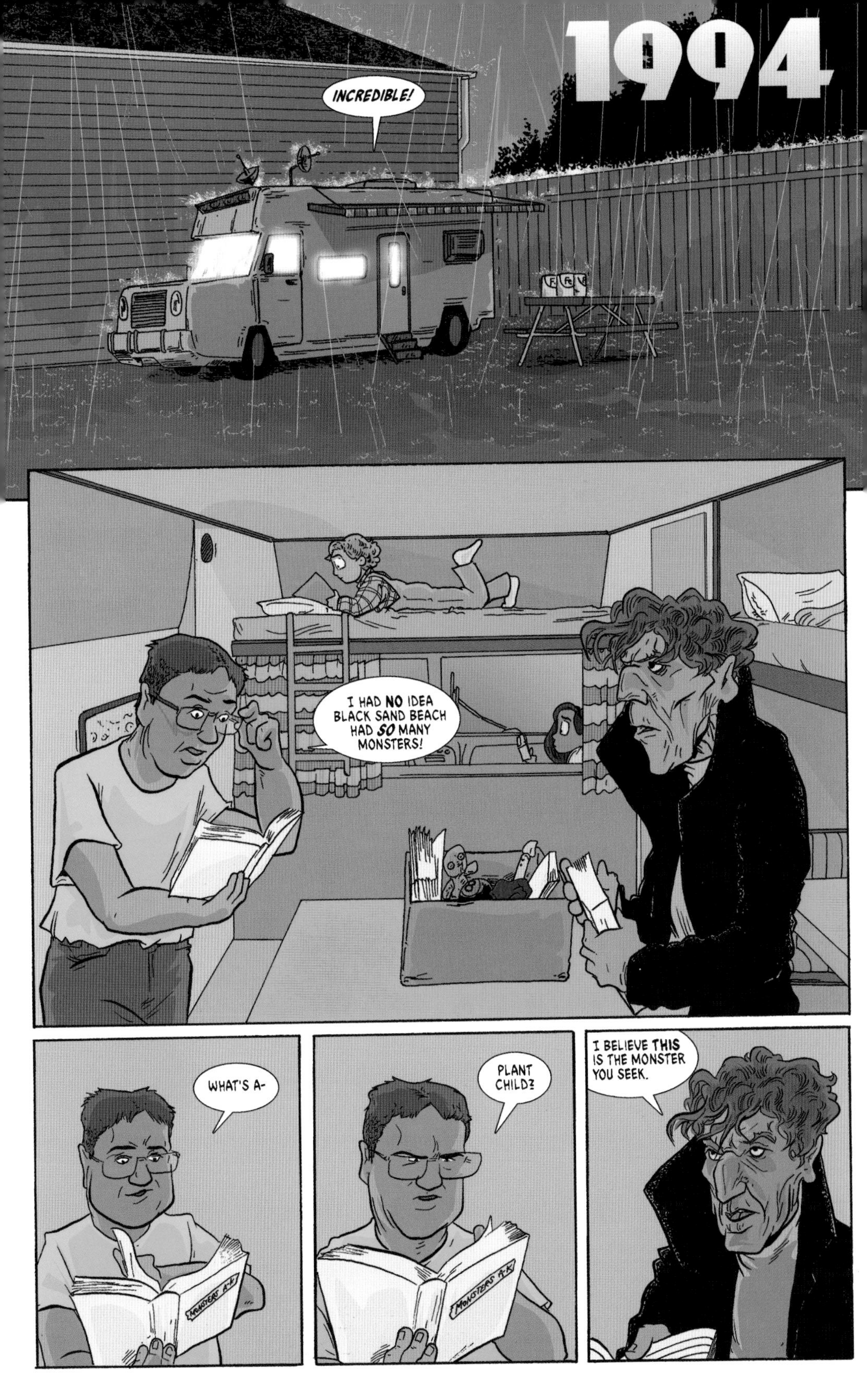
1994
INCREDIBLE!
I HAD NO IDEA BLACK SAND BEACH HAD SO MANY MONSTERS!
WHAT'S A-
PLANT CHILD?
I BELIEVE THIS IS THE MONSTER YOU SEEK.
MONSTERS A-K

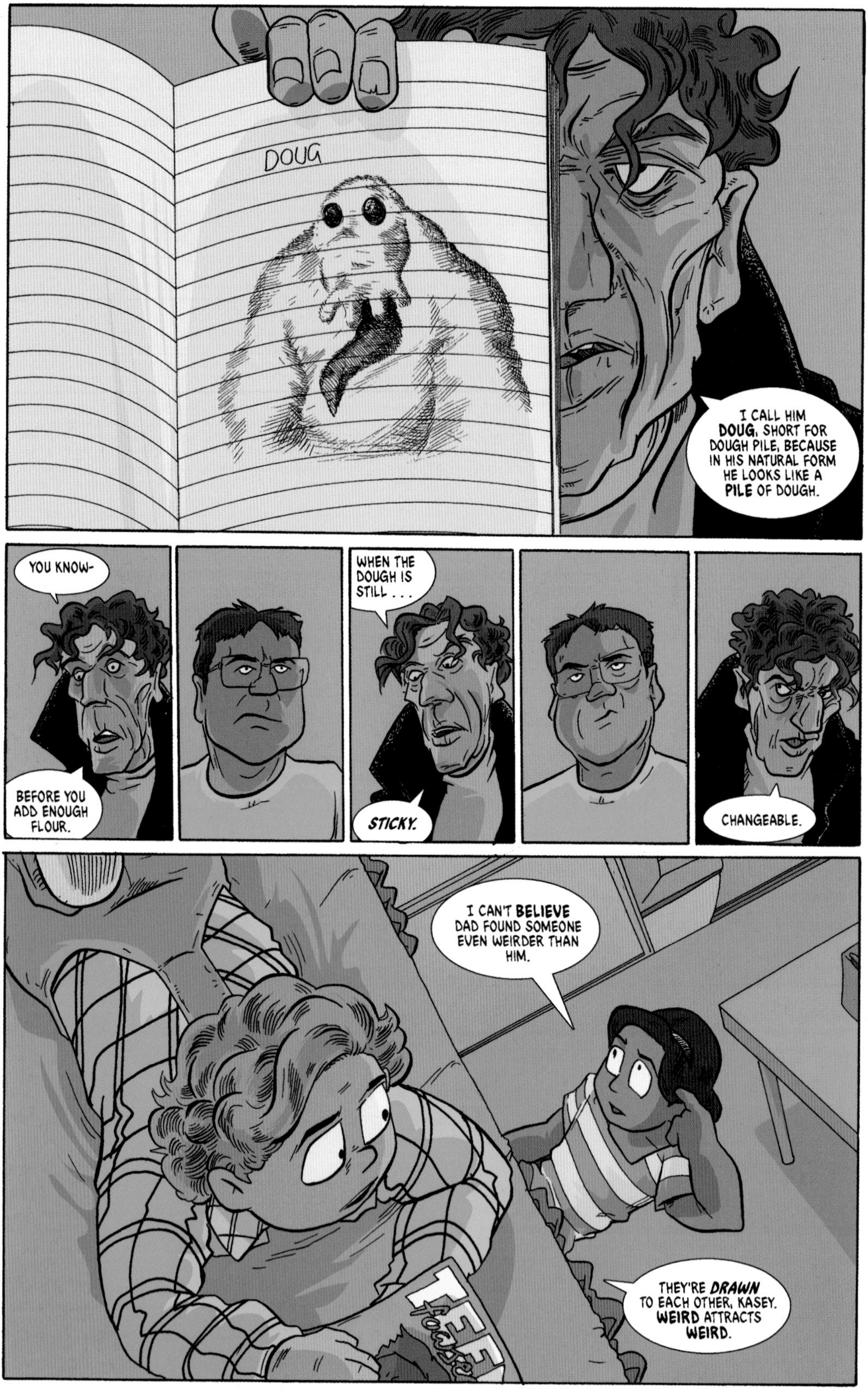
DOUG
I CALL HIM DOUG, SHORT FOR DOUGH PILE, BECAUSE IN HIS NATURAL FORM HE LOOKS LIKE A PILE OF DOUGH.
YOU KNOW-
BEFORE YOU ADD ENOUGH FLOUR.
WHEN THE DOUGH IS STILL . . .
STICKY.
CHANGEABLE.
I CAN'T BELIEVE DAD FOUND SOMEONE EVEN WEIRDER THAN HIM.
THEY'RE DRAWN TO EACH OTHER, KASEY. WEIRD ATTRACTS WEIRD.

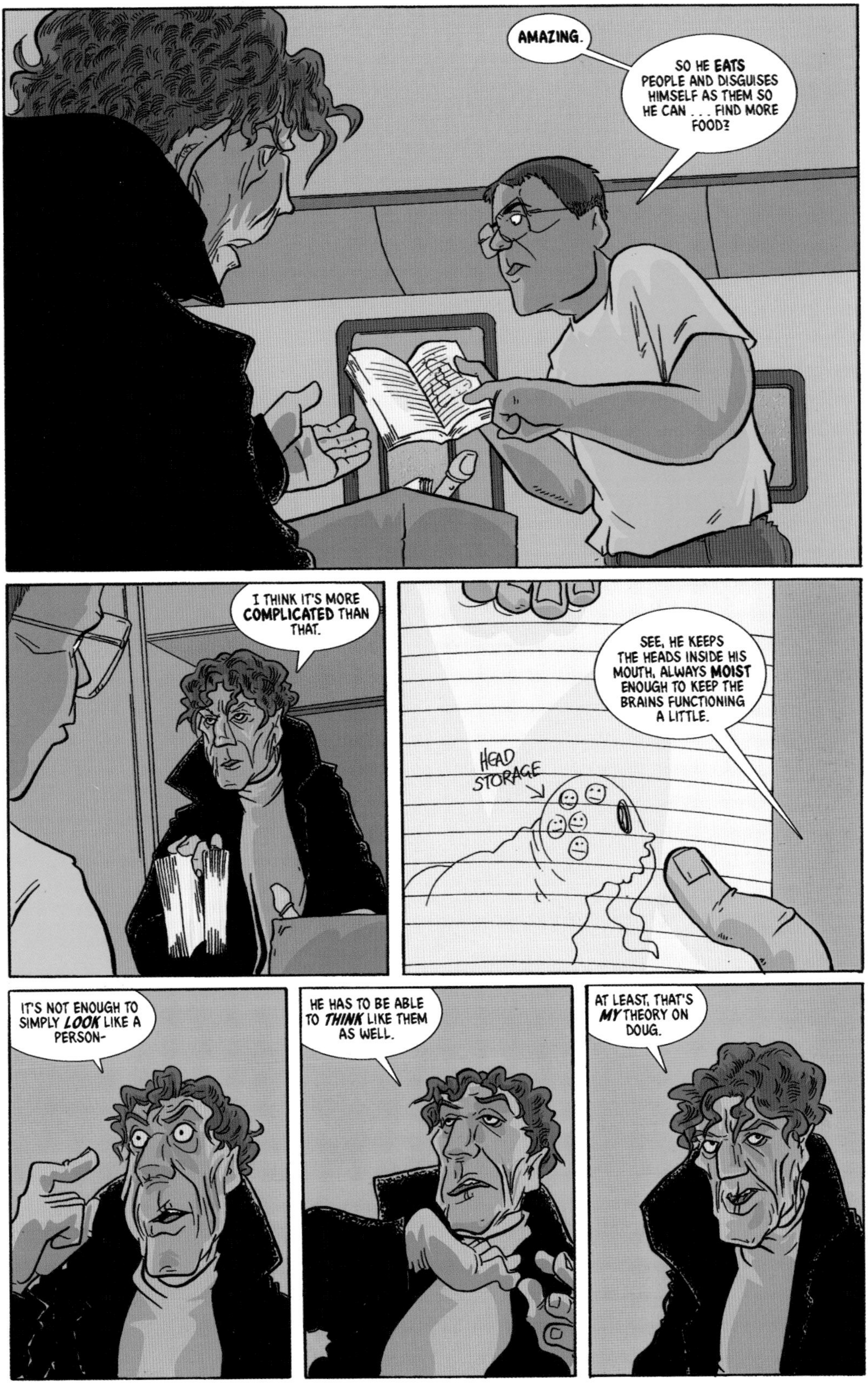
AMAZING.
SO HE EATS PEOPLE AND DISGUISES HIMSELF AS THEM SO HE CAN . . . FIND MORE FOOD?
I THINK IT'S MORE COMPLICATED THAN THAT.
SEE, HE KEEPS THE HEADS INSIDE HIS MOUTH, ALWAYS MOIST ENOUGH TO KEEP THE BRAINS FUNCTIONING A LITTLE.
HEAD STORAGE
IT'S NOT ENOUGH TO SIMPLY LOOK LIKE A PERSON-
HE HAS TO BE ABLE TO THINK LIKE THEM AS WELL.
AT LEAST, THAT'S MY THEORY ON DOUG.

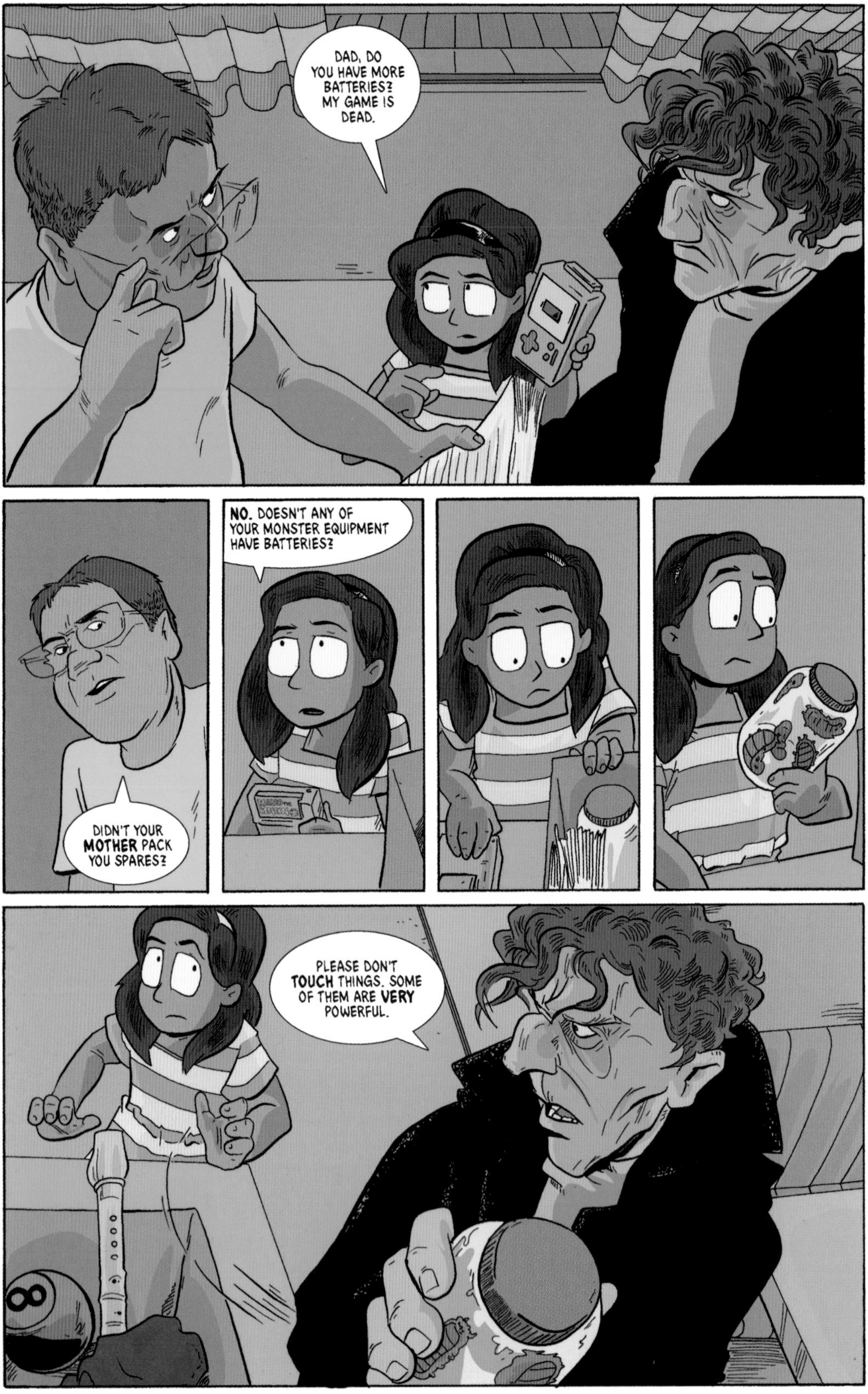
DAD, DO YOU HAVE MORE BATTERIES? MY GAME IS DEAD.
DIDN'T YOUR **MOTHER** PACK YOU SPARES?
NO. DOESN'T ANY OF YOUR MONSTER EQUIPMENT HAVE BATTERIES?
PLEASE DON'T **TOUCH** THINGS. SOME OF THEM ARE **VERY** POWERFUL.

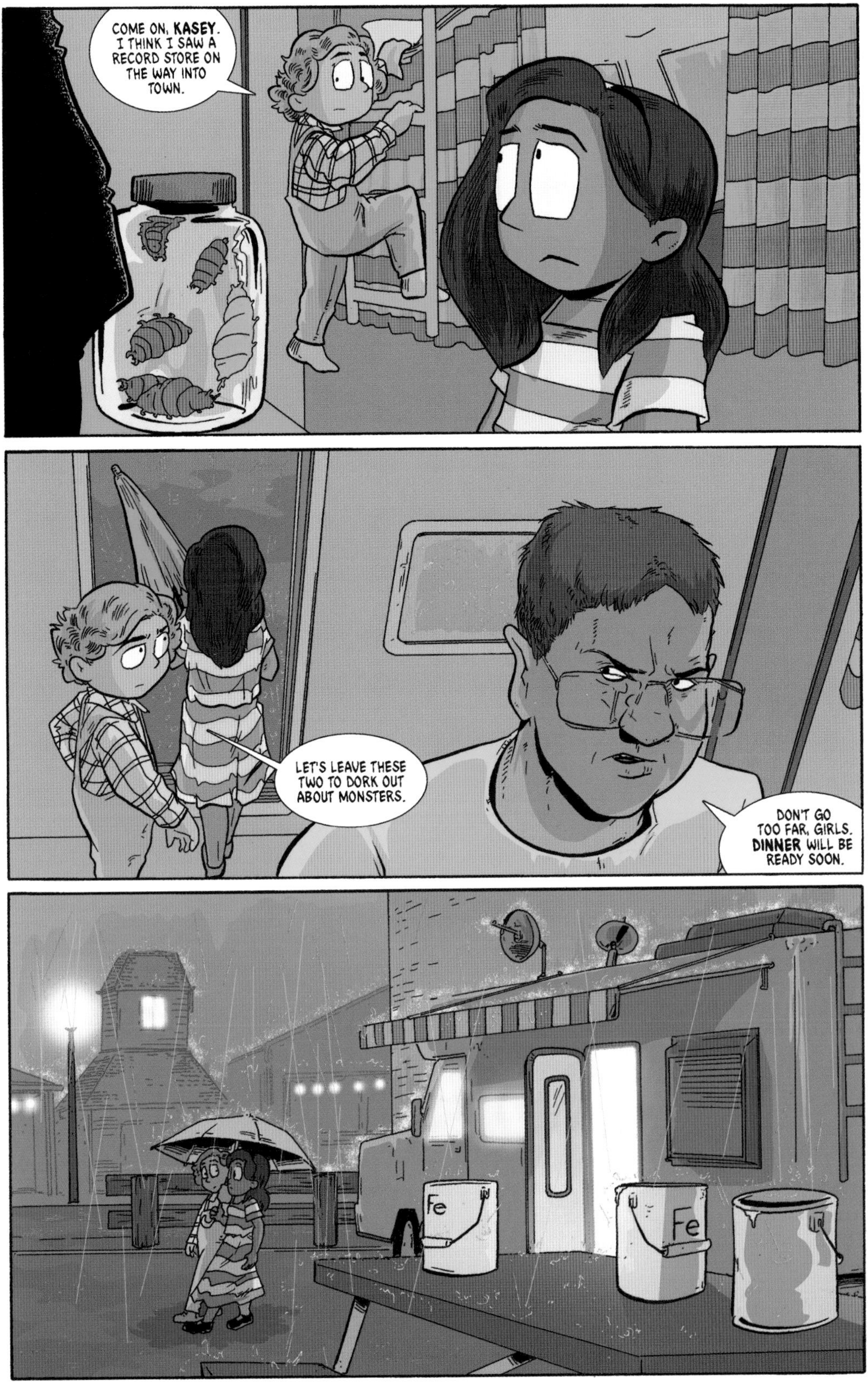
COME ON, KASEY. I THINK I SAW A RECORD STORE ON THE WAY INTO TOWN.
LET'S LEAVE THESE TWO TO DORK OUT ABOUT MONSTERS.
DON'T GO TOO FAR, GIRLS. DINNER WILL BE READY SOON.
Fe
Fe

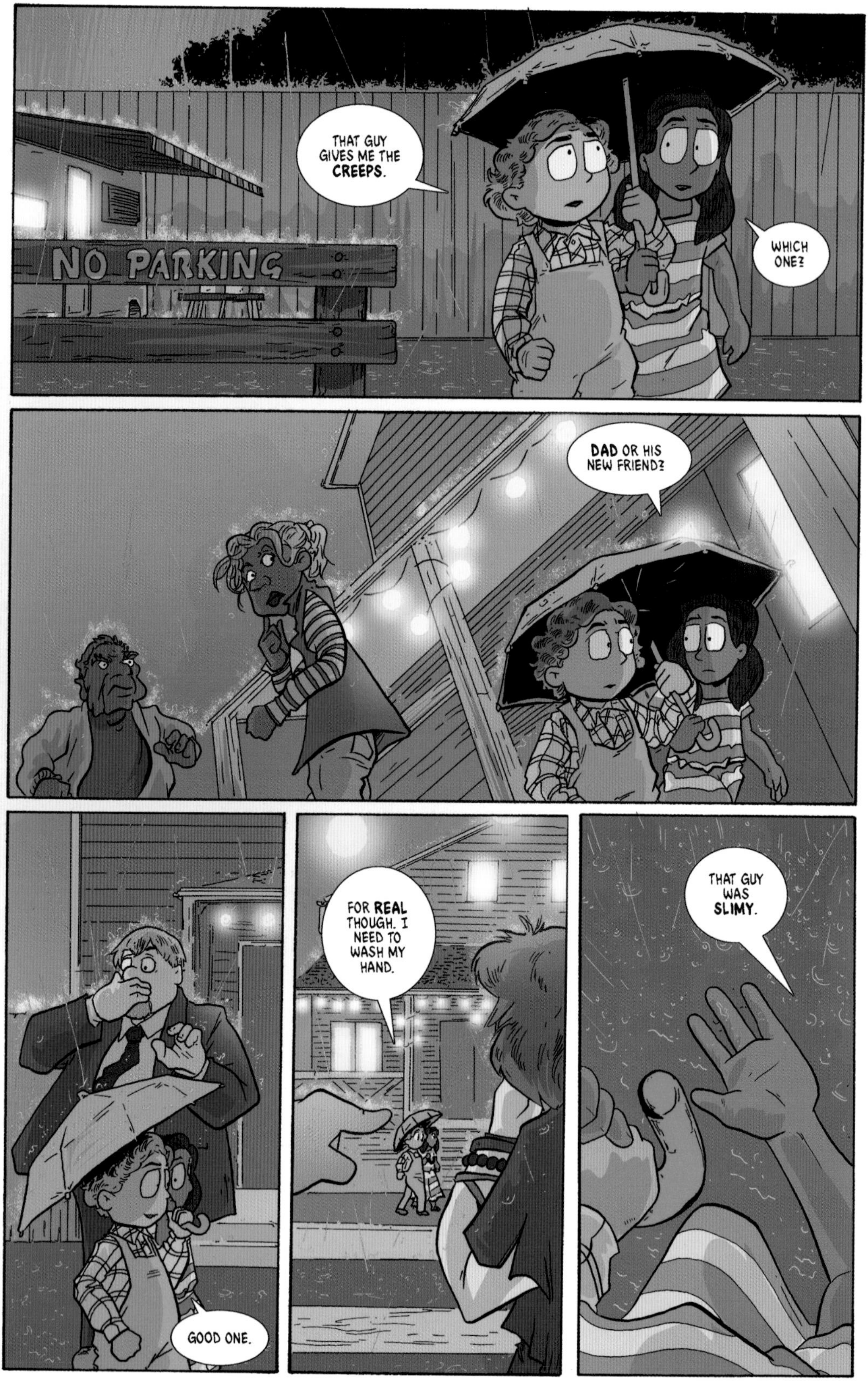
THAT GUY GIVES ME THE CREEPS.
WHICH ONE?
DAD OR HIS NEW FRIEND?
NO PARKING
GOOD ONE.
FOR REAL THOUGH. I NEED TO WASH MY HAND.
THAT GUY WAS SLIMY.

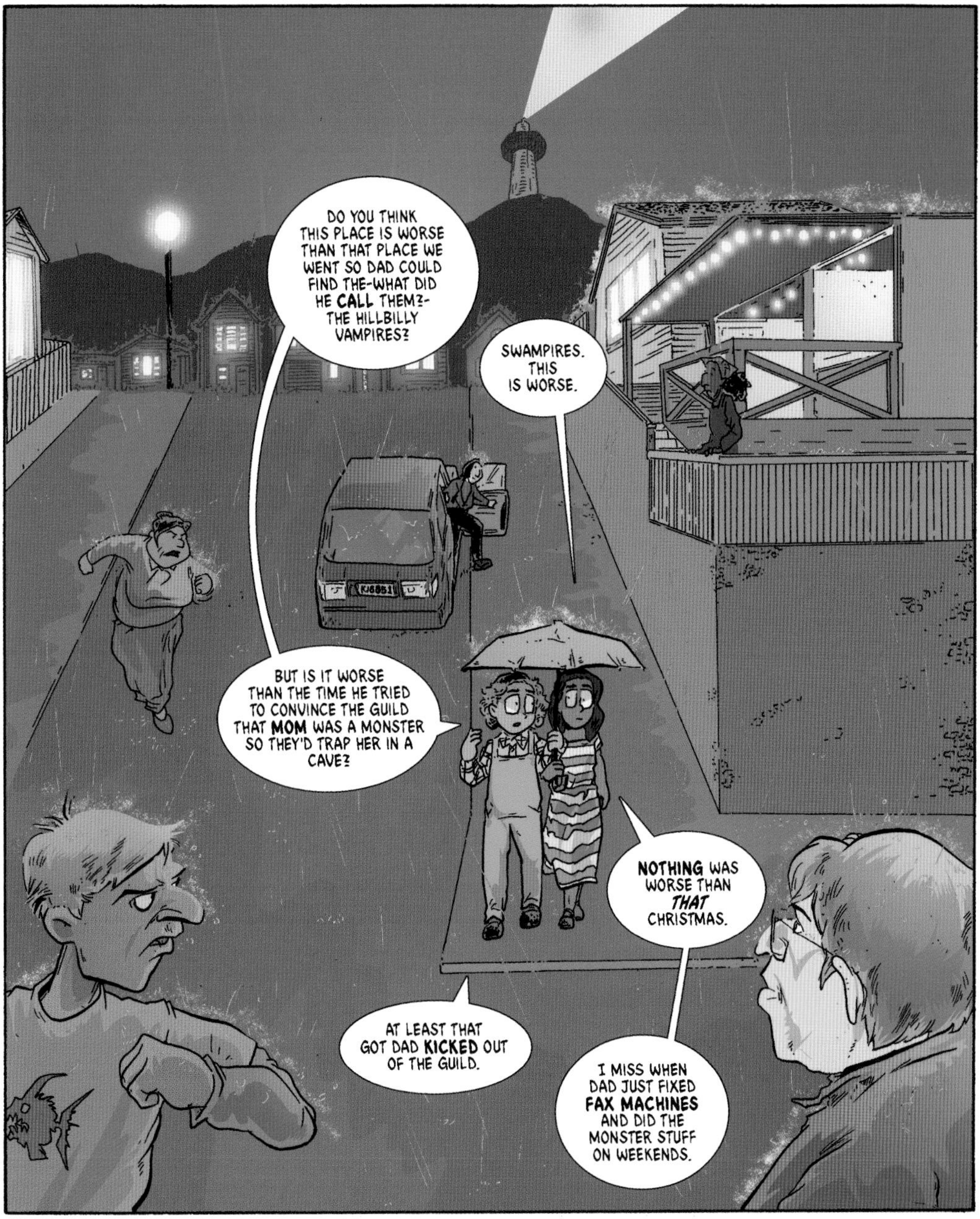
DO YOU THINK THIS PLACE IS WORSE THAN THAT PLACE WE WENT SO DAD COULD FIND THE—WHAT DID HE CALL THEM?—THE HILLBILLY VAMPIRES?
SWAMPIRES. THIS IS WORSE.
BUT IS IT WORSE THAN THE TIME HE TRIED TO CONVINCE THE GUILD THAT MOM WAS A MONSTER SO THEY'D TRAP HER IN A CAVE?
NOTHING WAS WORSE THAN THAT CHRISTMAS.
AT LEAST THAT GOT DAD KICKED OUT OF THE GUILD.
I MISS WHEN DAD JUST FIXED FAX MACHINES AND DID THE MONSTER STUFF ON WEEKENDS.

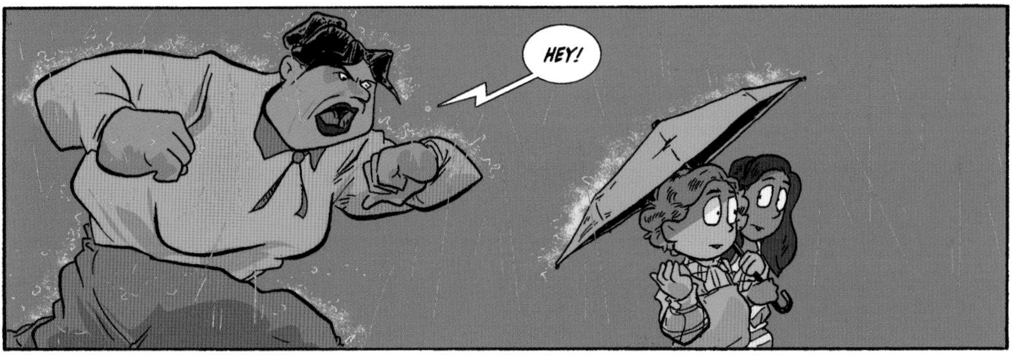
HEY!

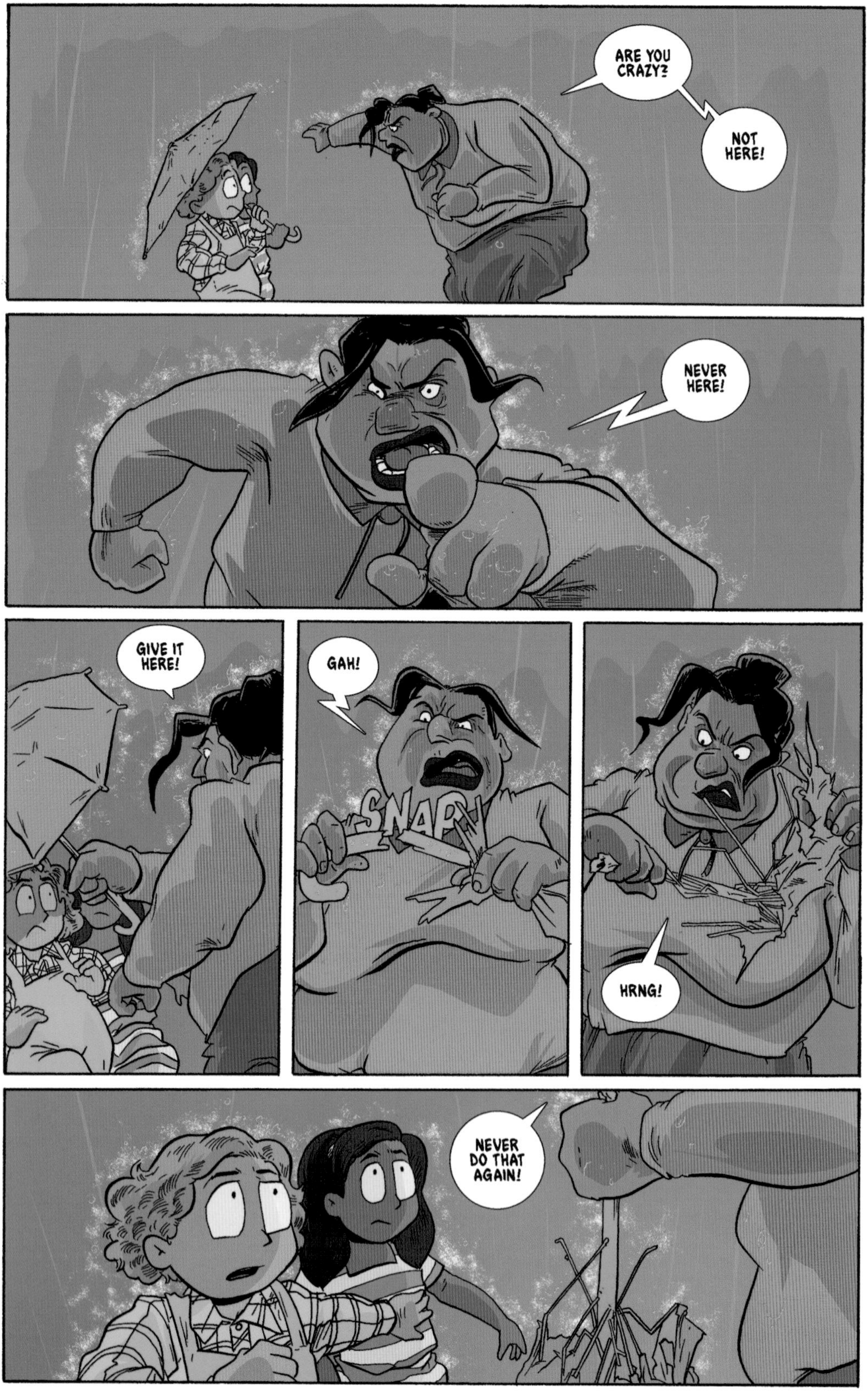
ARE YOU CRAZY?
NOT HERE!
NEVER HERE!
GIVE IT HERE!
GAH!
SNAP!
HRNG!
NEVER DO THAT AGAIN!

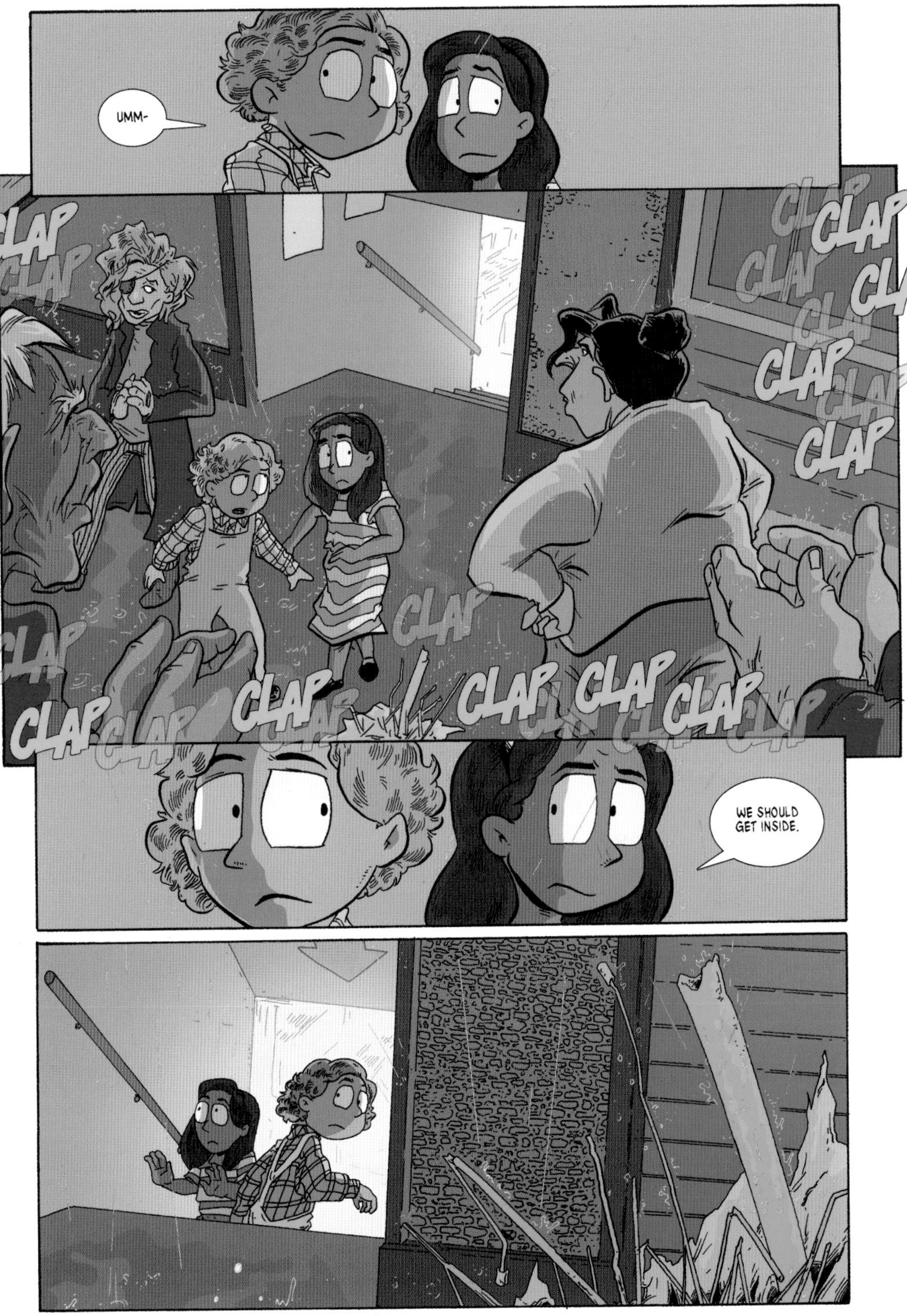
UMM-
CLAP CLAP CLAP CLAP CLAP CLAP CLAP CLAP CLAP CLAP CLAP CLAP CLAP CLAP CLAP CLAP
WE SHOULD GET INSIDE.

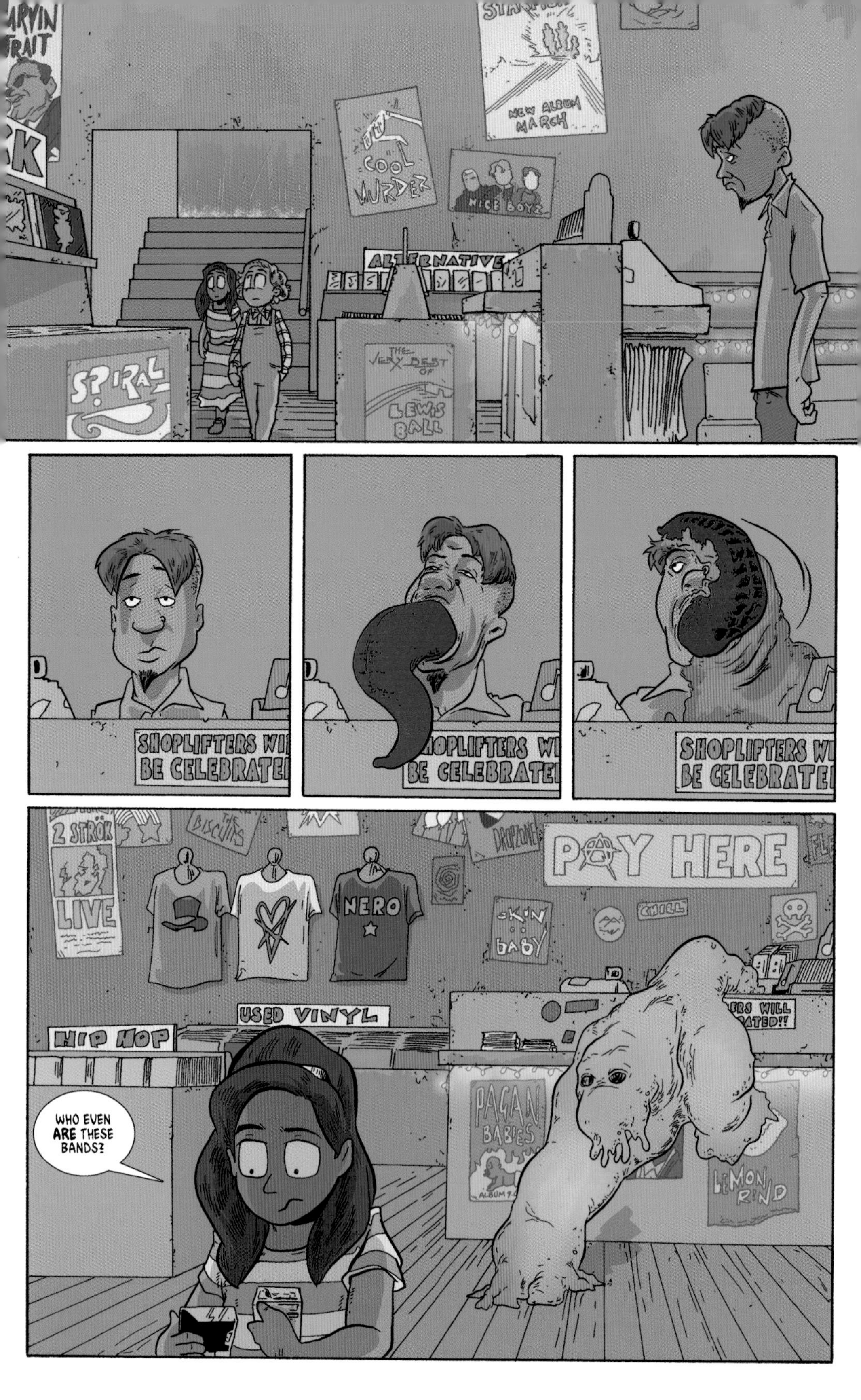
NEW ALBUM MARCH
COOL MURDER
NICE BOYZ
ALTERNATIVE
THE VERY BEST OF LEWIS BALL
SHOPLIFTERS WI
BE CELEBRATE
SHOPLIFTERS WI
BE CELEBRATE
SHOPLIFTERS WI
BE CELEBRATE
2 STRÖK LIVE
THE BISCUITS
PAY HERE
NERO
SKIN BABY
CHILL
USED VINYL
HIP HOP
PAGAN BABIES
LEMON RIND
WHO EVEN ARE THESE BANDS?

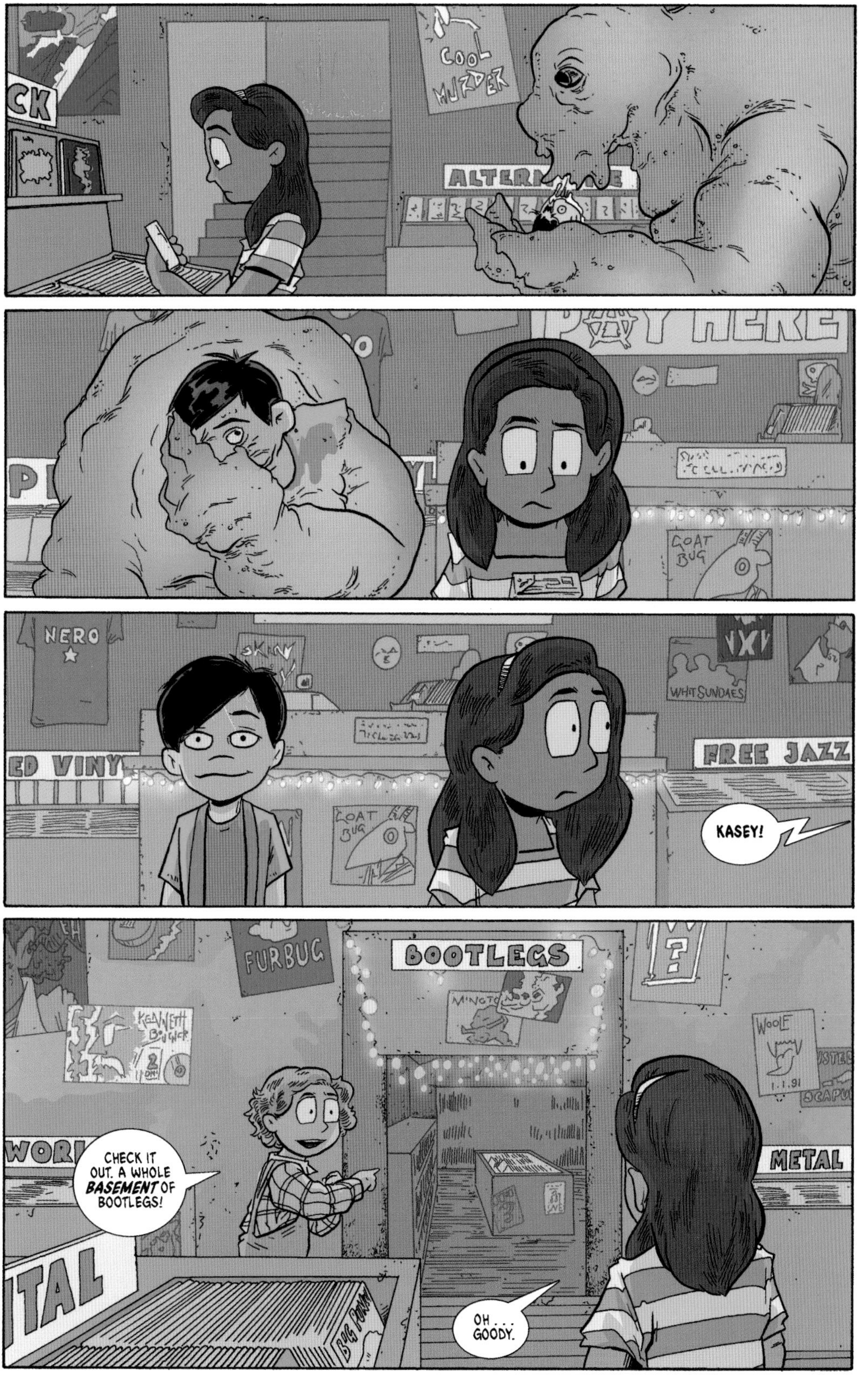
COOL MURDER
GOAT BUG
NERO
WHITSUNDAES
FREE JAZZ
GOAT BUG
KASEY!
FURBUG
BOOTLEGS
WOOLF 1.1.91
METAL
CHECK IT OUT. A WHOLE *BASEMENT* OF BOOTLEGS!
OH . . . GOODY.

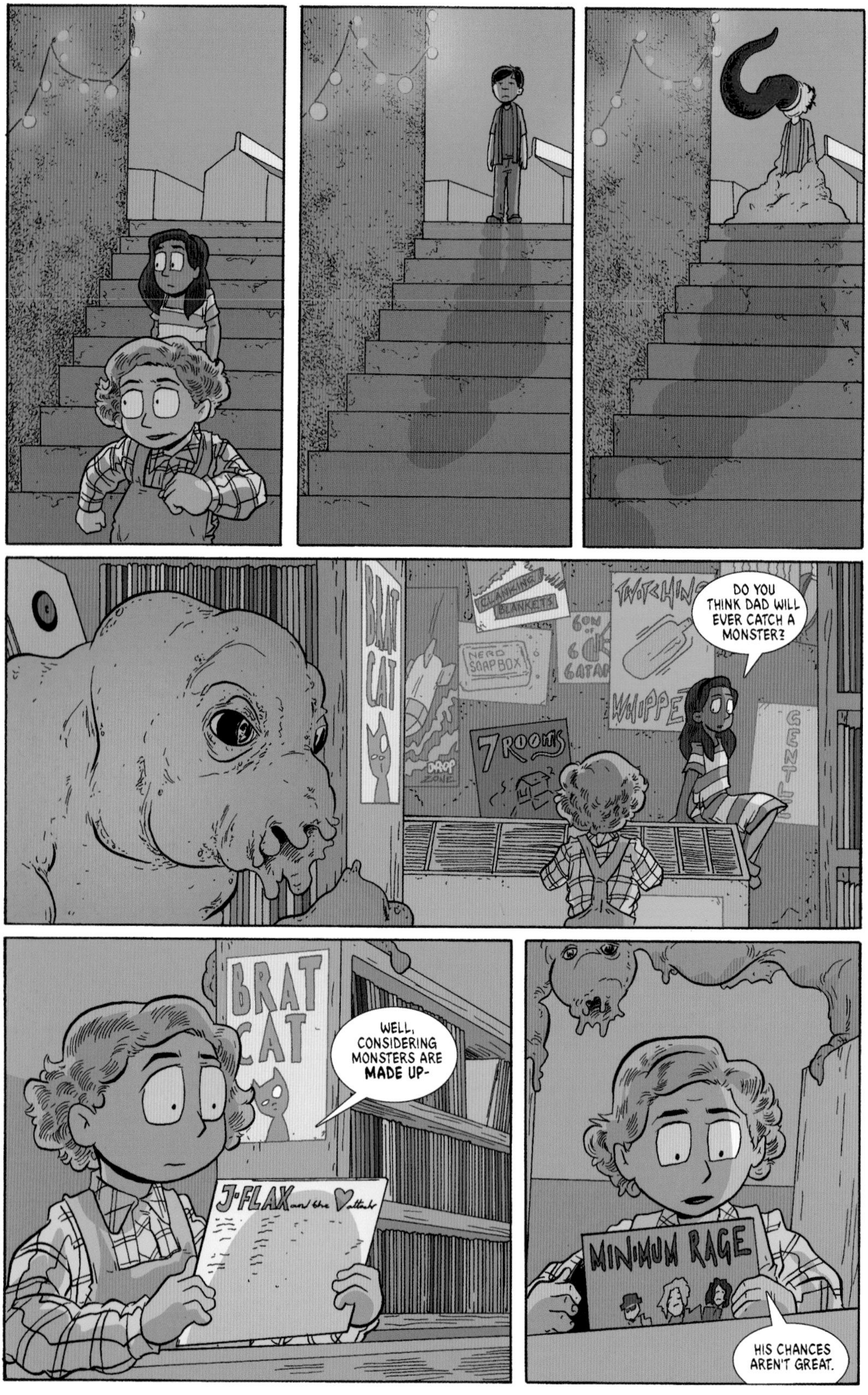
BRAT CAT
CLANKING BLANKETS
NERD SOAPBOX
TWITCHING WHIPPET
7 ROOMS
DROP ZONE
GENTLE
DO YOU THINK DAD WILL EVER CATCH A MONSTER?
BRAT CAT
J-FLAX and the Heart attacks
WELL, CONSIDERING MONSTERS ARE **MADE UP**-
MINIMUM RAGE
HIS CHANCES AREN'T GREAT.

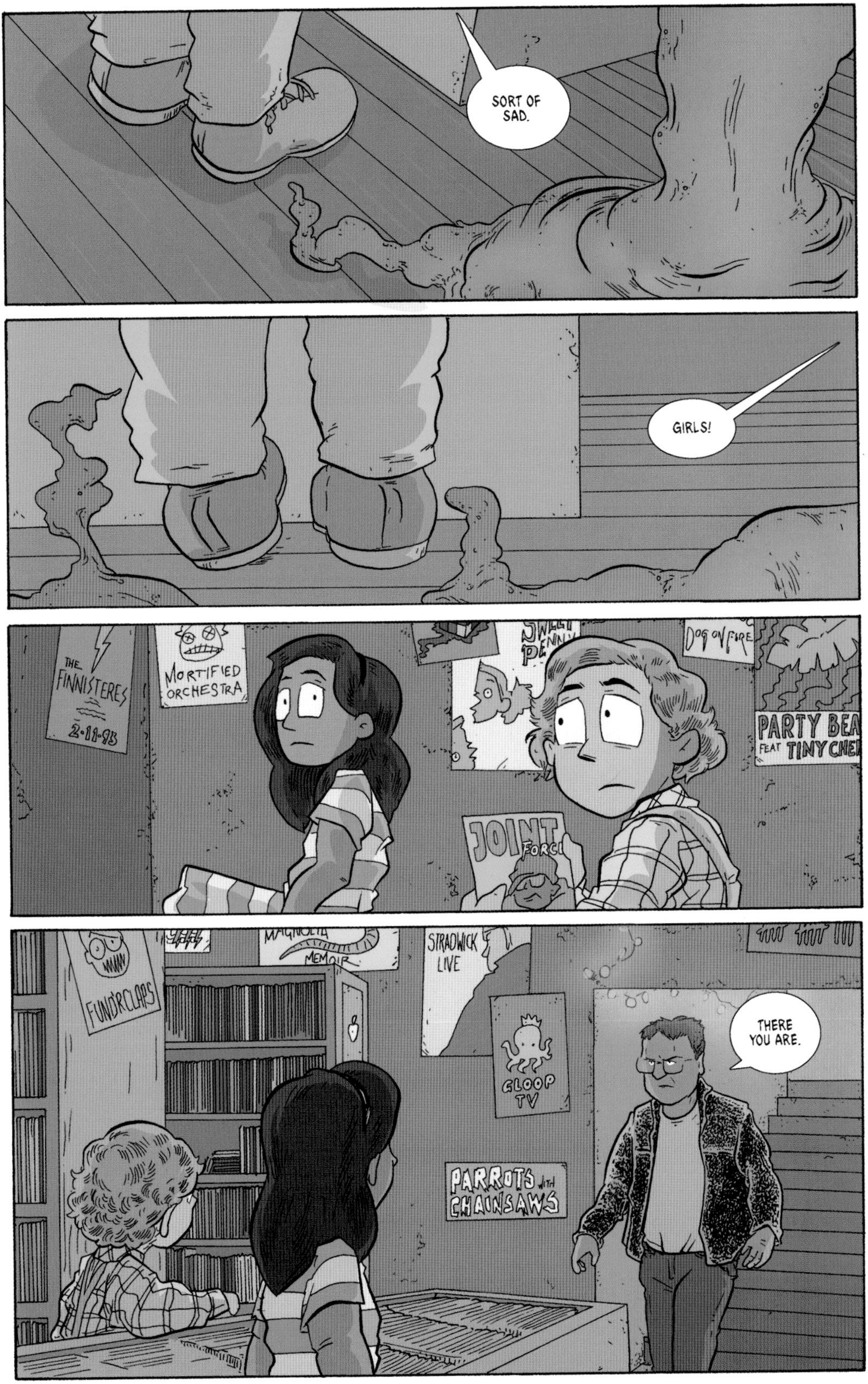

SORT OF SAD.
GIRLS!
THE FINNISTERES
2-11-93
MORTIFIED ORCHESTRA
DOG ON FIRE
STRADWICK LIVE
GLOOP TV
PARROTS WITH CHAINSAWS
THERE YOU ARE.

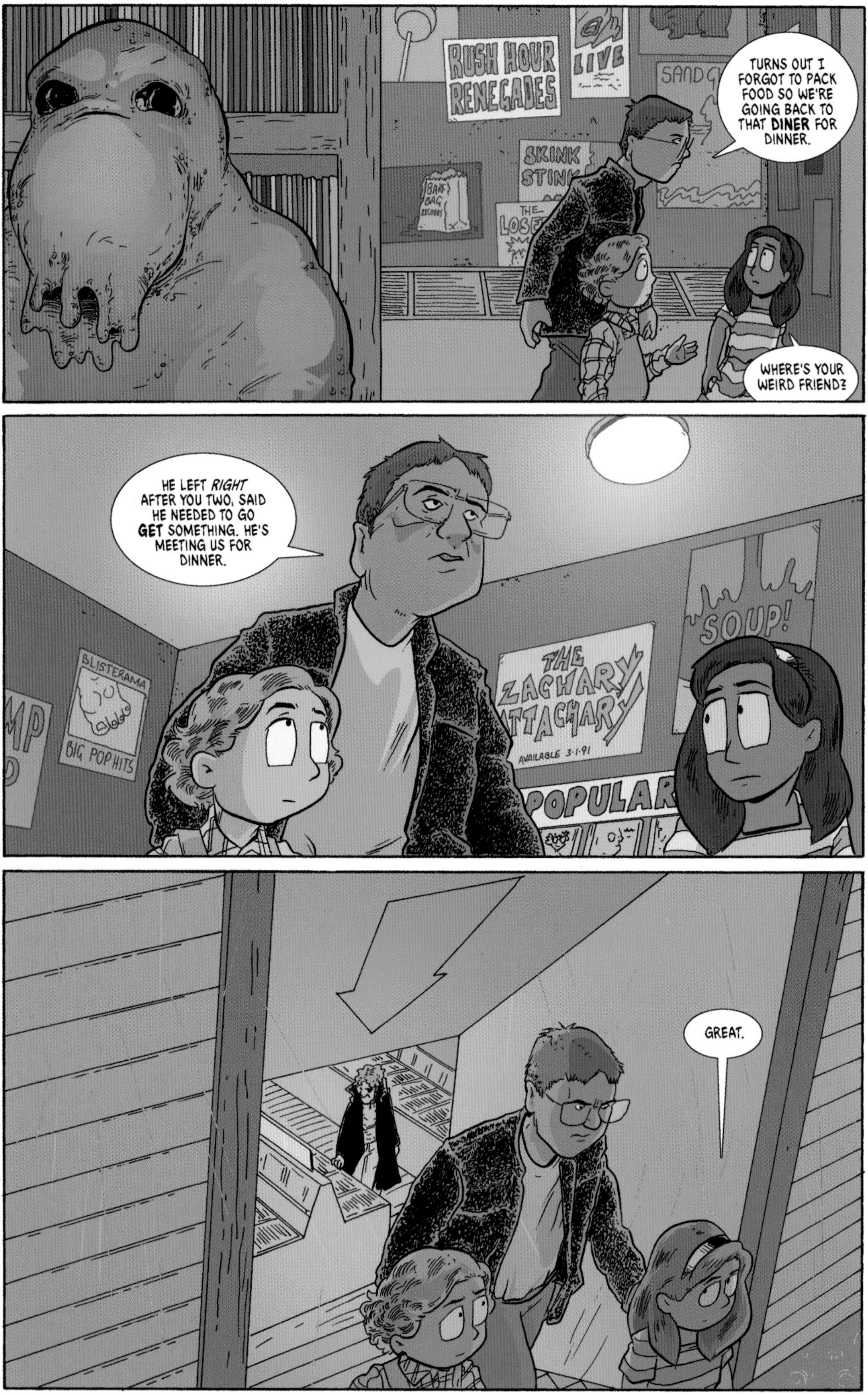
RUSH HOUR RENEGADES
LIVE
TURNS OUT I FORGOT TO PACK FOOD SO WE'RE GOING BACK TO THAT **DINER** FOR DINNER.
WHERE'S YOUR WEIRD FRIEND?
HE LEFT *RIGHT* AFTER YOU TWO, SAID HE NEEDED TO GO **GET** SOMETHING. HE'S MEETING US FOR DINNER.
BLISTERAMA
BIG POP HITS
THE ZACHARY ATTACHARY
AVAILABLE 3·1·91
SOUP!
POPULAR
GREAT.

TO BE CONTINUED.

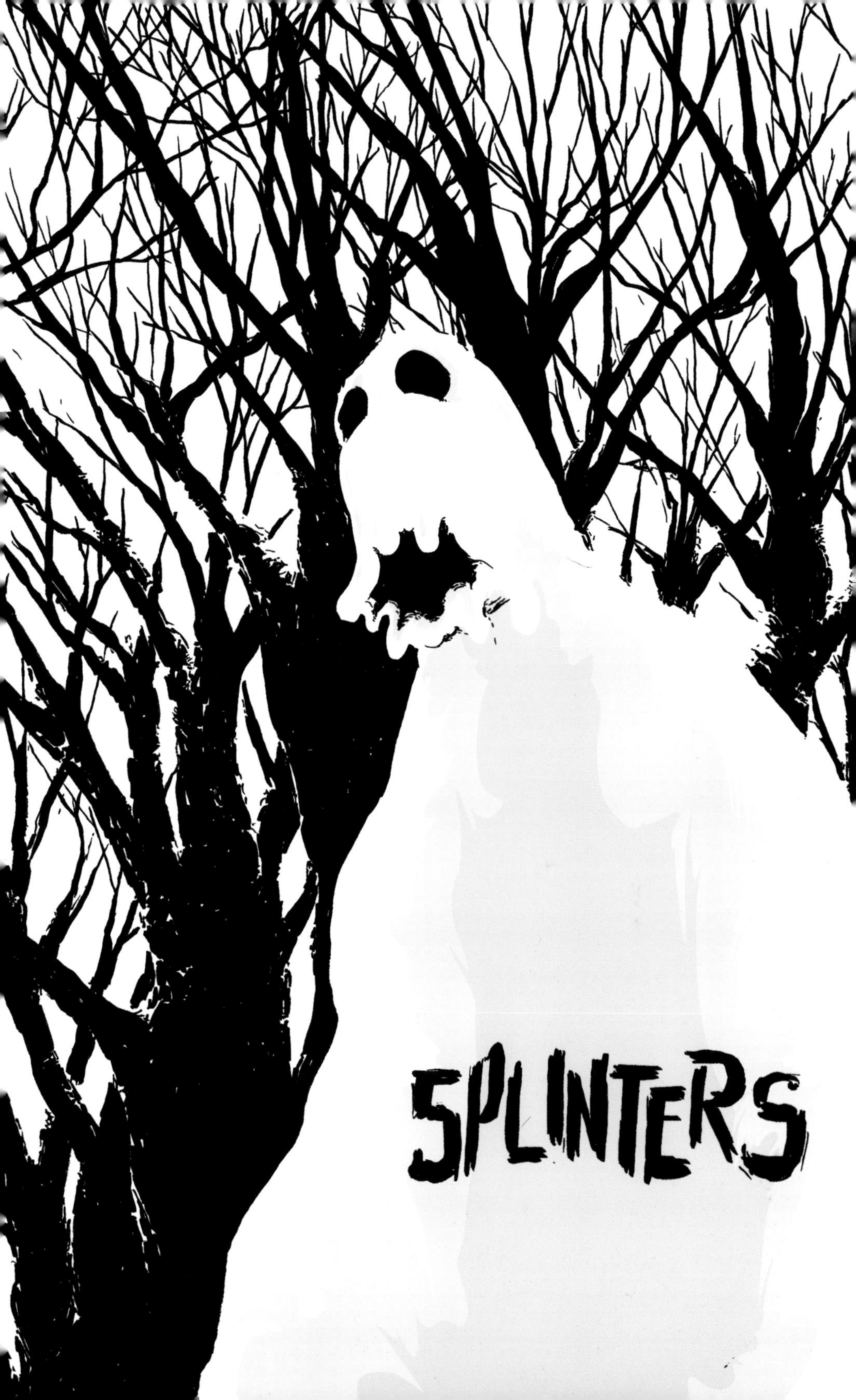
SPLINTERS

SPLINTERS

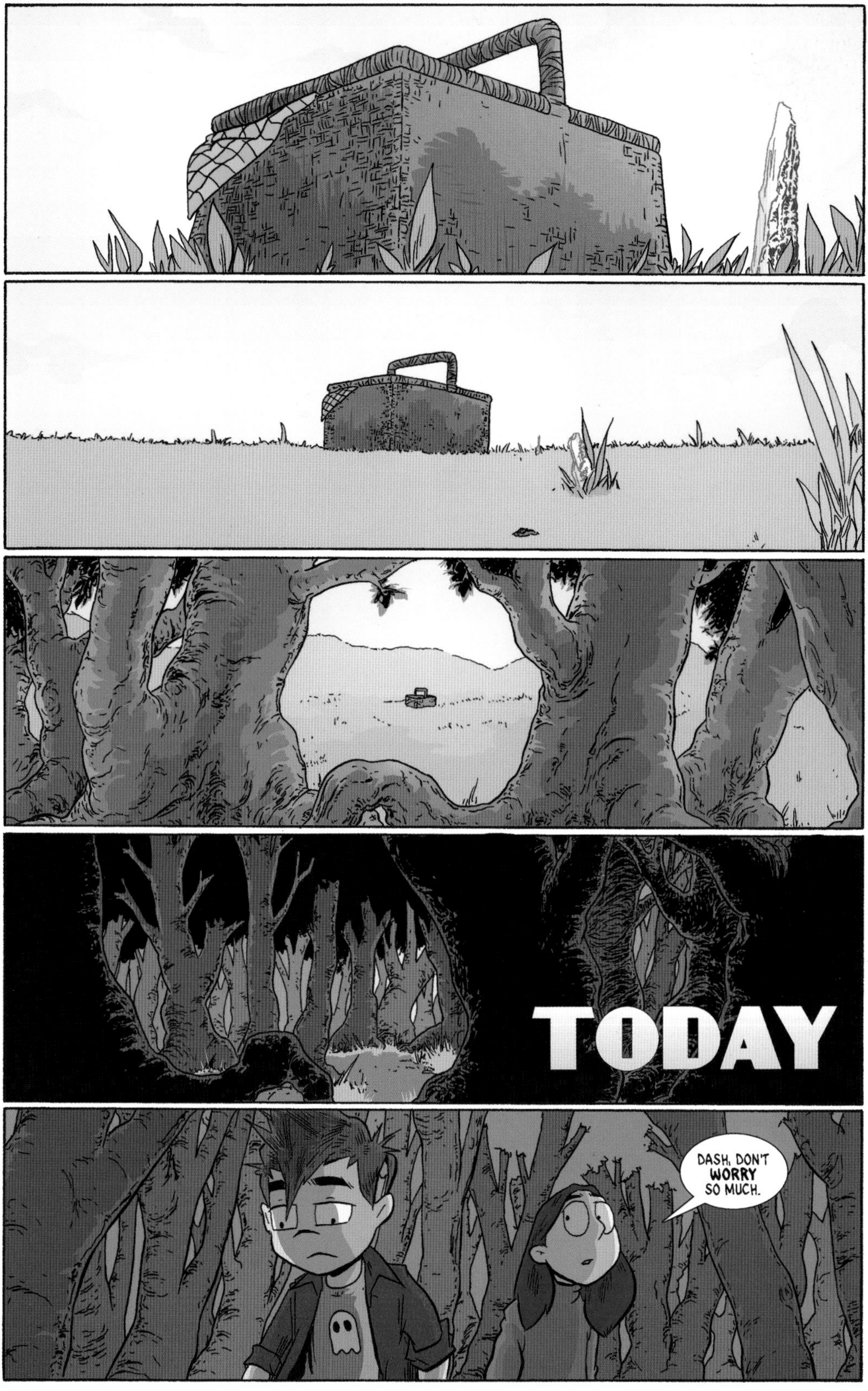
TODAY
DASH, DON'T WORRY SO MUCH.

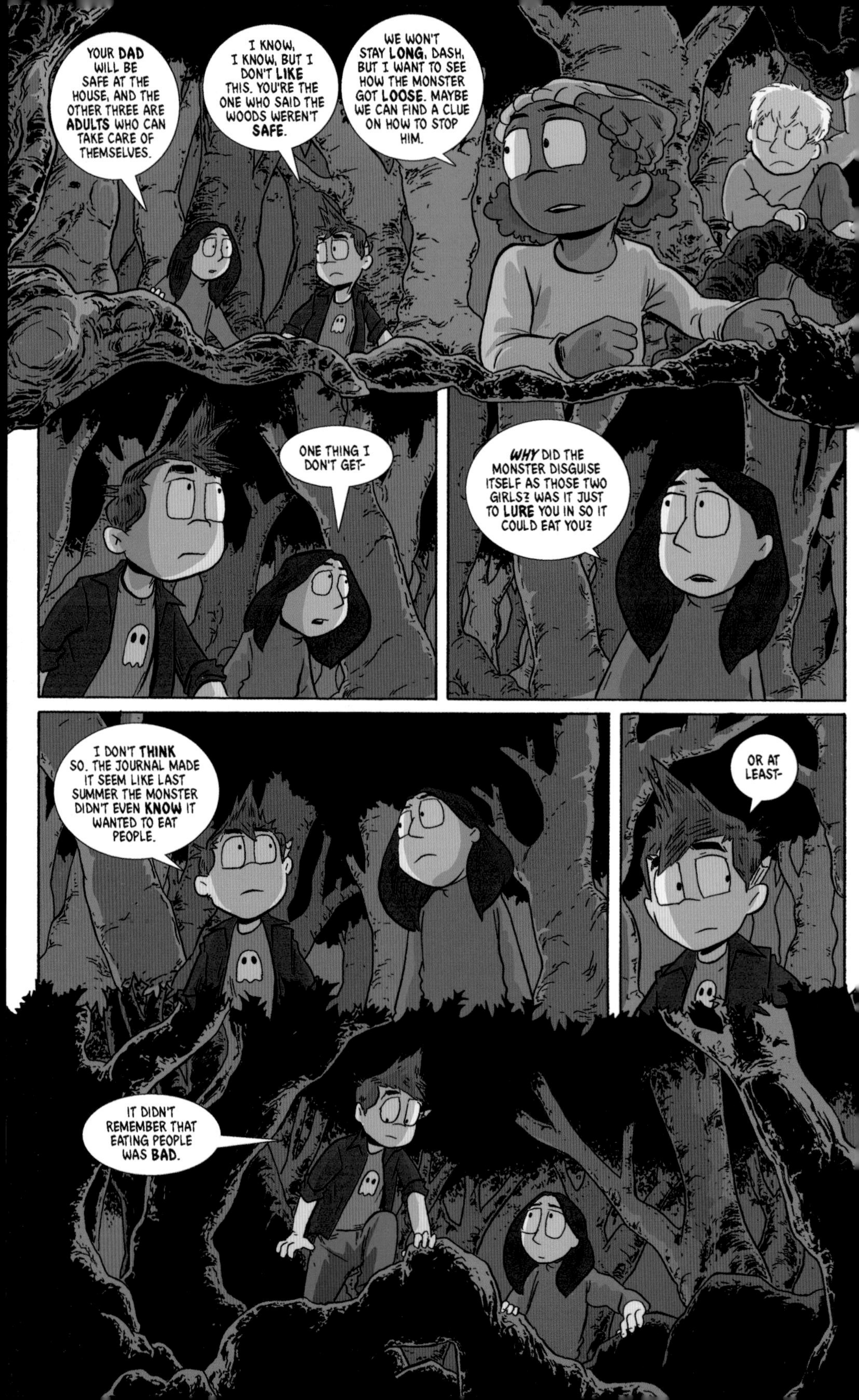
YOUR DAD WILL BE SAFE AT THE HOUSE, AND THE OTHER THREE ARE ADULTS WHO CAN TAKE CARE OF THEMSELVES.
I KNOW, I KNOW, BUT I DON'T LIKE THIS. YOU'RE THE ONE WHO SAID THE WOODS WEREN'T SAFE.
WE WON'T STAY LONG, DASH, BUT I WANT TO SEE HOW THE MONSTER GOT LOOSE. MAYBE WE CAN FIND A CLUE ON HOW TO STOP HIM.
ONE THING I DON'T GET-
WHY DID THE MONSTER DISGUISE ITSELF AS THOSE TWO GIRLS? WAS IT JUST TO LURE YOU IN SO IT COULD EAT YOU?
I DON'T THINK SO. THE JOURNAL MADE IT SEEM LIKE LAST SUMMER THE MONSTER DIDN'T EVEN KNOW IT WANTED TO EAT PEOPLE.
OR AT LEAST-
IT DIDN'T REMEMBER THAT EATING PEOPLE WAS BAD.

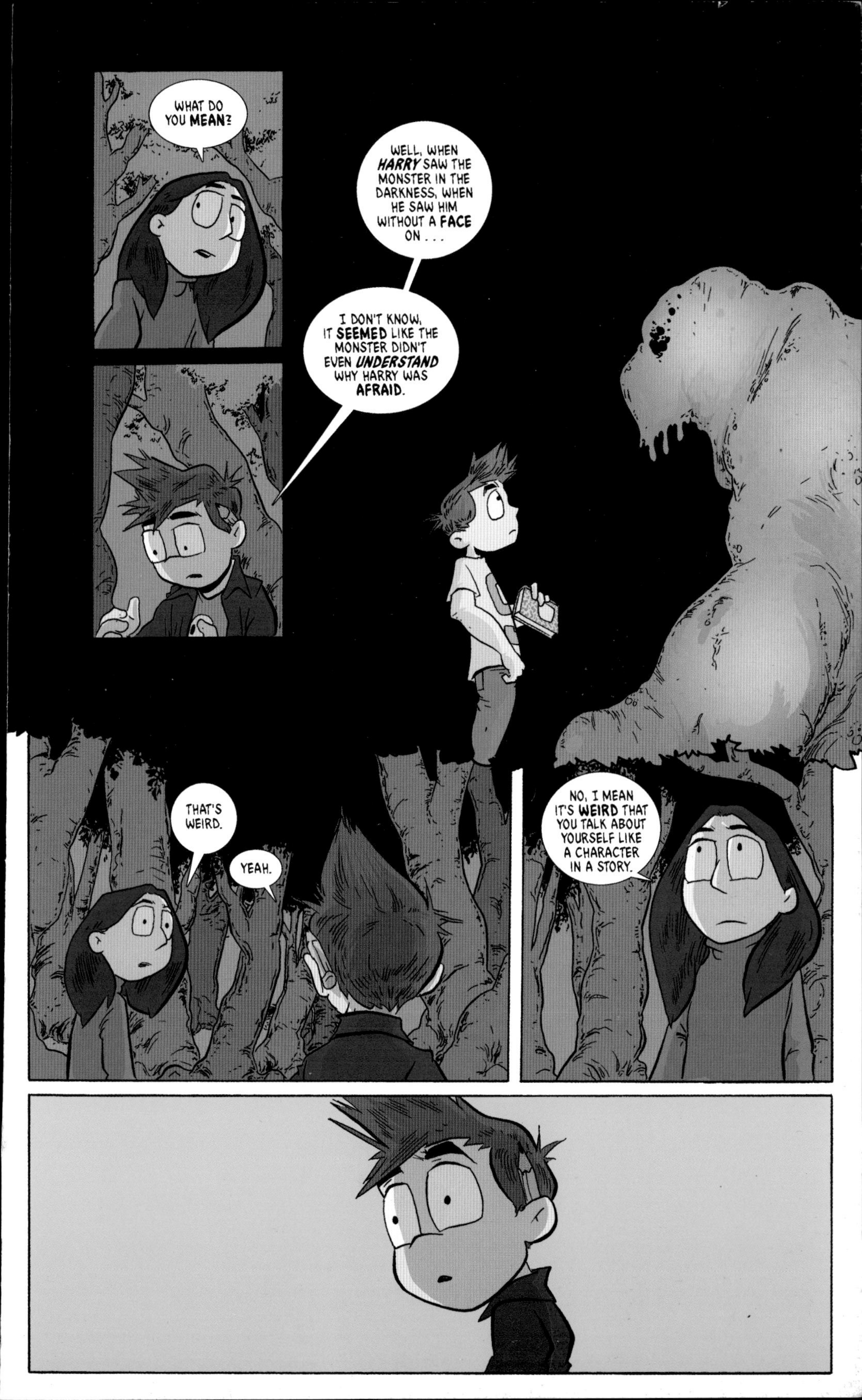
WHAT DO YOU MEAN?
WELL, WHEN HARRY SAW THE MONSTER IN THE DARKNESS, WHEN HE SAW HIM WITHOUT A FACE ON . . .
I DON'T KNOW, IT SEEMED LIKE THE MONSTER DIDN'T EVEN UNDERSTAND WHY HARRY WAS AFRAID.
THAT'S WEIRD.
YEAH.
NO, I MEAN IT'S WEIRD THAT YOU TALK ABOUT YOURSELF LIKE A CHARACTER IN A STORY.

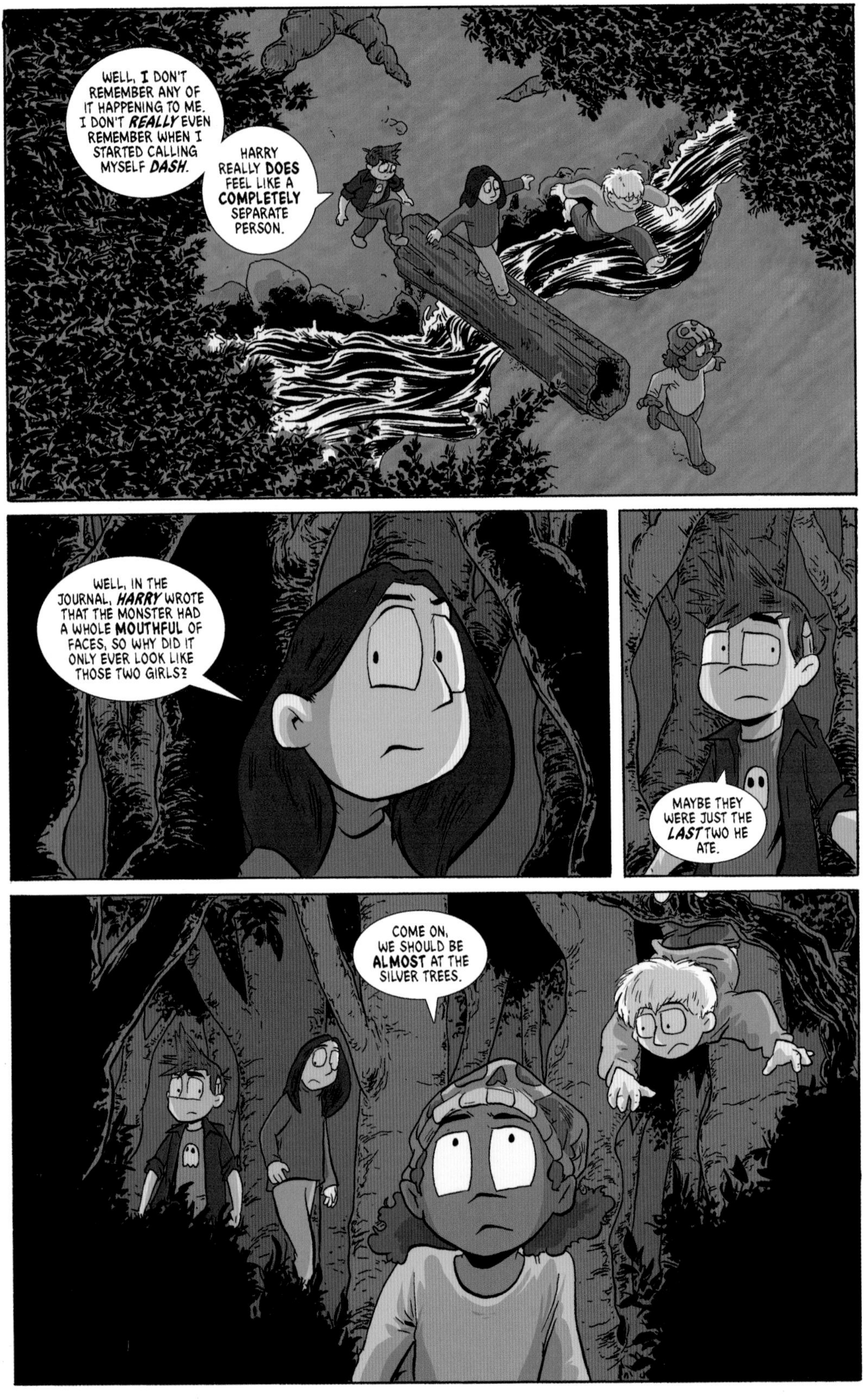
WELL, I DON'T REMEMBER ANY OF IT HAPPENING TO ME. I DON'T REALLY EVEN REMEMBER WHEN I STARTED CALLING MYSELF DASH.
HARRY REALLY DOES FEEL LIKE A COMPLETELY SEPARATE PERSON.
WELL, IN THE JOURNAL, HARRY WROTE THAT THE MONSTER HAD A WHOLE MOUTHFUL OF FACES, SO WHY DID IT ONLY EVER LOOK LIKE THOSE TWO GIRLS?
MAYBE THEY WERE JUST THE LAST TWO HE ATE.
COME ON, WE SHOULD BE ALMOST AT THE SILVER TREES.

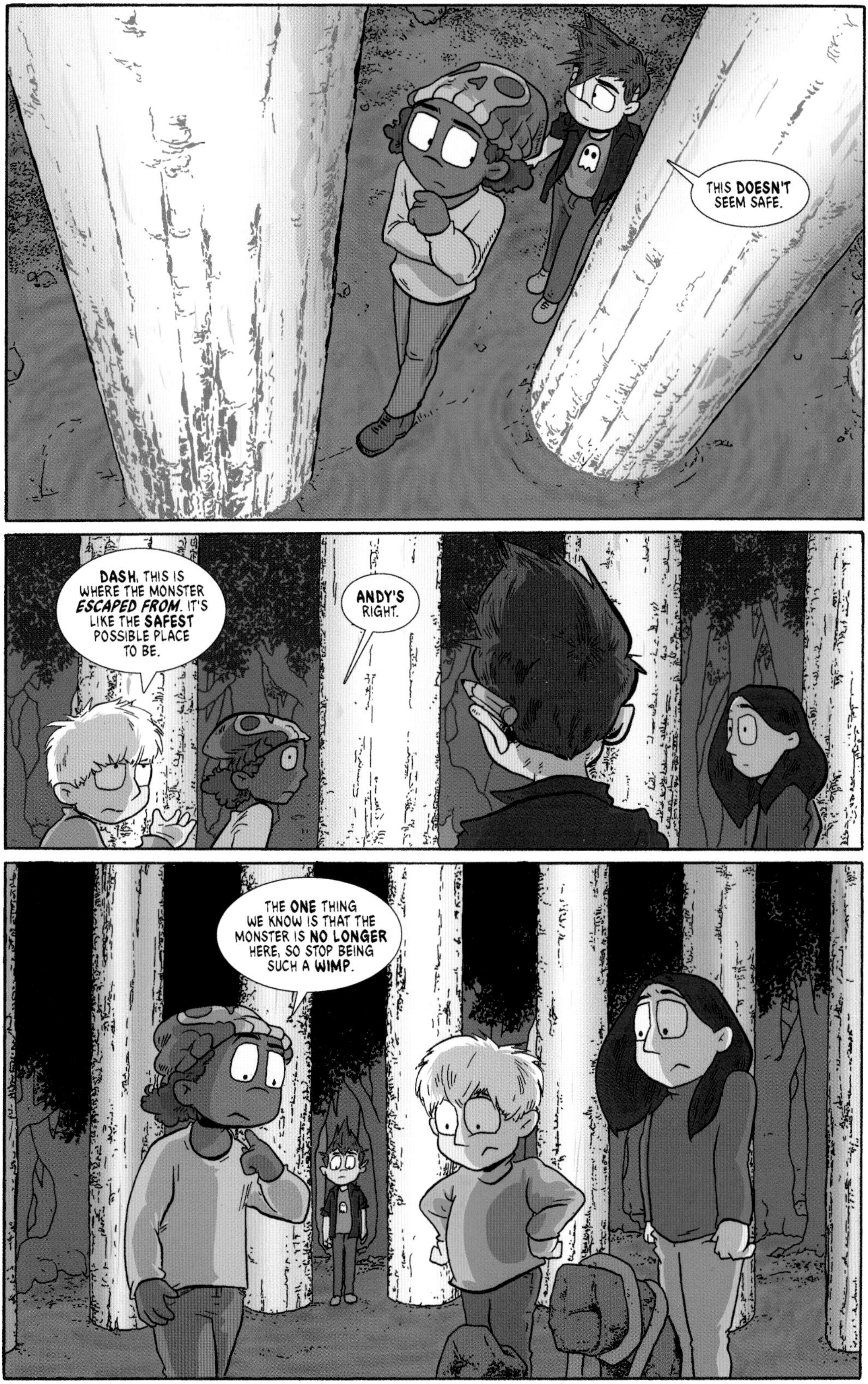
THIS DOESN'T SEEM SAFE.
DASH, THIS IS WHERE THE MONSTER ESCAPED FROM. IT'S LIKE THE SAFEST POSSIBLE PLACE TO BE.
ANDY'S RIGHT.
THE ONE THING WE KNOW IS THAT THE MONSTER IS NO LONGER HERE, SO STOP BEING SUCH A WIMP.

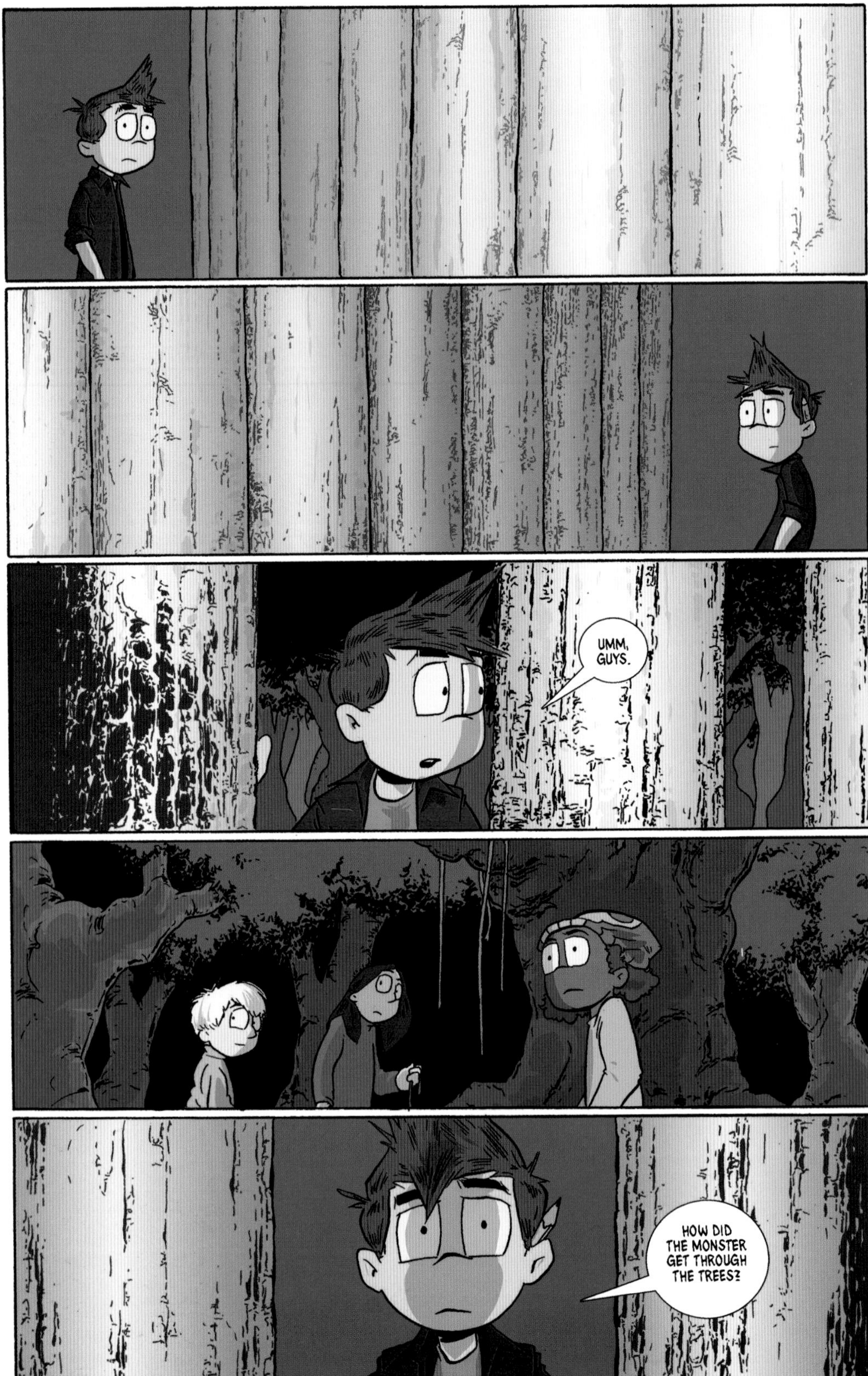
UMM, GUYS.
HOW DID THE MONSTER GET THROUGH THE TREES?

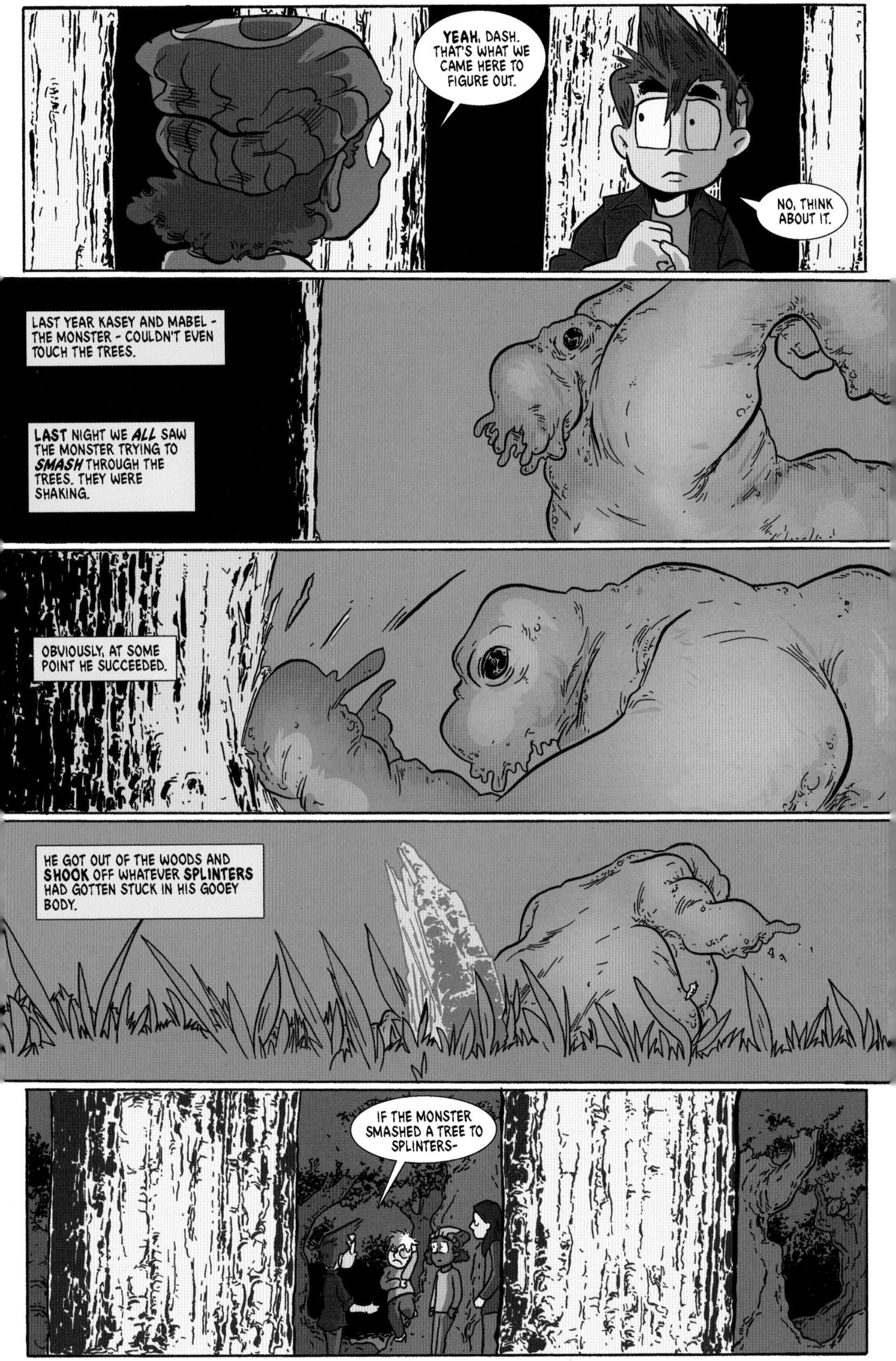

YEAH, DASH. THAT'S WHAT WE CAME HERE TO FIGURE OUT.
NO, THINK ABOUT IT.
LAST YEAR KASEY AND MABEL - THE MONSTER - COULDN'T EVEN TOUCH THE TREES.
LAST NIGHT WE ALL SAW THE MONSTER TRYING TO SMASH THROUGH THE TREES. THEY WERE SHAKING.
OBVIOUSLY, AT SOME POINT HE SUCCEEDED.
HE GOT OUT OF THE WOODS AND SHOOK OFF WHATEVER SPLINTERS HAD GOTTEN STUCK IN HIS GOOEY BODY.
IF THE MONSTER SMASHED A TREE TO SPLINTERS-

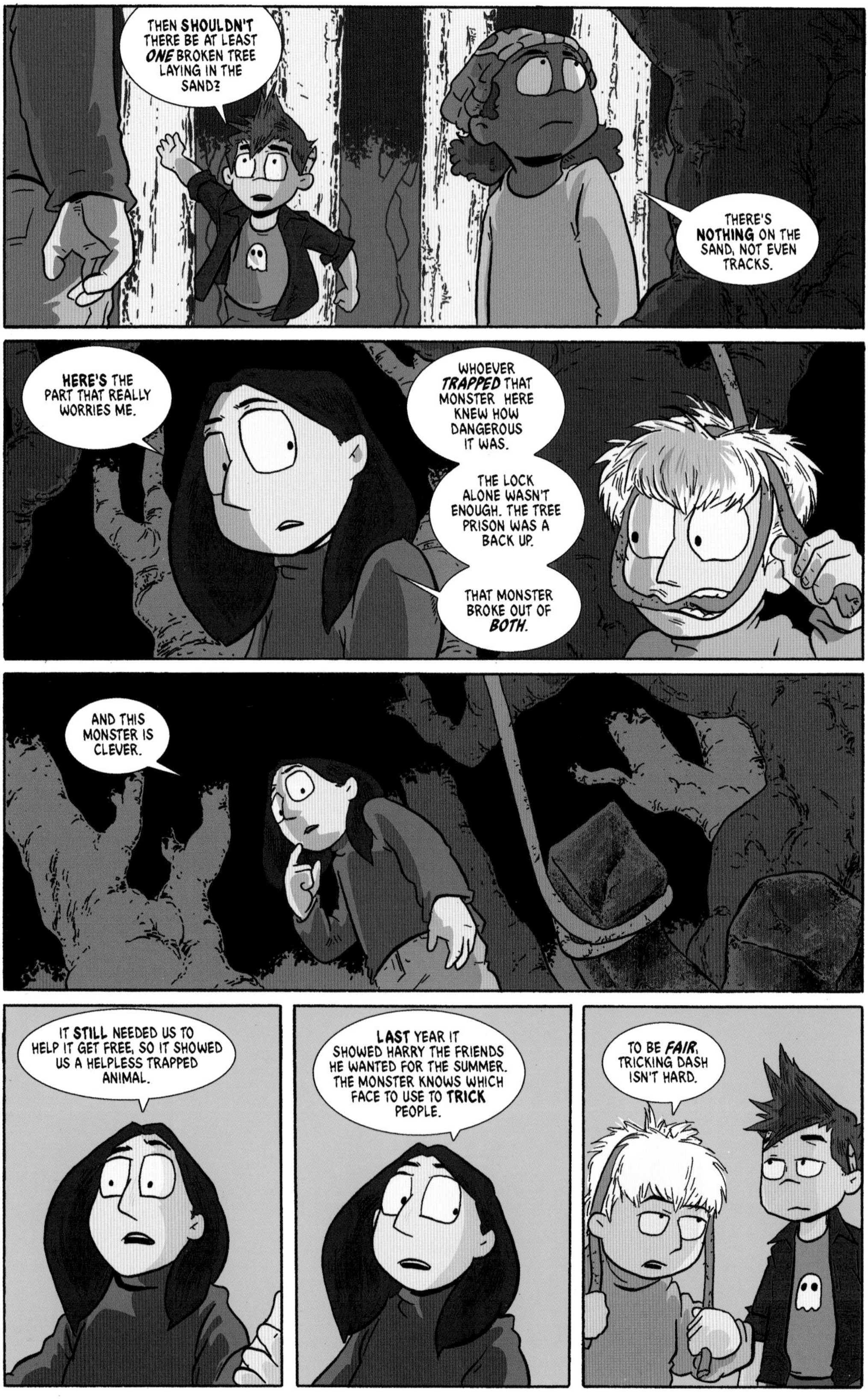
THEN SHOULDN'T THERE BE AT LEAST ONE BROKEN TREE LAYING IN THE SAND?
THERE'S NOTHING ON THE SAND, NOT EVEN TRACKS.
HERE'S THE PART THAT REALLY WORRIES ME.
WHOEVER TRAPPED THAT MONSTER HERE KNEW HOW DANGEROUS IT WAS.
THE LOCK ALONE WASN'T ENOUGH. THE TREE PRISON WAS A BACK UP.
THAT MONSTER BROKE OUT OF BOTH.
AND THIS MONSTER IS CLEVER.
IT STILL NEEDED US TO HELP IT GET FREE, SO IT SHOWED US A HELPLESS TRAPPED ANIMAL.
LAST YEAR IT SHOWED HARRY THE FRIENDS HE WANTED FOR THE SUMMER. THE MONSTER KNOWS WHICH FACE TO USE TO TRICK PEOPLE.
TO BE FAIR, TRICKING DASH ISN'T HARD.

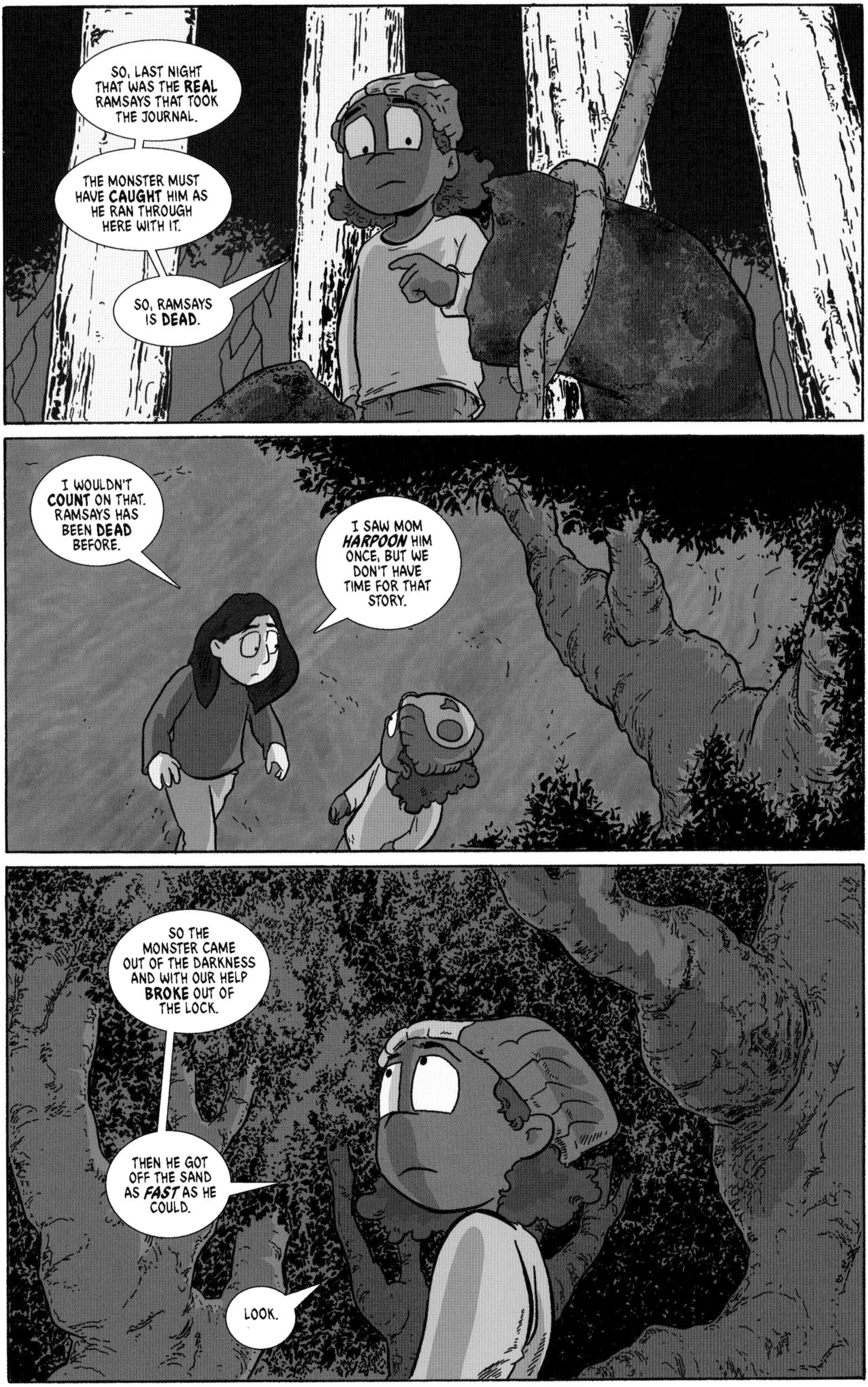
SO, LAST NIGHT THAT WAS THE **REAL** RAMSAYS THAT TOOK THE JOURNAL.
THE MONSTER MUST HAVE **CAUGHT** HIM AS HE RAN THROUGH HERE WITH IT.
SO, RAMSAYS IS **DEAD**.
I WOULDN'T **COUNT** ON THAT. RAMSAYS HAS BEEN **DEAD** BEFORE.
I SAW MOM ***HARPOON*** HIM ONCE, BUT WE DON'T HAVE TIME FOR THAT STORY.
SO THE MONSTER CAME OUT OF THE DARKNESS AND WITH OUR HELP **BROKE** OUT OF THE LOCK.
THEN HE GOT OFF THE SAND AS ***FAST*** AS HE COULD.
LOOK.

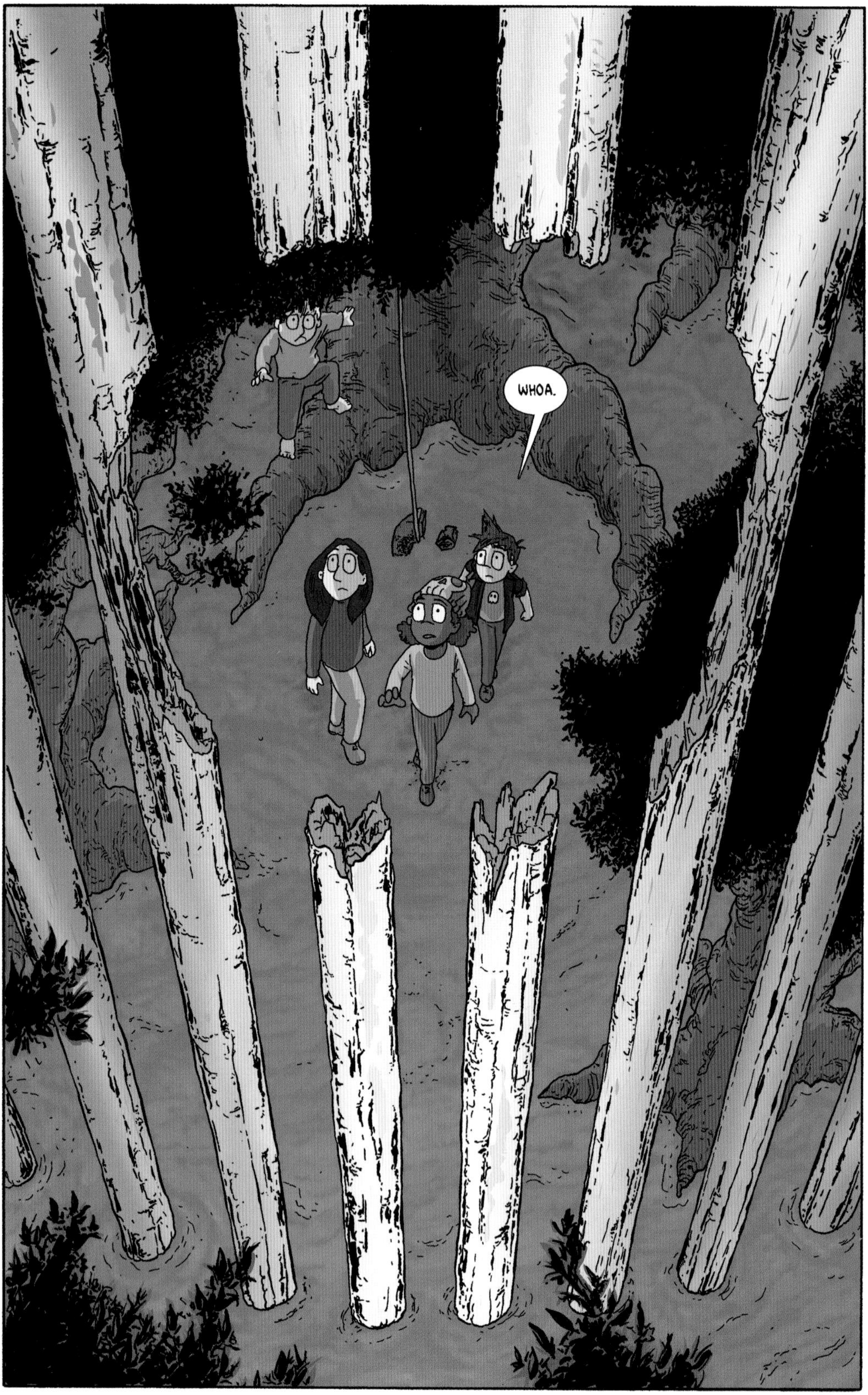
WHOA.

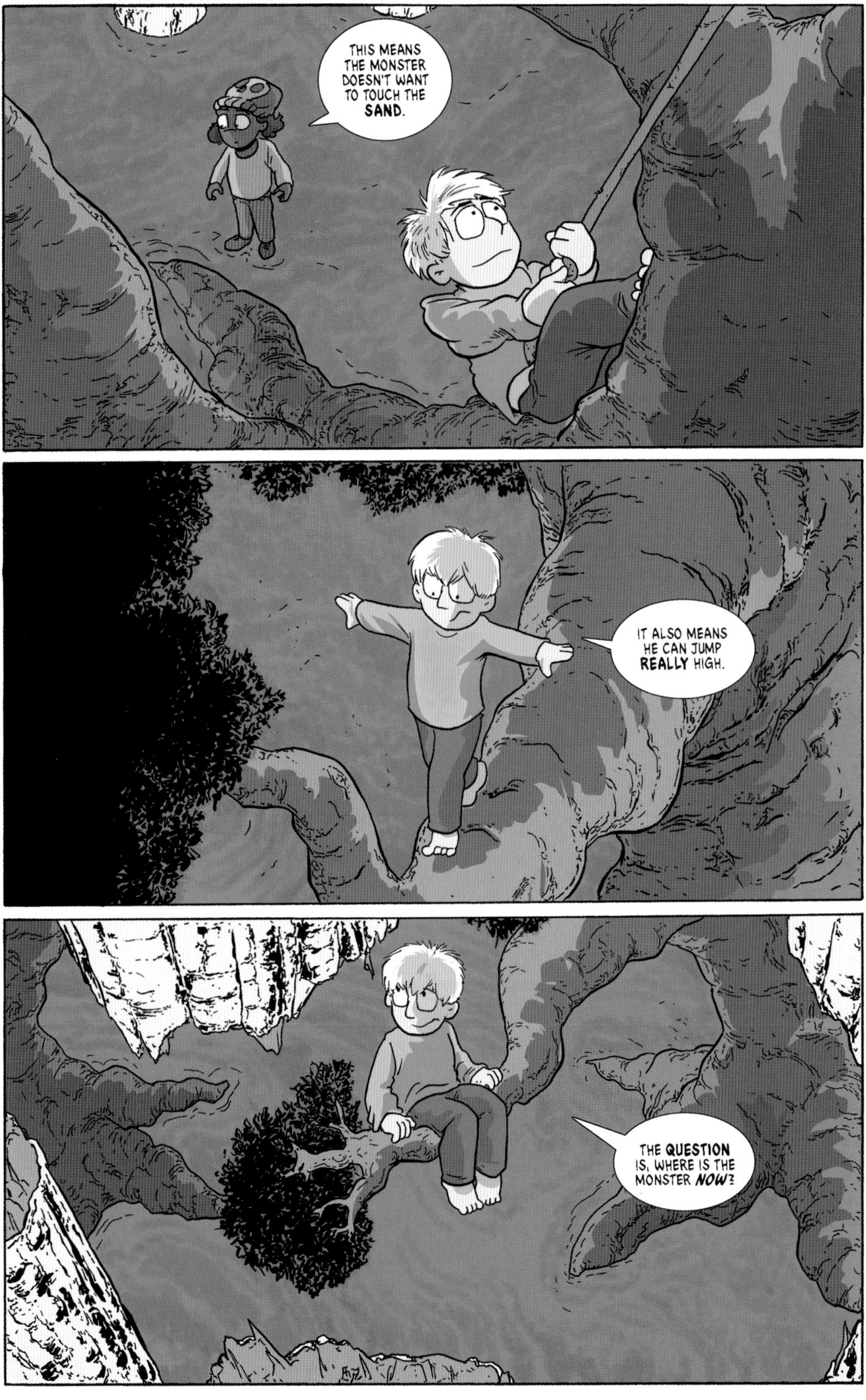
THIS MEANS THE MONSTER DOESN'T WANT TO TOUCH THE SAND.
IT ALSO MEANS HE CAN JUMP REALLY HIGH.
THE QUESTION IS, WHERE IS THE MONSTER NOW?

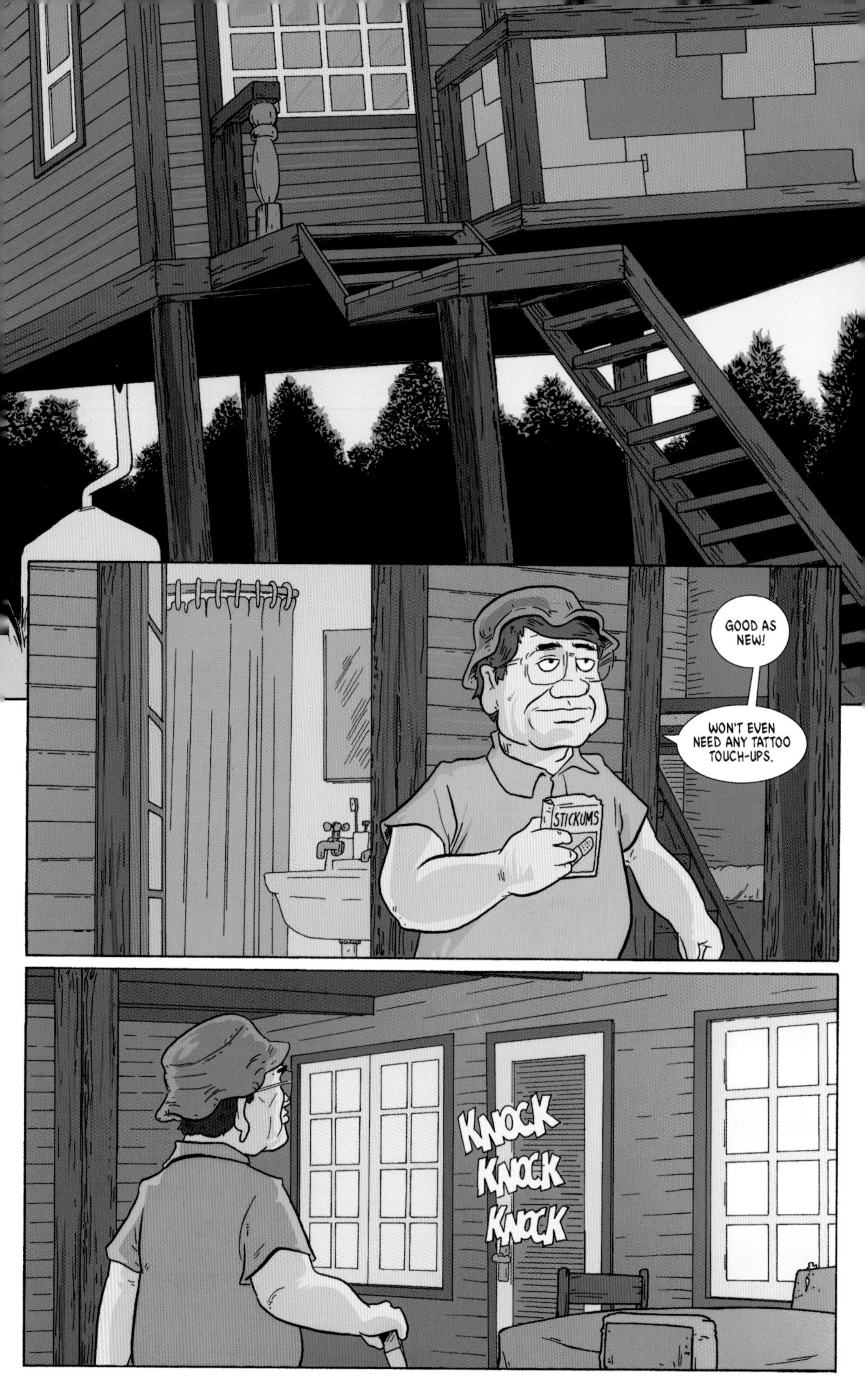
GOOD AS NEW!
WON'T EVEN NEED ANY TATTOO TOUCH-UPS.
STICKUMS
KNOCK
KNOCK
KNOCK

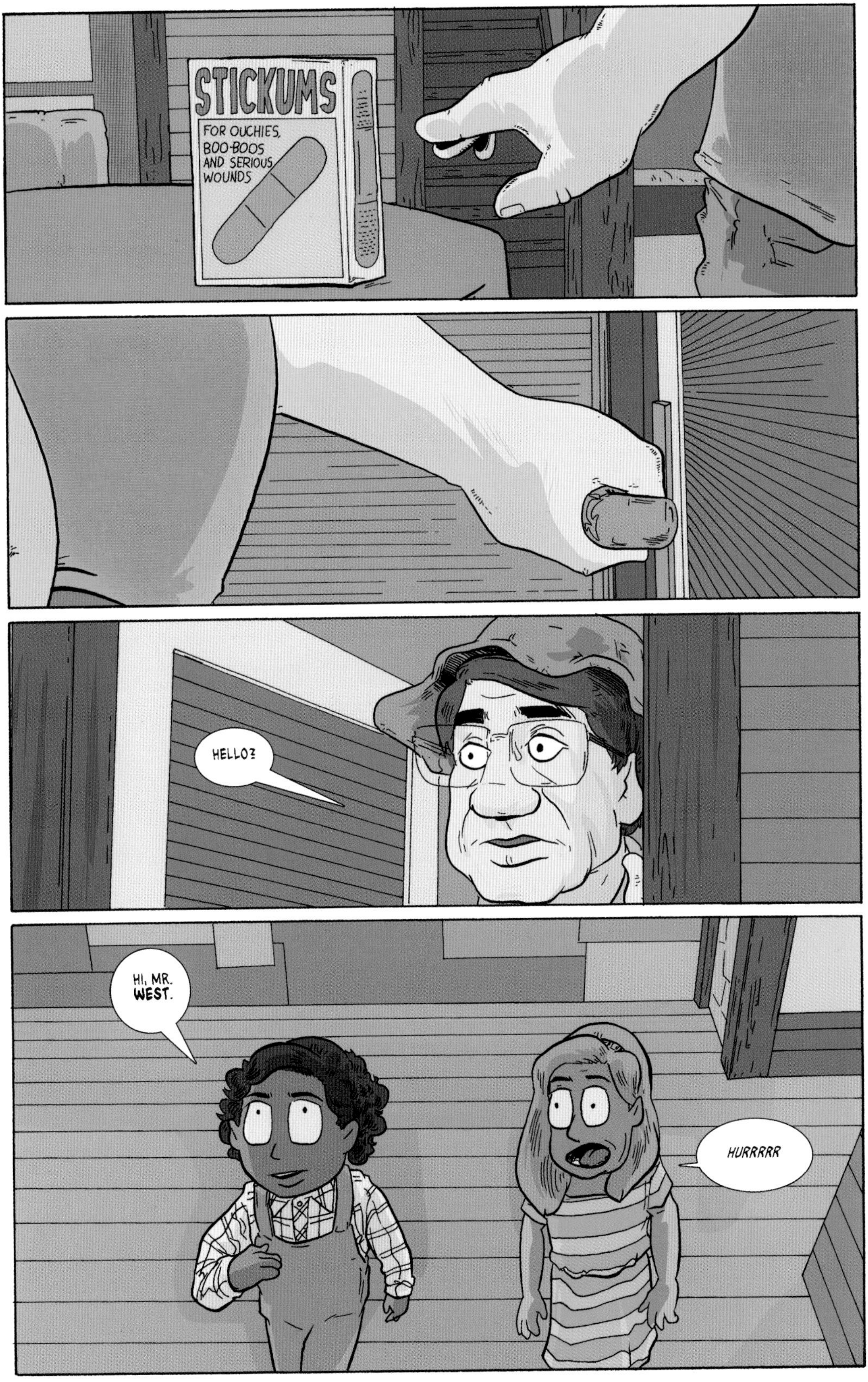
STICKUMS
FOR OUCHIES, BOO-BOOS AND SERIOUS WOUNDS
HELLO?
HI, MR. WEST.
HURRRRR

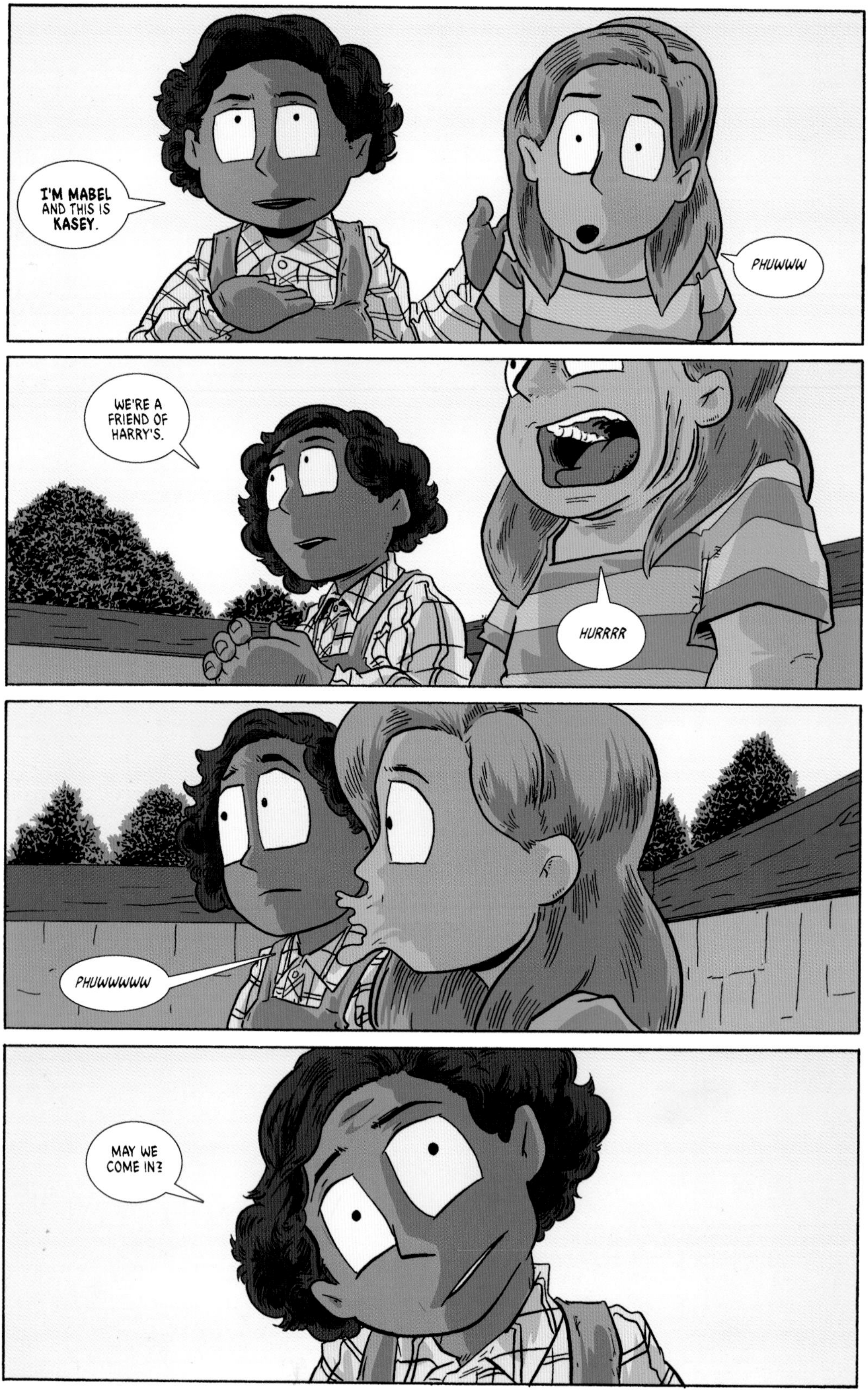
I'M MABEL AND THIS IS KASEY.
PHUWWW
WE'RE A FRIEND OF HARRY'S.
HURRRR
PHUWWWWW
MAY WE COME IN?

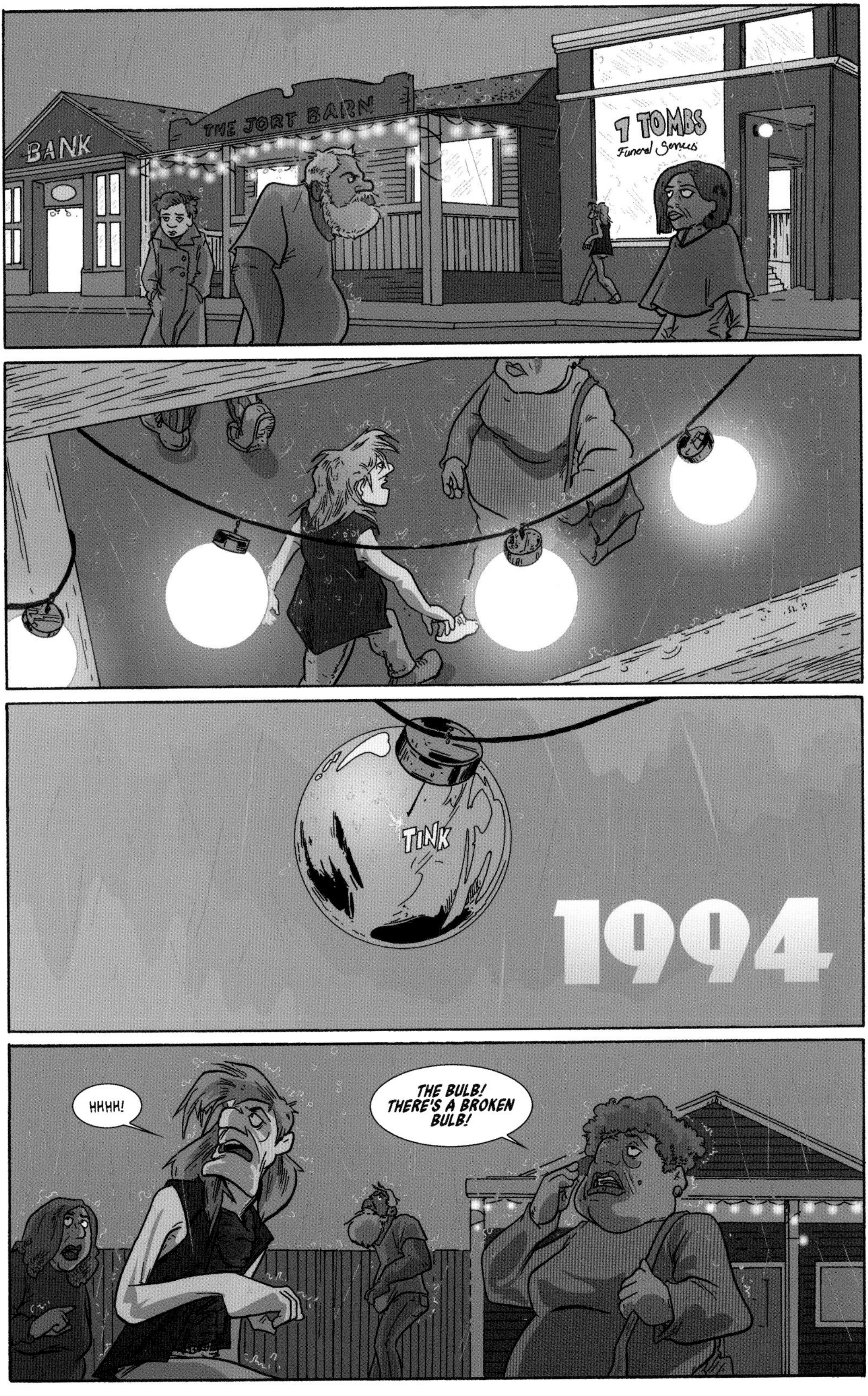
BANK
THE JORT BARN
7 TOMBS
Funeral Services
TINK
1994
HHHH!
THE BULB! THERE'S A BROKEN BULB!

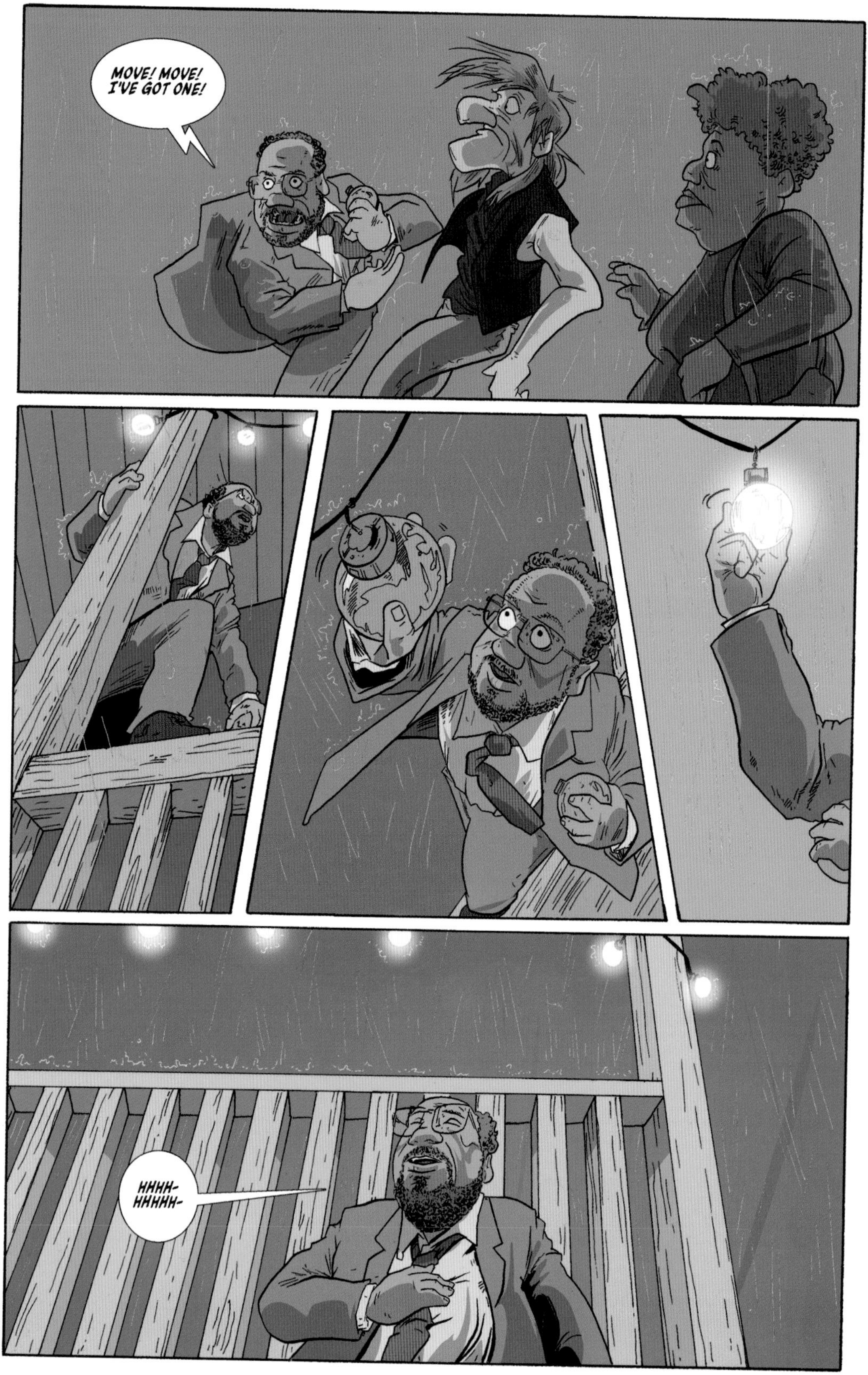
MOVE! MOVE!
I'VE GOT ONE!
HHHH-
HHHHH-

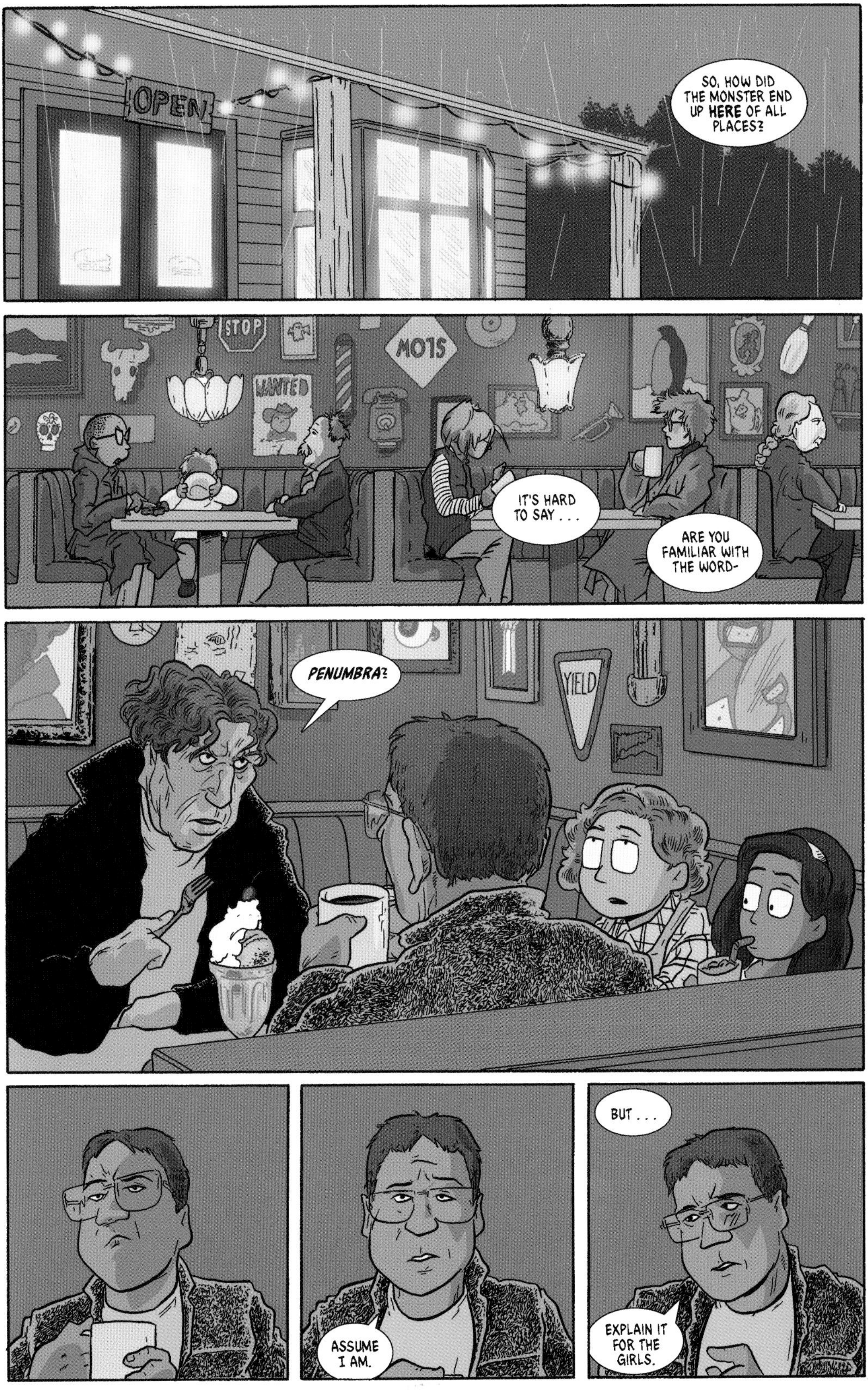
OPEN
SO, HOW DID THE MONSTER END UP **HERE** OF ALL PLACES?
STOP
SLOW
WANTED
IT'S HARD TO SAY . . .
ARE YOU FAMILIAR WITH THE WORD-
PENUMBRA?
YIELD
ASSUME I AM.
BUT . . .
EXPLAIN IT FOR THE GIRLS.

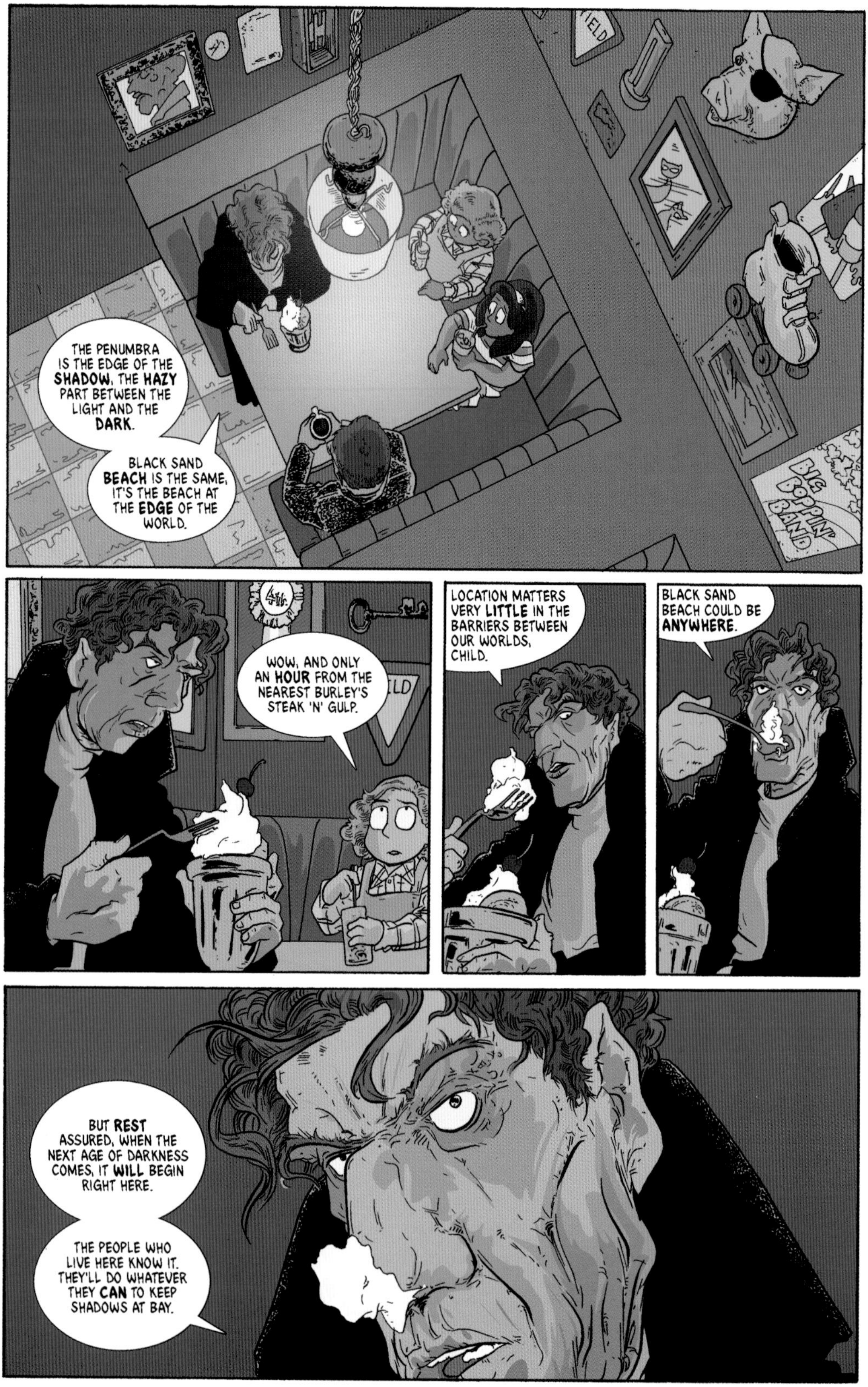
FIELD
THE PENUMBRA IS THE EDGE OF THE SHADOW, THE HAZY PART BETWEEN THE LIGHT AND THE DARK.
BLACK SAND BEACH IS THE SAME, IT'S THE BEACH AT THE EDGE OF THE WORLD.
BIG BOPPIN' BAND
WOW, AND ONLY AN HOUR FROM THE NEAREST BURLEY'S STEAK 'N' GULP.
LOCATION MATTERS VERY LITTLE IN THE BARRIERS BETWEEN OUR WORLDS, CHILD.
BLACK SAND BEACH COULD BE ANYWHERE.
BUT REST ASSURED, WHEN THE NEXT AGE OF DARKNESS COMES, IT WILL BEGIN RIGHT HERE.
THE PEOPLE WHO LIVE HERE KNOW IT. THEY'LL DO WHATEVER THEY CAN TO KEEP SHADOWS AT BAY.

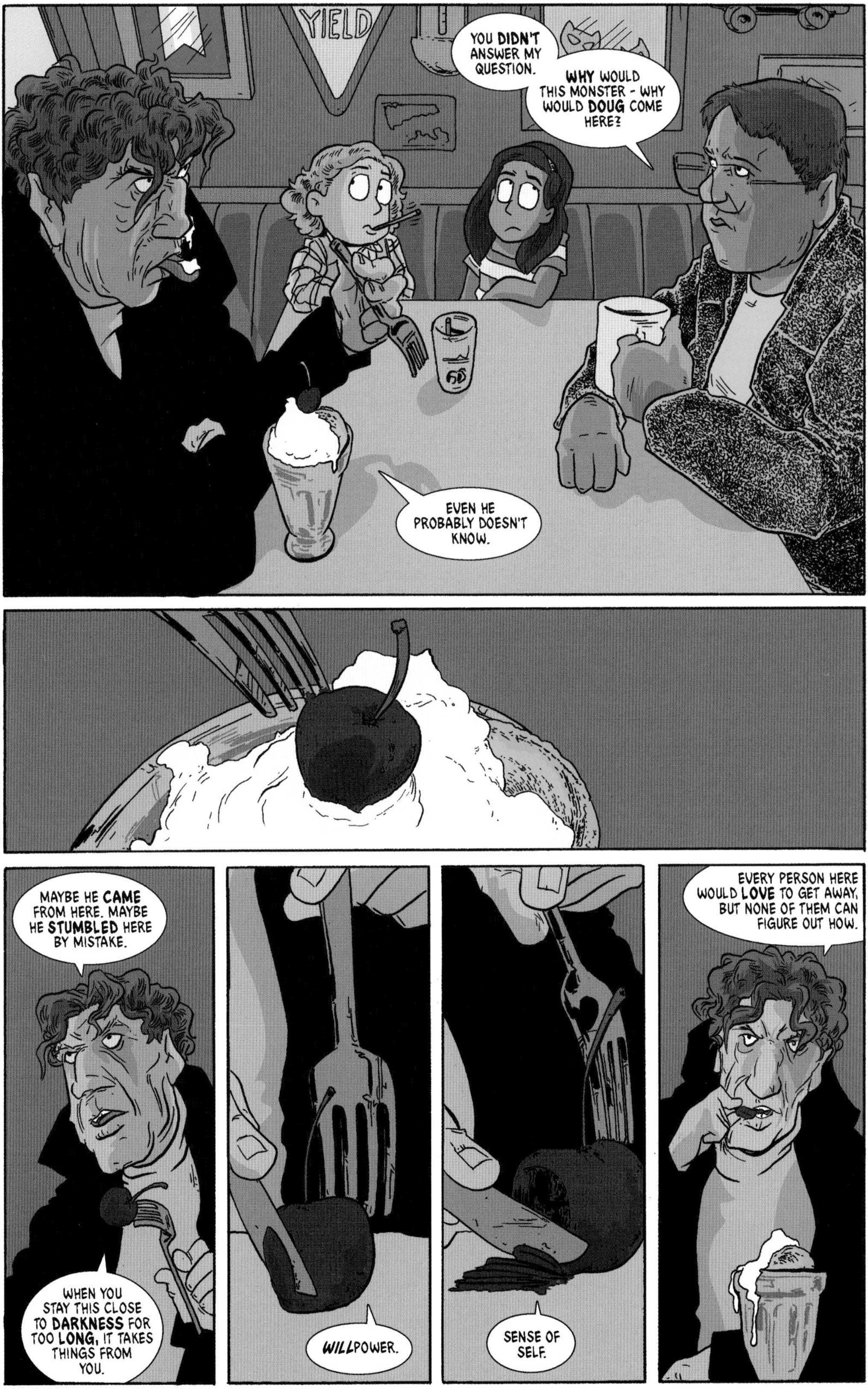
YIELD
YOU DIDN'T ANSWER MY QUESTION.
WHY WOULD THIS MONSTER - WHY WOULD DOUG COME HERE?
EVEN HE PROBABLY DOESN'T KNOW.
MAYBE HE CAME FROM HERE. MAYBE HE STUMBLED HERE BY MISTAKE.
WHEN YOU STAY THIS CLOSE TO DARKNESS FOR TOO LONG, IT TAKES THINGS FROM YOU.
WILLPOWER.
SENSE OF SELF.
EVERY PERSON HERE WOULD LOVE TO GET AWAY, BUT NONE OF THEM CAN FIGURE OUT HOW.

WELL THEN OF COURSE HE'D STAY HERE.
PLENTY OF PEOPLE TO EAT WHO HE KNOWS CAN'T GET FAR.
NO, DOUG WOULD RELISH THE CHANCE TO LEAVE. TOUCHING THE DARKNESS CAUSES HIM IMMENSE PAIN.
BUT DOUG'S SURVIVAL RELIES ON HIM STAYING HIDDEN, UNNOTICED.
FOR DOUG TO GET AWAY, HE'D NEED TO ABSORB SOMEONE WITH A MIND UNCLOUDED BY BLACK SAND BEACH.
AN OUTSIDER.

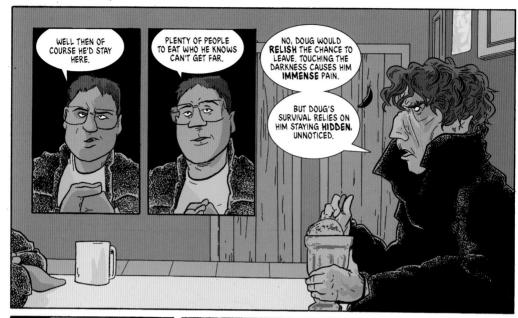

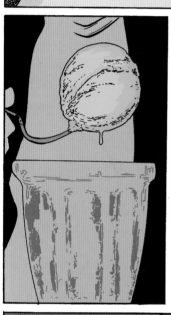

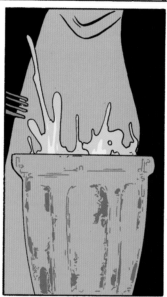

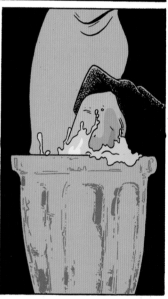

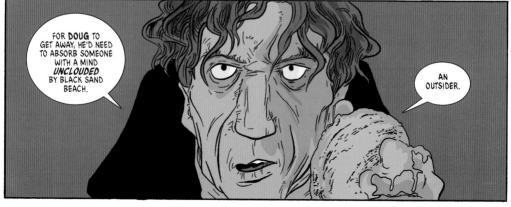

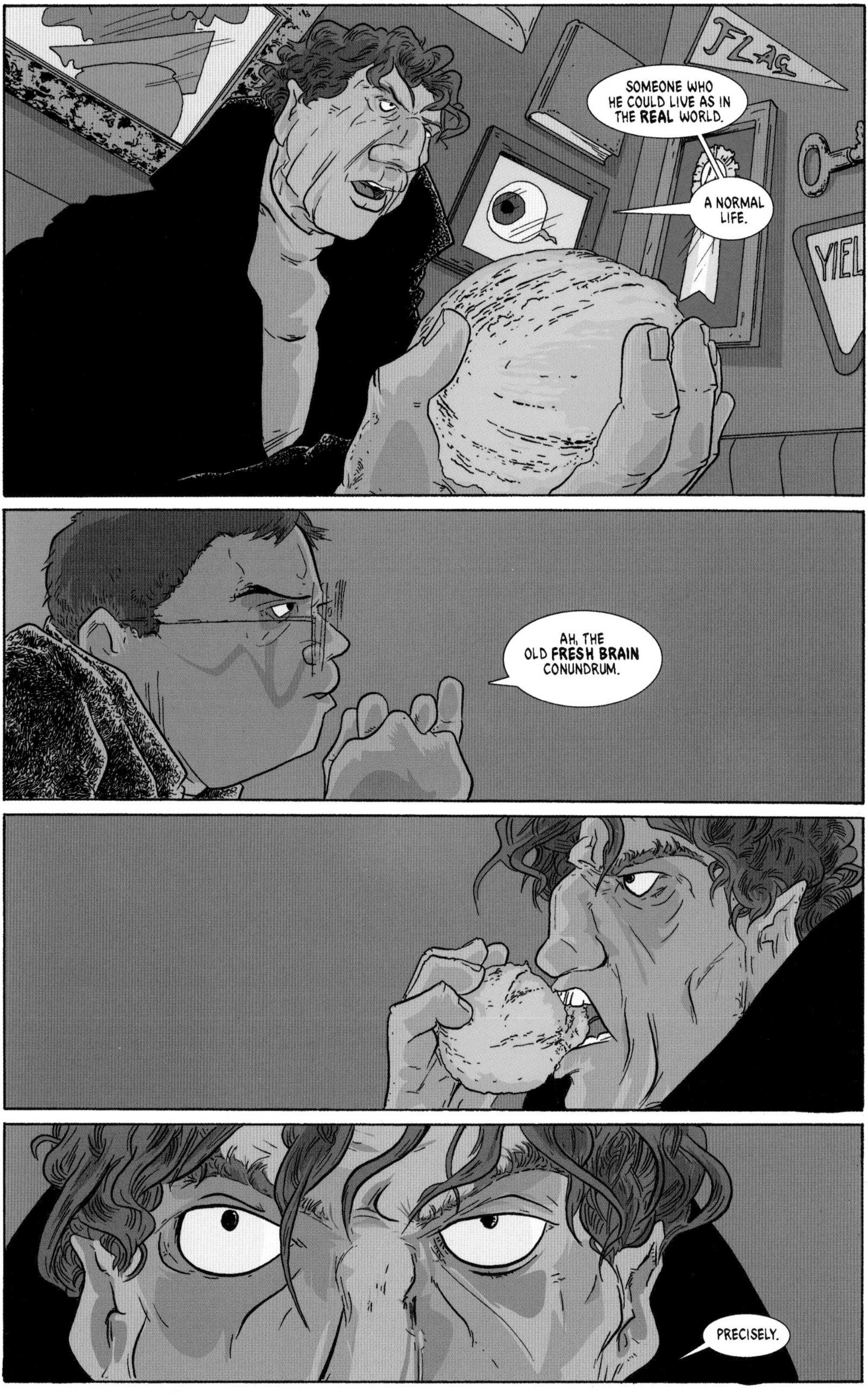
SOMEONE WHO HE COULD LIVE AS IN THE REAL WORLD.
A NORMAL LIFE.
AH, THE OLD FRESH BRAIN CONUNDRUM.
PRECISELY.

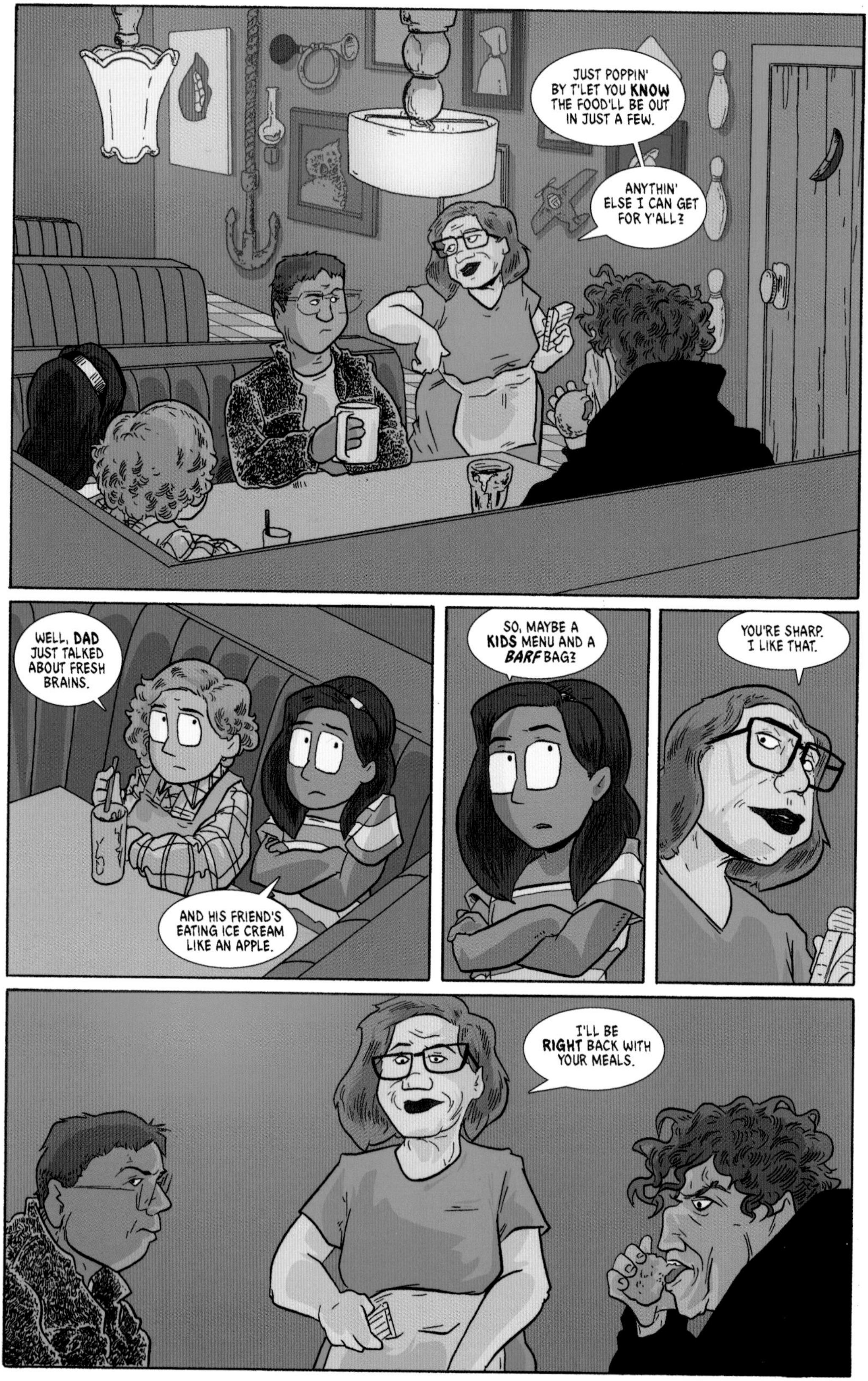

JUST POPPIN' BY T'LET YOU KNOW THE FOOD'LL BE OUT IN JUST A FEW.
ANYTHIN' ELSE I CAN GET FOR Y'ALL?
WELL, DAD JUST TALKED ABOUT FRESH BRAINS.
AND HIS FRIEND'S EATING ICE CREAM LIKE AN APPLE.
SO, MAYBE A KIDS MENU AND A BARF BAG?
YOU'RE SHARP. I LIKE THAT.
I'LL BE RIGHT BACK WITH YOUR MEALS.

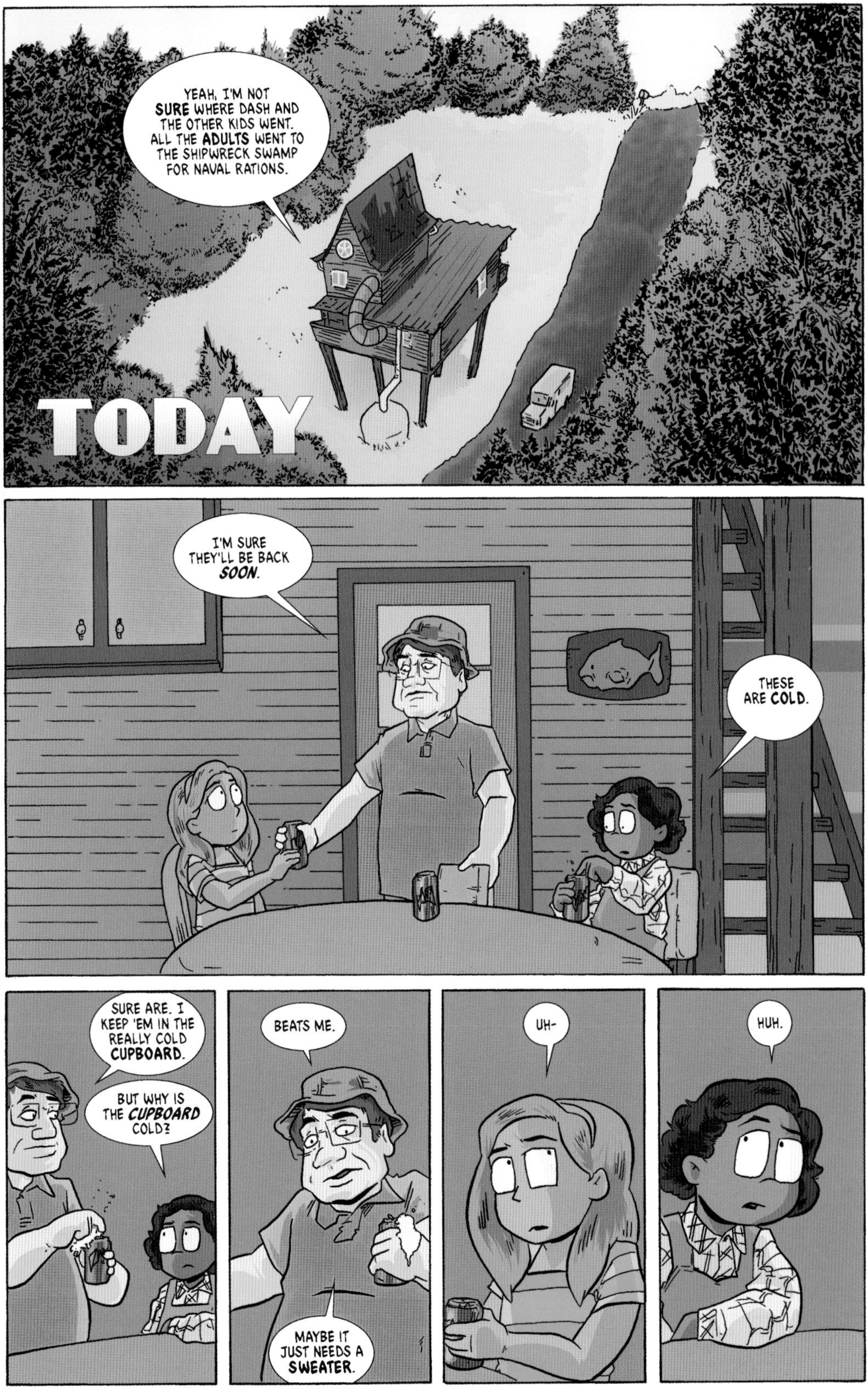
YEAH, I'M NOT SURE WHERE DASH AND THE OTHER KIDS WENT. ALL THE ADULTS WENT TO THE SHIPWRECK SWAMP FOR NAVAL RATIONS.
TODAY
I'M SURE THEY'LL BE BACK SOON.
THESE ARE COLD.
SURE ARE. I KEEP 'EM IN THE REALLY COLD CUPBOARD.
BUT WHY IS THE CUPBOARD COLD?
BEATS ME.
MAYBE IT JUST NEEDS A SWEATER.
UH-
HUH.

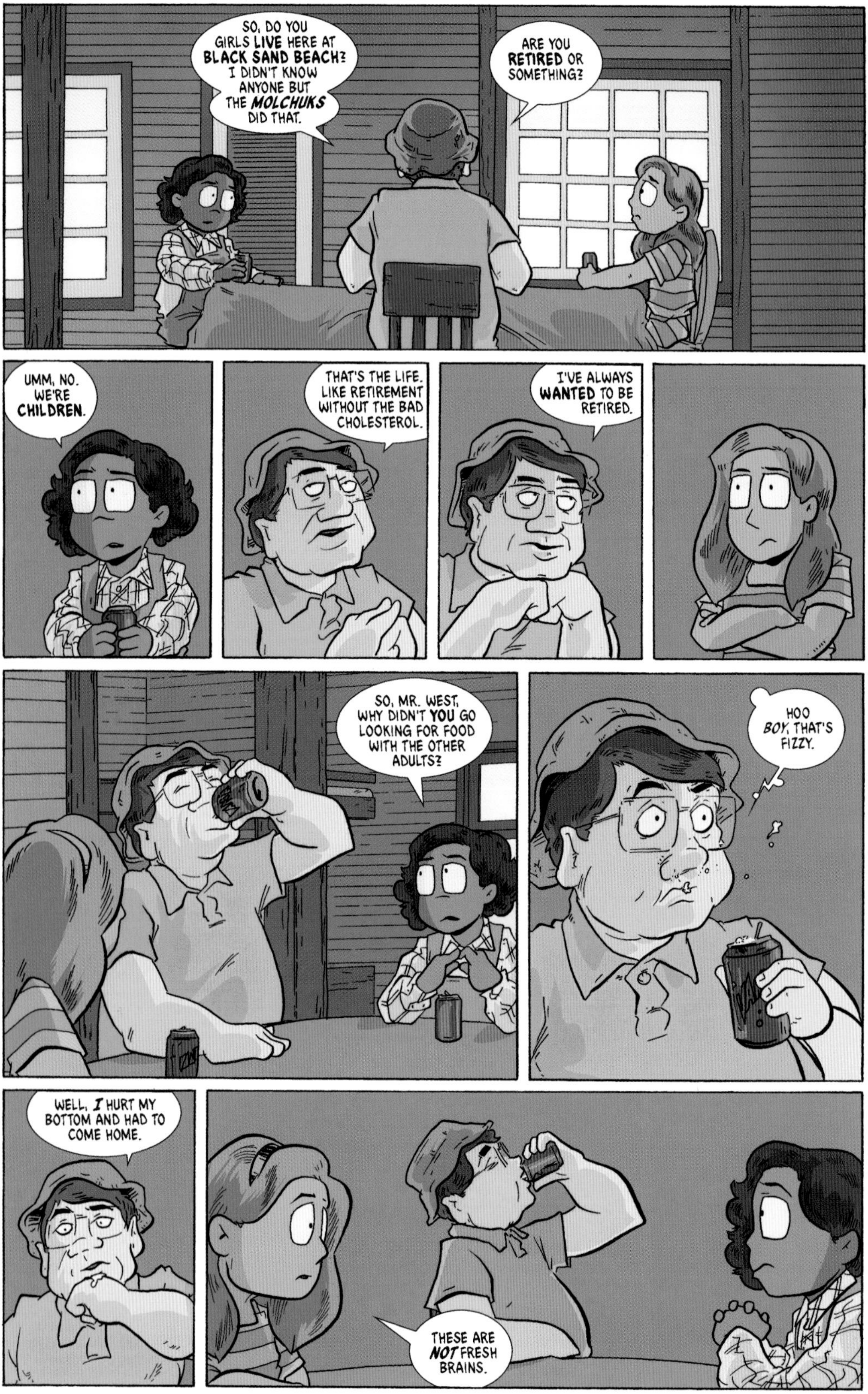
SO, DO YOU GIRLS LIVE HERE AT BLACK SAND BEACH? I DIDN'T KNOW ANYONE BUT THE MOLCHUKS DID THAT.
ARE YOU RETIRED OR SOMETHING?
UMM, NO. WE'RE CHILDREN.
THAT'S THE LIFE. LIKE RETIREMENT WITHOUT THE BAD CHOLESTEROL.
I'VE ALWAYS WANTED TO BE RETIRED.
SO, MR. WEST, WHY DIDN'T YOU GO LOOKING FOR FOOD WITH THE OTHER ADULTS?
HOO BOY, THAT'S FIZZY.
WELL, I HURT MY BOTTOM AND HAD TO COME HOME.
THESE ARE NOT FRESH BRAINS.

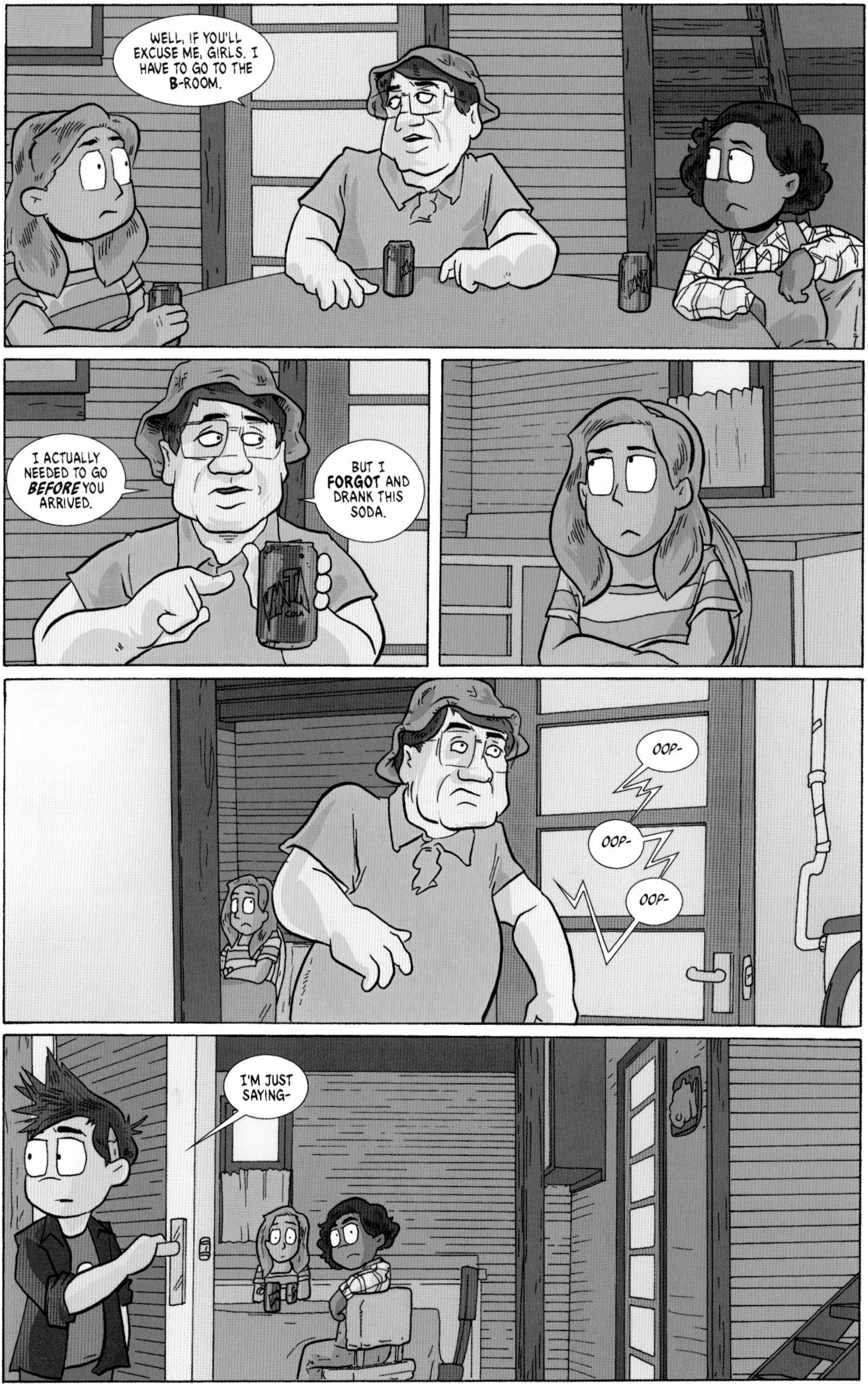
WELL, IF YOU'LL EXCUSE ME, GIRLS. I HAVE TO GO TO THE B-ROOM.
I ACTUALLY NEEDED TO GO BEFORE YOU ARRIVED.
BUT I FORGOT AND DRANK THIS SODA.
OOP-
OOP-
OOP-
I'M JUST SAYING-

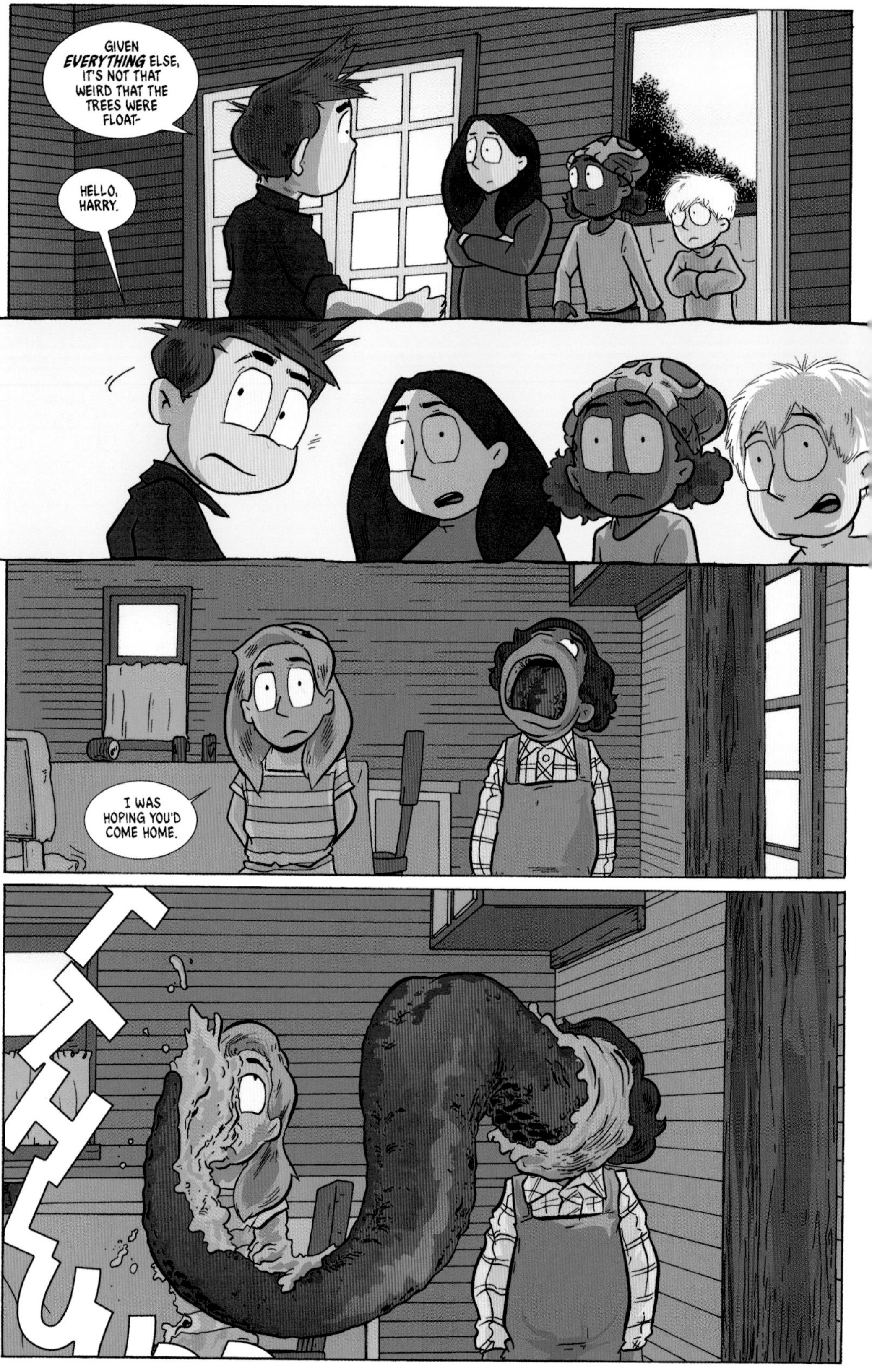
GIVEN EVERYTHING ELSE, IT'S NOT THAT WEIRD THAT THE TREES WERE FLOAT-
HELLO, HARRY.
I WAS HOPING YOU'D COME HOME.

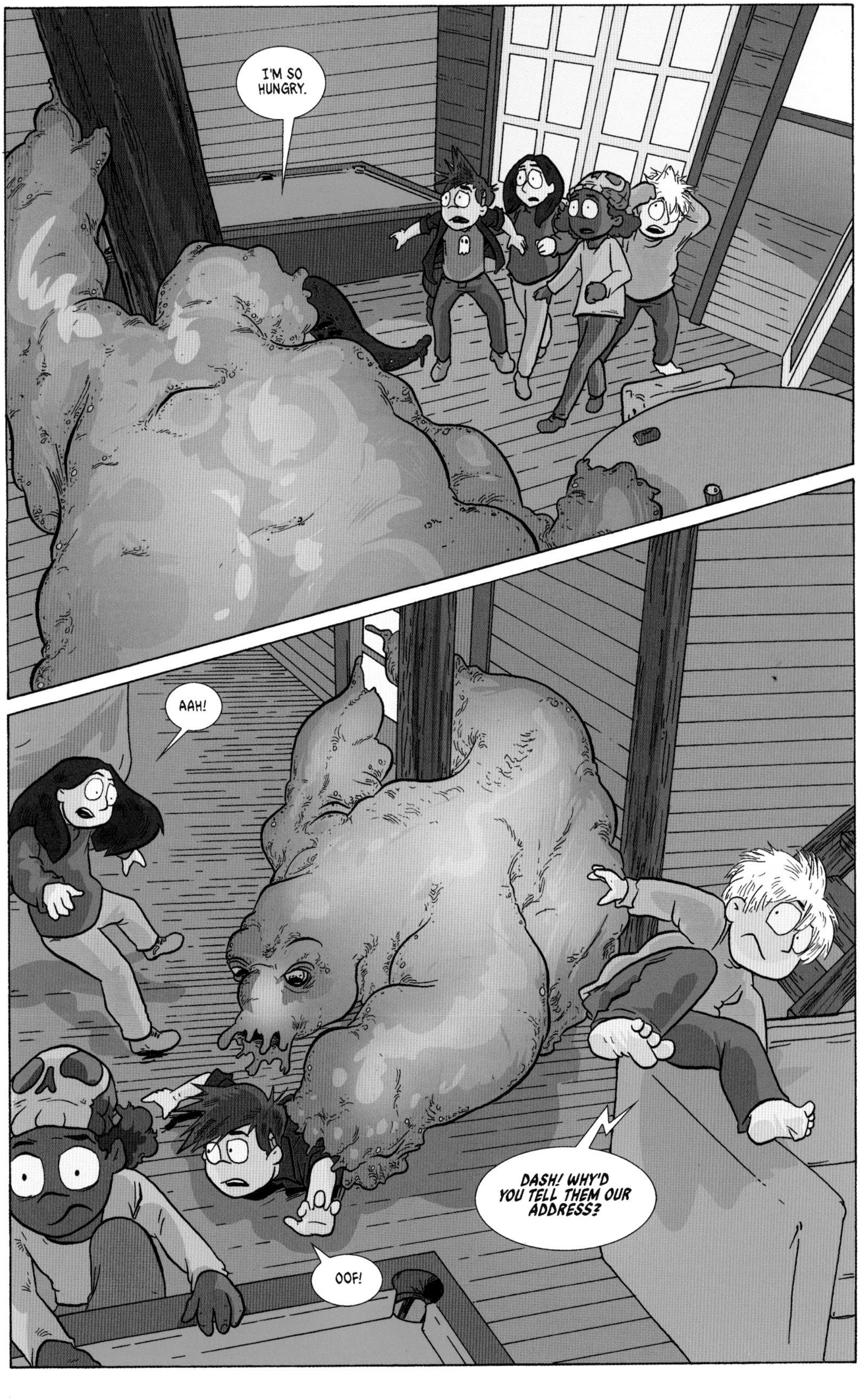
I'M SO HUNGRY.
AAH!
DASH! WHY'D YOU TELL THEM OUR ADDRESS?
OOF!

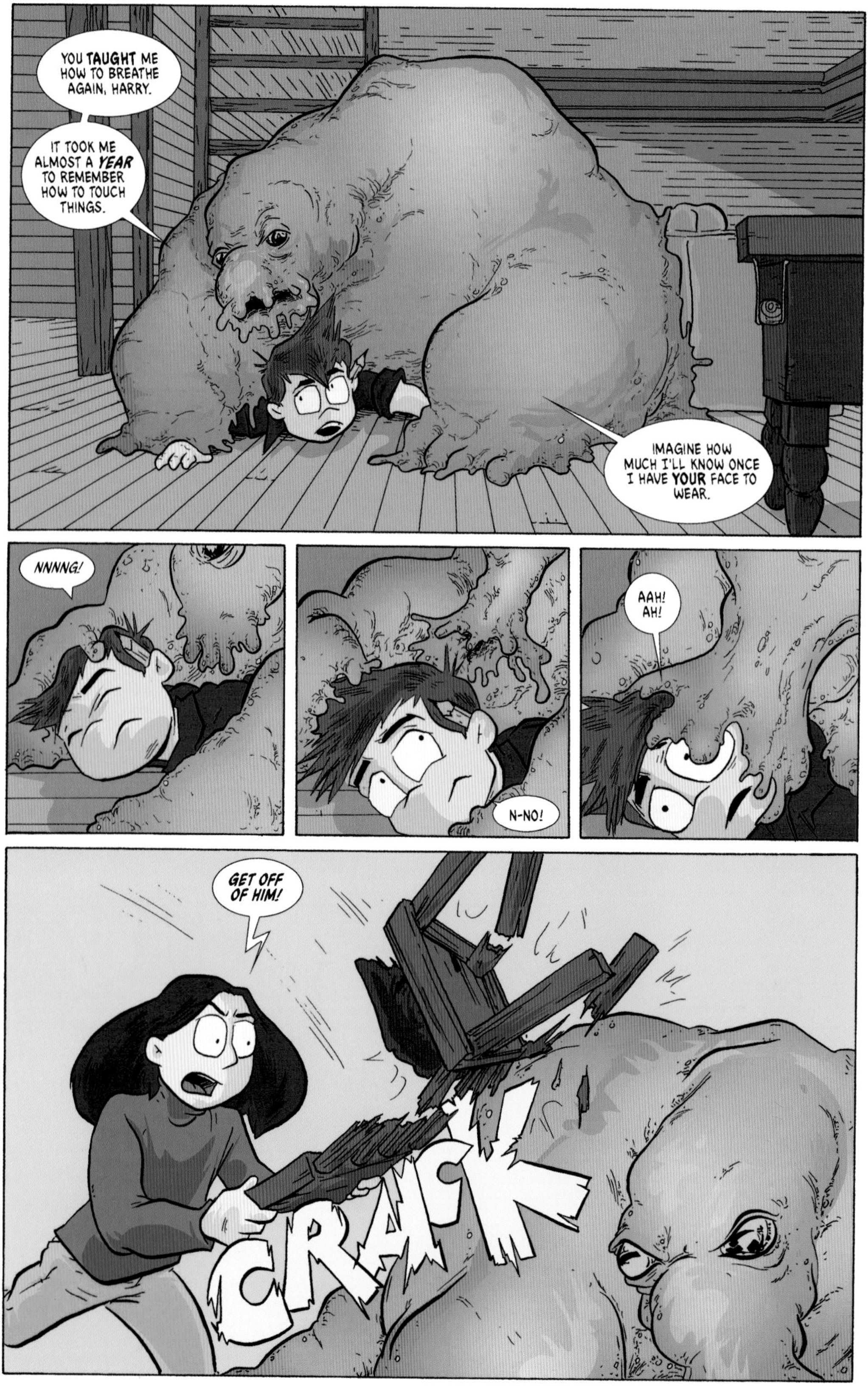
YOU TAUGHT ME HOW TO BREATHE AGAIN, HARRY.
IT TOOK ME ALMOST A YEAR TO REMEMBER HOW TO TOUCH THINGS.
IMAGINE HOW MUCH I'LL KNOW ONCE I HAVE YOUR FACE TO WEAR.
NNNNG!
N-NO!
AAH! AH!
GET OFF OF HIM!
CRACK

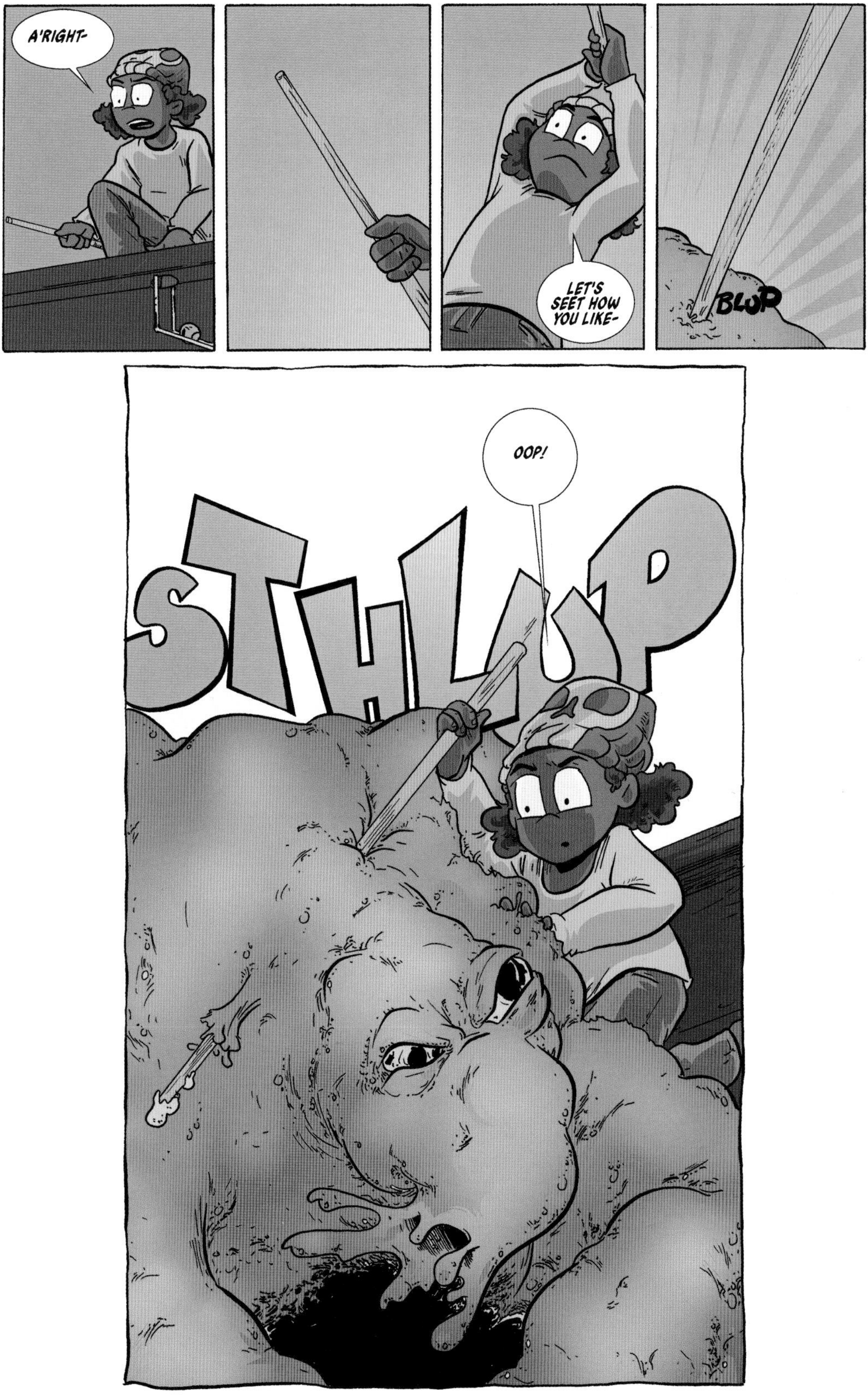
A'RIGHT-
LET'S SEET HOW YOU LIKE-
BLUP
OOP!
STHLUP

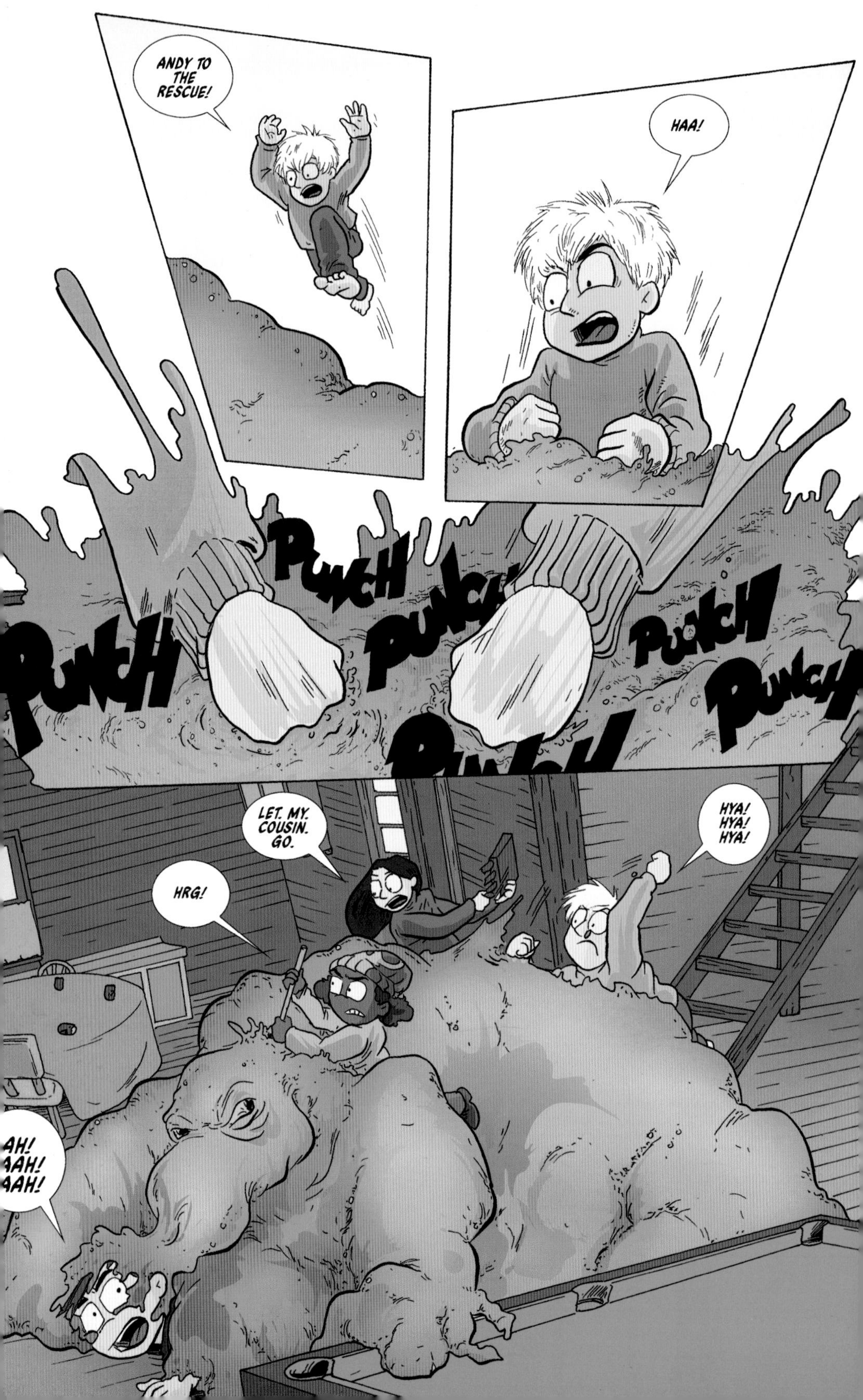
ANDY TO THE RESCUE!
HAA!
PUNCH
PUNCH
PUNCH
PUNCH
PUNCH
PUNCH
LET. MY. COUSIN. GO.
HYA! HYA! HYA!
HRG!
AH! AAH! AAH!

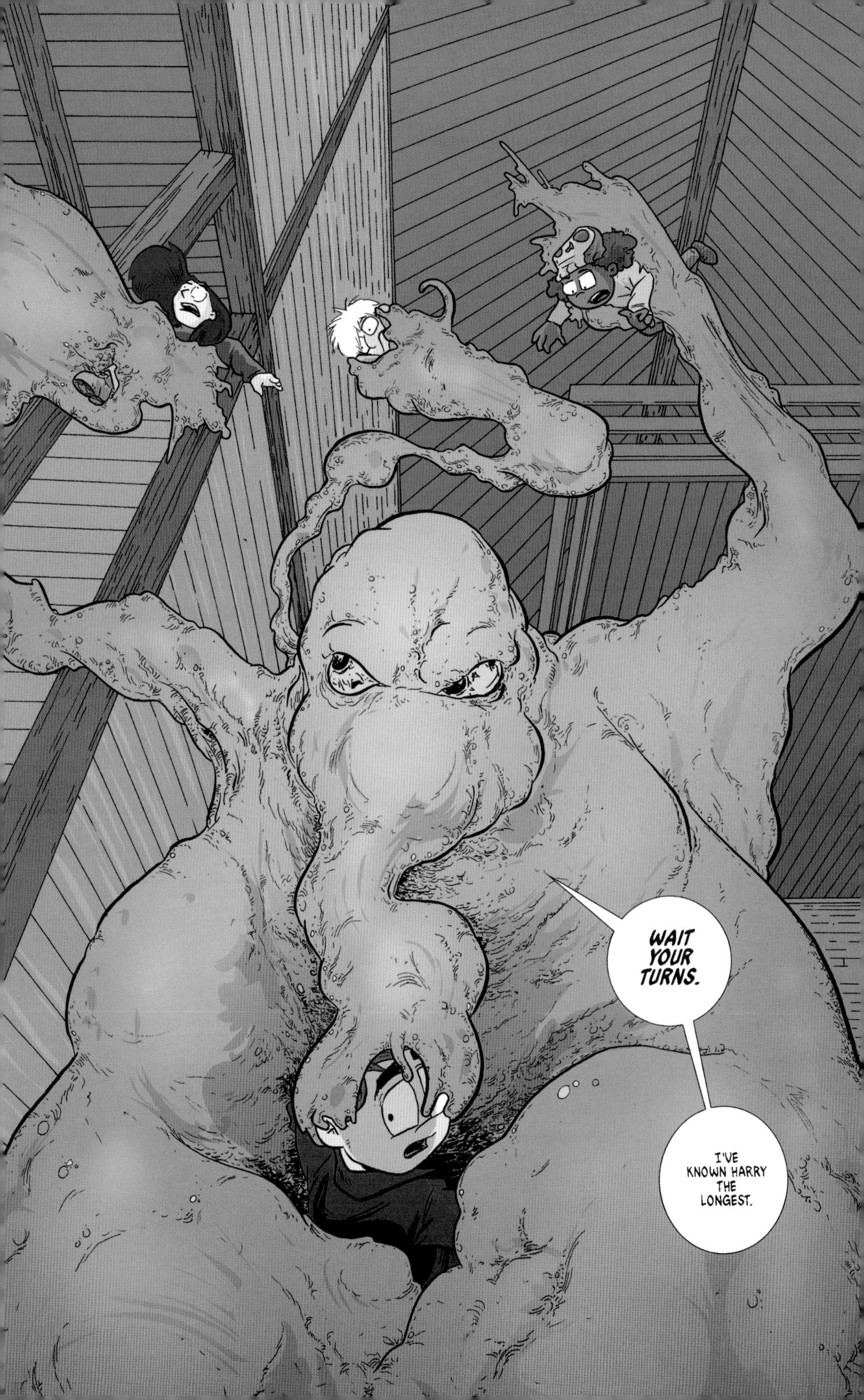
WAIT YOUR TURNS.
I'VE KNOWN HARRY THE LONGEST.

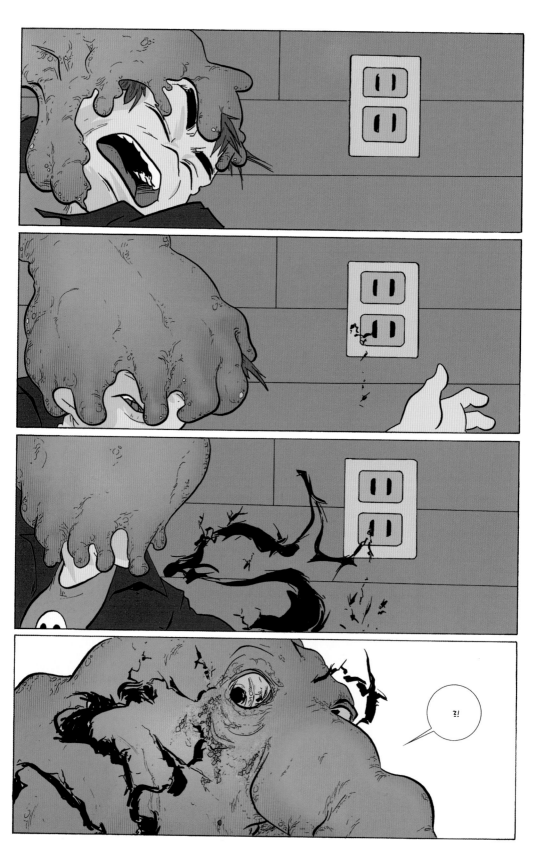

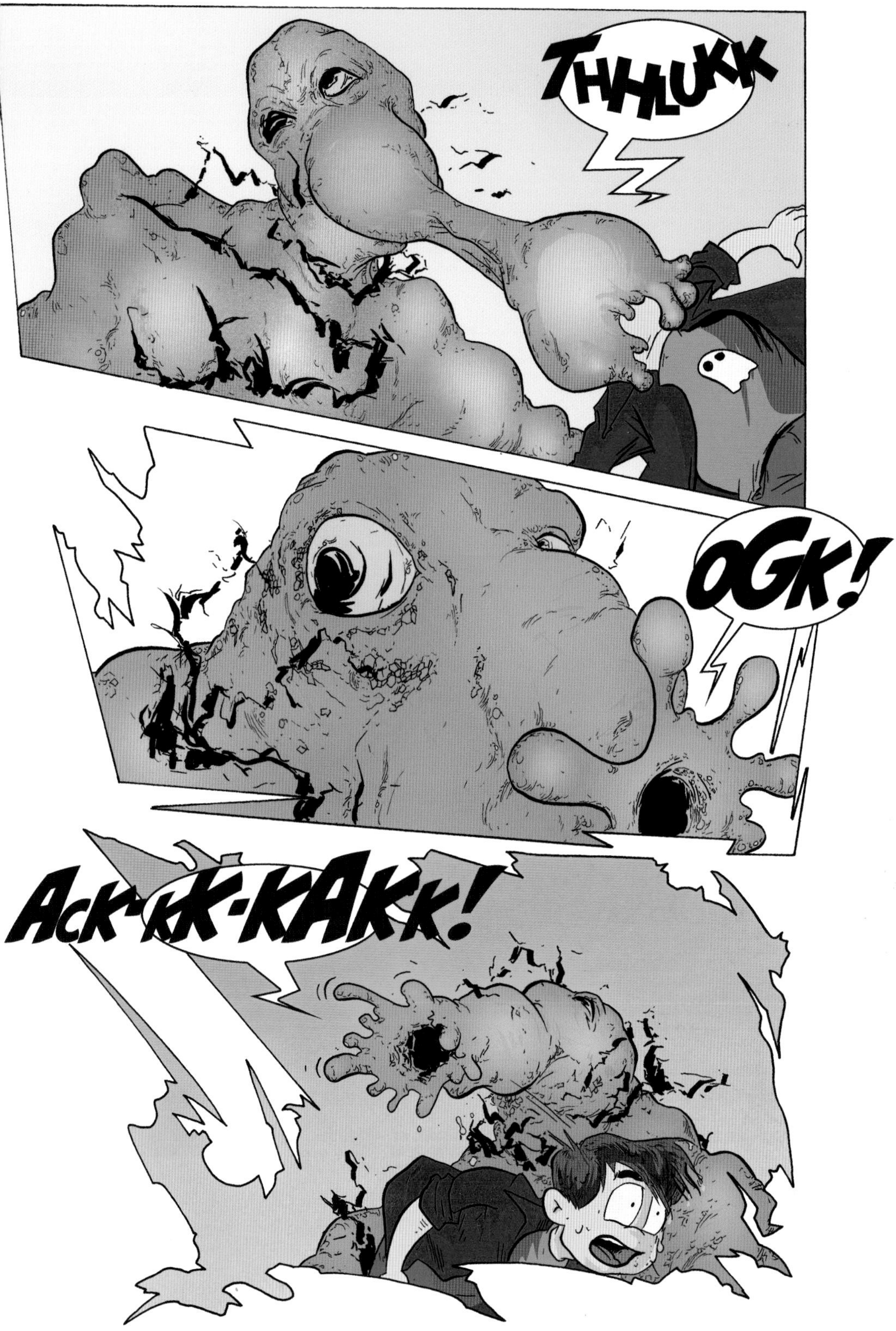
THHLUKK
OGK!
ACK-KK-KAKK!

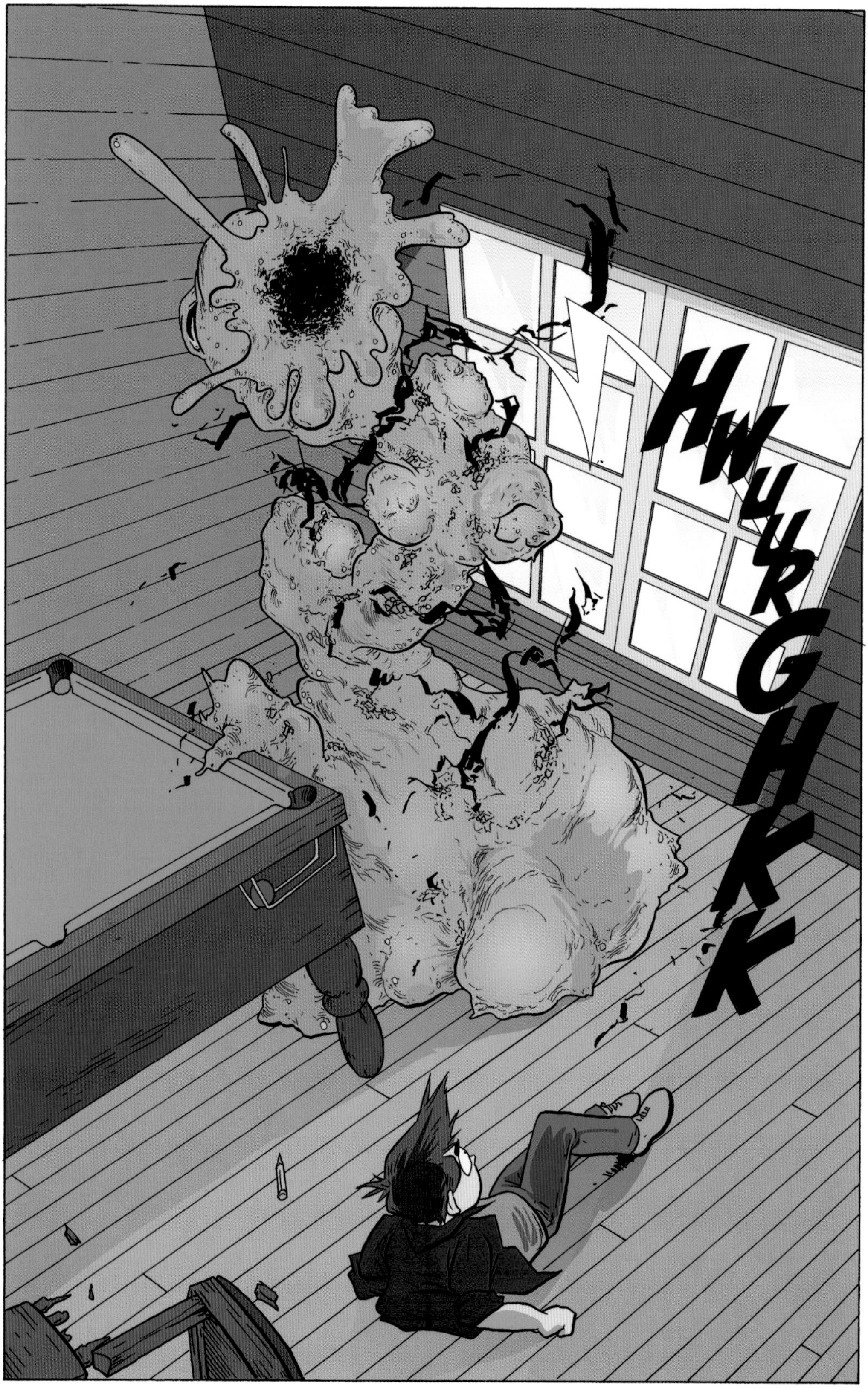
HWURGHKK

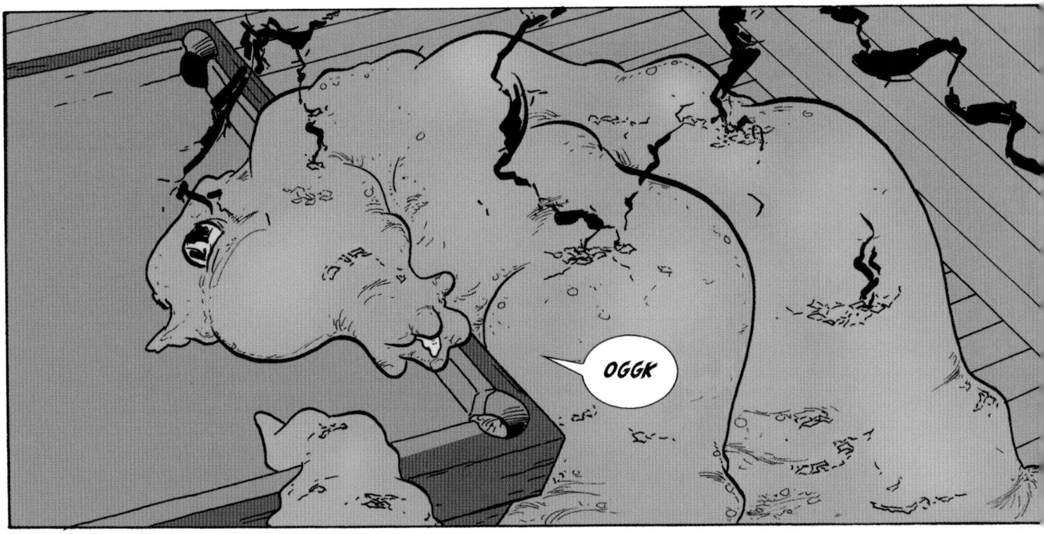
OGGK

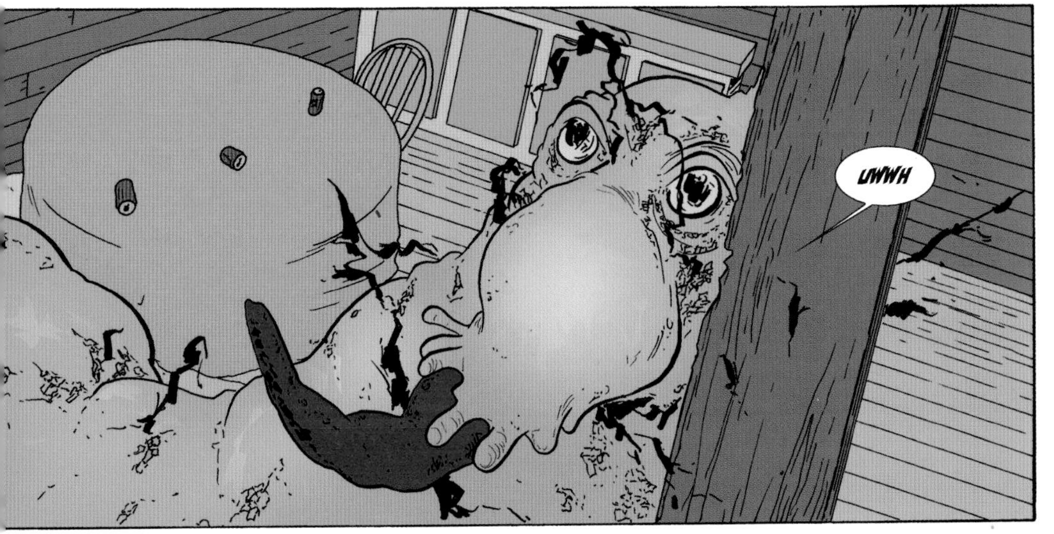
UWWH

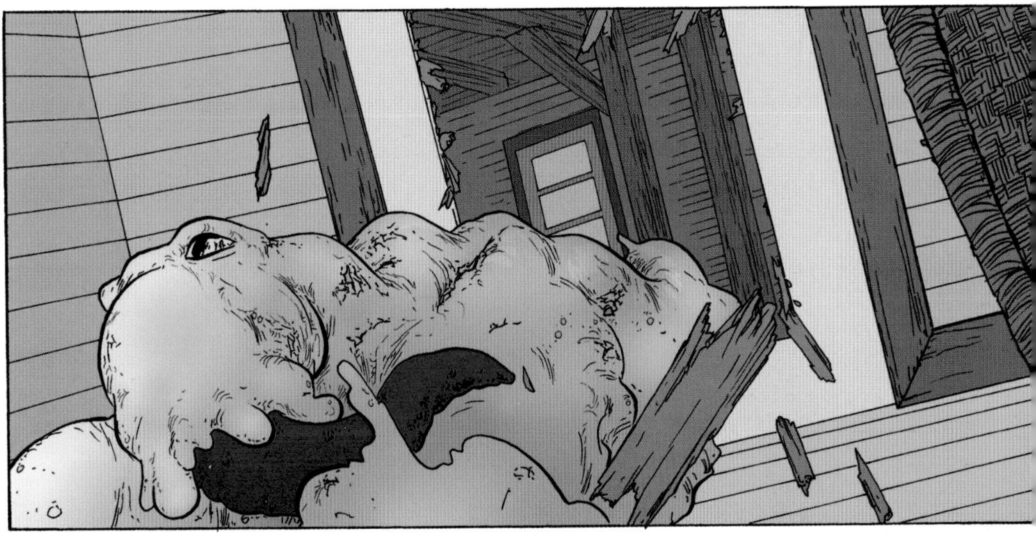

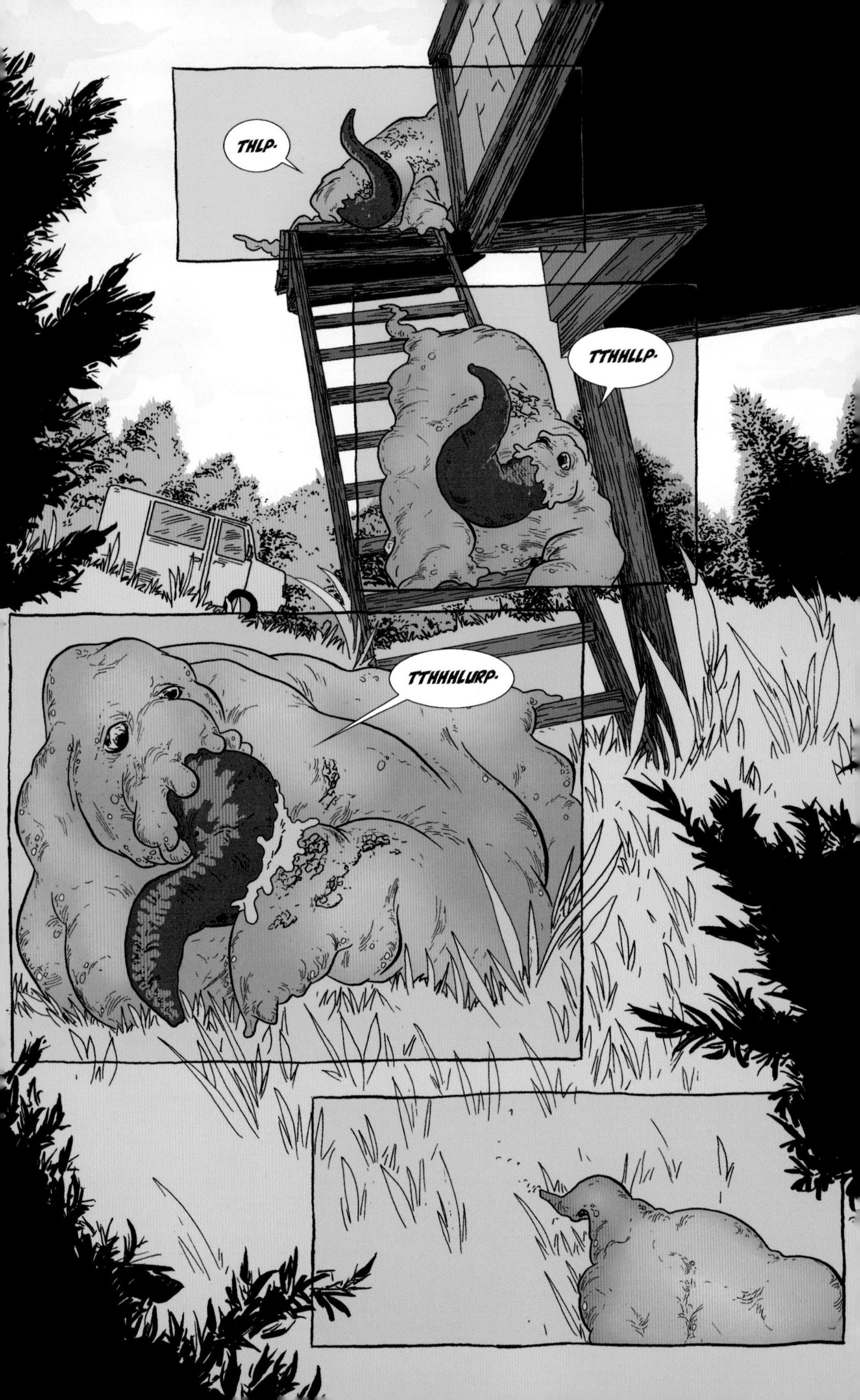
THLP.
TTHHLLP.
TTHHHLURP.

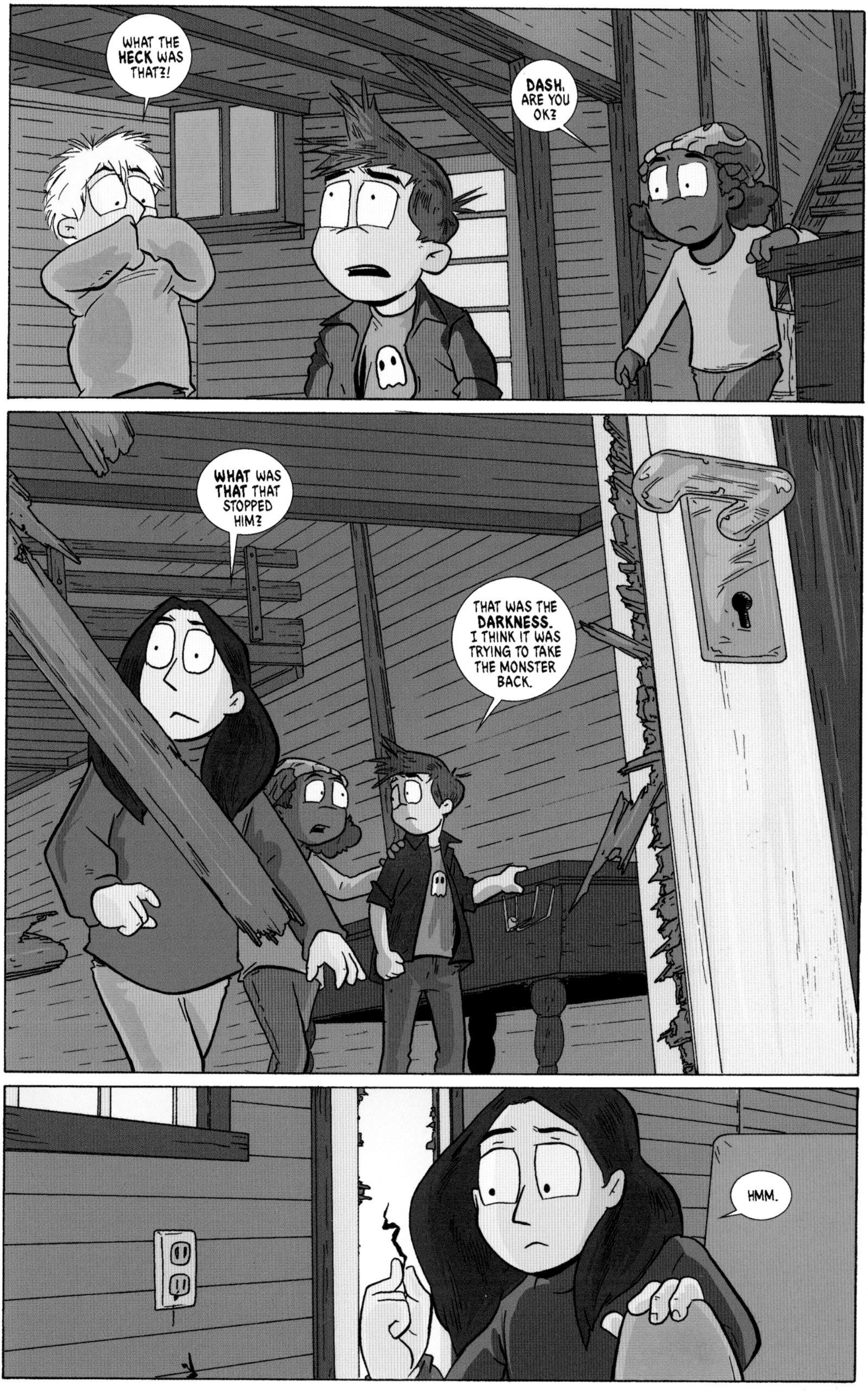
WHAT THE HECK WAS THAT?!
DASH, ARE YOU OK?
WHAT WAS THAT THAT STOPPED HIM?
THAT WAS THE DARKNESS. I THINK IT WAS TRYING TO TAKE THE MONSTER BACK.
HMM.

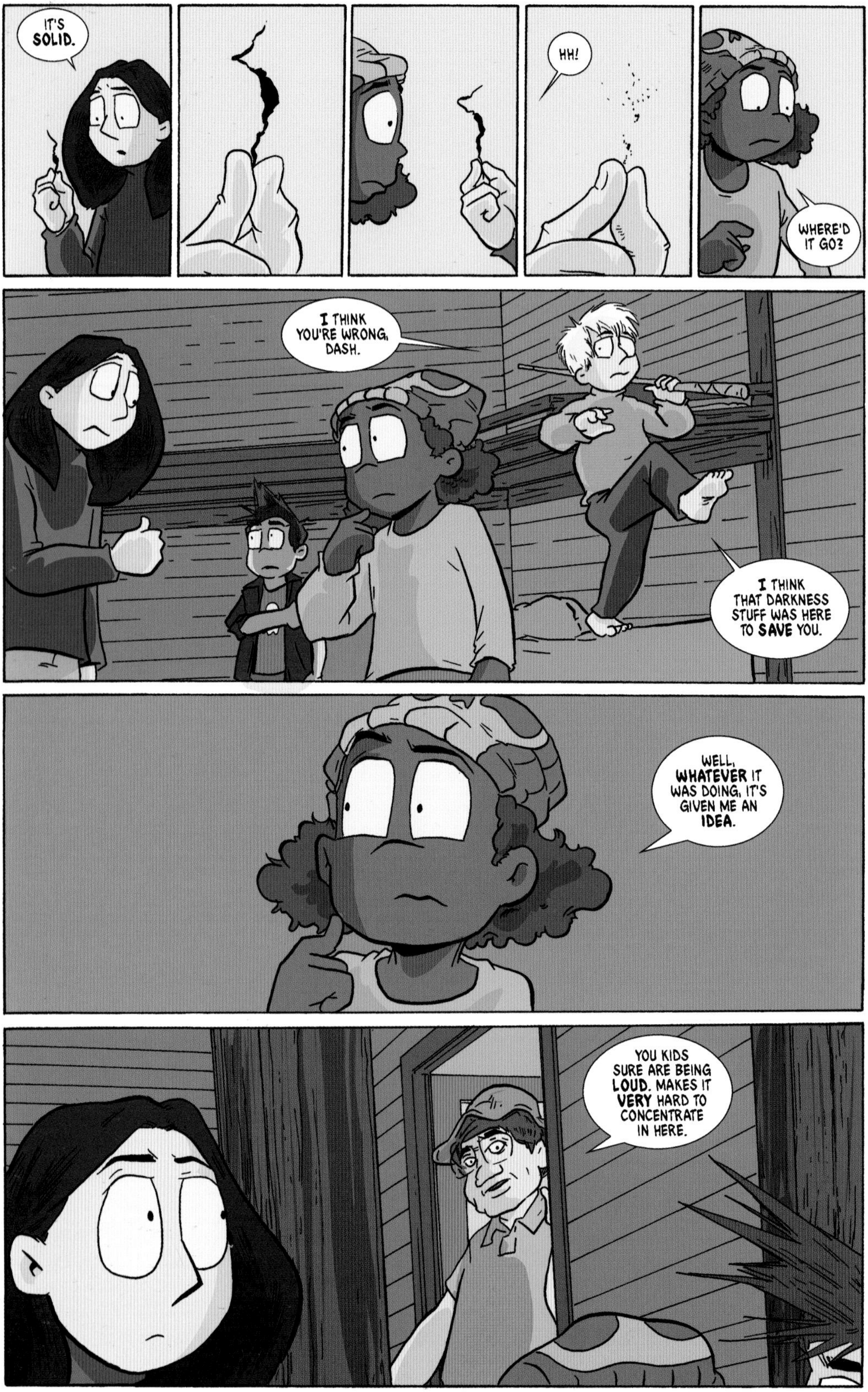
IT'S SOLID.
HH!
WHERE'D IT GO?
I THINK YOU'RE WRONG, DASH.
I THINK THAT DARKNESS STUFF WAS HERE TO SAVE YOU.
WELL, WHATEVER IT WAS DOING, IT'S GIVEN ME AN IDEA.
YOU KIDS SURE ARE BEING LOUD. MAKES IT VERY HARD TO CONCENTRATE IN HERE.

TO BE CONTINUED.

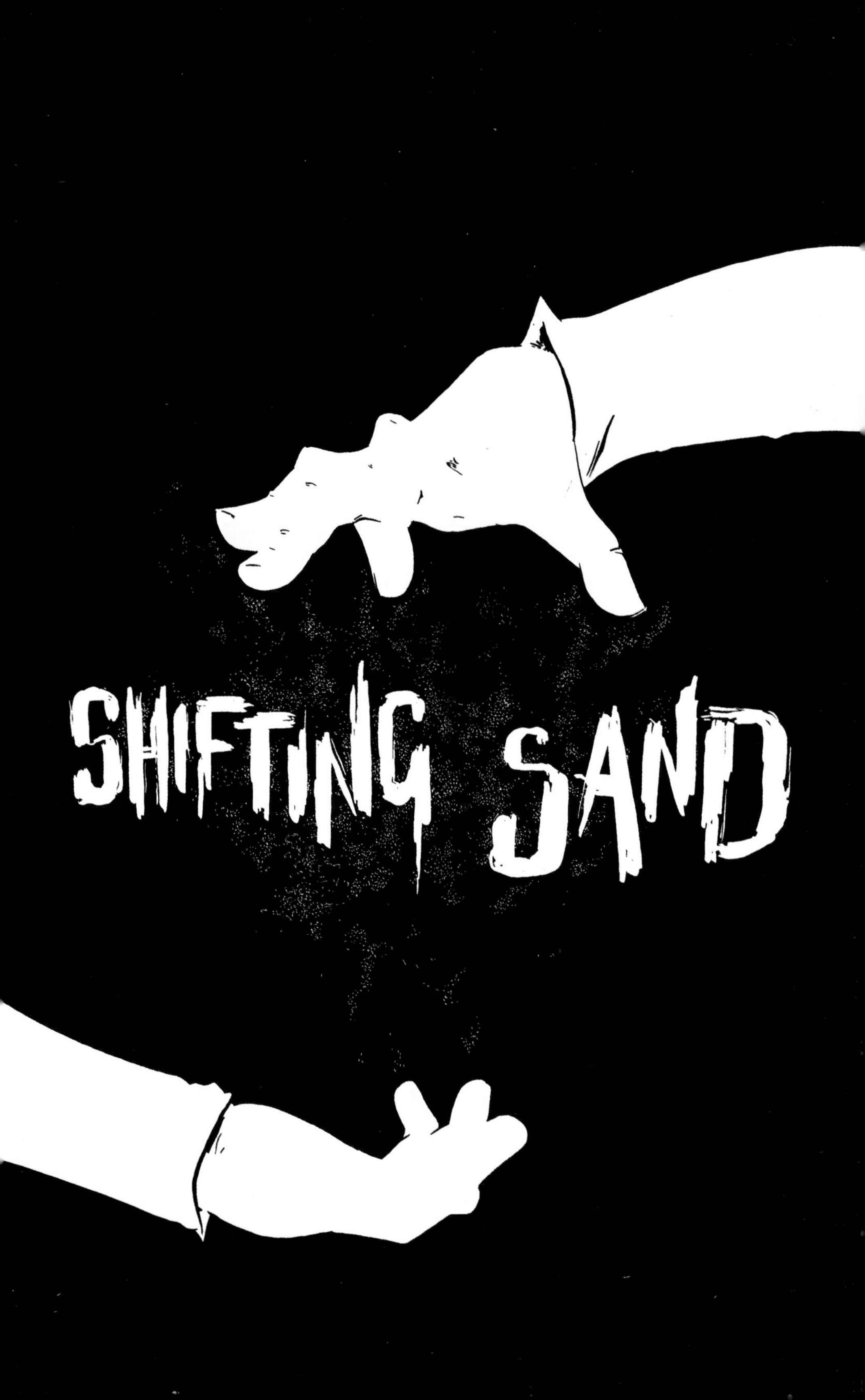
SHIFTING SAND

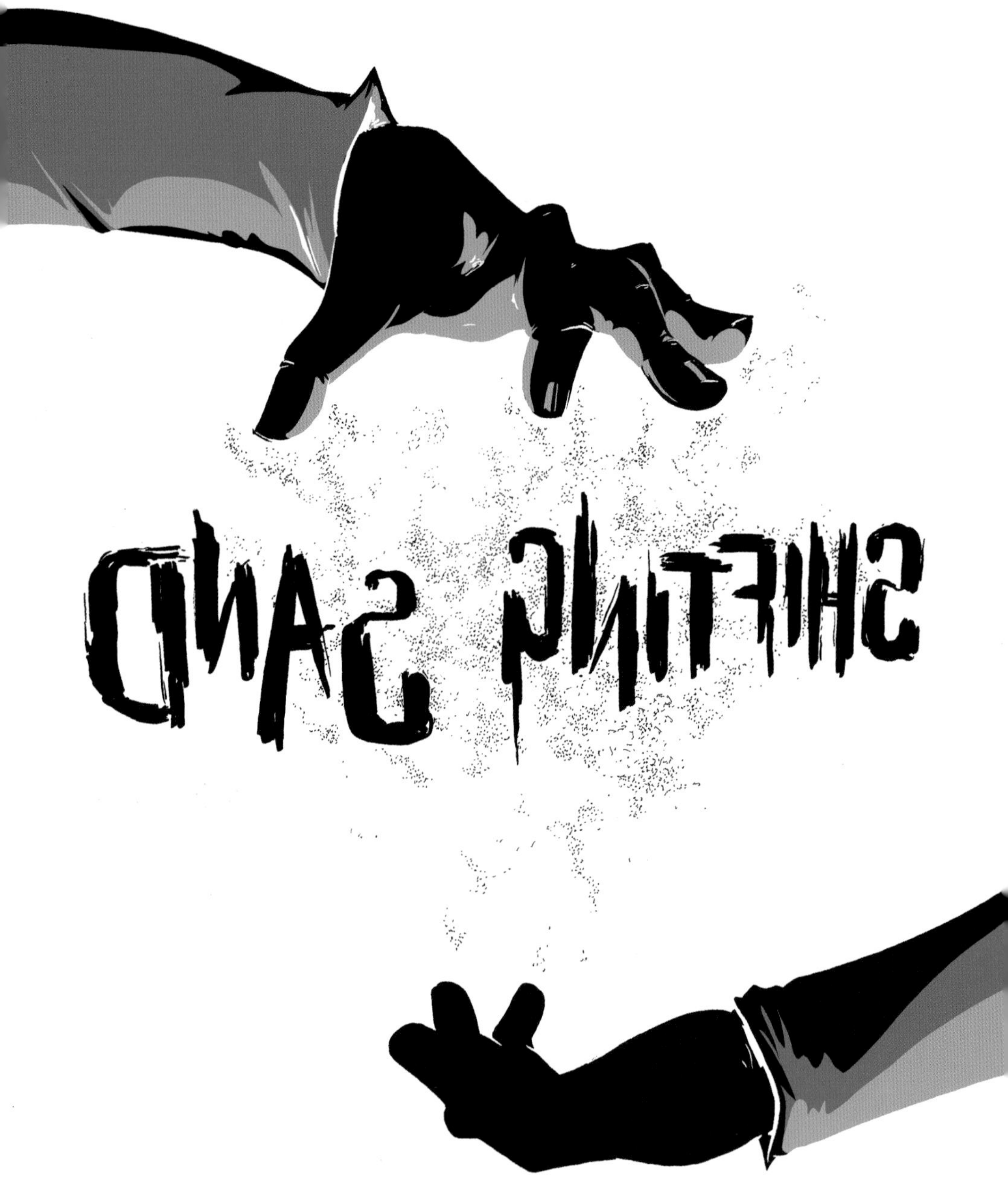
SHIFTING SAND

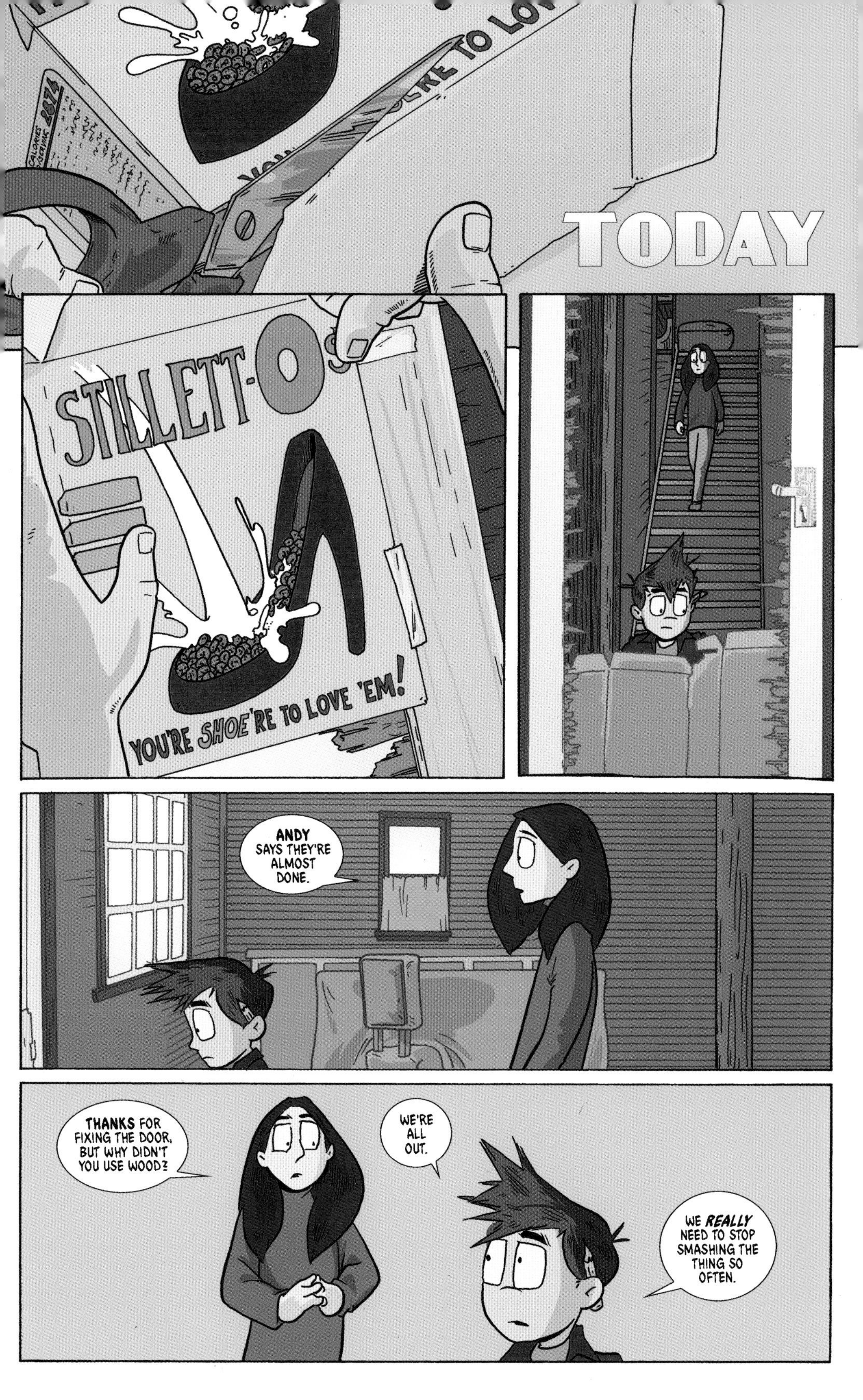
TODAY
STILLETT-O's
YOU'RE SHOE'RE TO LOVE 'EM!
ANDY SAYS THEY'RE ALMOST DONE.
THANKS FOR FIXING THE DOOR, BUT WHY DIDN'T YOU USE WOOD?
WE'RE ALL OUT.
WE REALLY NEED TO STOP SMASHING THE THING SO OFTEN.

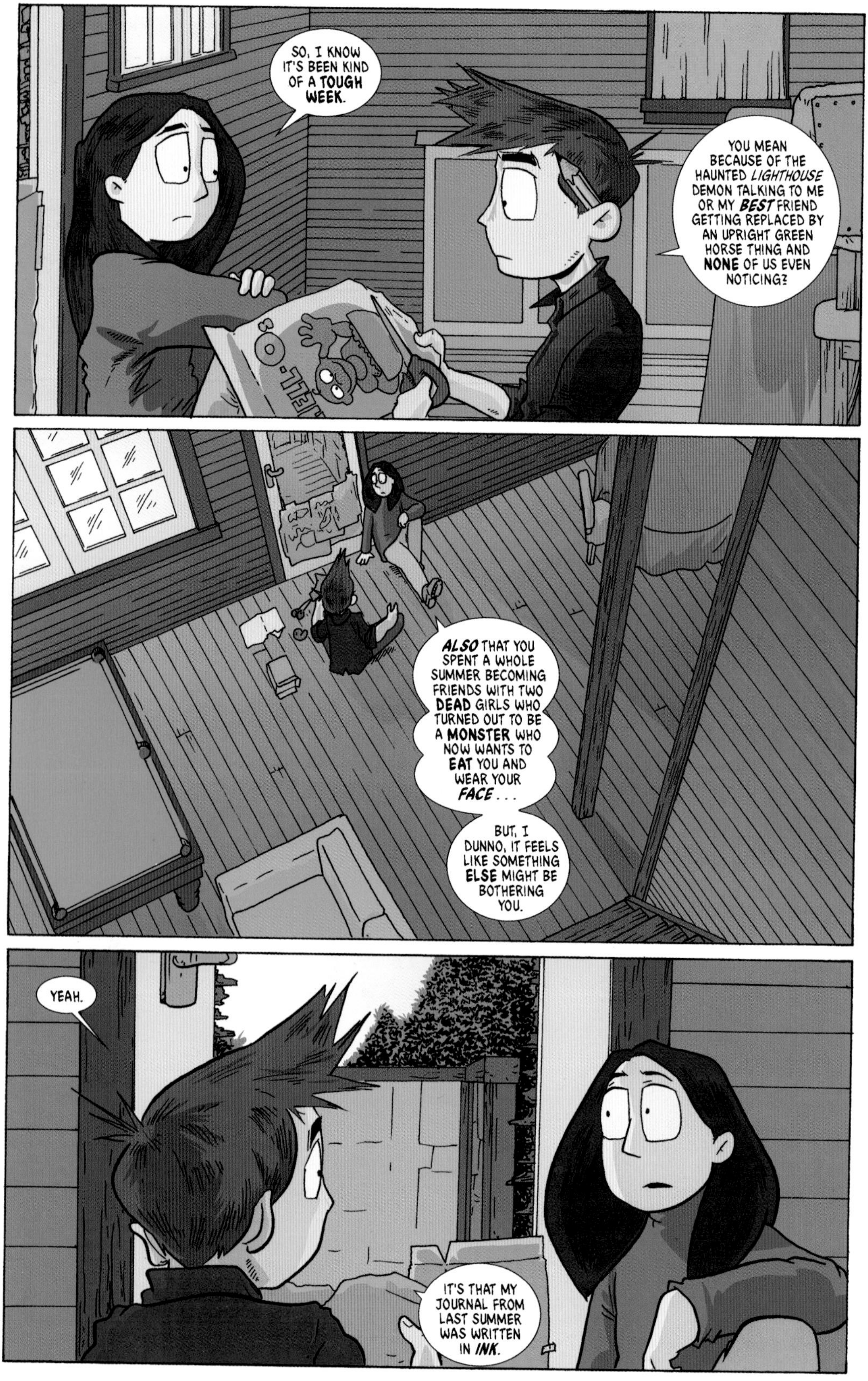
SO, I KNOW IT'S BEEN KIND OF A TOUGH WEEK.
YOU MEAN BECAUSE OF THE HAUNTED LIGHTHOUSE DEMON TALKING TO ME OR MY BEST FRIEND GETTING REPLACED BY AN UPRIGHT GREEN HORSE THING AND NONE OF US EVEN NOTICING?
ALSO THAT YOU SPENT A WHOLE SUMMER BECOMING FRIENDS WITH TWO DEAD GIRLS WHO TURNED OUT TO BE A MONSTER WHO NOW WANTS TO EAT YOU AND WEAR YOUR FACE . . .
BUT, I DUNNO, IT FEELS LIKE SOMETHING ELSE MIGHT BE BOTHERING YOU.
YEAH.
IT'S THAT MY JOURNAL FROM LAST SUMMER WAS WRITTEN IN INK.

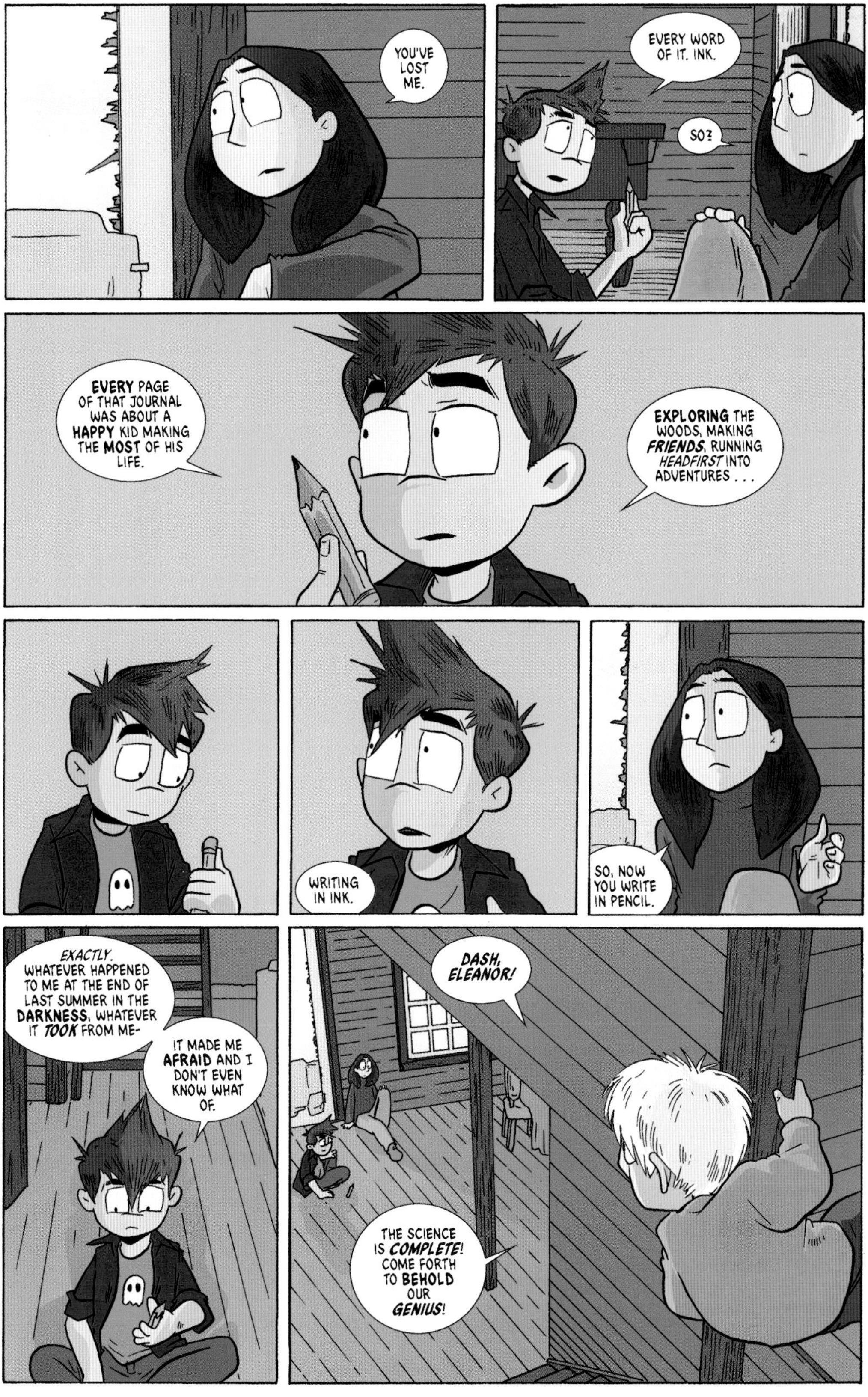
YOU'VE LOST ME.
EVERY WORD OF IT. INK.
SO?
EVERY PAGE OF THAT JOURNAL WAS ABOUT A HAPPY KID MAKING THE MOST OF HIS LIFE.
EXPLORING THE WOODS, MAKING FRIENDS, RUNNING HEADFIRST INTO ADVENTURES . . .
WRITING IN INK.
SO, NOW YOU WRITE IN PENCIL.
EXACTLY. WHATEVER HAPPENED TO ME AT THE END OF LAST SUMMER IN THE DARKNESS, WHATEVER IT TOOK FROM ME-
IT MADE ME AFRAID AND I DON'T EVEN KNOW WHAT OF.
DASH, ELEANOR!
THE SCIENCE IS COMPLETE! COME FORTH TO BEHOLD OUR GENIUS!

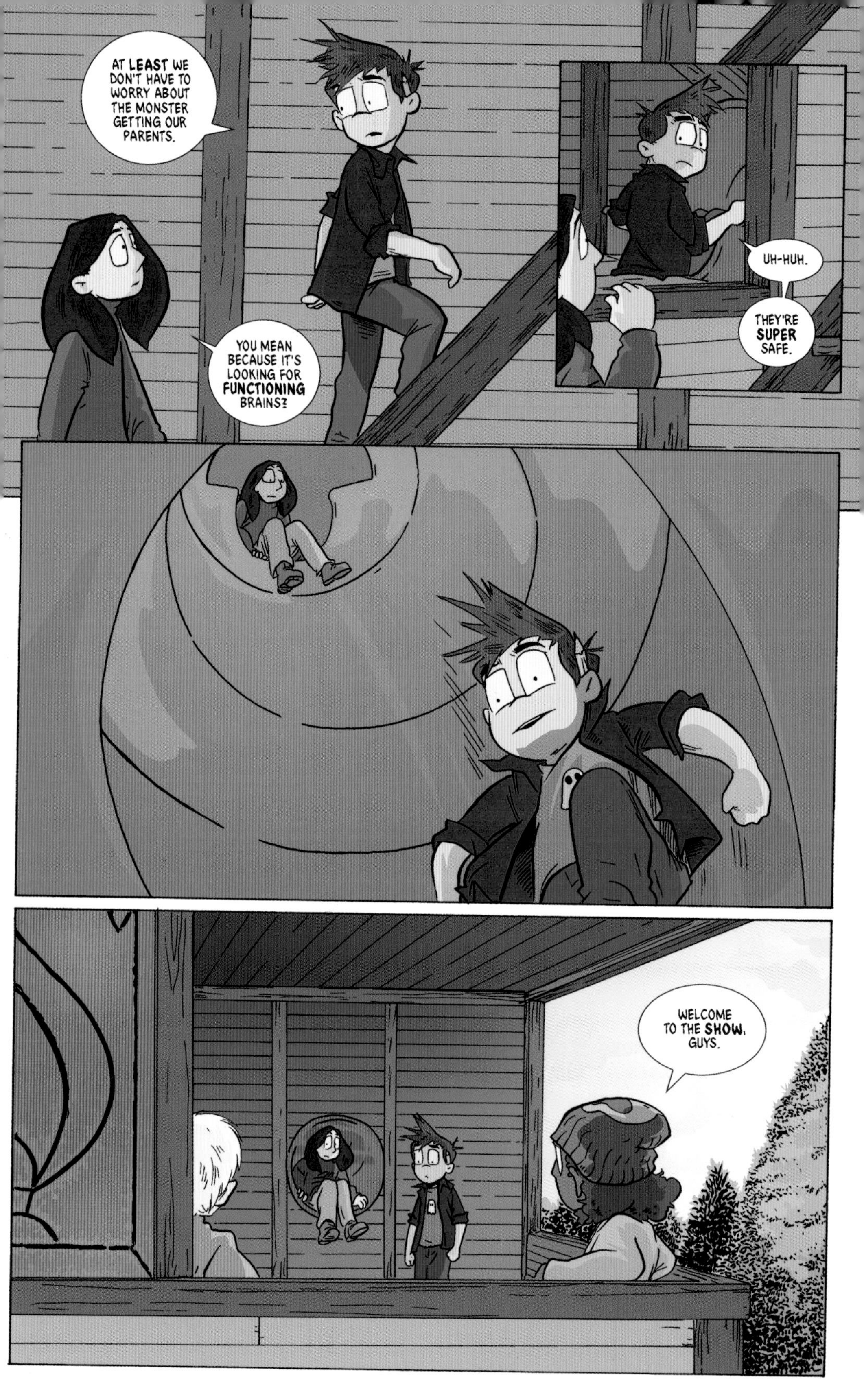
AT LEAST WE DON'T HAVE TO WORRY ABOUT THE MONSTER GETTING OUR PARENTS.
YOU MEAN BECAUSE IT'S LOOKING FOR FUNCTIONING BRAINS?
UH-HUH.
THEY'RE SUPER SAFE.
WELCOME TO THE SHOW, GUYS.

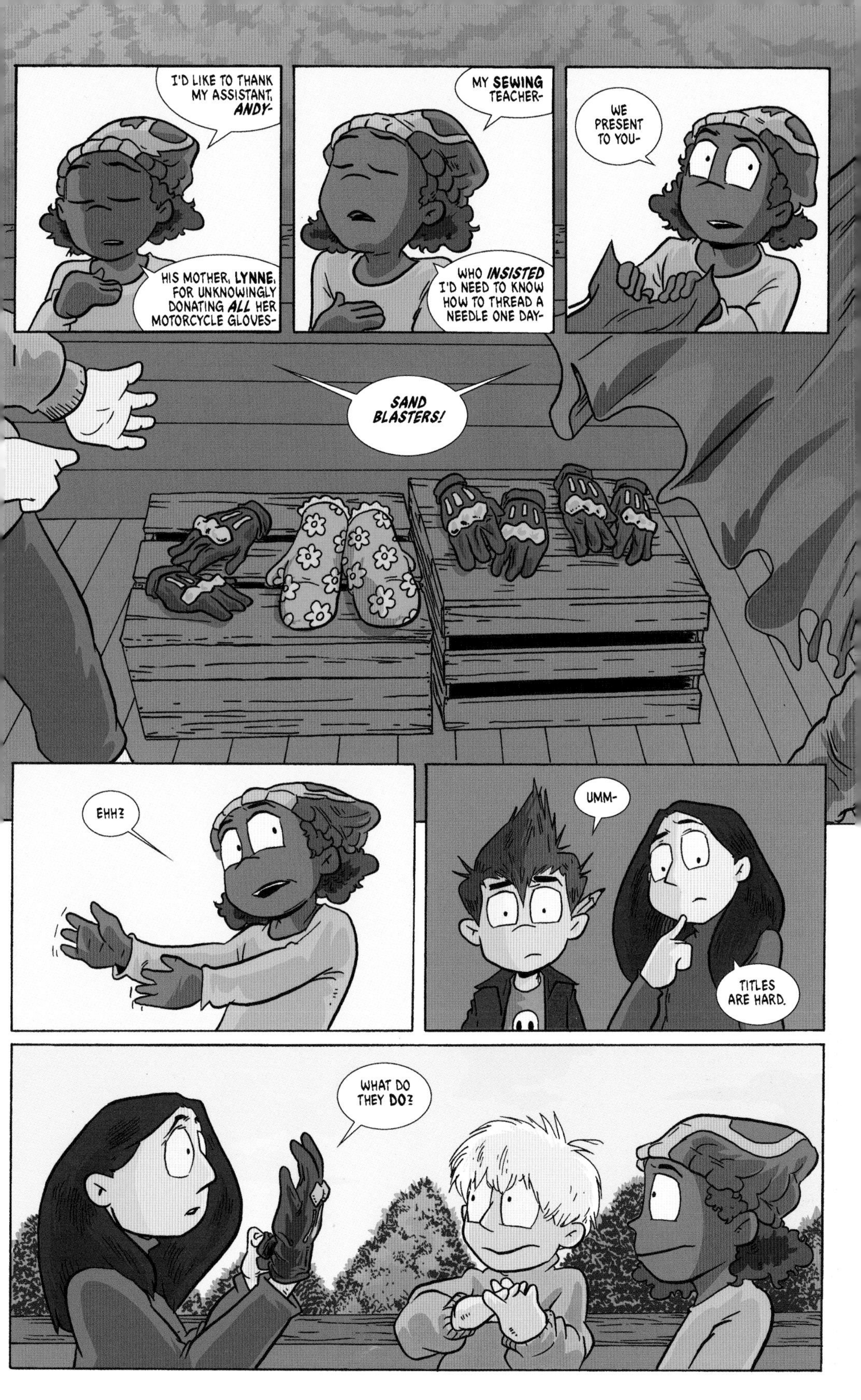

I'D LIKE TO THANK MY ASSISTANT, ANDY-
HIS MOTHER, LYNNE, FOR UNKNOWINGLY DONATING ALL HER MOTORCYCLE GLOVES-
MY SEWING TEACHER-
WHO INSISTED I'D NEED TO KNOW HOW TO THREAD A NEEDLE ONE DAY-
WE PRESENT TO YOU-
SAND BLASTERS!
EHH?
UMM-
TITLES ARE HARD.
WHAT DO THEY DO?

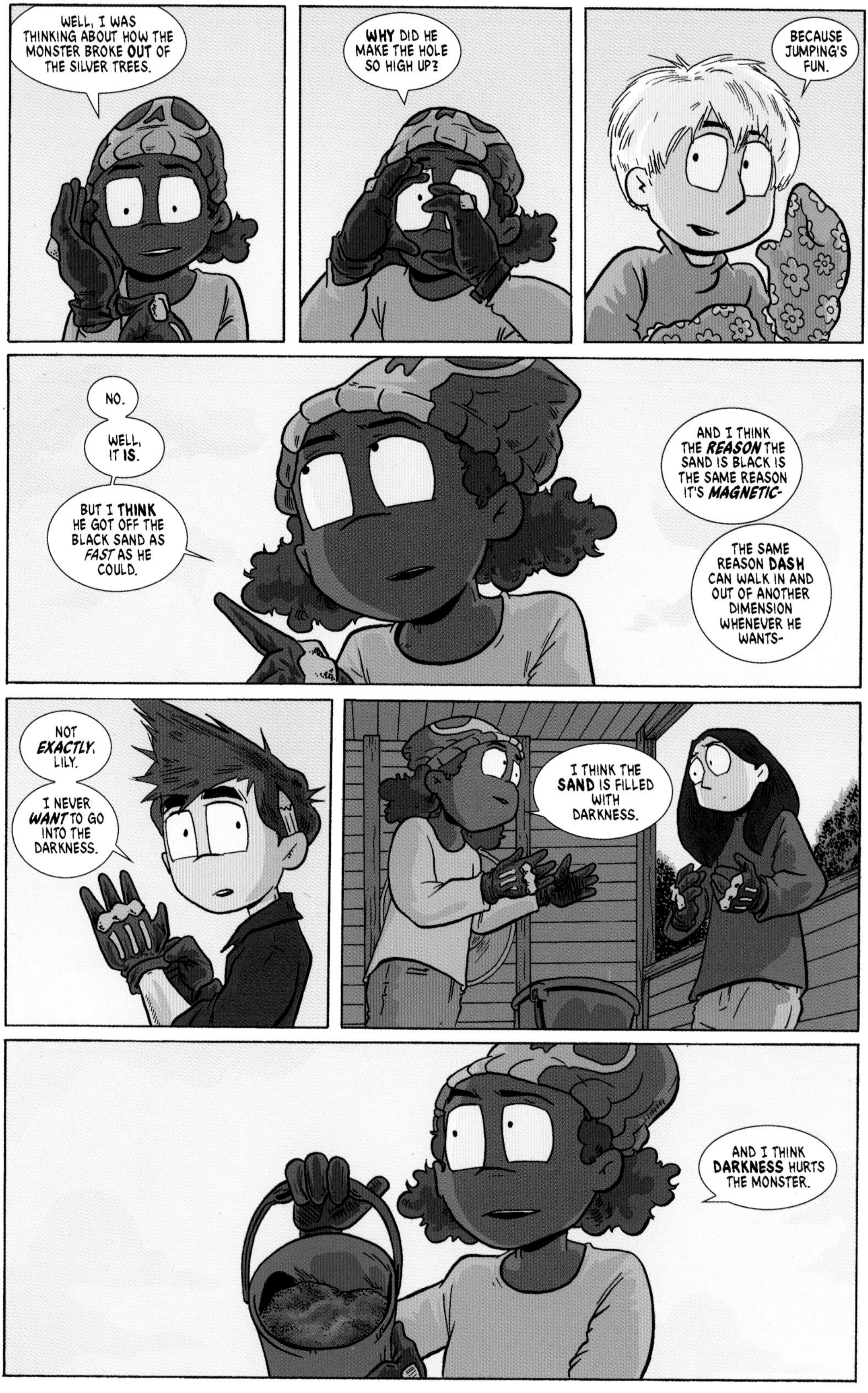
WELL, I WAS THINKING ABOUT HOW THE MONSTER BROKE OUT OF THE SILVER TREES.
WHY DID HE MAKE THE HOLE SO HIGH UP?
BECAUSE JUMPING'S FUN.
NO.
WELL, IT IS.
BUT I THINK HE GOT OFF THE BLACK SAND AS FAST AS HE COULD.
AND I THINK THE REASON THE SAND IS BLACK IS THE SAME REASON IT'S MAGNETIC-
THE SAME REASON DASH CAN WALK IN AND OUT OF ANOTHER DIMENSION WHENEVER HE WANTS-
NOT EXACTLY, LILY.
I NEVER WANT TO GO INTO THE DARKNESS.
I THINK THE SAND IS FILLED WITH DARKNESS.
AND I THINK DARKNESS HURTS THE MONSTER.

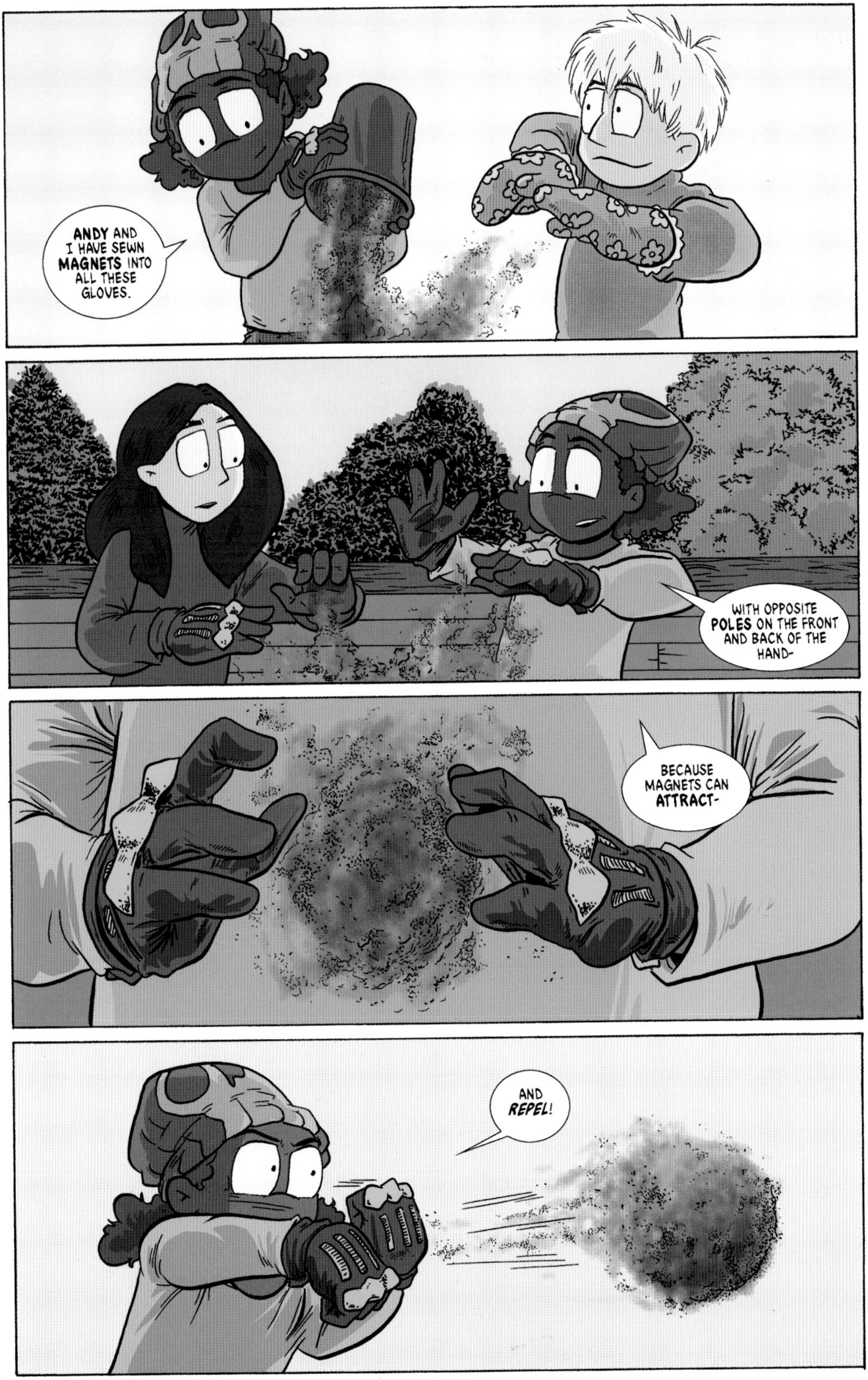
ANDY AND I HAVE SEWN MAGNETS INTO ALL THESE GLOVES.
WITH OPPOSITE POLES ON THE FRONT AND BACK OF THE HAND-
BECAUSE MAGNETS CAN ATTRACT-
AND REPEL!

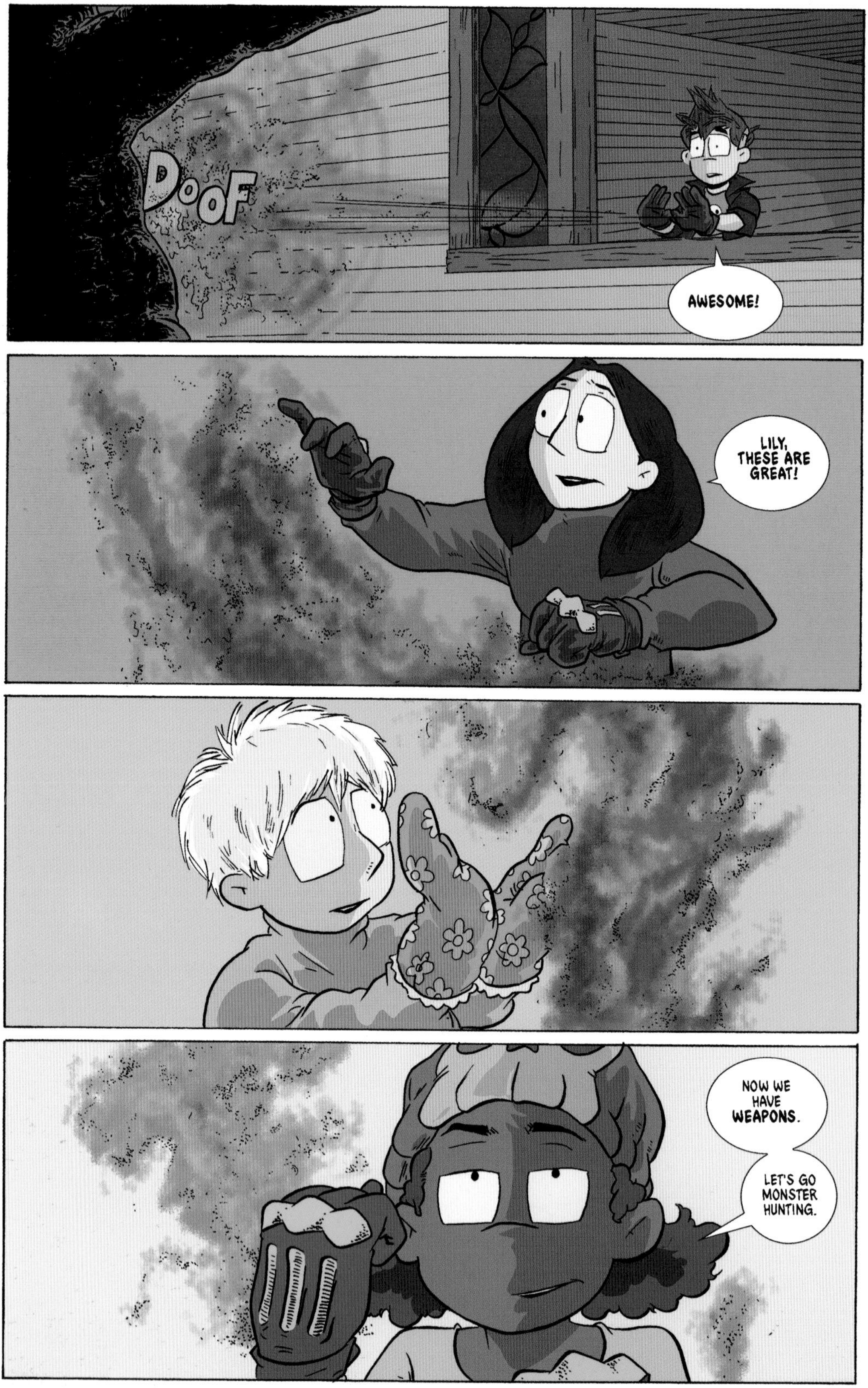
DOOF
AWESOME!
LILY, THESE ARE GREAT!
NOW WE HAVE WEAPONS.
LET'S GO MONSTER HUNTING.

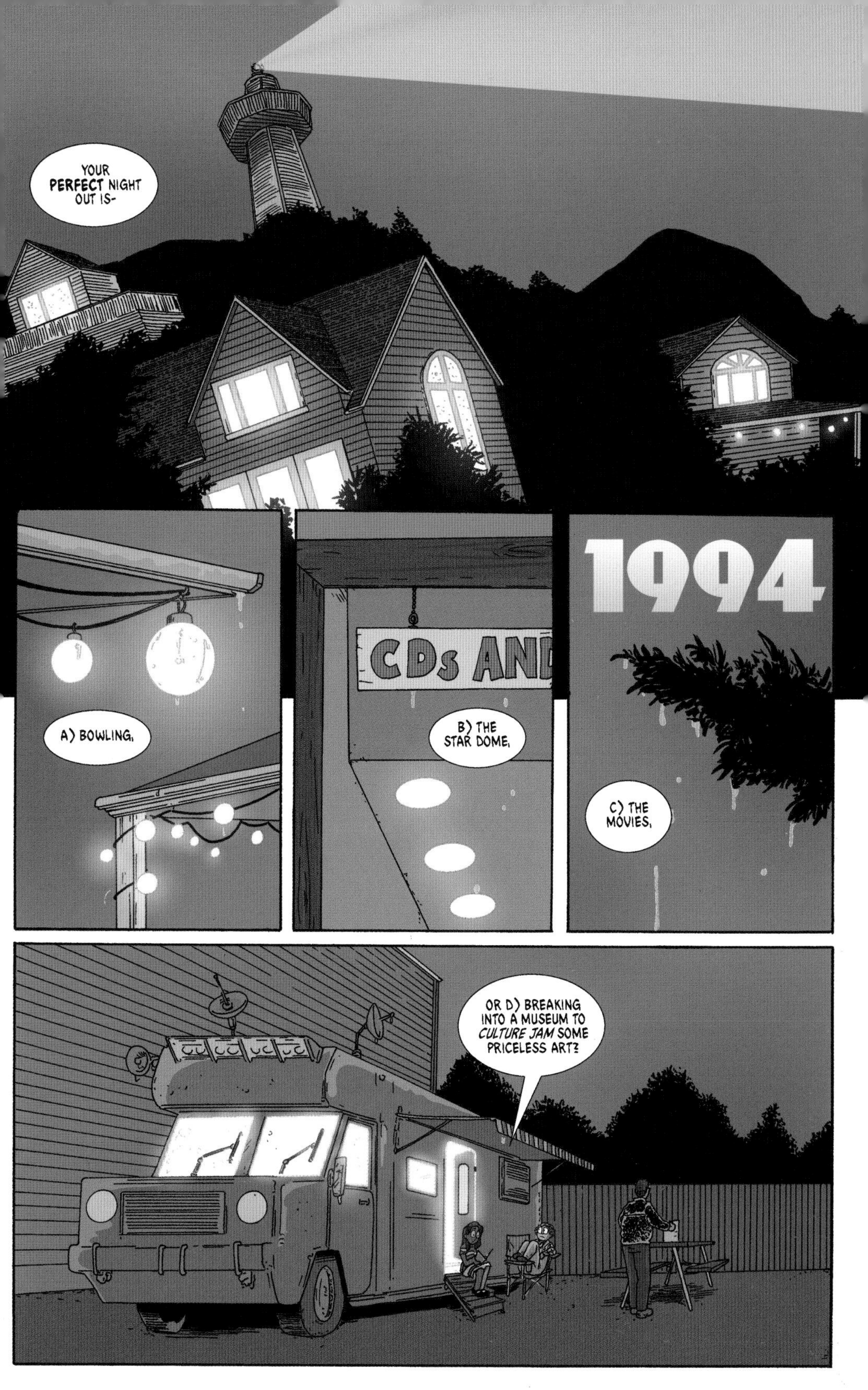
YOUR PERFECT NIGHT OUT IS-
1994
CDs AND
A) BOWLING,
B) THE STAR DOME,
C) THE MOVIES,
OR D) BREAKING INTO A MUSEUM TO *CULTURE JAM* SOME PRICELESS ART?

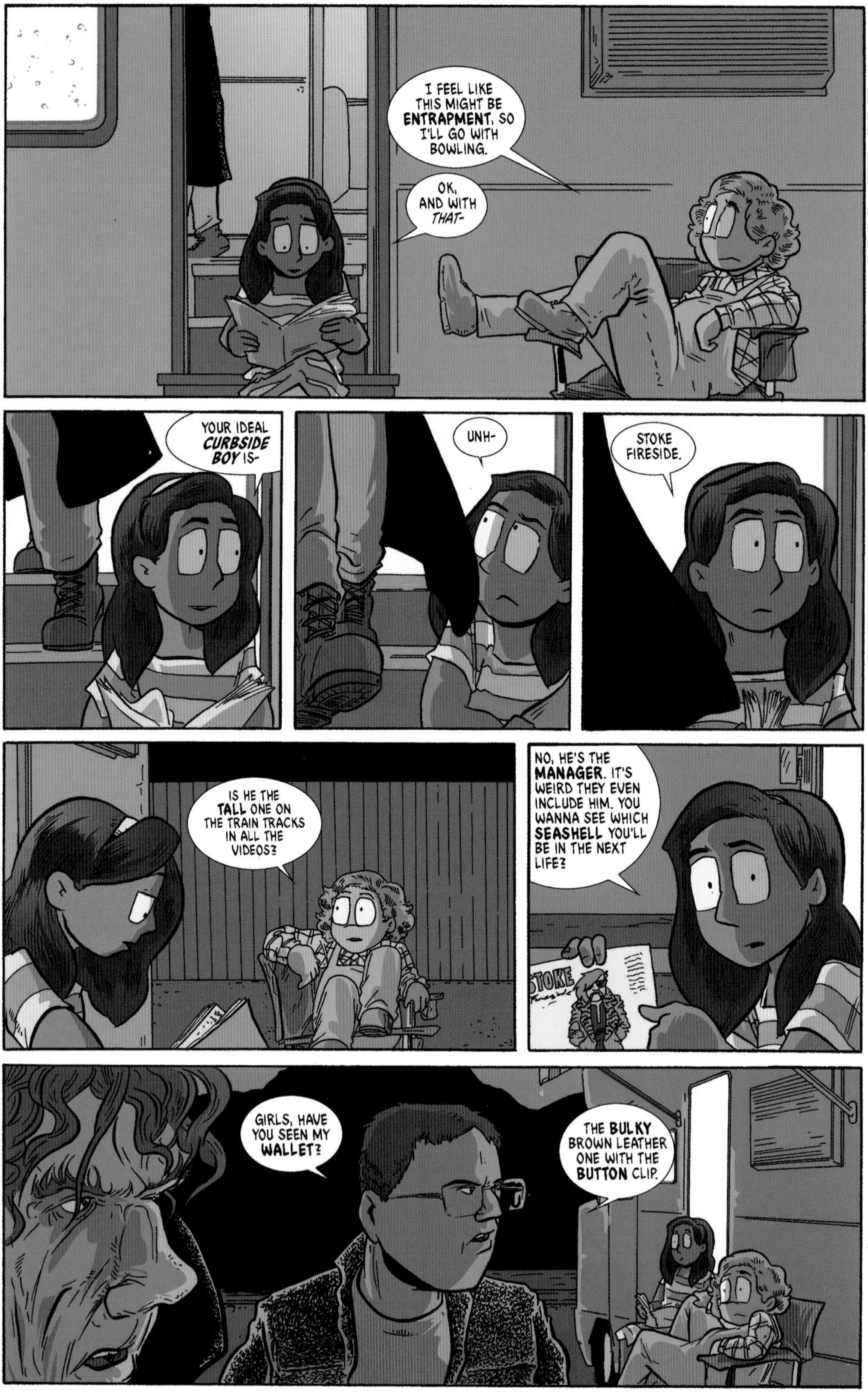
I FEEL LIKE THIS MIGHT BE ENTRAPMENT, SO I'LL GO WITH BOWLING.
OK, AND WITH THAT-
YOUR IDEAL CURBSIDE BOY IS-
UNH-
STOKE FIRESIDE.
IS HE THE TALL ONE ON THE TRAIN TRACKS IN ALL THE VIDEOS?
NO, HE'S THE MANAGER. IT'S WEIRD THEY EVEN INCLUDE HIM. YOU WANNA SEE WHICH SEASHELL YOU'LL BE IN THE NEXT LIFE?
STOKE
GIRLS, HAVE YOU SEEN MY WALLET?
THE BULKY BROWN LEATHER ONE WITH THE BUTTON CLIP.

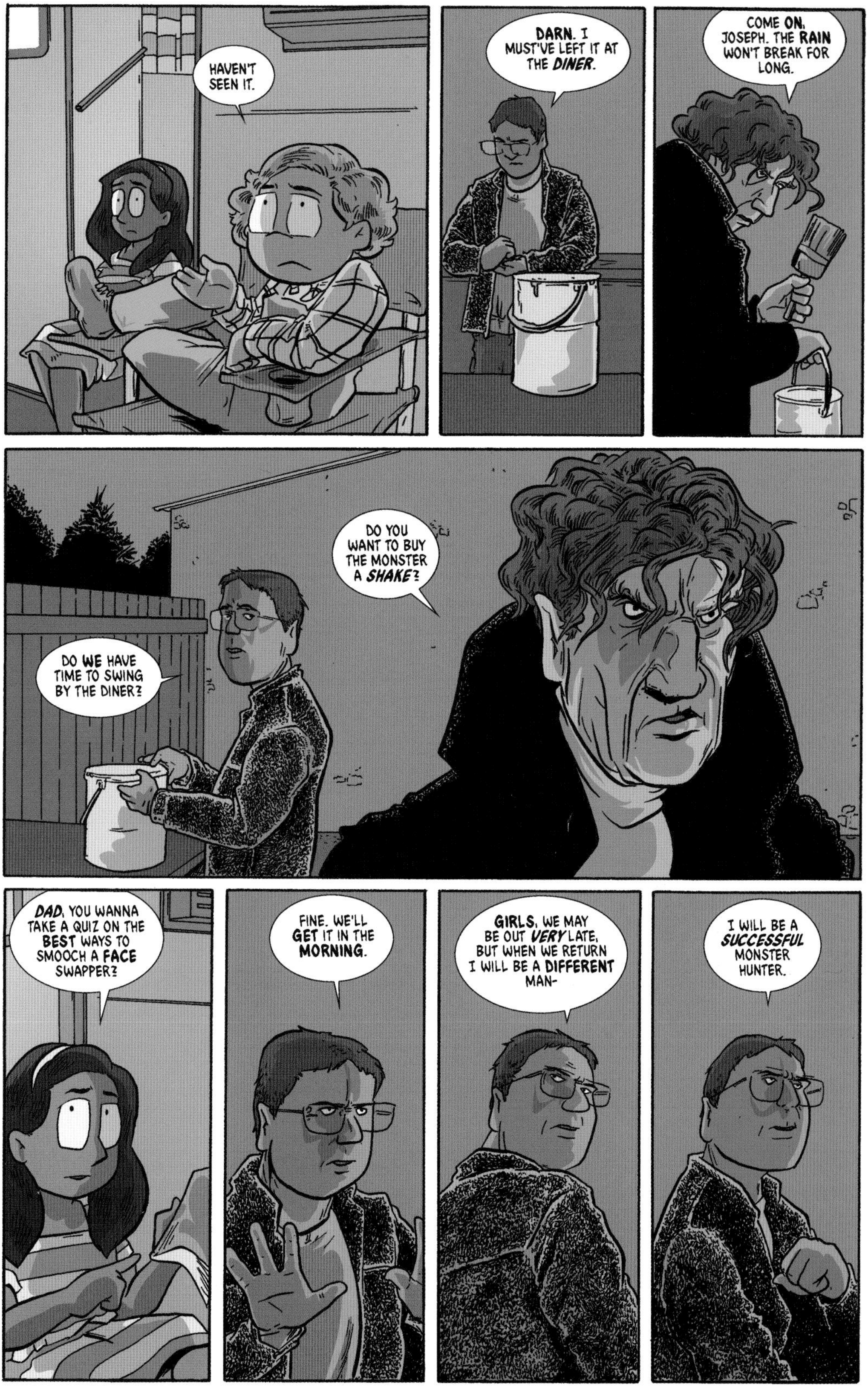
HAVEN'T SEEN IT.
DARN. I MUST'VE LEFT IT AT THE DINER.
COME ON, JOSEPH. THE RAIN WON'T BREAK FOR LONG.
DO YOU WANT TO BUY THE MONSTER A SHAKE?
DO WE HAVE TIME TO SWING BY THE DINER?
DAD, YOU WANNA TAKE A QUIZ ON THE BEST WAYS TO SMOOCH A FACE SWAPPER?
FINE. WE'LL GET IT IN THE MORNING.
GIRLS, WE MAY BE OUT VERY LATE, BUT WHEN WE RETURN I WILL BE A DIFFERENT MAN-
I WILL BE A SUCCESSFUL MONSTER HUNTER.

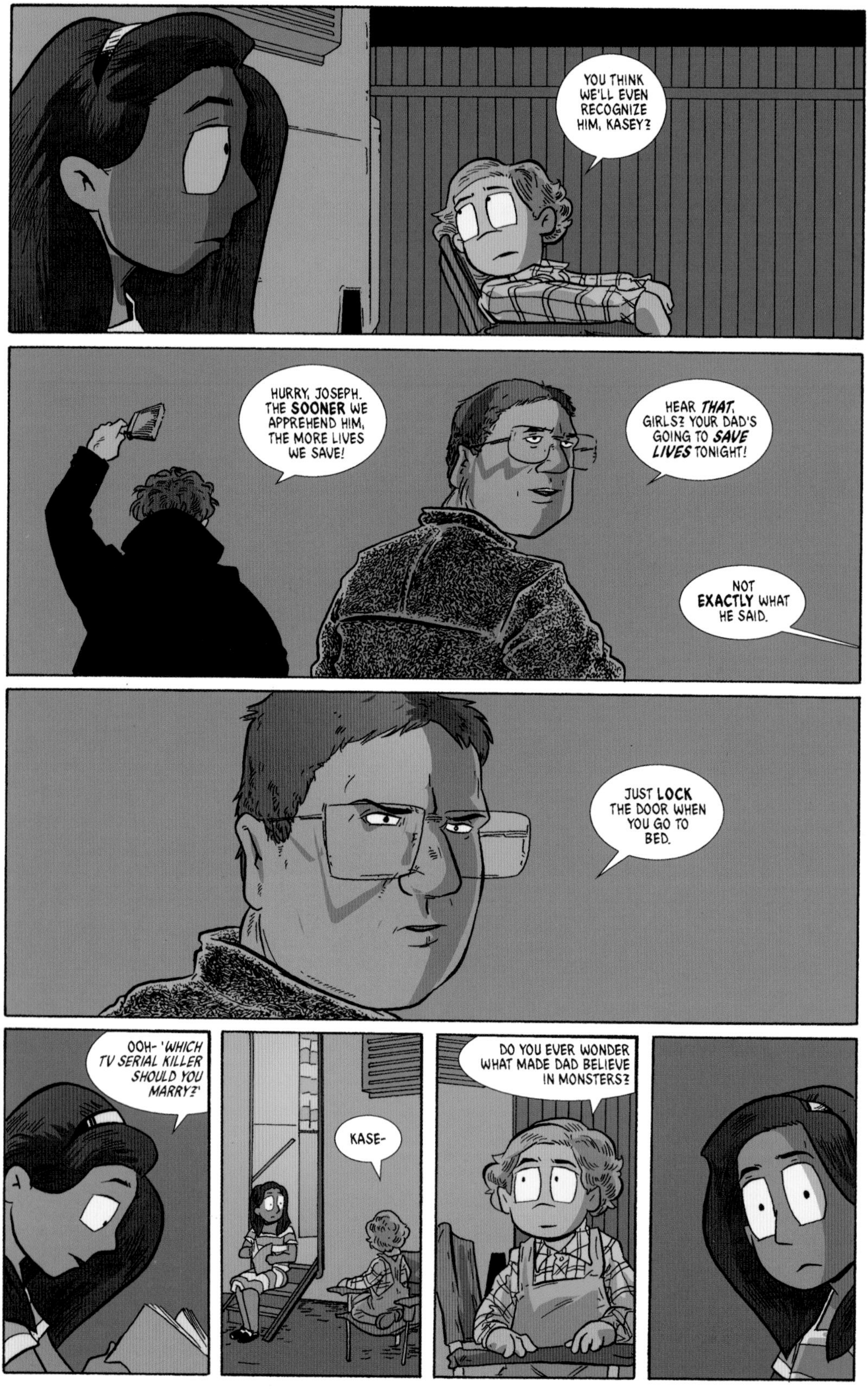
YOU THINK WE'LL EVEN RECOGNIZE HIM, KASEY?
HURRY, JOSEPH. THE **SOONER** WE APPREHEND HIM, THE MORE LIVES WE SAVE!
HEAR ***THAT***, GIRLS? YOUR DAD'S GOING TO ***SAVE LIVES*** TONIGHT!
NOT **EXACTLY** WHAT HE SAID.
JUST **LOCK** THE DOOR WHEN YOU GO TO BED.
OOH- '*WHICH TV SERIAL KILLER SHOULD YOU MARRY?*'
KASE-
DO YOU EVER WONDER WHAT MADE DAD BELIEVE IN MONSTERS?

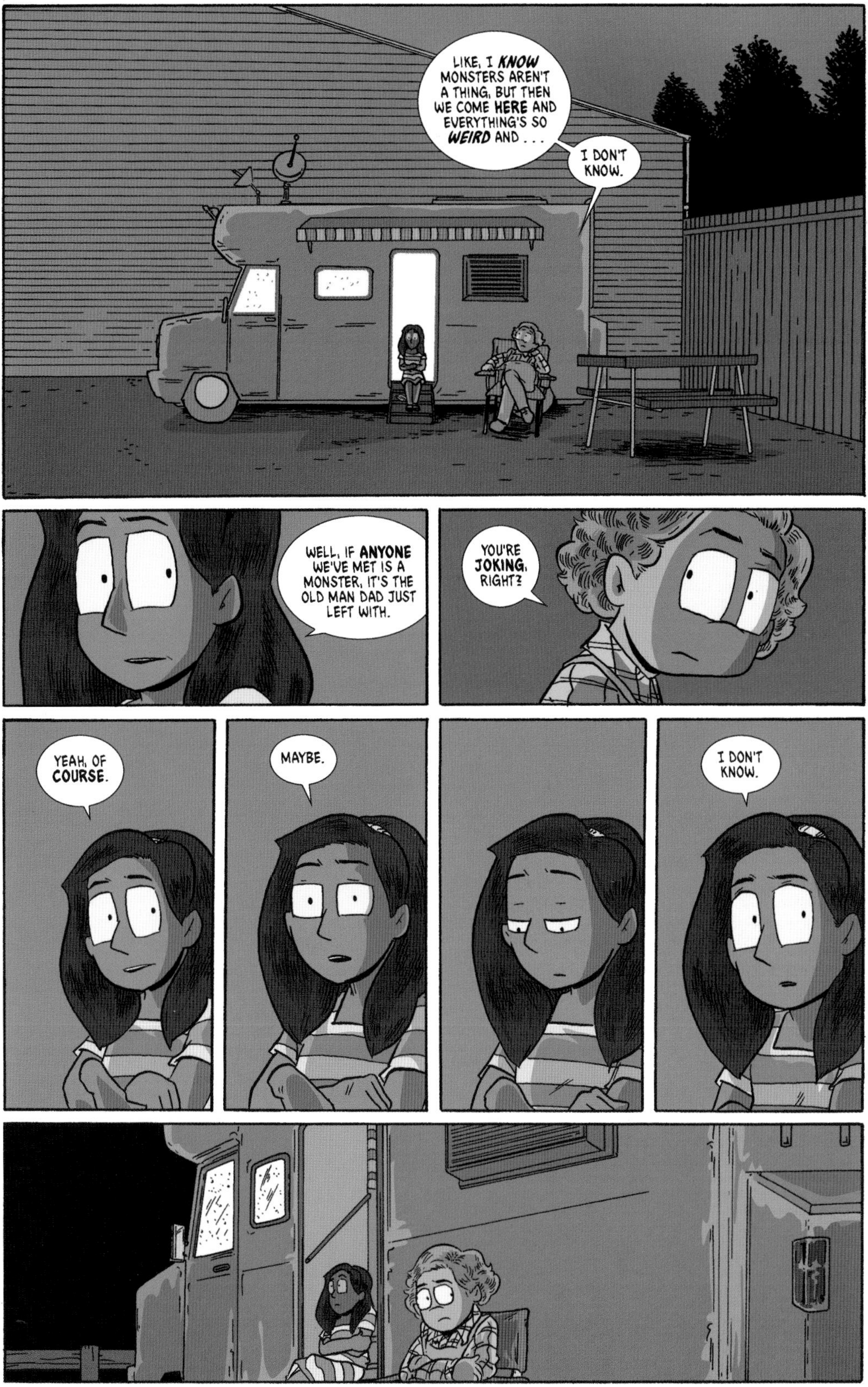
LIKE, I KNOW MONSTERS AREN'T A THING, BUT THEN WE COME HERE AND EVERYTHING'S SO WEIRD AND . . .
I DON'T KNOW.
WELL, IF ANYONE WE'VE MET IS A MONSTER, IT'S THE OLD MAN DAD JUST LEFT WITH.
YOU'RE JOKING, RIGHT?
YEAH, OF COURSE.
MAYBE.
I DON'T KNOW.

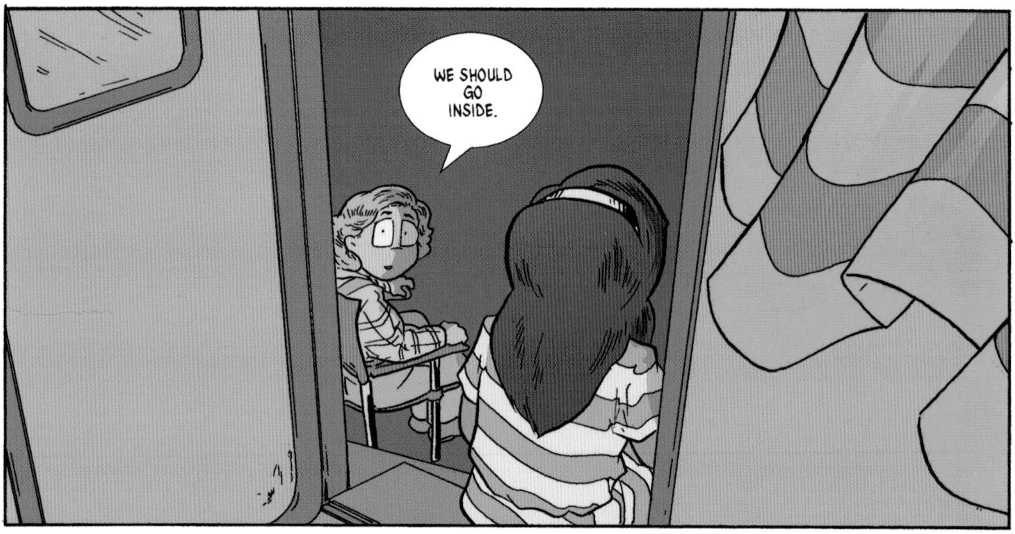
WE SHOULD GO INSIDE.

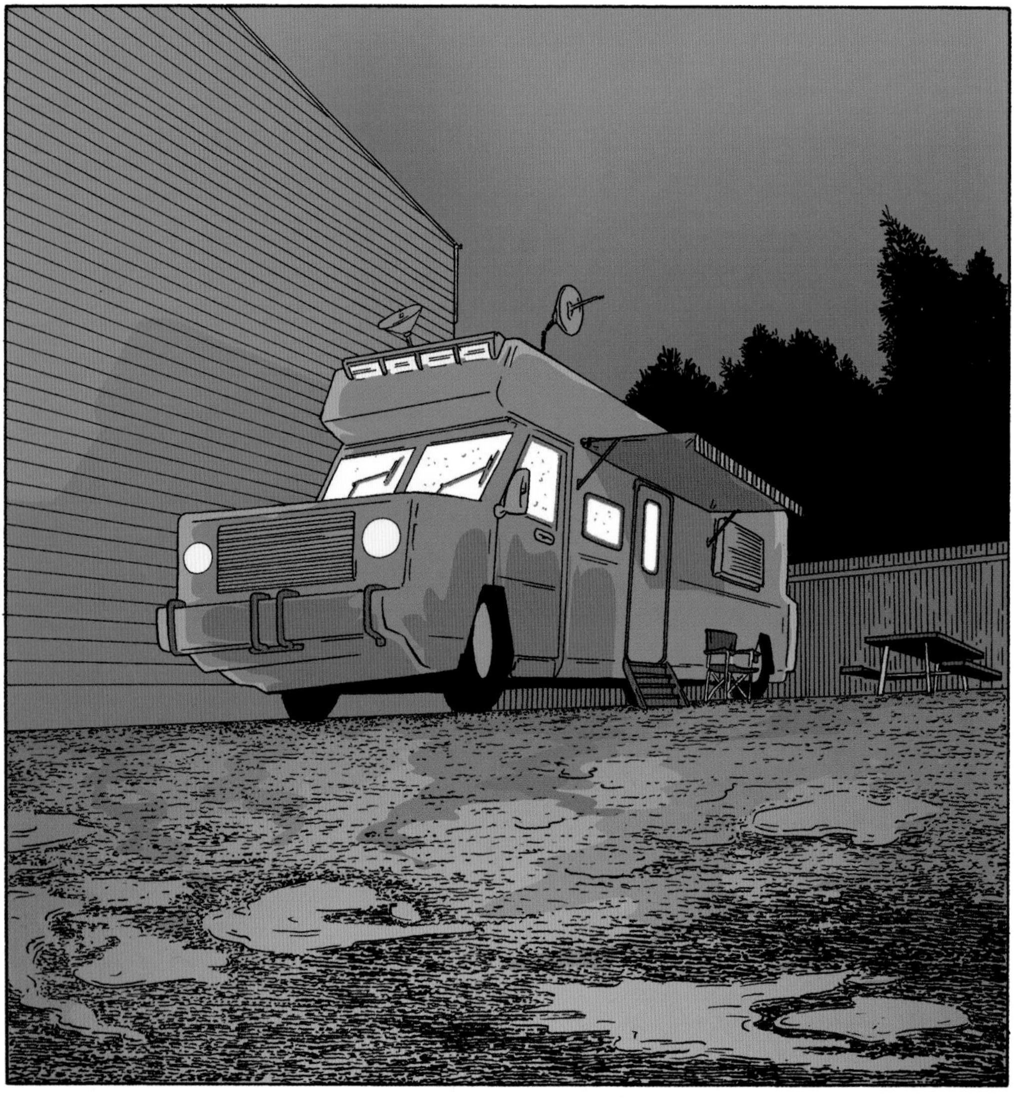

KNOCK
KNOCK
KNOCK
KNOCK
KNOCK

WAAAAH!

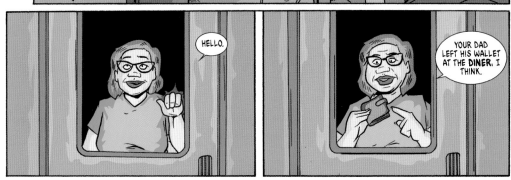

HELLO.

YOUR DAD LEFT HIS WALLET AT THE **DINER**, I THINK.

THERE'RE A LOT OF MEMBERSHIP CARDS TO **VIDEO STORES** THAT I DON'T RECOGNIZE AND YOU WERE THE ONLY *OUT-OF-TOWN* CUSTOMERS I SERVED TONIGHT.

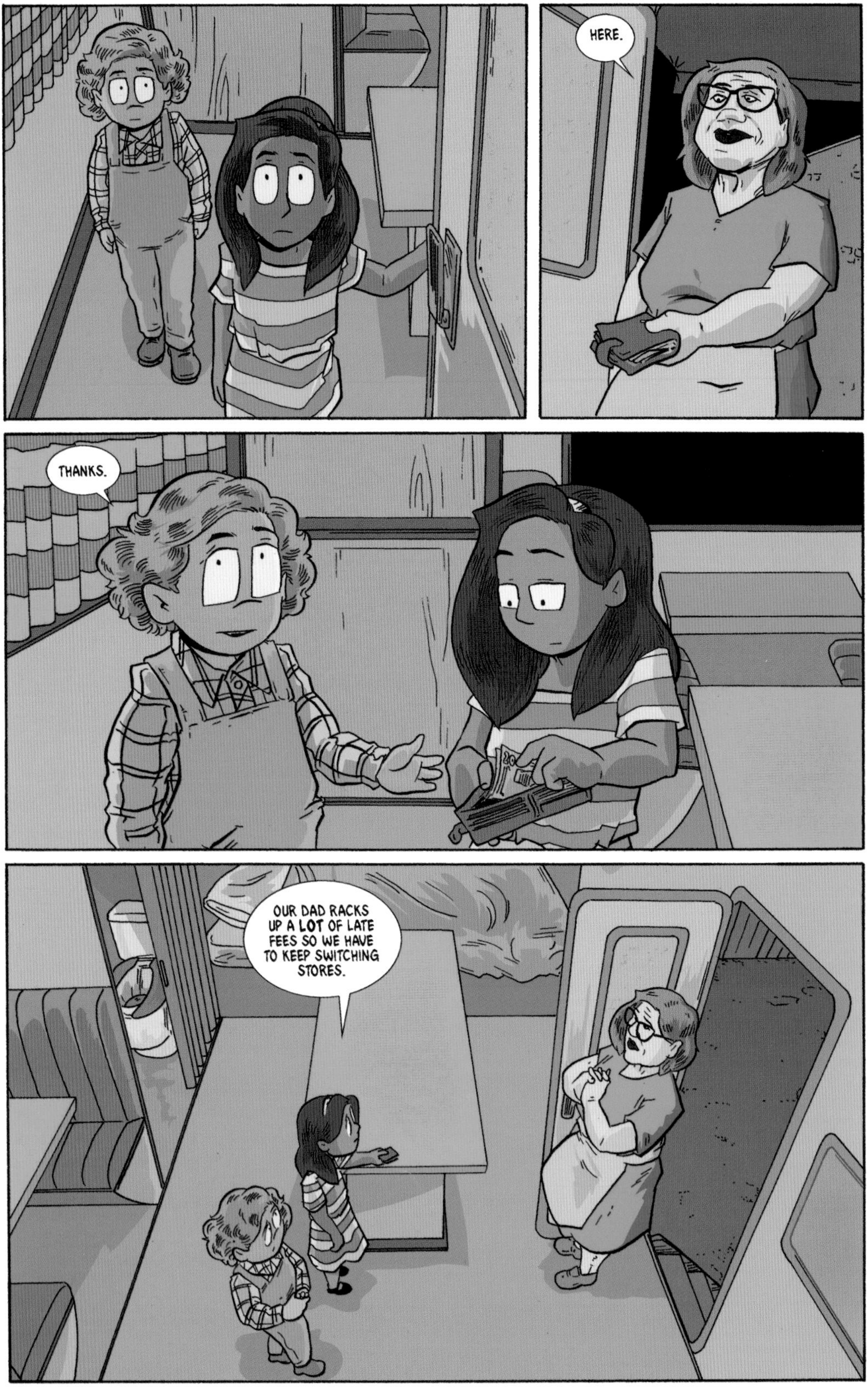
HERE.
THANKS.
OUR DAD RACKS UP A **LOT** OF LATE FEES SO WE HAVE TO KEEP SWITCHING STORES.

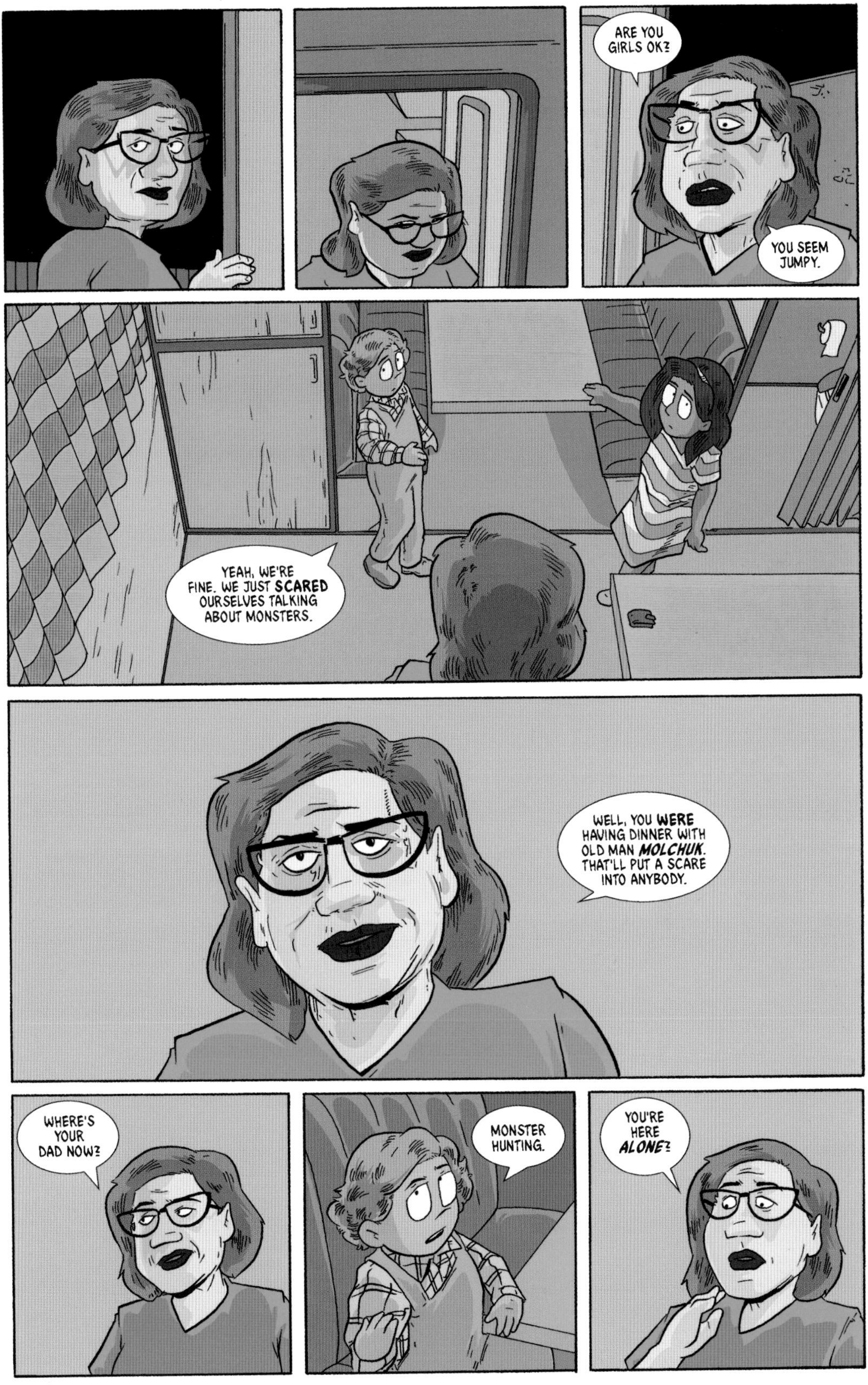
ARE YOU GIRLS OK?
YOU SEEM JUMPY.
YEAH, WE'RE FINE. WE JUST SCARED OURSELVES TALKING ABOUT MONSTERS.
WELL, YOU WERE HAVING DINNER WITH OLD MAN MOLCHUK. THAT'LL PUT A SCARE INTO ANYBODY.
WHERE'S YOUR DAD NOW?
MONSTER HUNTING.
YOU'RE HERE ALONE?

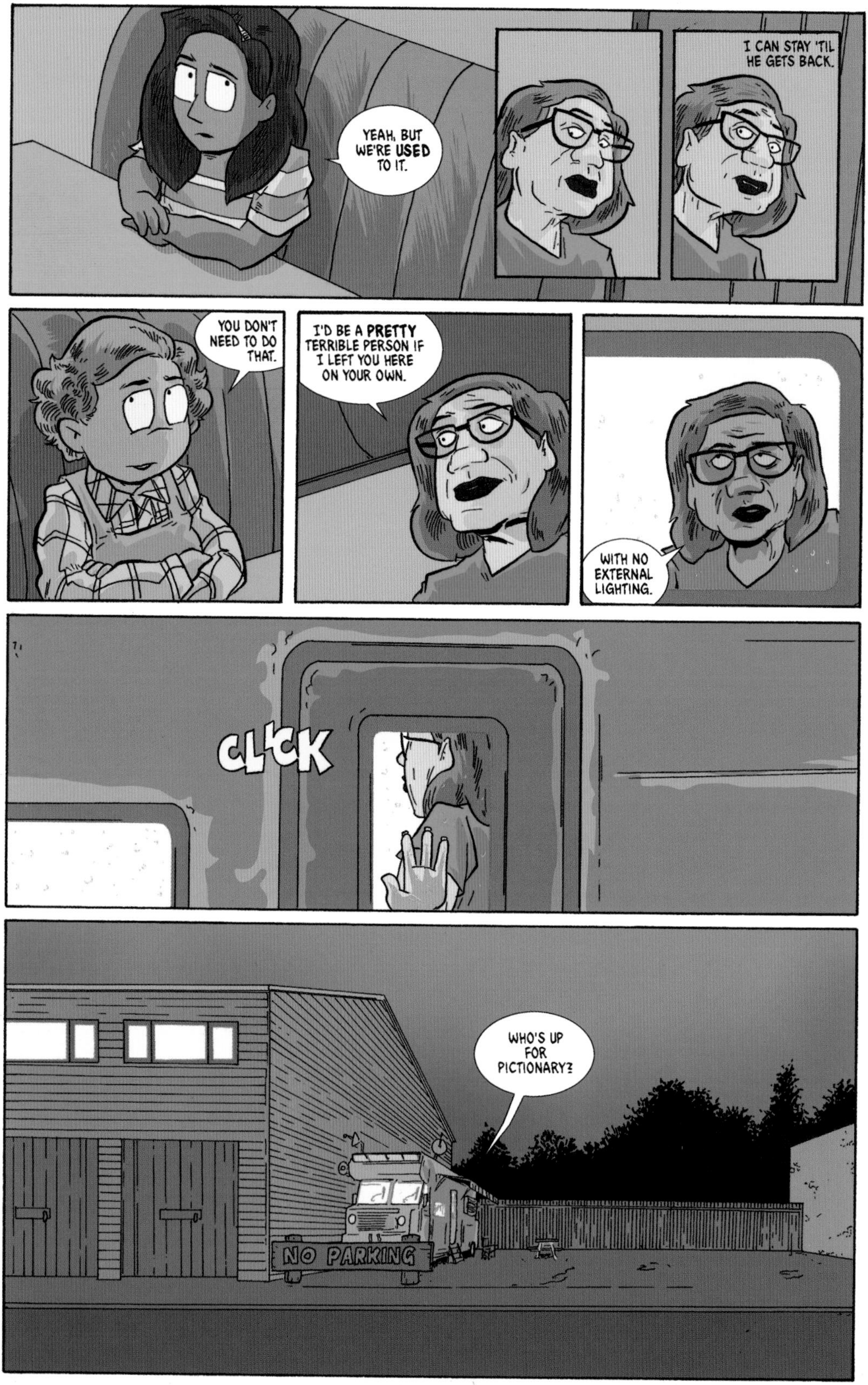
YEAH, BUT WE'RE USED TO IT.
I CAN STAY 'TIL HE GETS BACK.
YOU DON'T NEED TO DO THAT.
I'D BE A PRETTY TERRIBLE PERSON IF I LEFT YOU HERE ON YOUR OWN.
WITH NO EXTERNAL LIGHTING.
CLICK
NO PARKING
WHO'S UP FOR PICTIONARY?

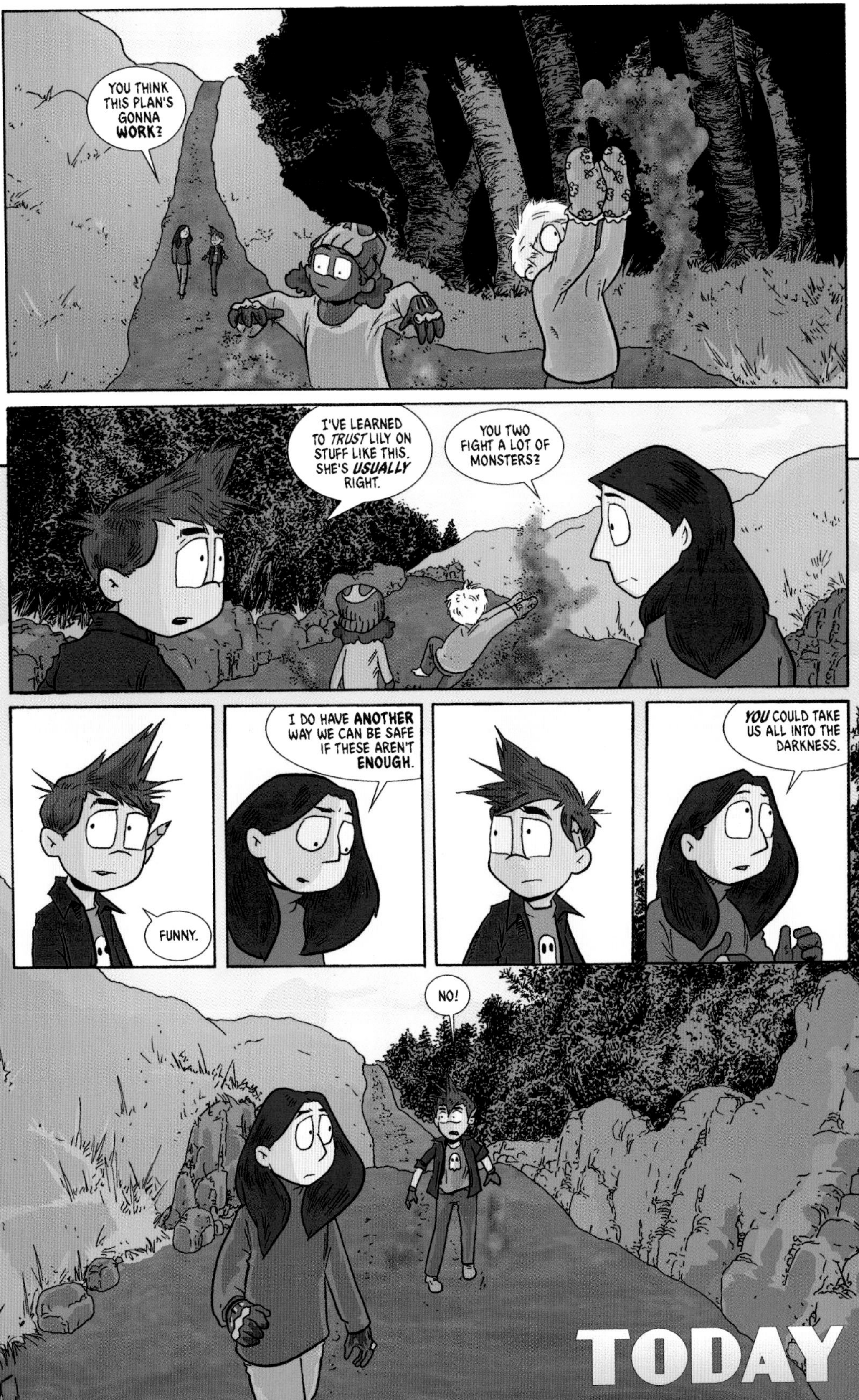
YOU THINK THIS PLAN'S GONNA WORK?
I'VE LEARNED TO TRUST LILY ON STUFF LIKE THIS. SHE'S USUALLY RIGHT.
YOU TWO FIGHT A LOT OF MONSTERS?
FUNNY.
I DO HAVE ANOTHER WAY WE CAN BE SAFE IF THESE AREN'T ENOUGH.
YOU COULD TAKE US ALL INTO THE DARKNESS.
NO!
TODAY

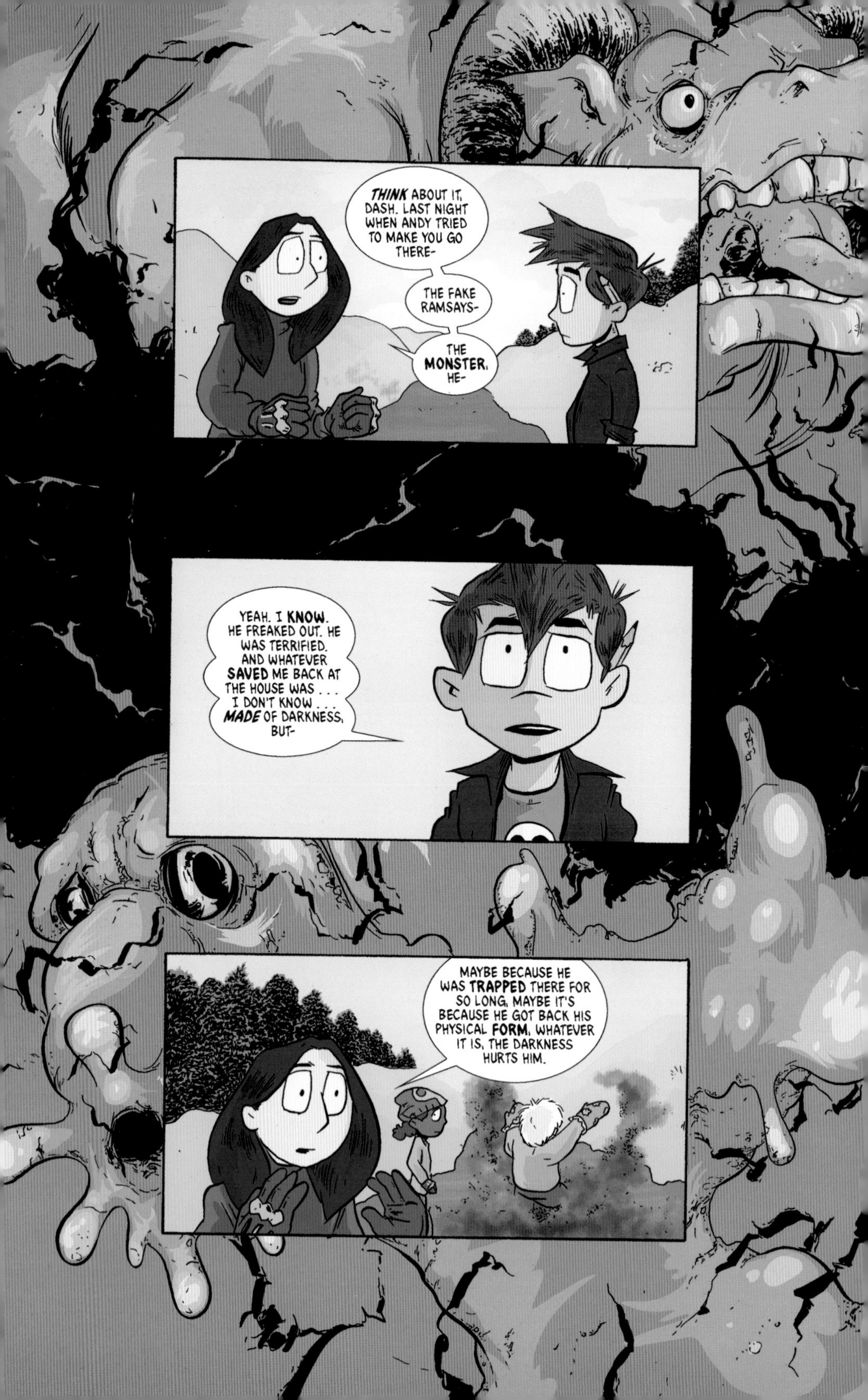
THINK ABOUT IT, DASH. LAST NIGHT WHEN ANDY TRIED TO MAKE YOU GO THERE-
THE FAKE RAMSAYS-
THE MONSTER, HE-
YEAH. I KNOW. HE FREAKED OUT. HE WAS TERRIFIED. AND WHATEVER SAVED ME BACK AT THE HOUSE WAS . . . I DON'T KNOW . . . MADE OF DARKNESS, BUT-
MAYBE BECAUSE HE WAS TRAPPED THERE FOR SO LONG, MAYBE IT'S BECAUSE HE GOT BACK HIS PHYSICAL FORM, WHATEVER IT IS, THE DARKNESS HURTS HIM.

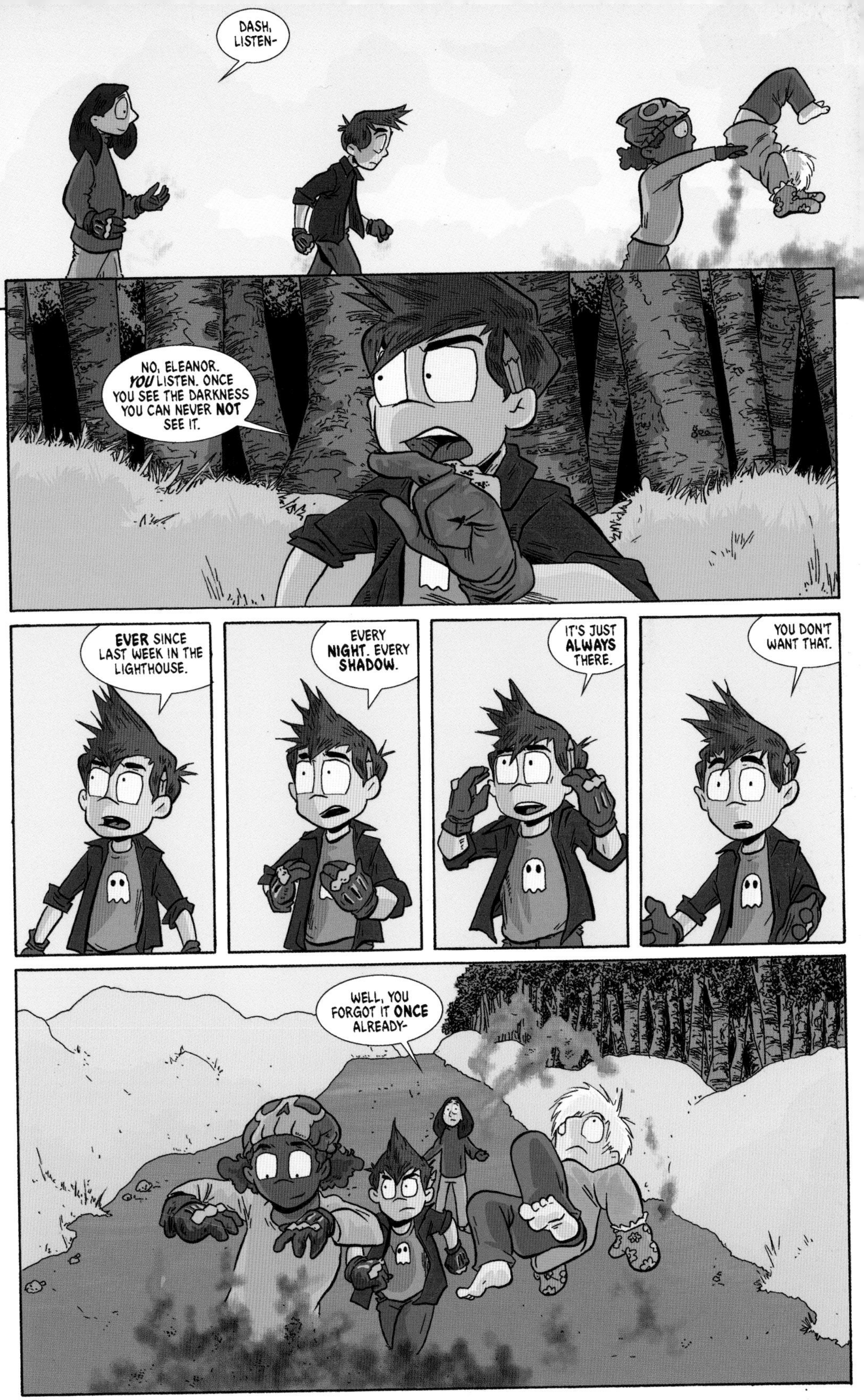
DASH, LISTEN-
NO, ELEANOR. YOU LISTEN. ONCE YOU SEE THE DARKNESS YOU CAN NEVER NOT SEE IT.
EVER SINCE LAST WEEK IN THE LIGHTHOUSE.
EVERY NIGHT. EVERY SHADOW.
IT'S JUST ALWAYS THERE.
YOU DON'T WANT THAT.
WELL, YOU FORGOT IT ONCE ALREADY-

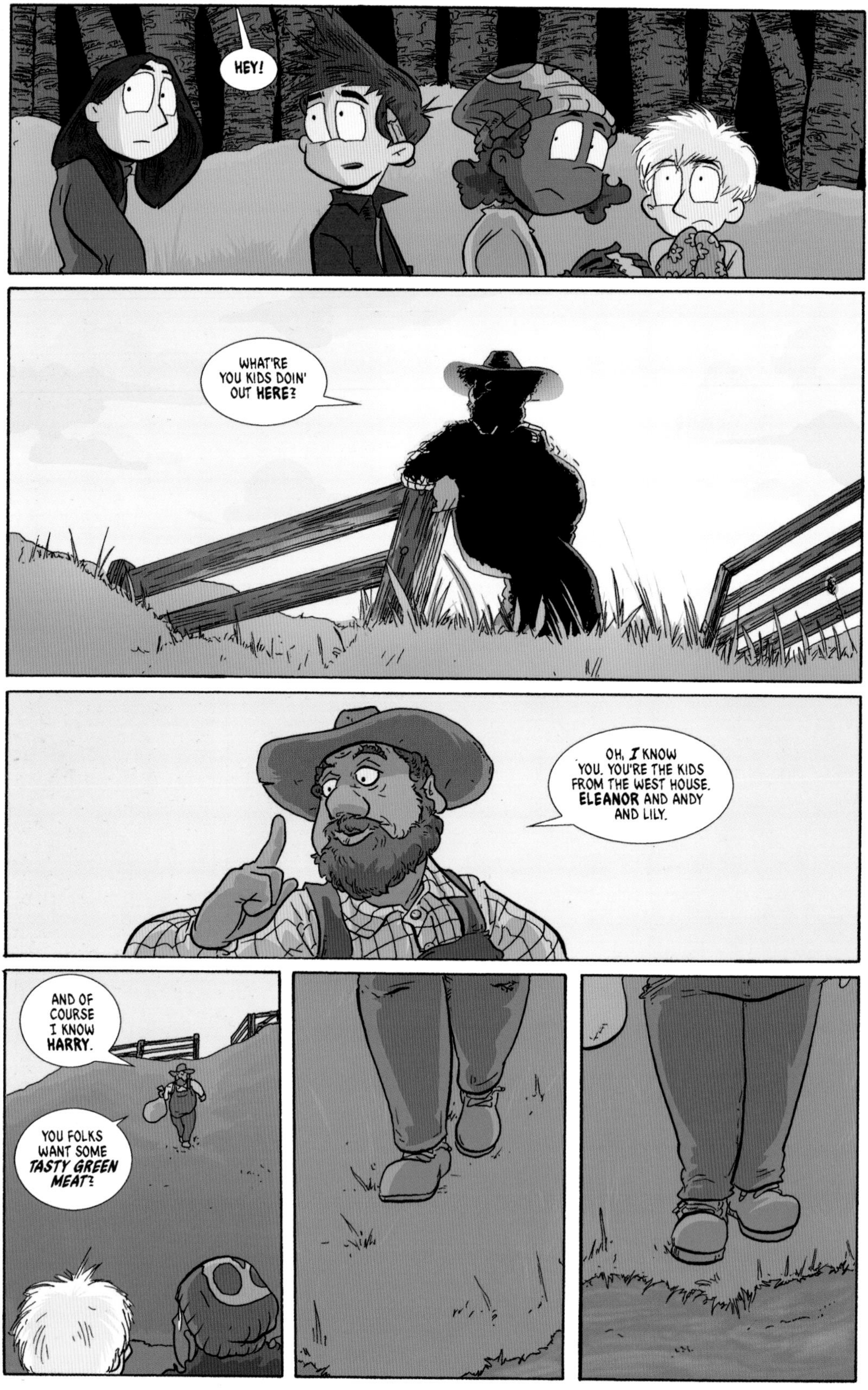
HEY!
WHAT'RE YOU KIDS DOIN' OUT HERE?
OH, I KNOW YOU. YOU'RE THE KIDS FROM THE WEST HOUSE. ELEANOR AND ANDY AND LILY.
AND OF COURSE I KNOW HARRY.
YOU FOLKS WANT SOME TASTY GREEN MEAT?

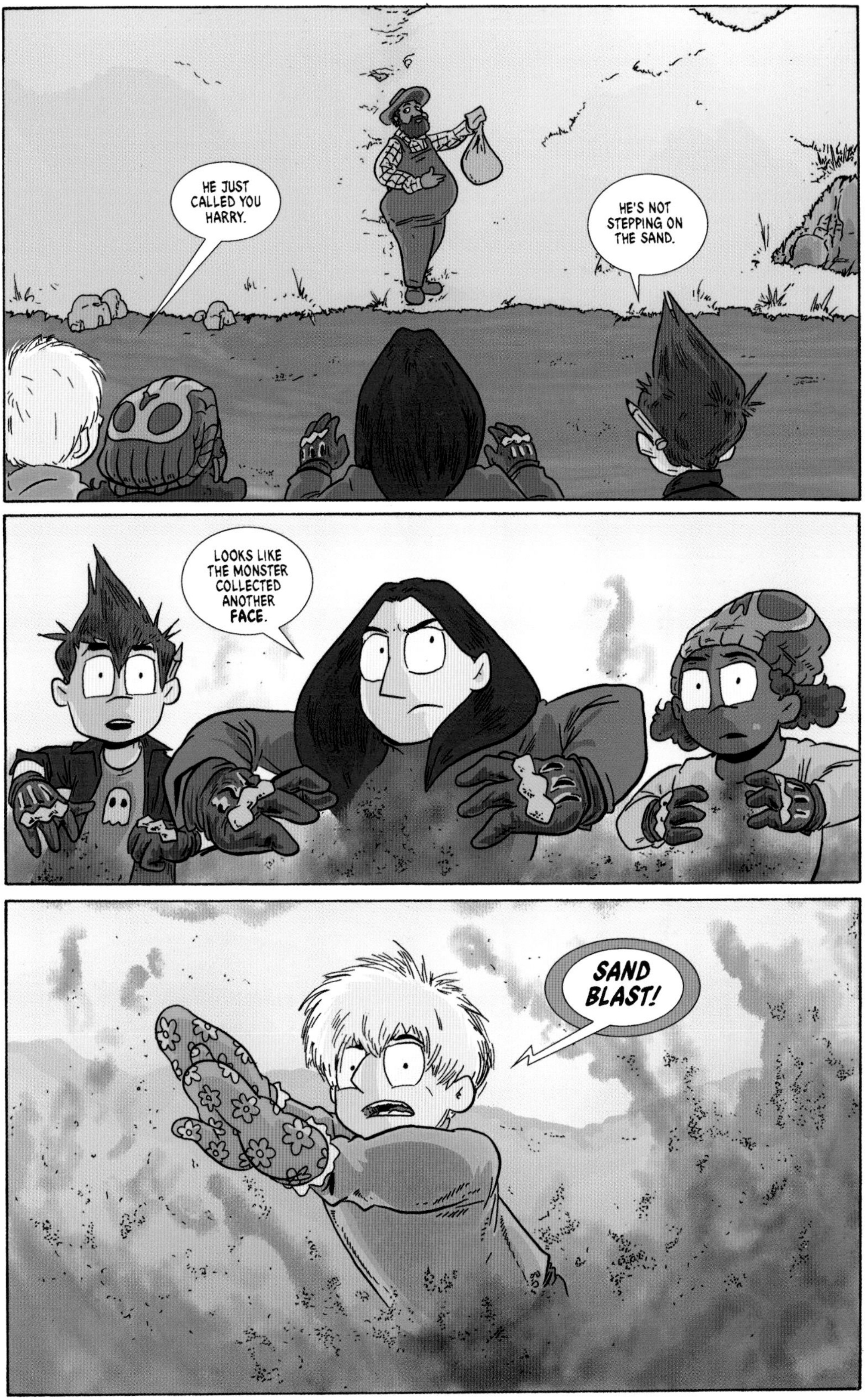
HE JUST CALLED YOU HARRY.
HE'S NOT STEPPING ON THE SAND.
LOOKS LIKE THE MONSTER COLLECTED ANOTHER FACE.
SAND BLAST!

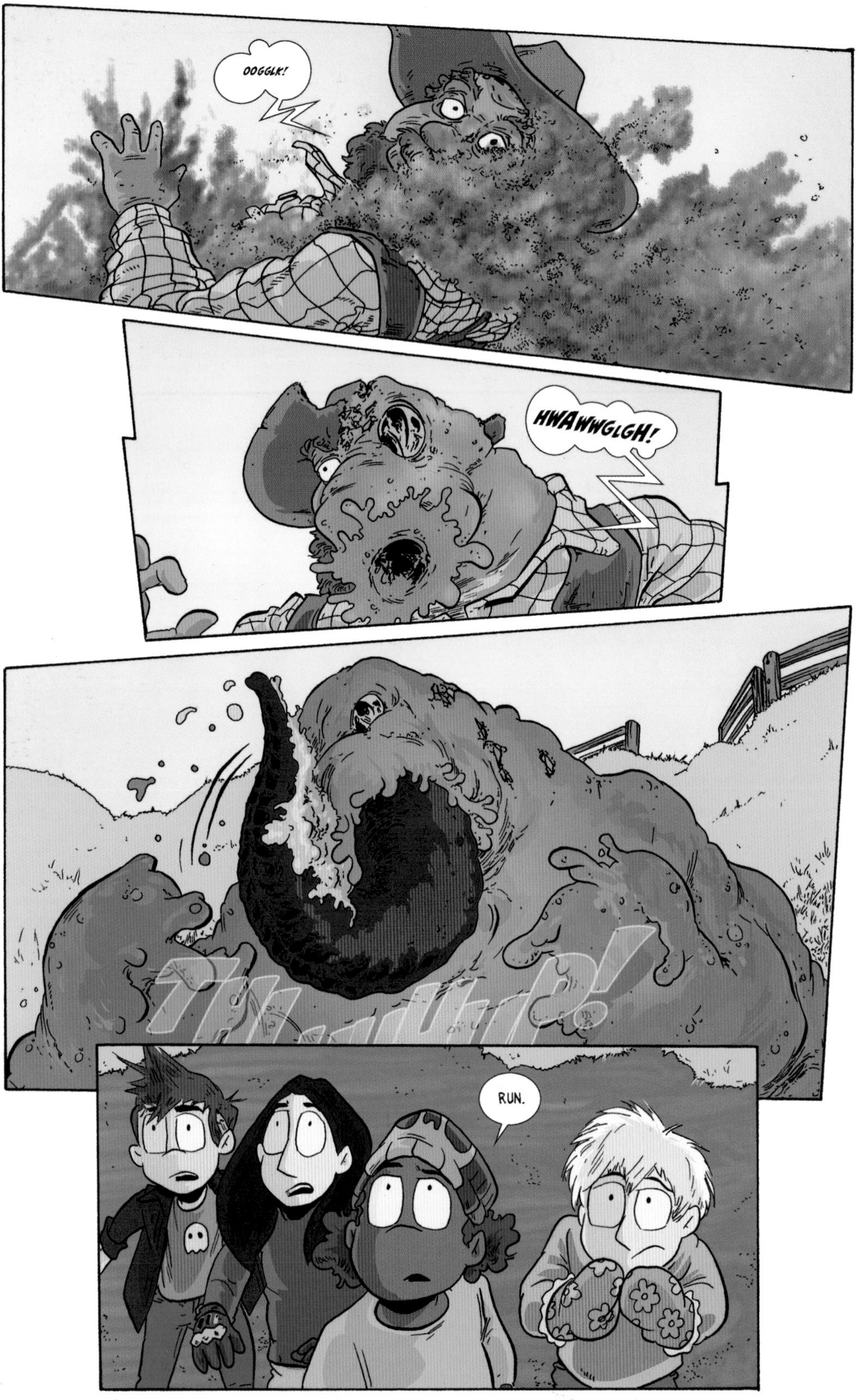
OOGGLK!
HWAWWGLGH!
RUN.

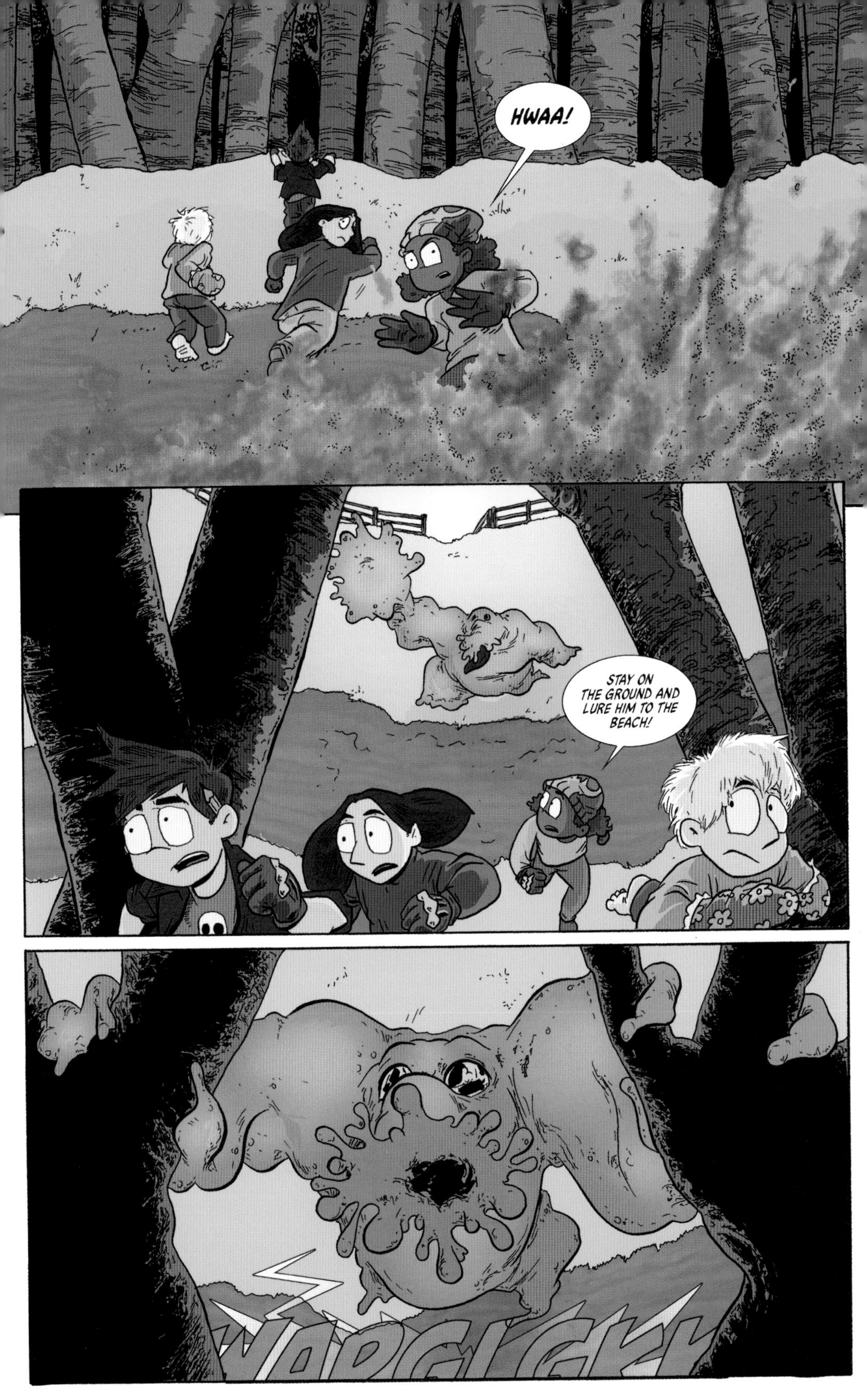
HWAA!
STAY ON THE GROUND AND LURE HIM TO THE BEACH!

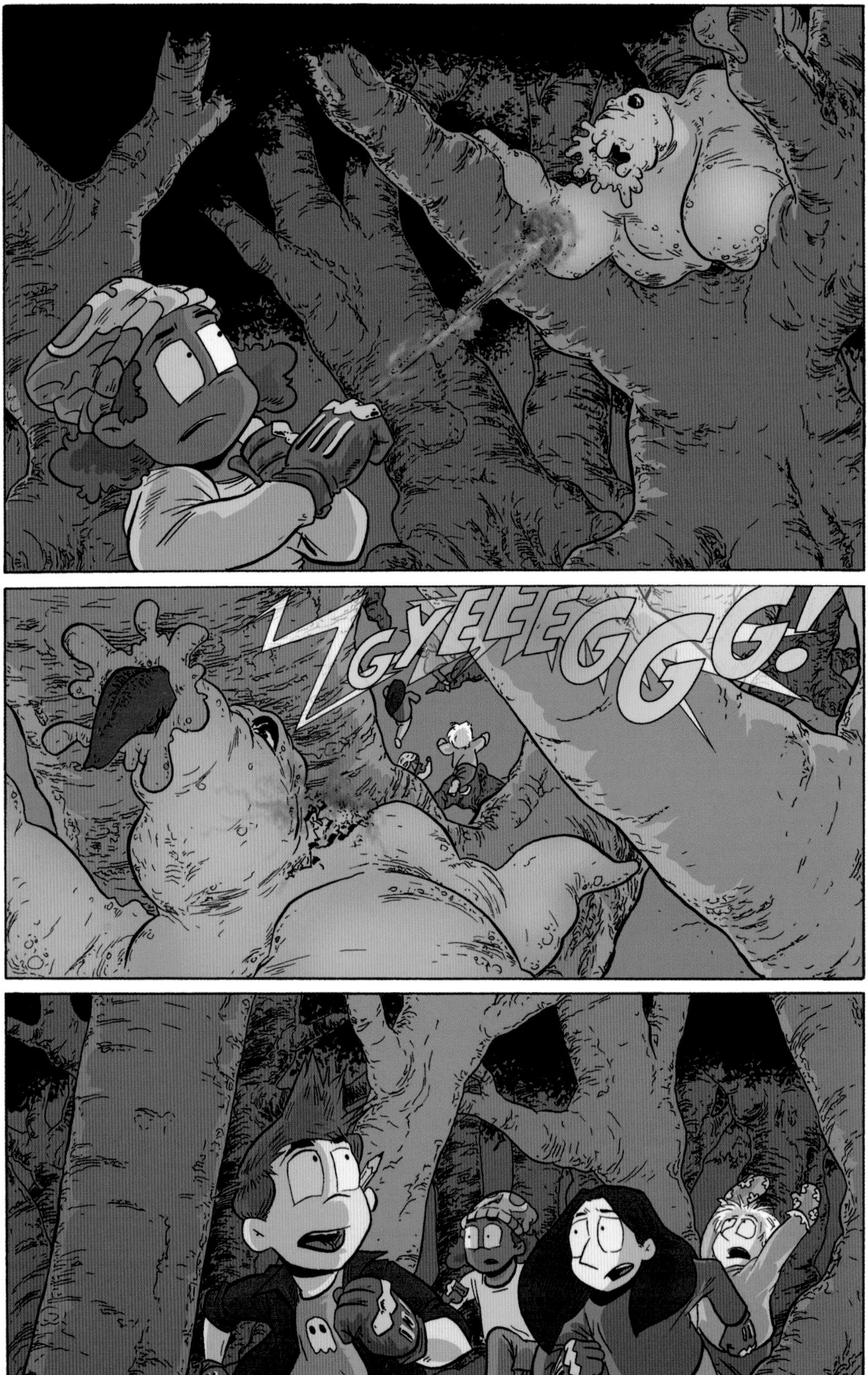
GYEEEGGG!

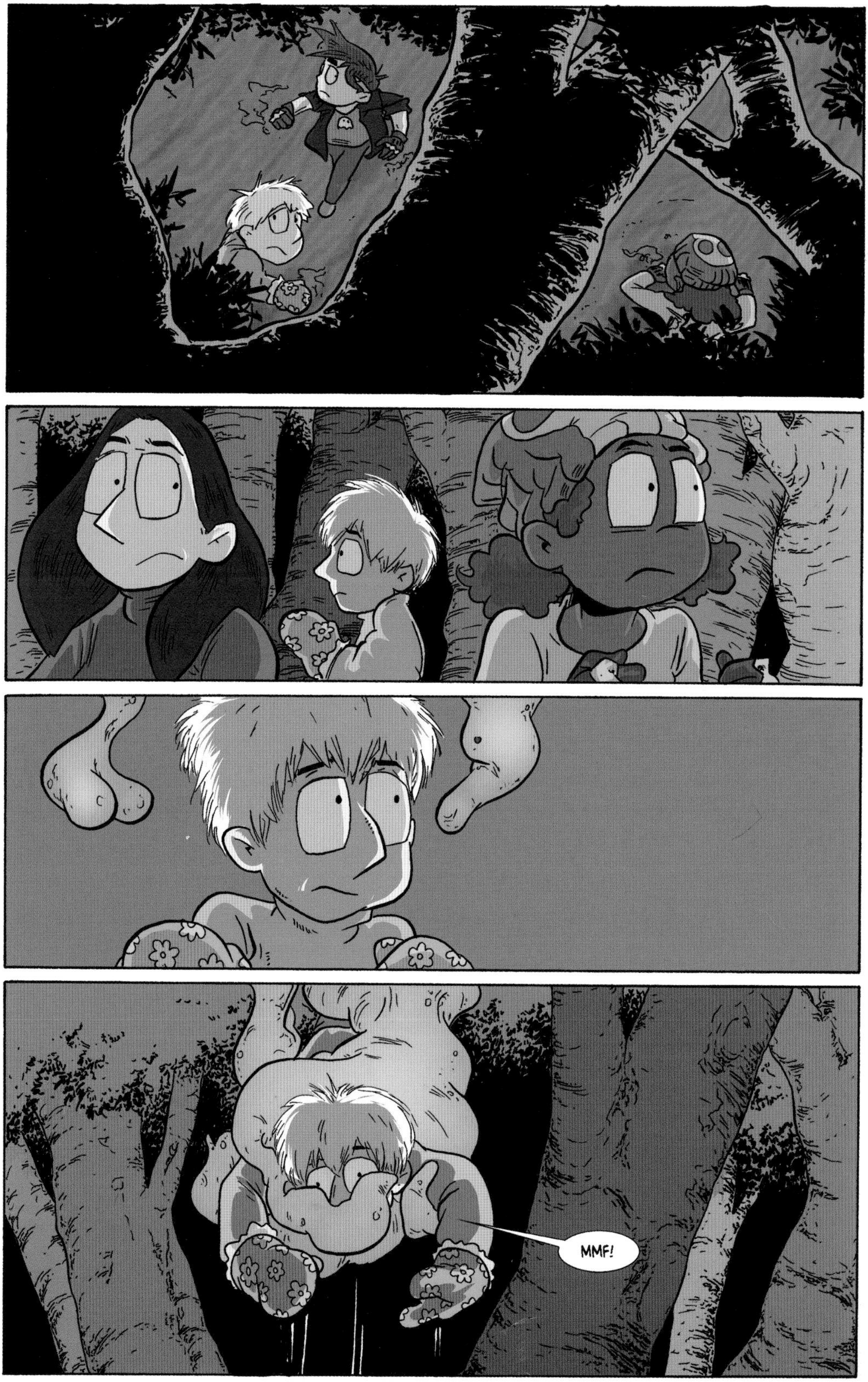
MMF!

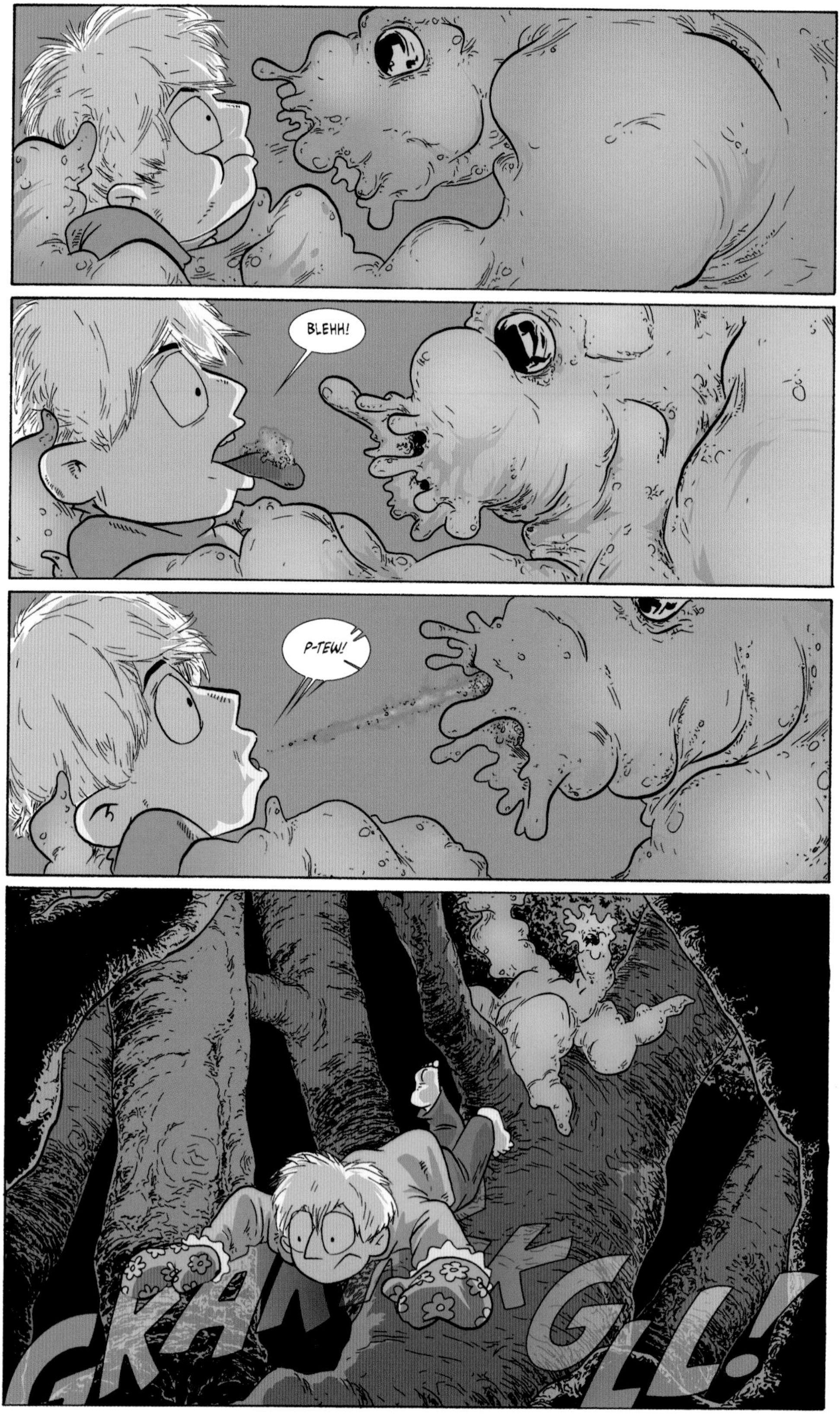
BLEHH!
P-TEW!
GKAKGLL!

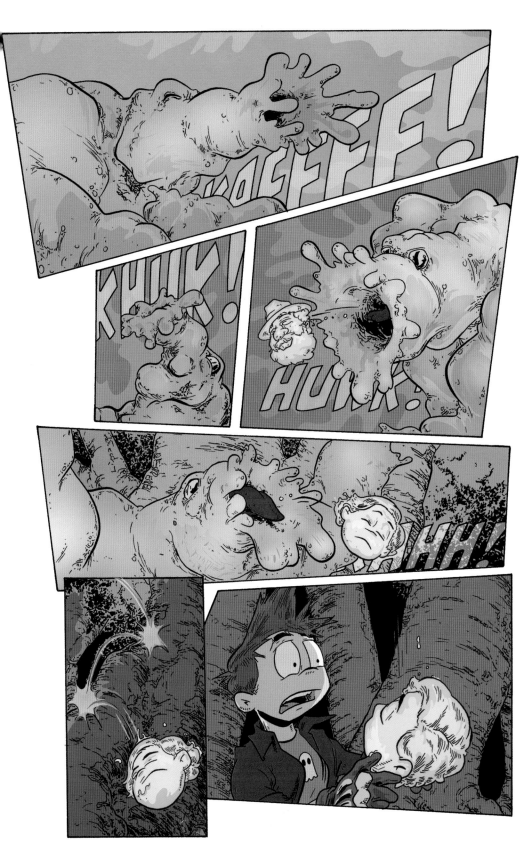

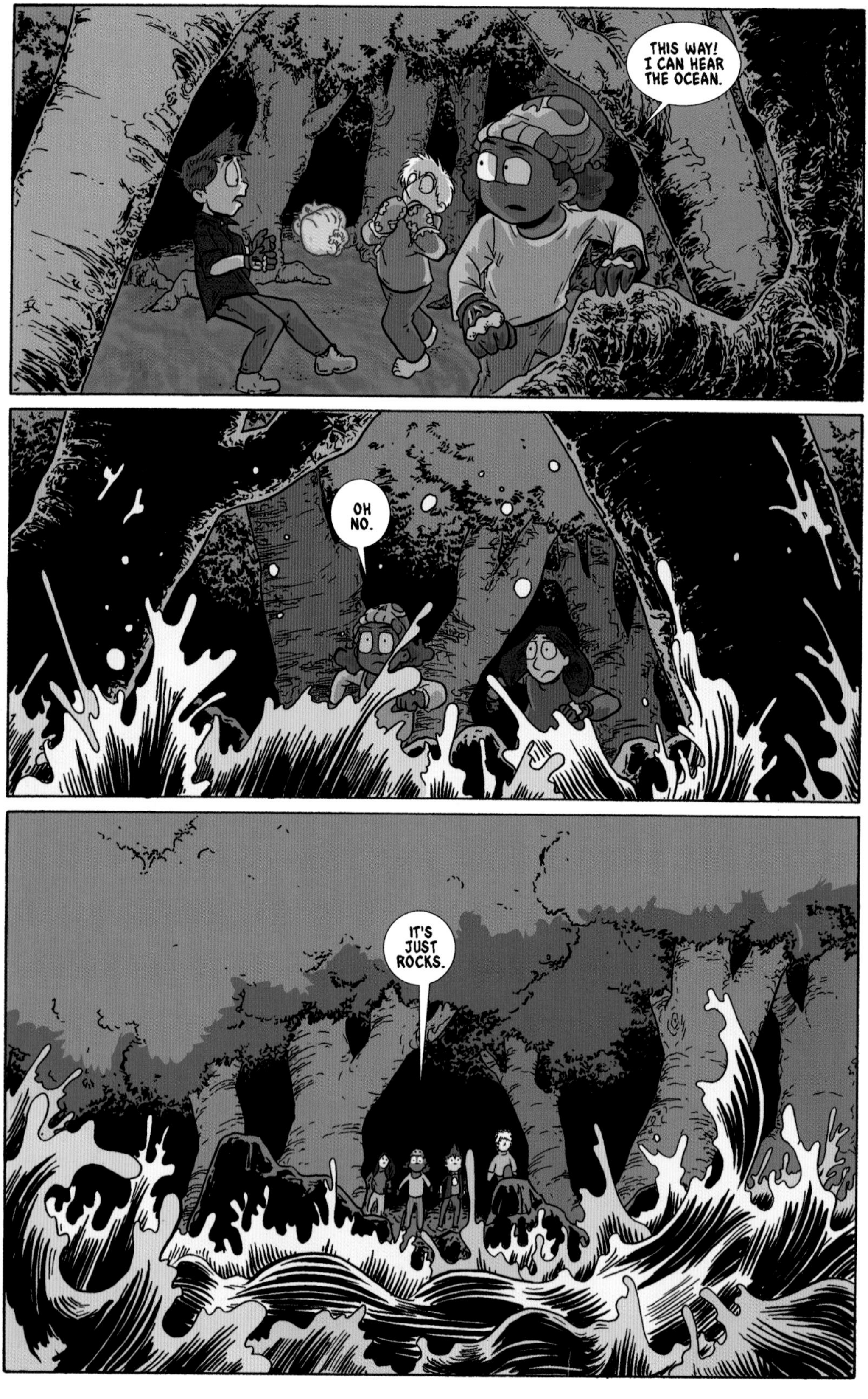
THIS WAY! I CAN HEAR THE OCEAN.
OH NO.
IT'S JUST ROCKS.

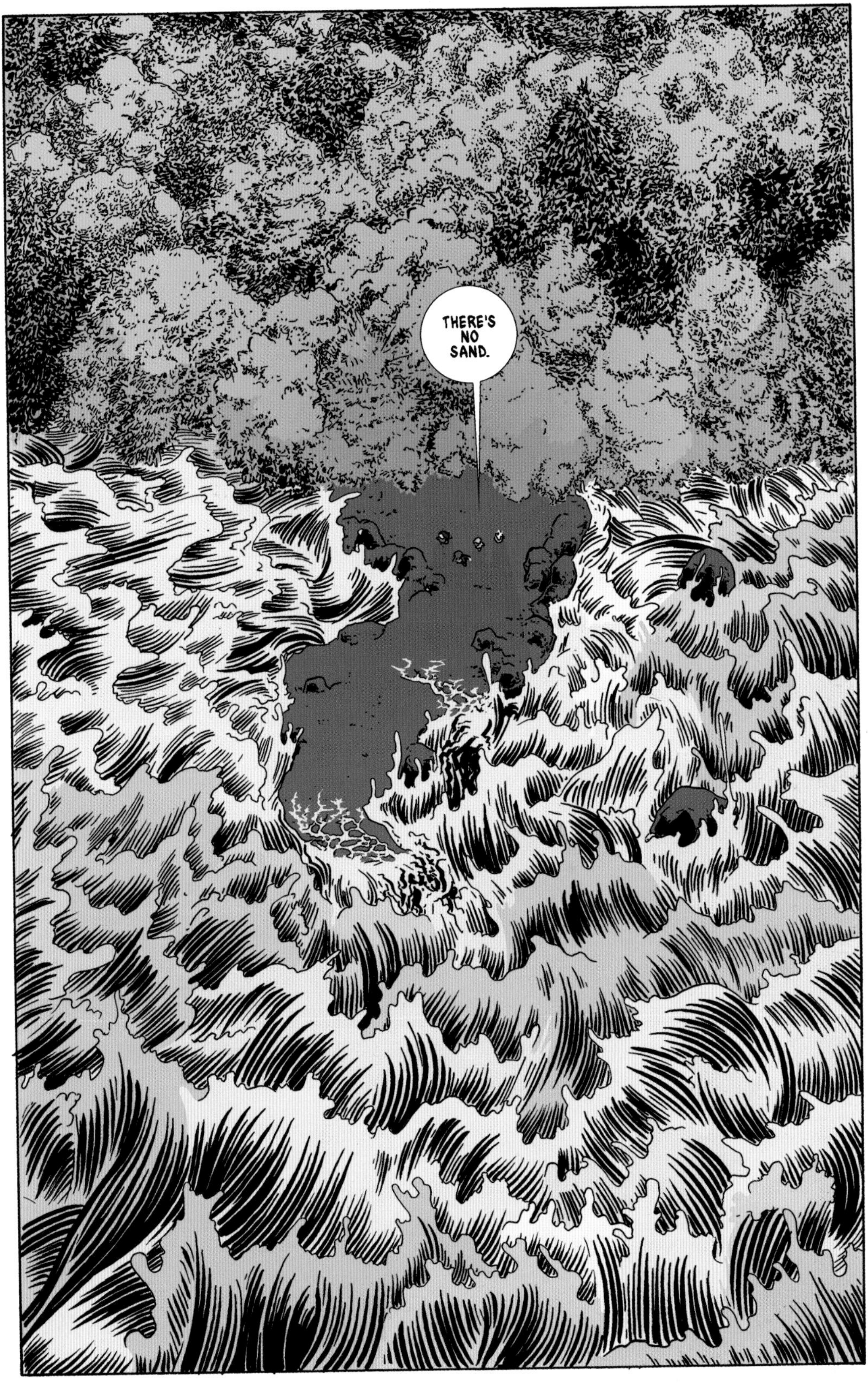
THERE'S NO SAND.

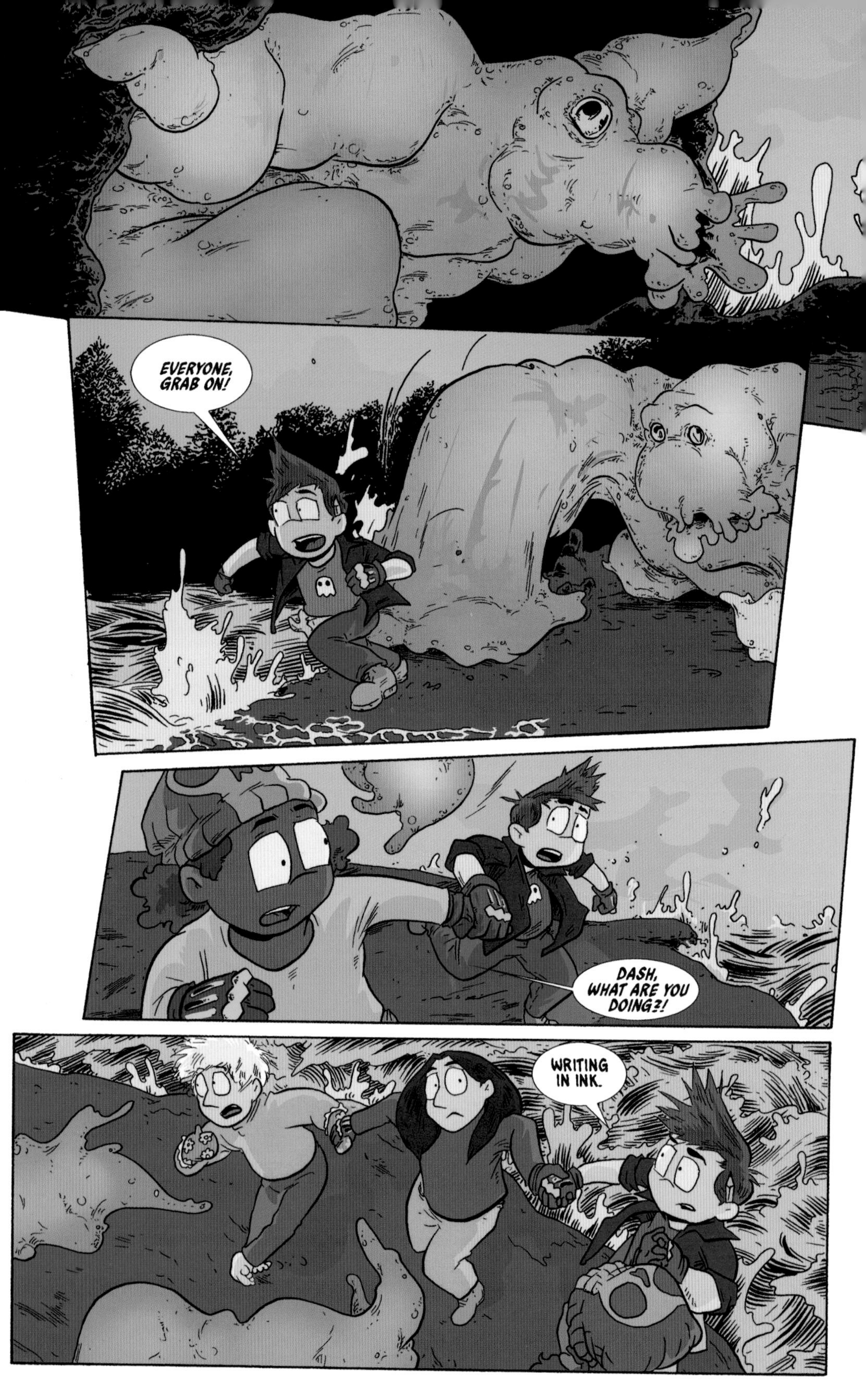
EVERYONE, GRAB ON!
DASH, WHAT ARE YOU DOING?!
WRITING IN INK.

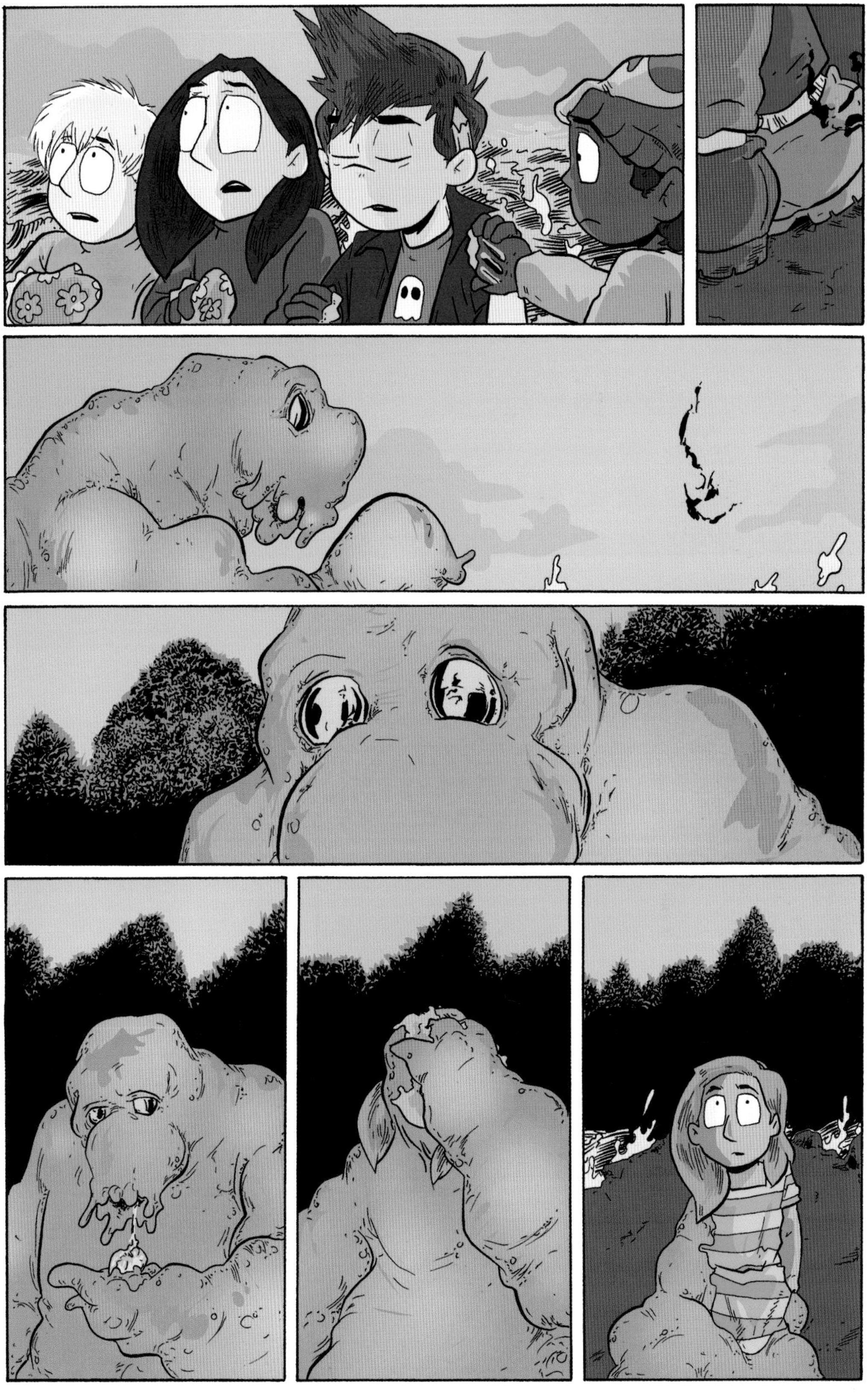

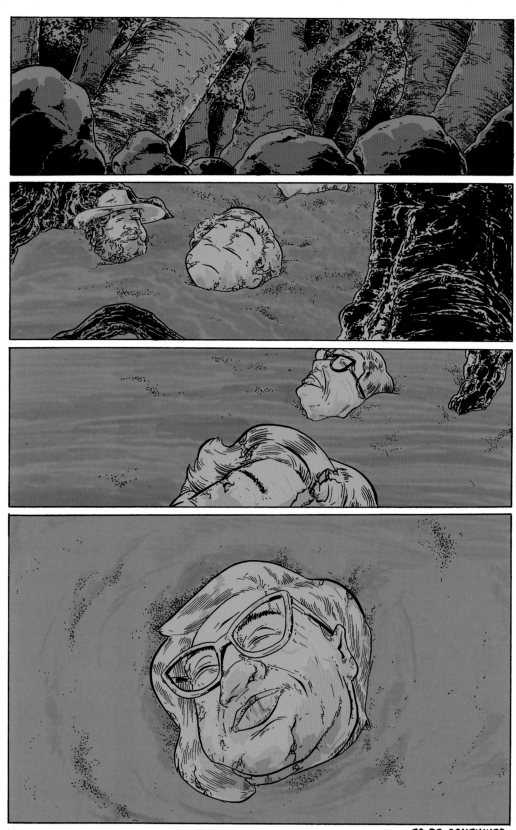

TO BE CONTINUED.

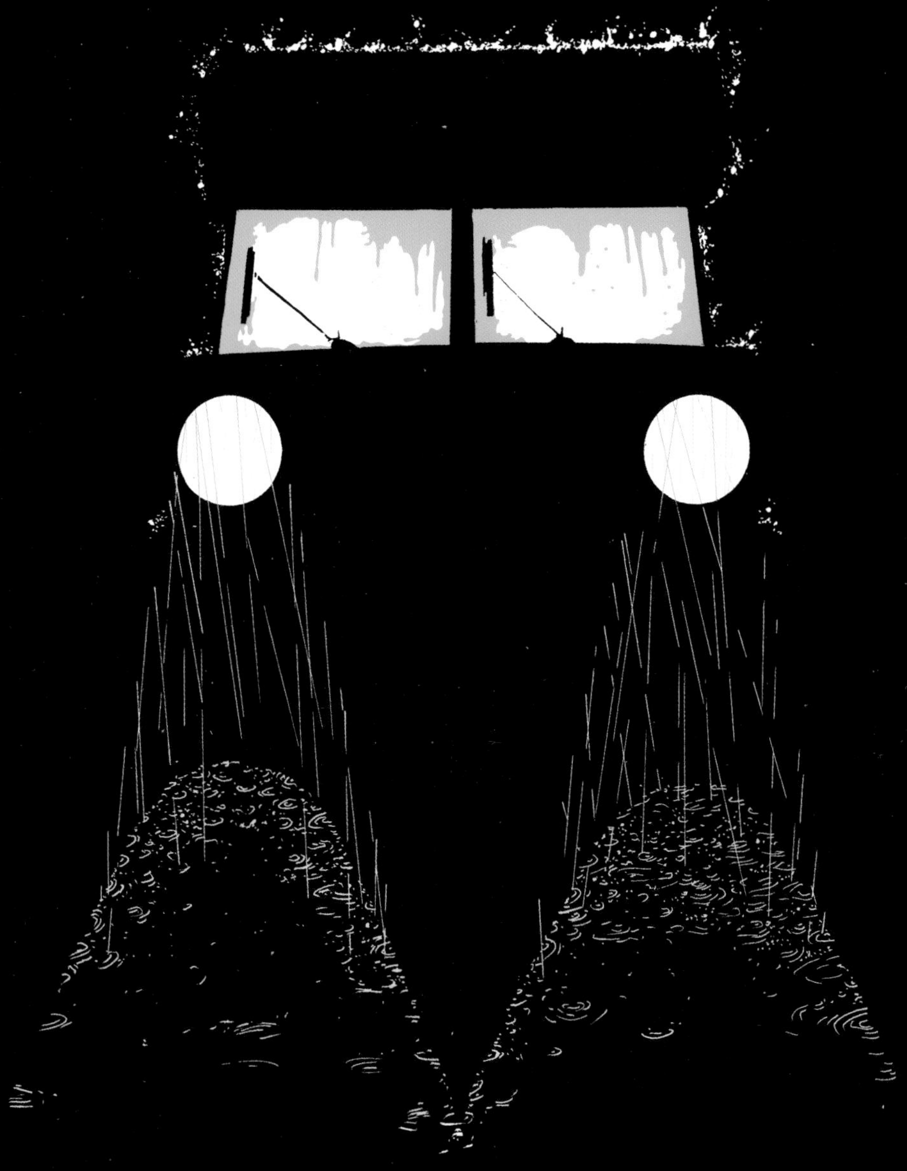

BAIT $ SWITCH

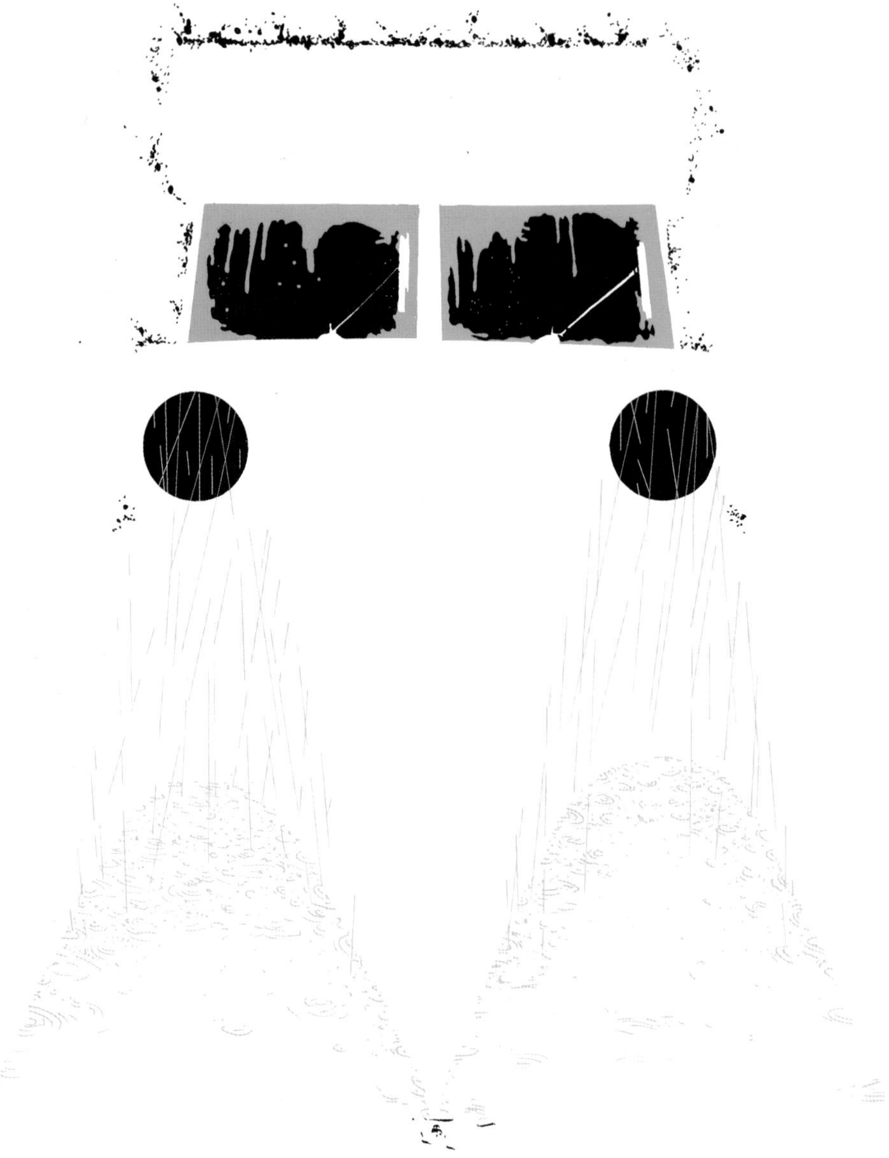

BAIT $ SWITCH

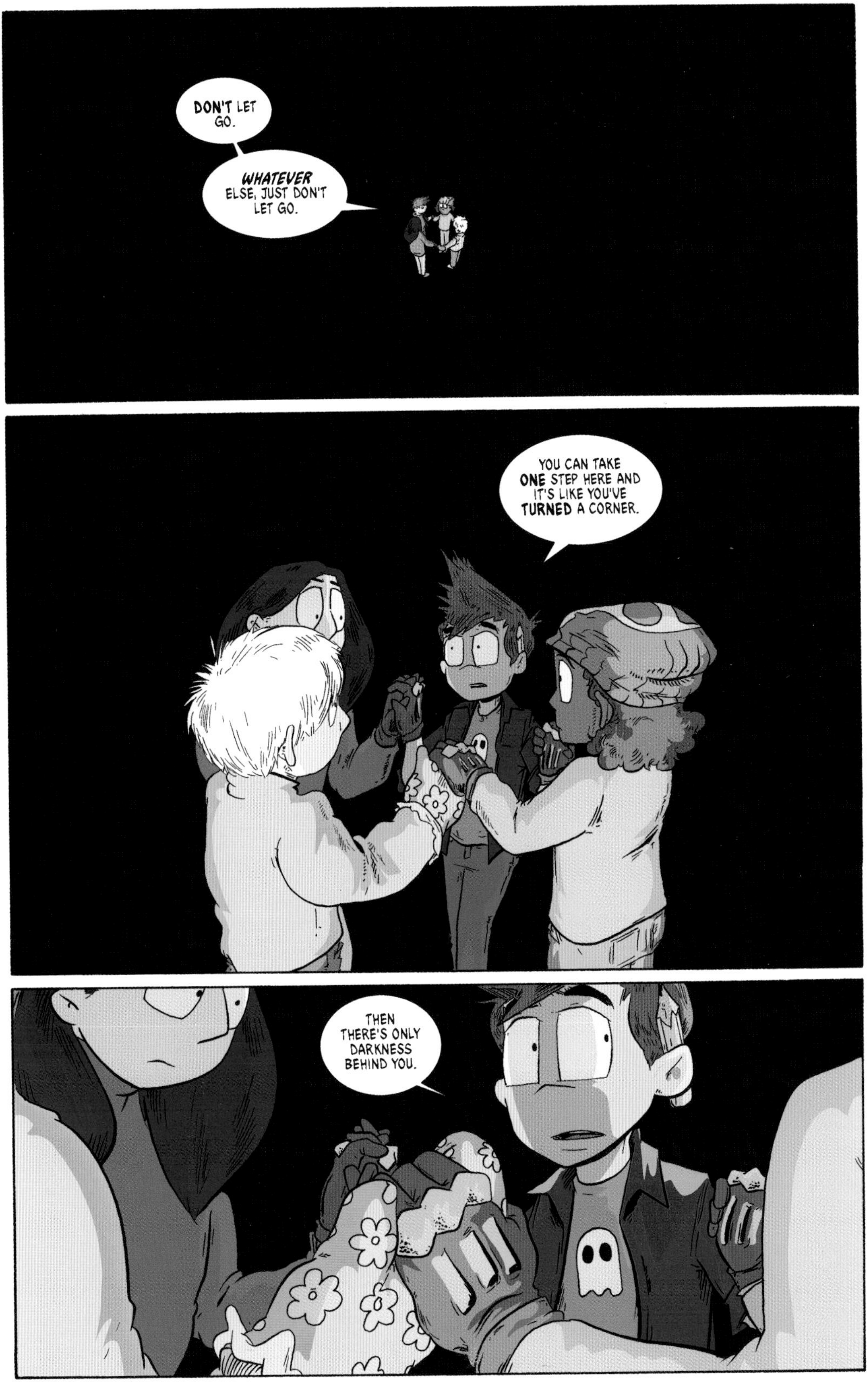
DON'T LET GO.
WHATEVER ELSE, JUST DON'T LET GO.
YOU CAN TAKE ONE STEP HERE AND IT'S LIKE YOU'VE TURNED A CORNER.
THEN THERE'S ONLY DARKNESS BEHIND YOU.

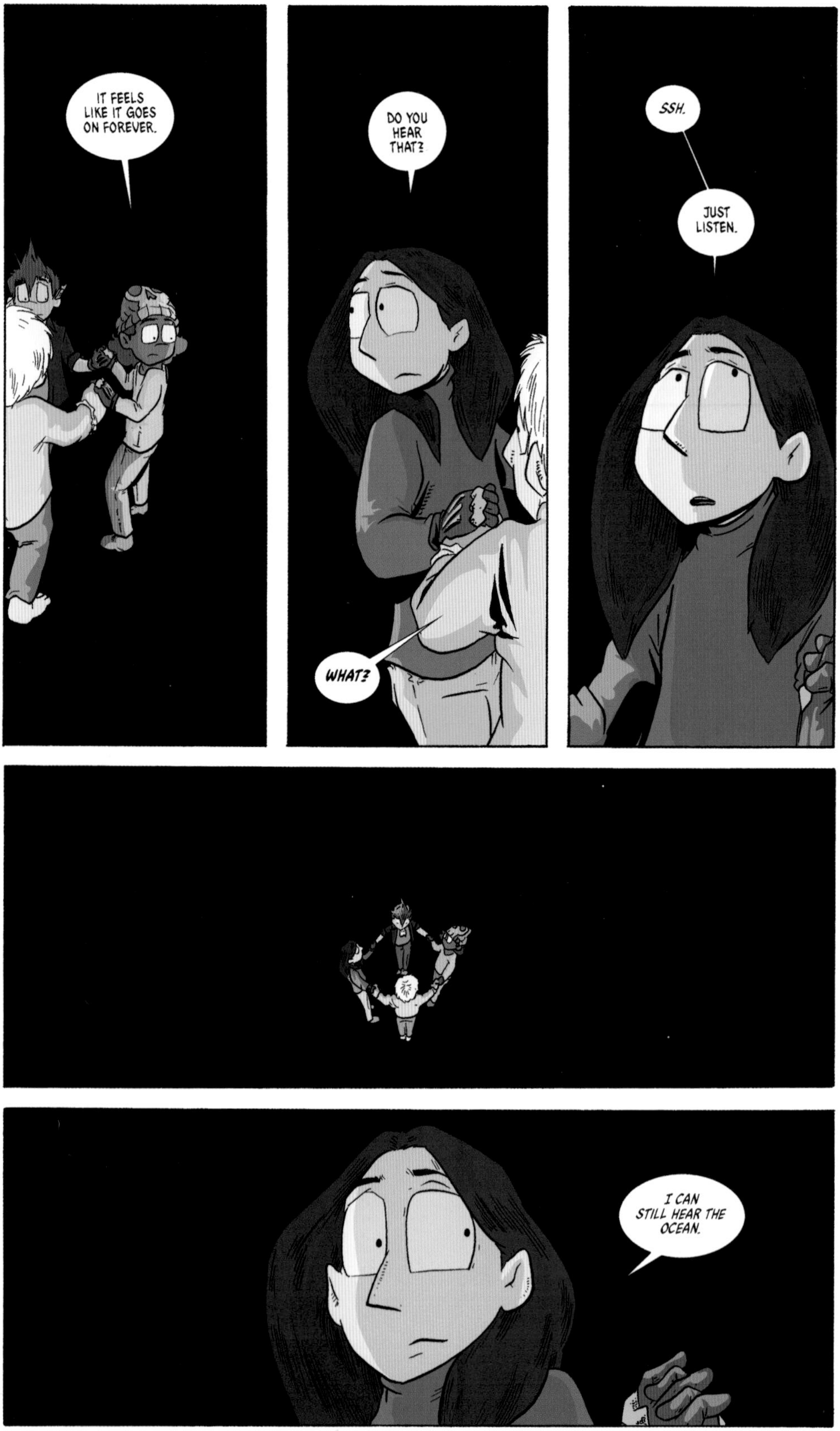
IT FEELS LIKE IT GOES ON FOREVER.
DO YOU HEAR THAT?
WHAT?
SSH.
JUST LISTEN.
I CAN STILL HEAR THE OCEAN.

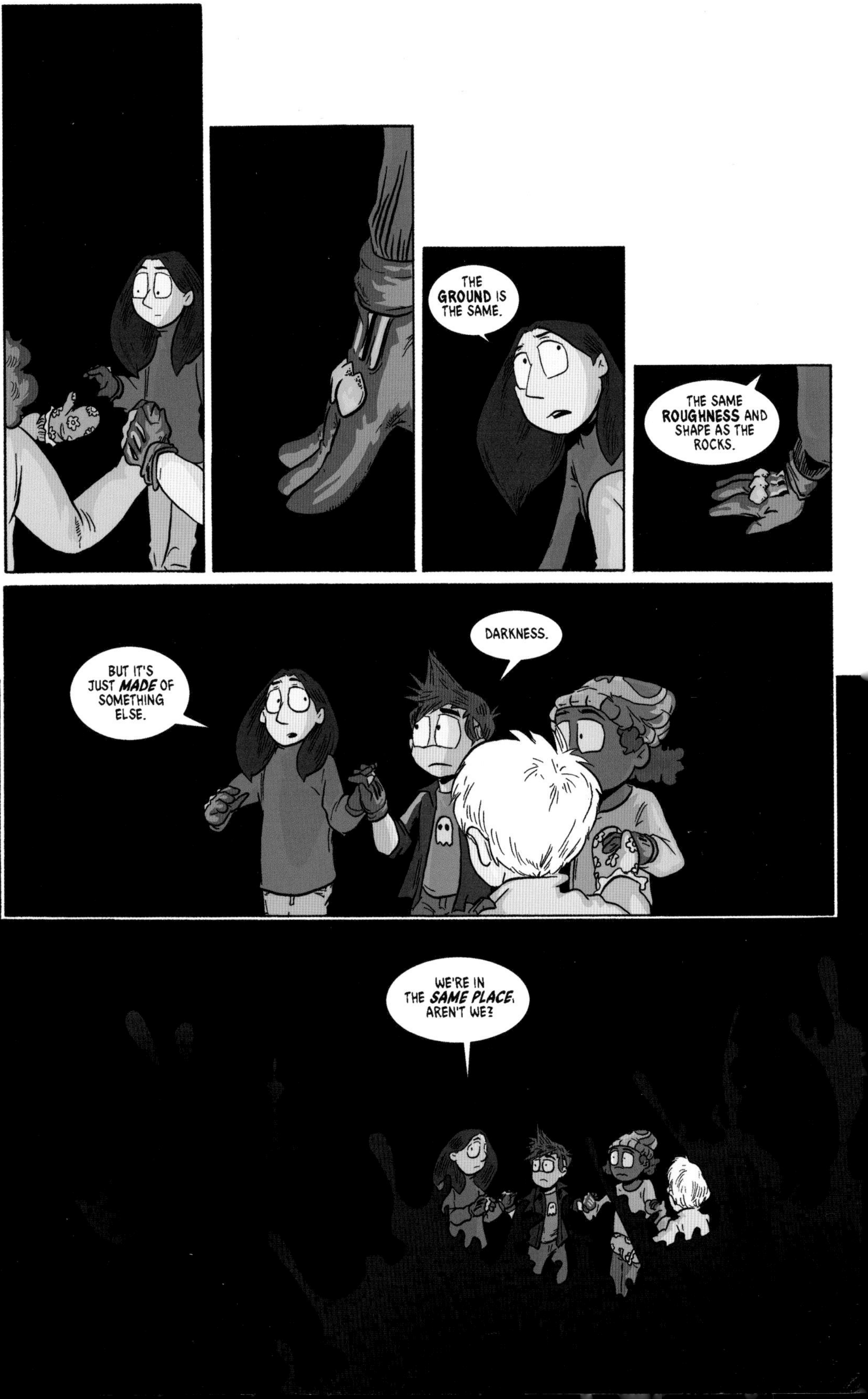
THE GROUND IS THE SAME.
THE SAME ROUGHNESS AND SHAPE AS THE ROCKS.
DARKNESS.
BUT IT'S JUST MADE OF SOMETHING ELSE.
WE'RE IN THE SAME PLACE, AREN'T WE?

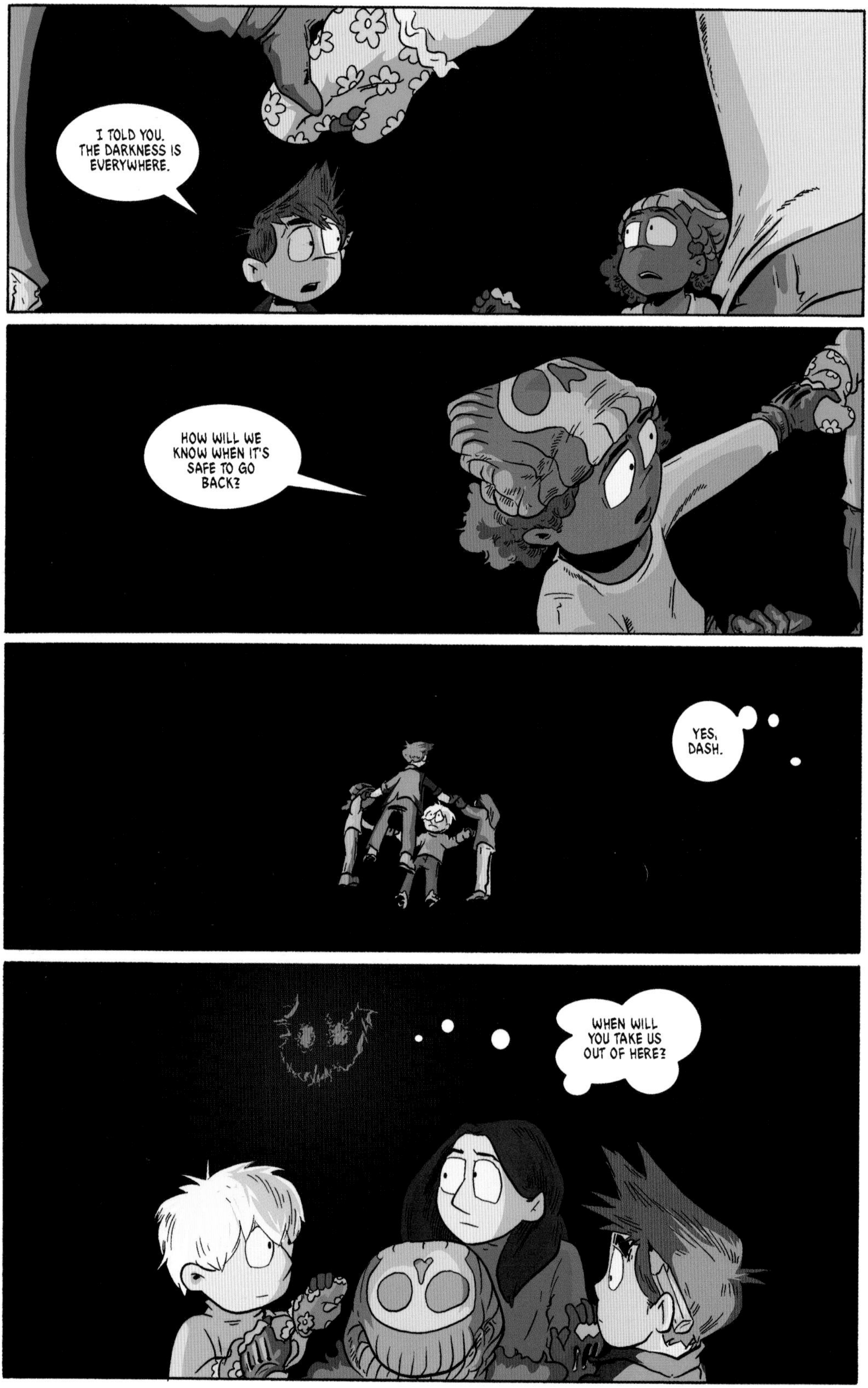
I TOLD YOU. THE DARKNESS IS EVERYWHERE.
HOW WILL WE KNOW WHEN IT'S SAFE TO GO BACK?
YES, DASH.
WHEN WILL YOU TAKE US OUT OF HERE?

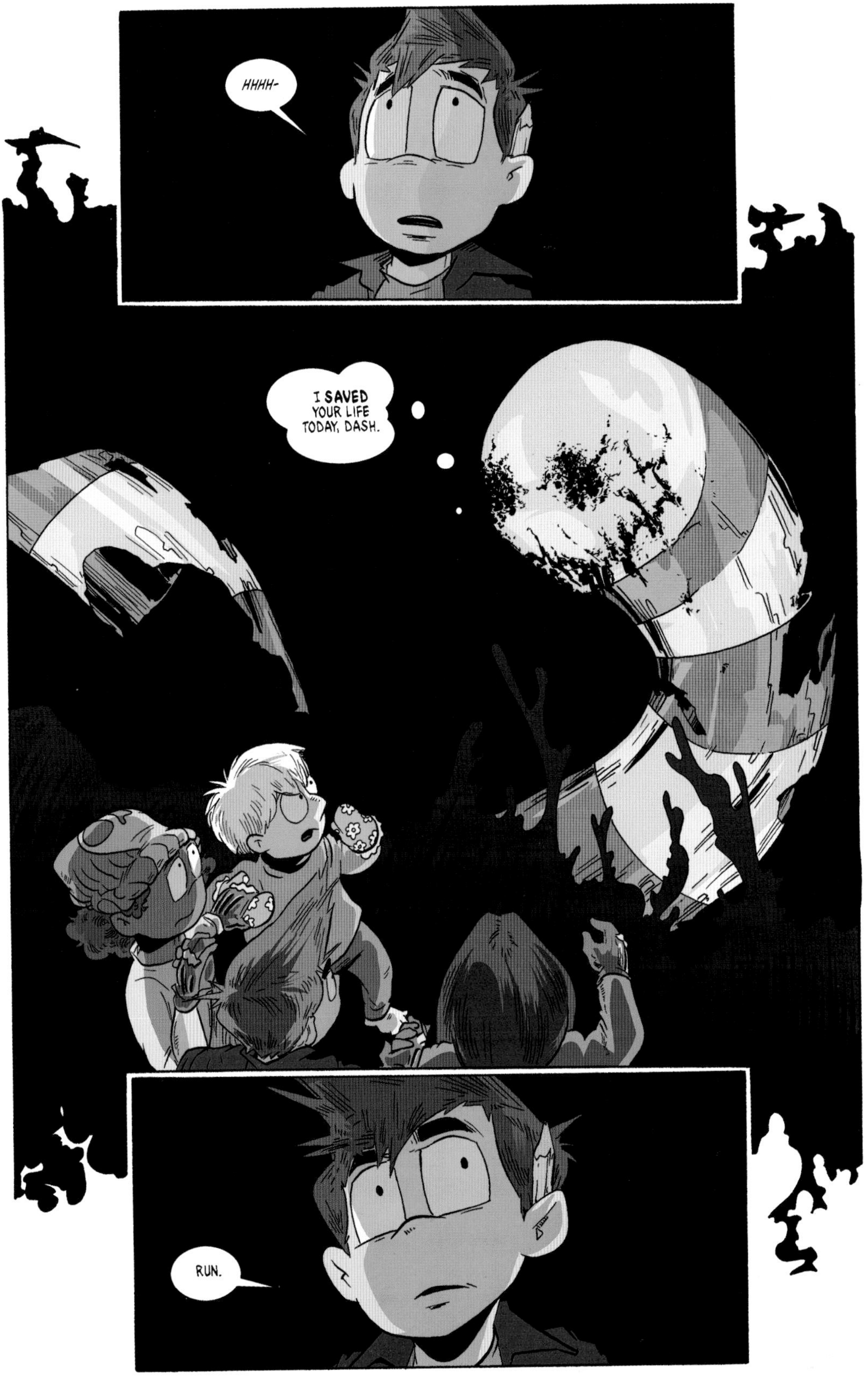
HHHH-
I SAVED YOUR LIFE TODAY, DASH.
RUN.

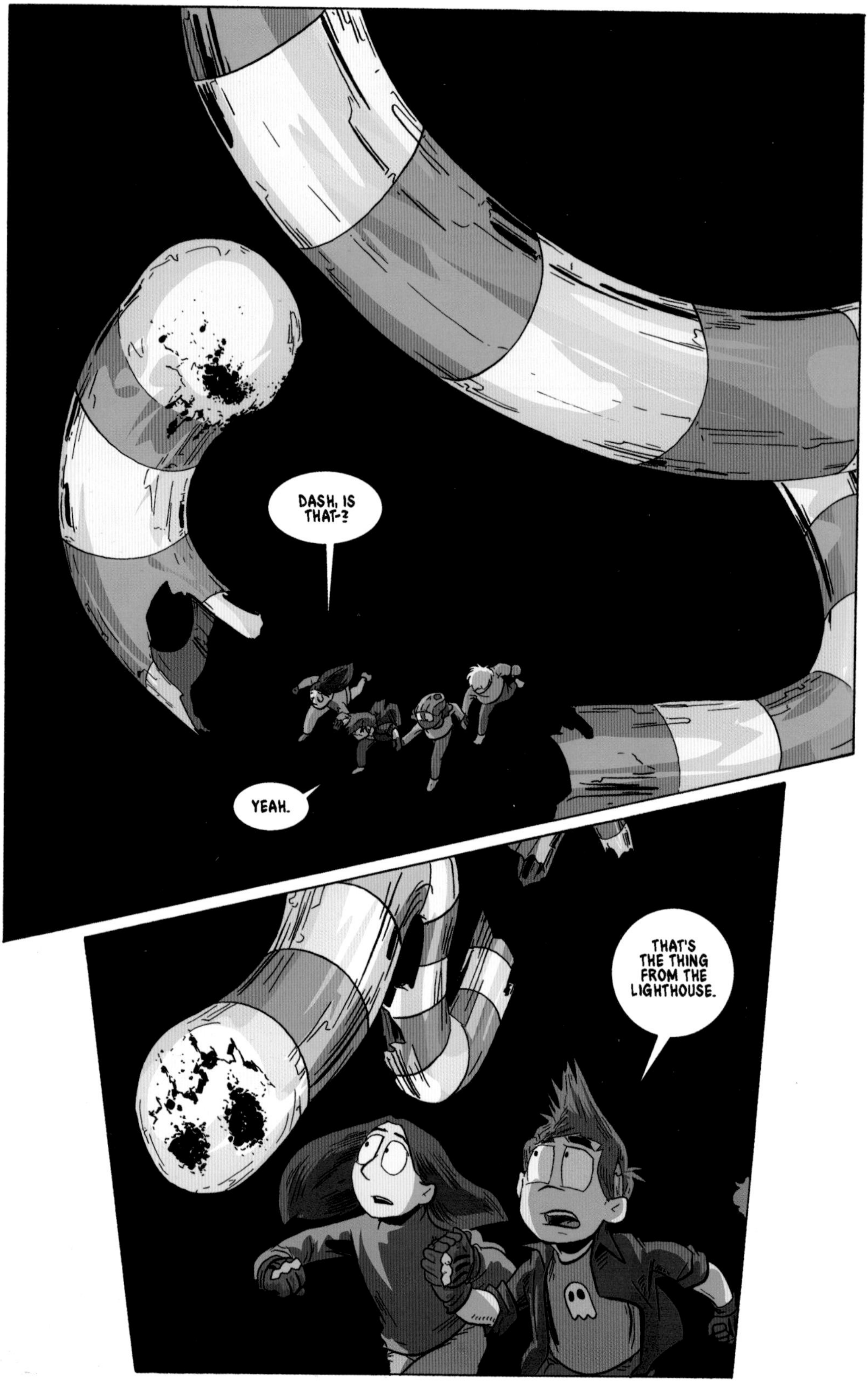
DASH, IS THAT-?
YEAH.
THAT'S THE THING FROM THE LIGHTHOUSE.

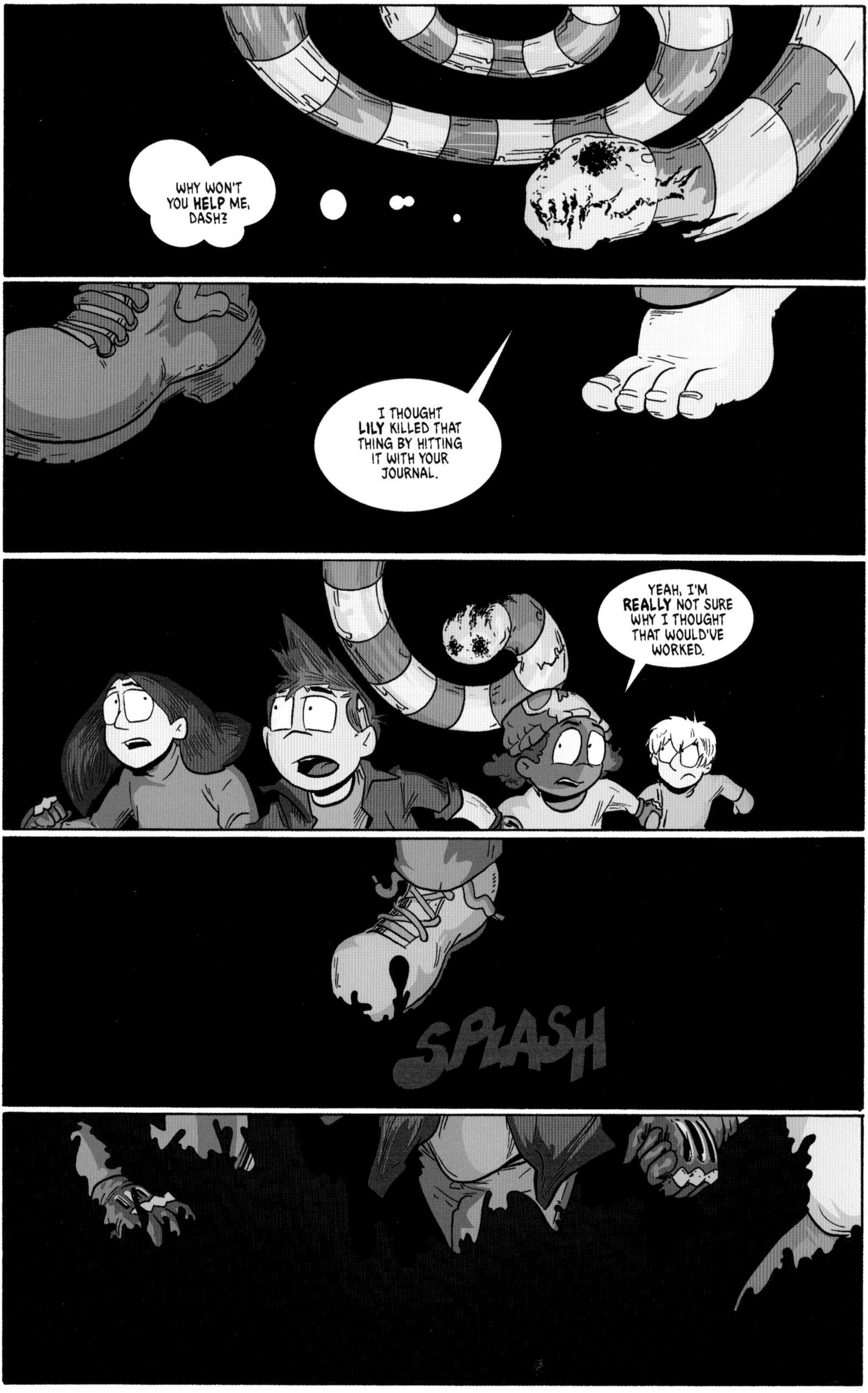
WHY WON'T YOU HELP ME, DASH?
I THOUGHT LILY KILLED THAT THING BY HITTING IT WITH YOUR JOURNAL.
YEAH, I'M REALLY NOT SURE WHY I THOUGHT THAT WOULD'VE WORKED.
SPLASH

DASH,
GET US OUT
OF HERE!

JUST HOLD
ON.

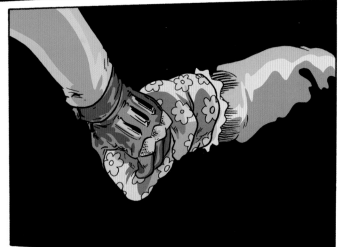

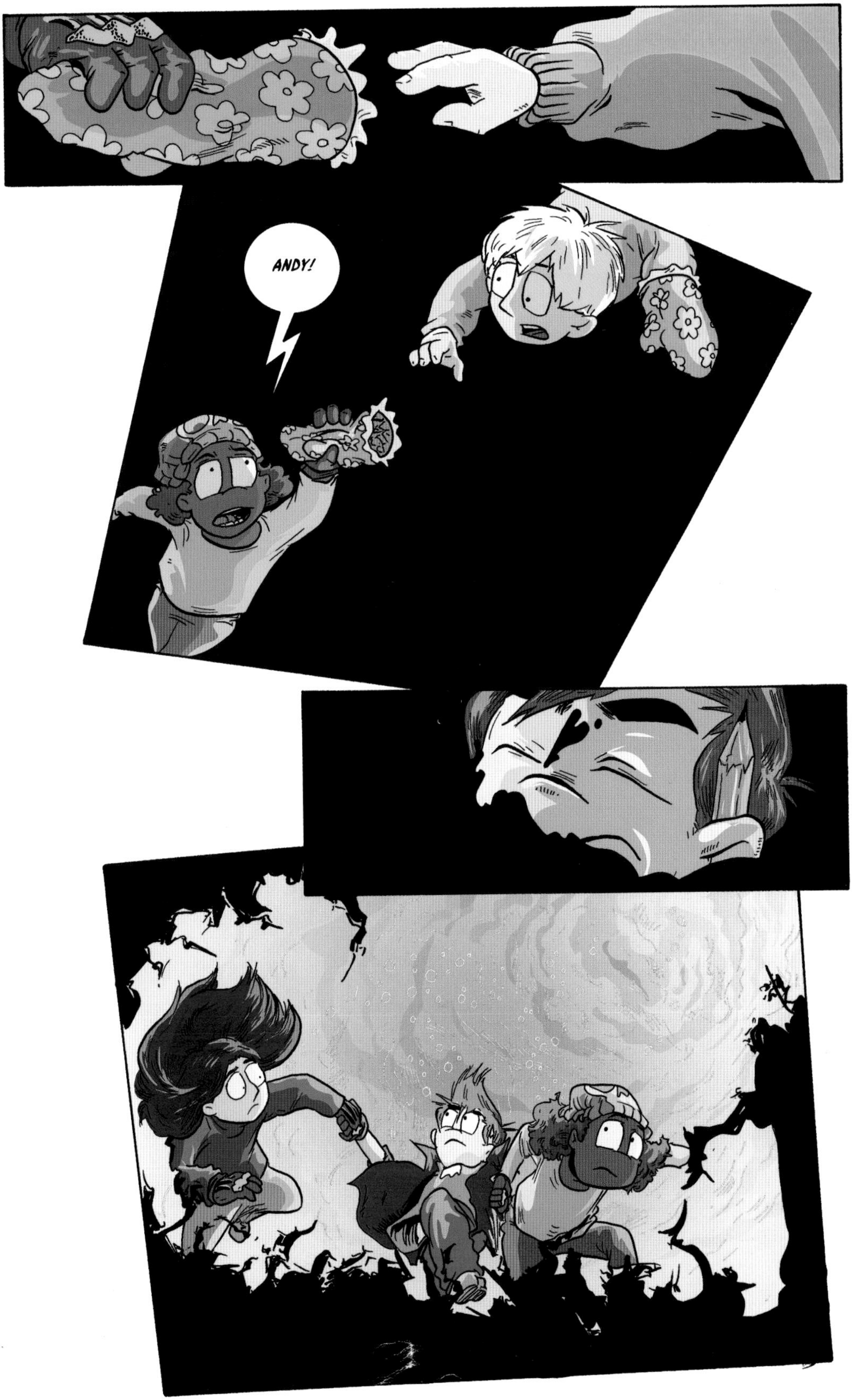
ANDY!

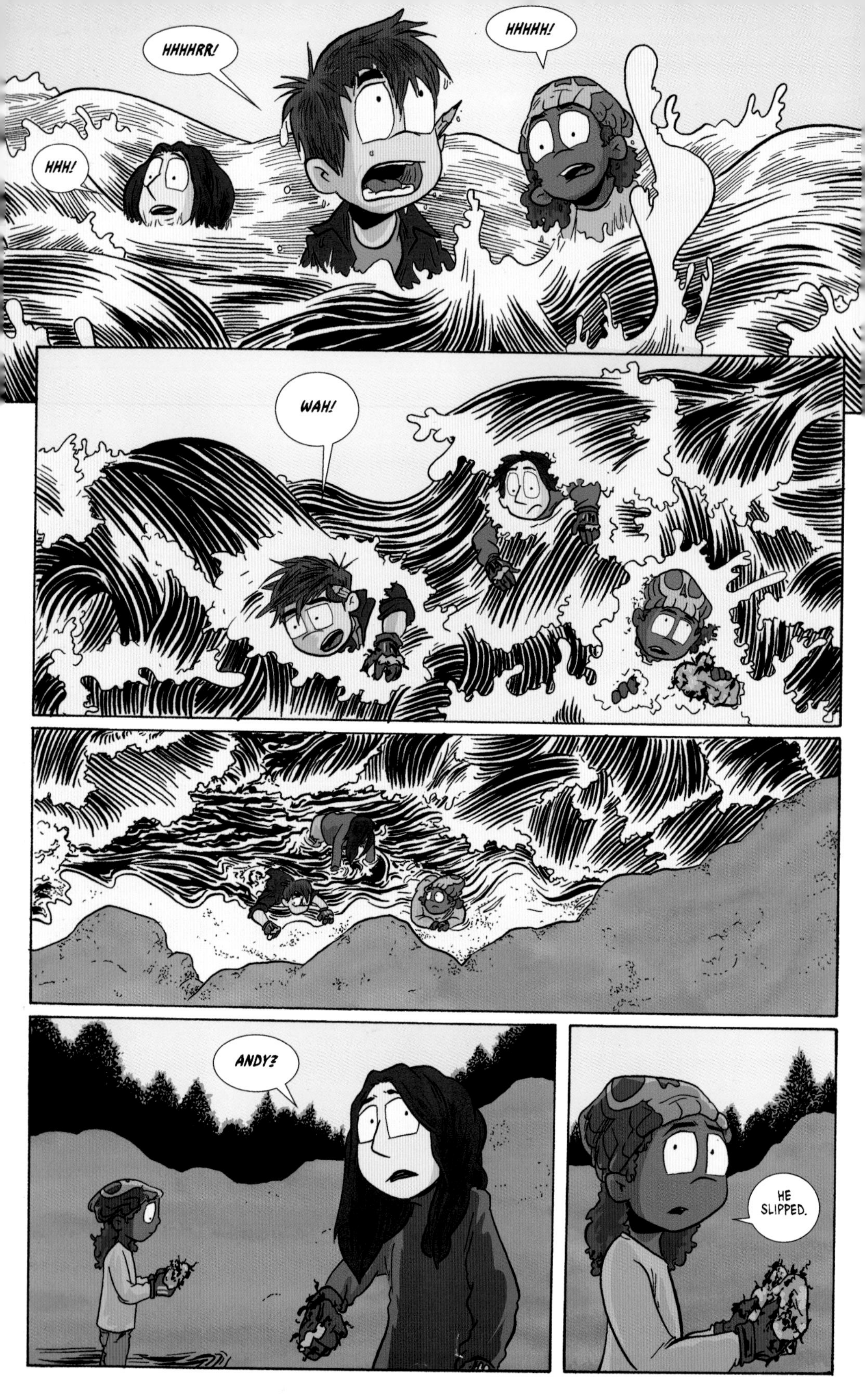
HHHHRR!
HHHHH!
HHH!
WAH!
ANDY?
HE SLIPPED.

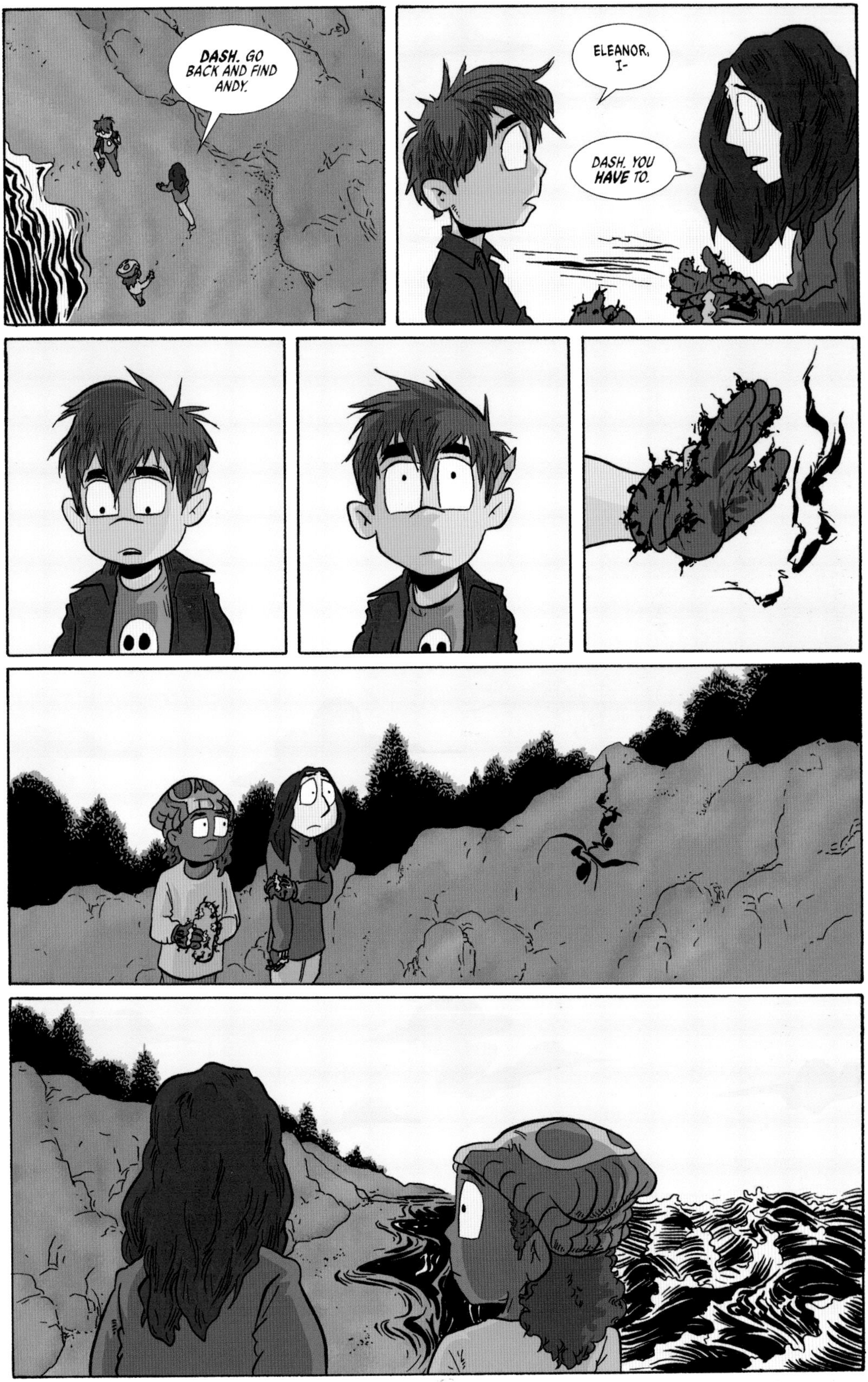
DASH. GO BACK AND FIND ANDY.
ELEANOR, I-
DASH. YOU HAVE TO.

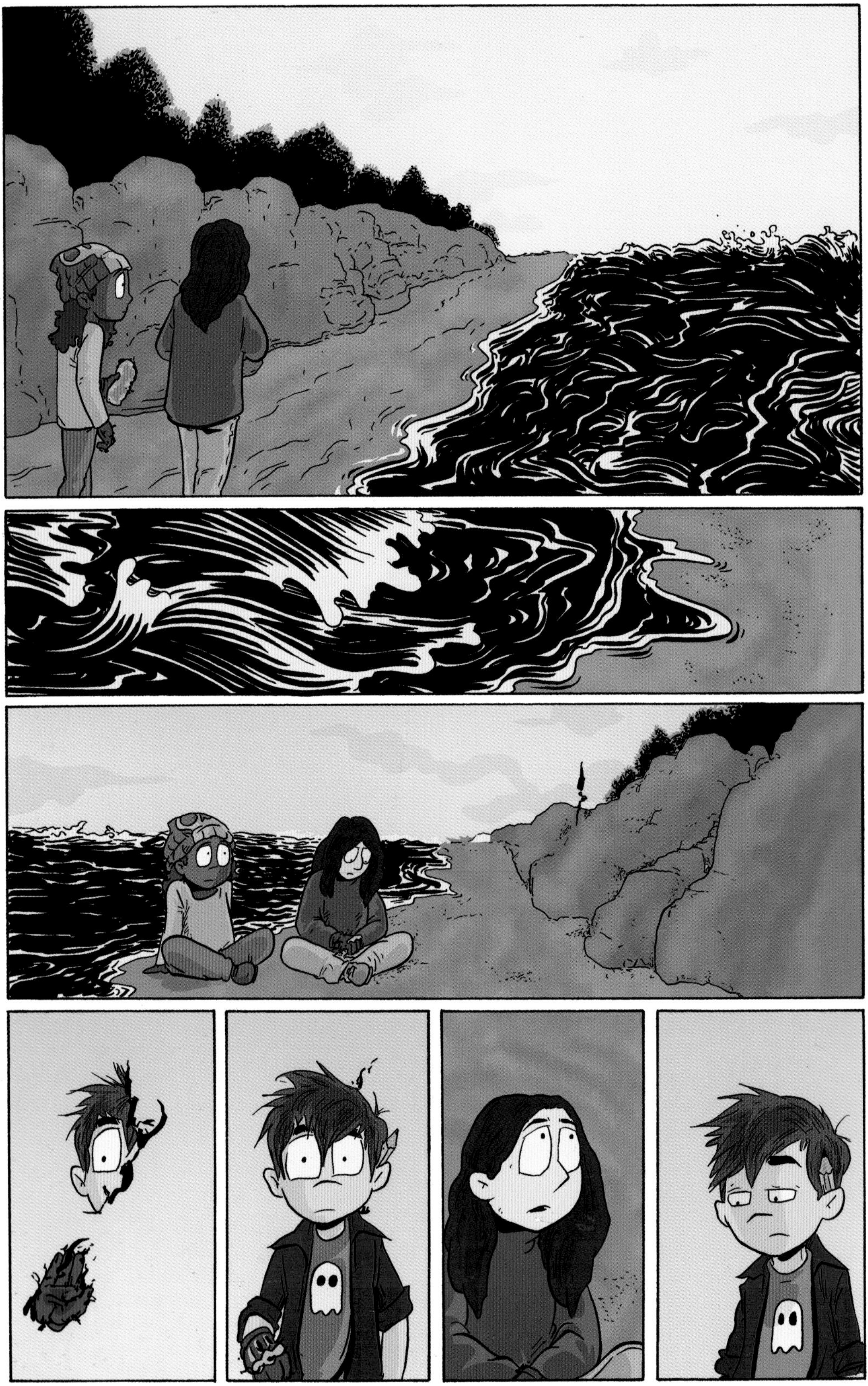

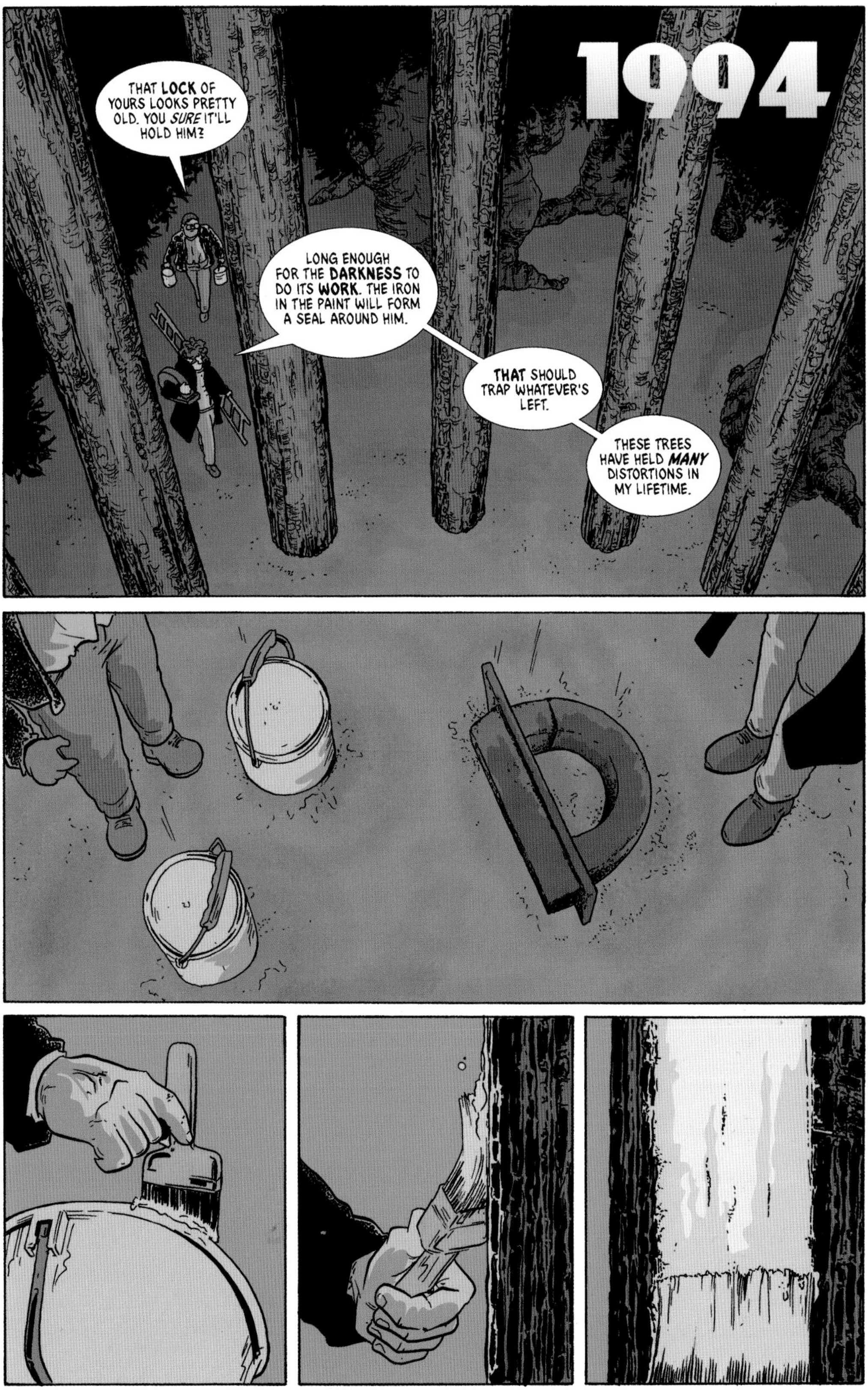
1994
THAT LOCK OF YOURS LOOKS PRETTY OLD. YOU SURE IT'LL HOLD HIM?
LONG ENOUGH FOR THE DARKNESS TO DO ITS WORK. THE IRON IN THE PAINT WILL FORM A SEAL AROUND HIM.
THAT SHOULD TRAP WHATEVER'S LEFT.
THESE TREES HAVE HELD MANY DISTORTIONS IN MY LIFETIME.

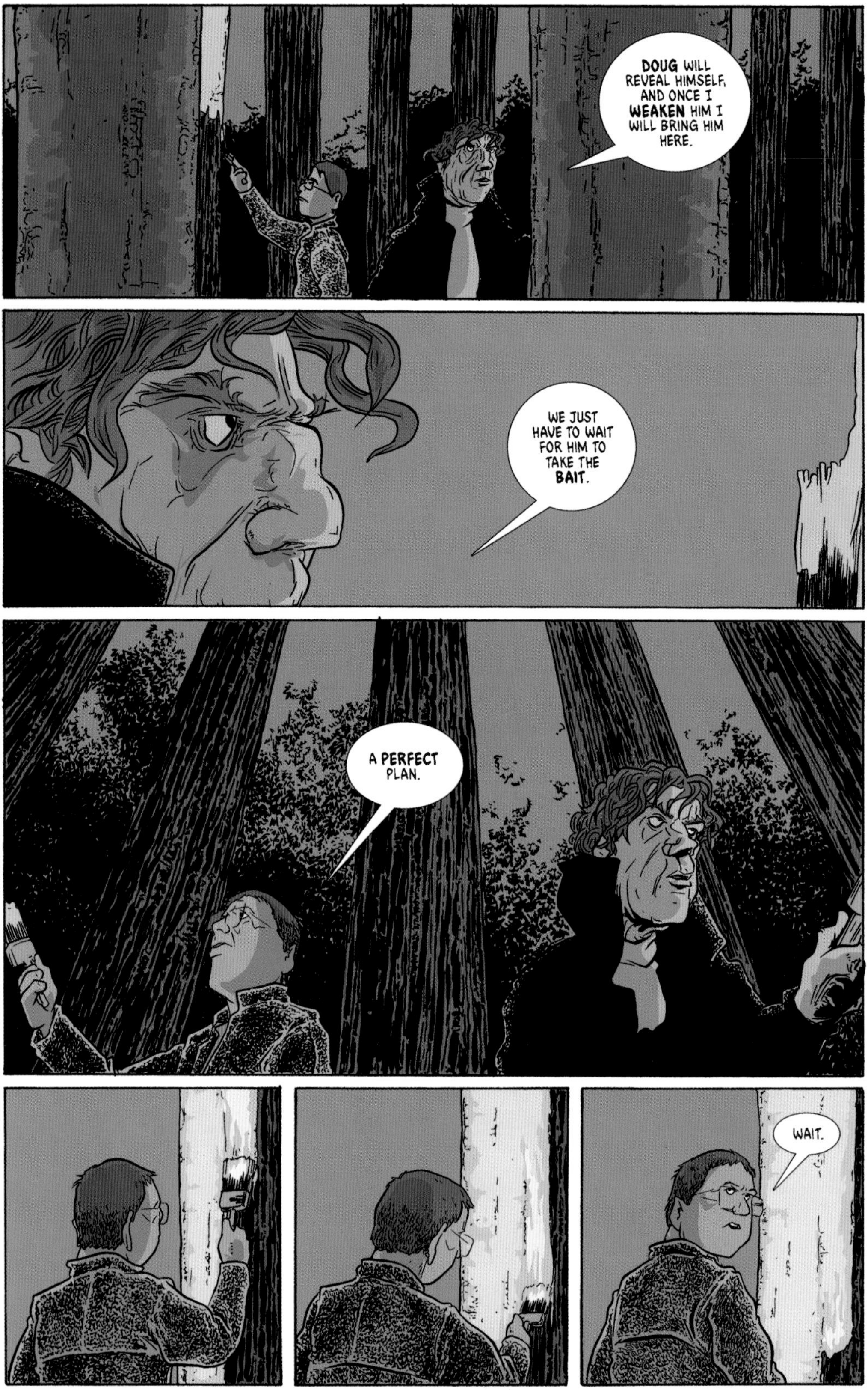
DOUG WILL REVEAL HIMSELF, AND ONCE I WEAKEN HIM I WILL BRING HIM HERE.
WE JUST HAVE TO WAIT FOR HIM TO TAKE THE BAIT.
A PERFECT PLAN.
WAIT.

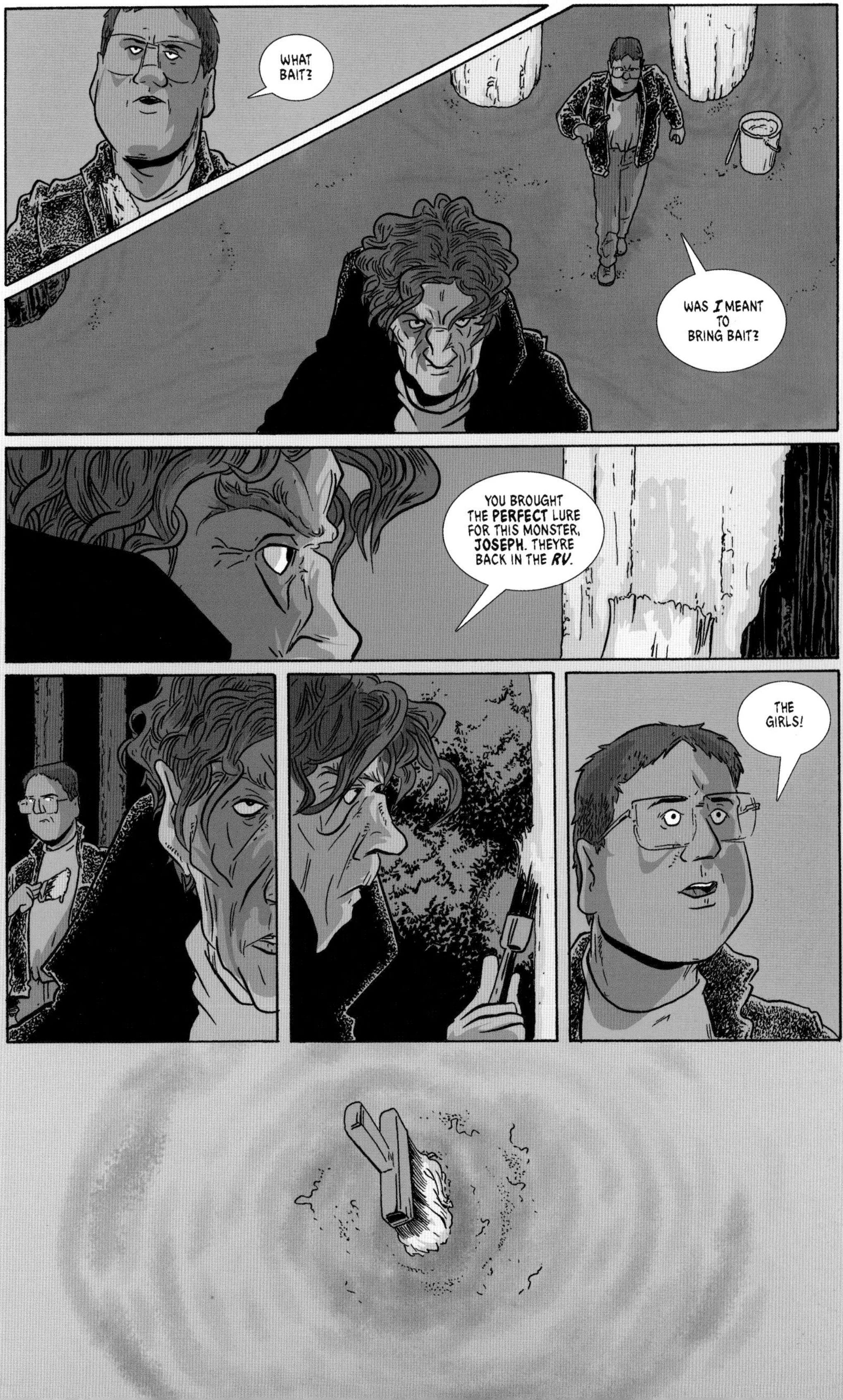
WHAT BAIT?
WAS I MEANT TO BRING BAIT?
YOU BROUGHT THE PERFECT LURE FOR THIS MONSTER, JOSEPH. THEYRE BACK IN THE RV.
THE GIRLS!

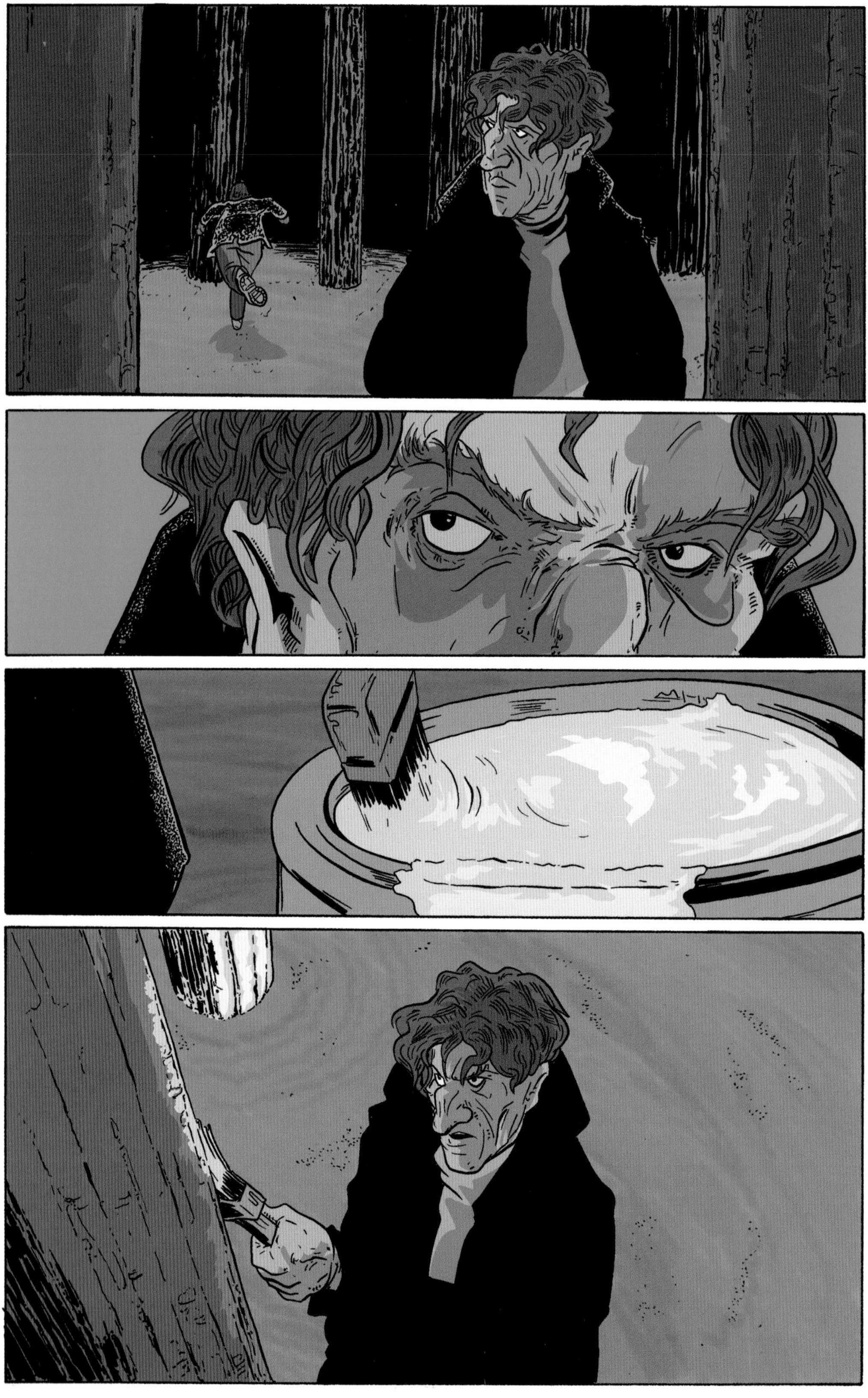

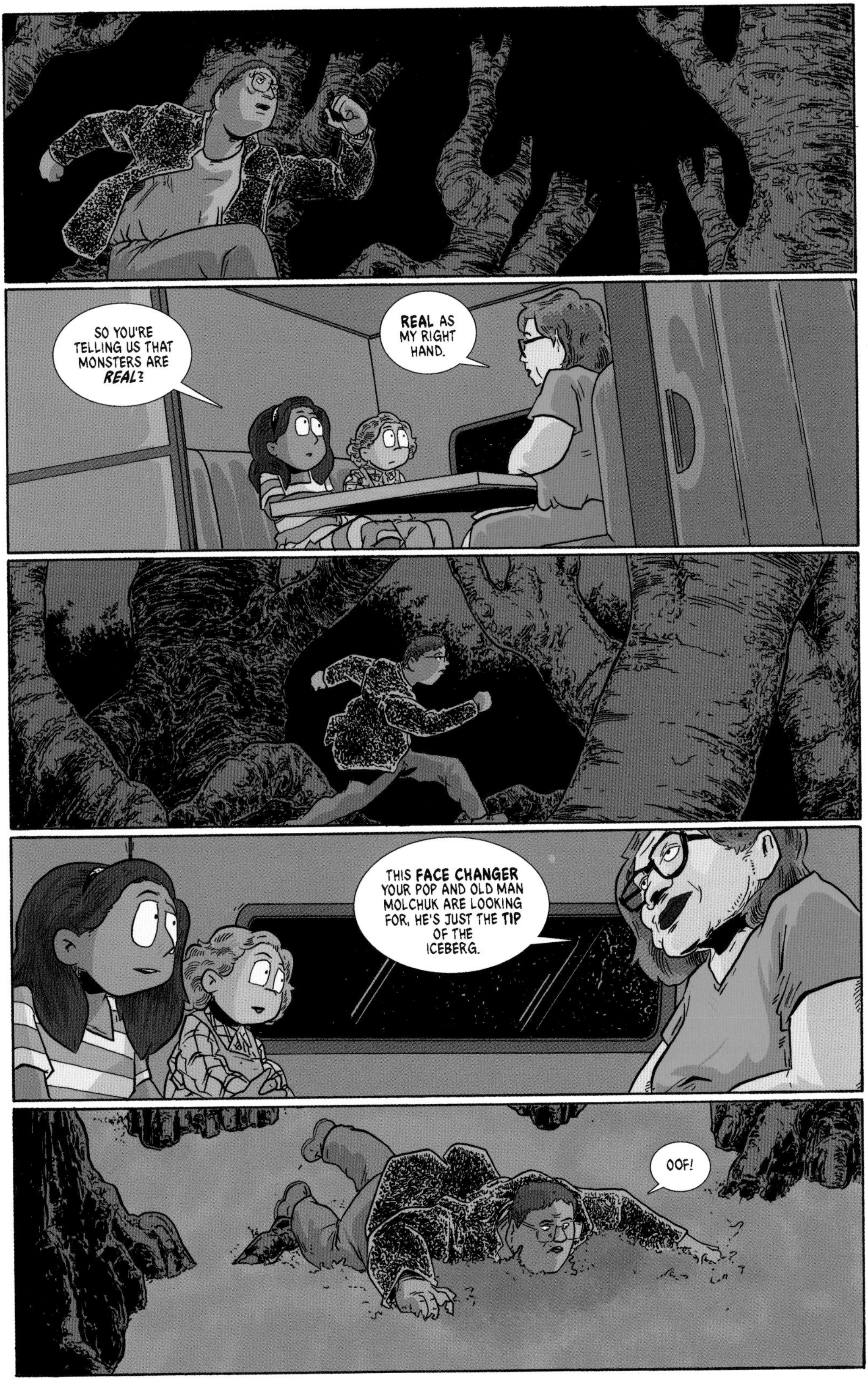

SO YOU'RE TELLING US THAT MONSTERS ARE *REAL*?
REAL AS MY RIGHT HAND.
THIS **FACE CHANGER** YOUR POP AND OLD MAN MOLCHUK ARE LOOKING FOR, HE'S JUST THE **TIP** OF THE ICEBERG.
OOF!

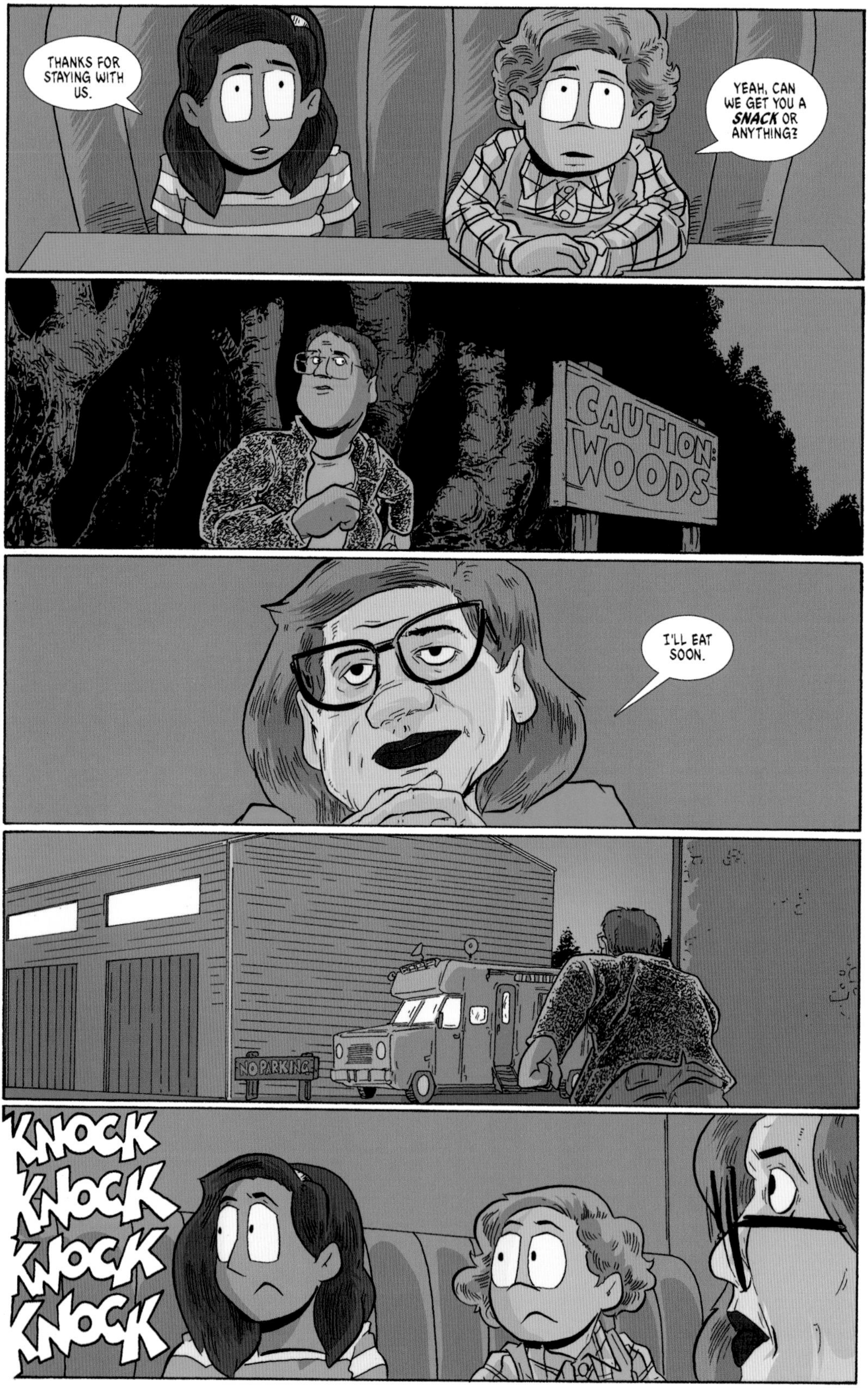
THANKS FOR STAYING WITH US.
YEAH, CAN WE GET YOU A SNACK OR ANYTHING?
CAUTION: WOODS
I'LL EAT SOON.
NO PARKING
KNOCK KNOCK KNOCK KNOCK

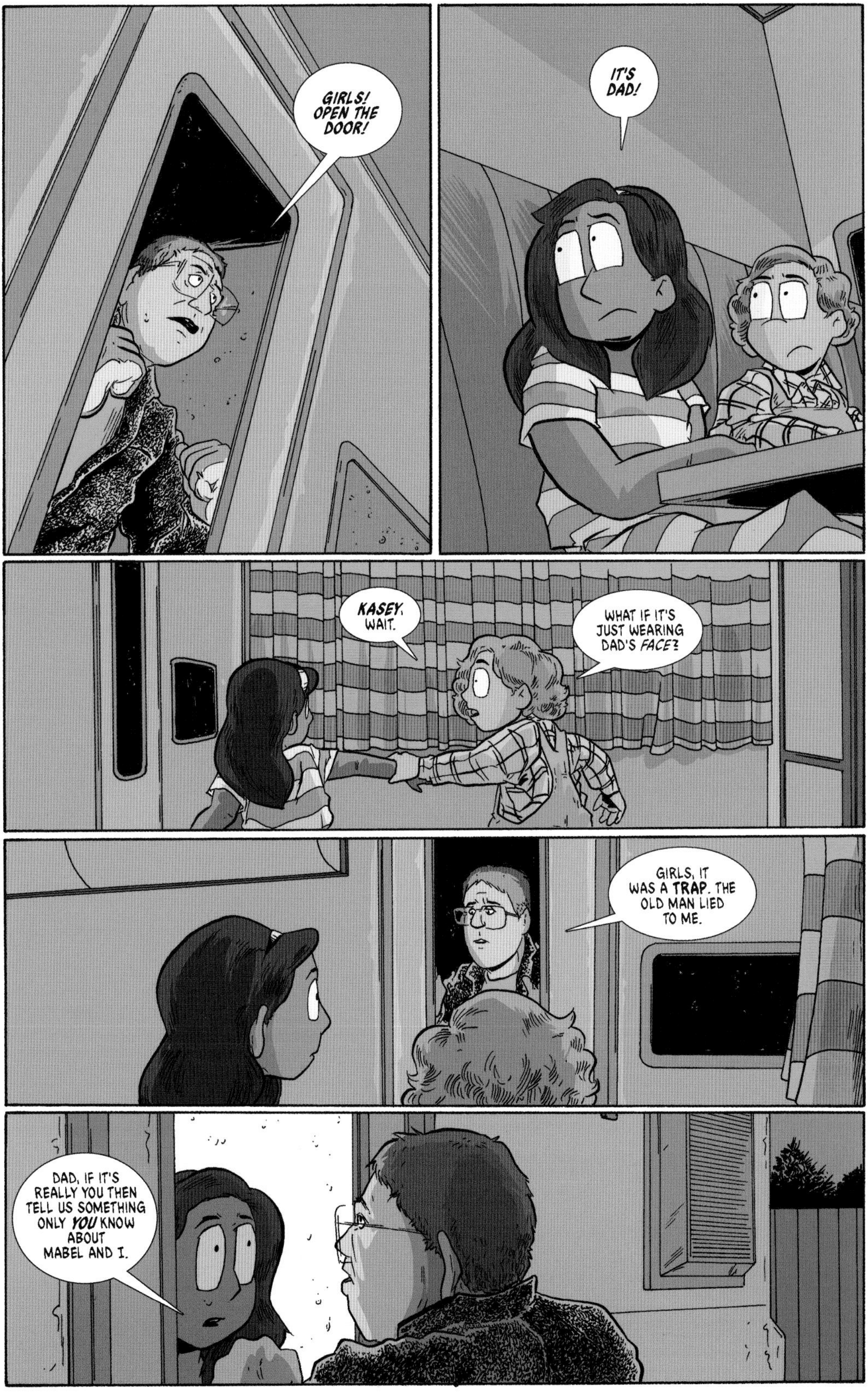
GIRLS! OPEN THE DOOR!
IT'S DAD!
KASEY, WAIT.
WHAT IF IT'S JUST WEARING DAD'S FACE?
GIRLS, IT WAS A TRAP. THE OLD MAN LIED TO ME.
DAD, IF IT'S REALLY YOU THEN TELL US SOMETHING ONLY YOU KNOW ABOUT MABEL AND I.

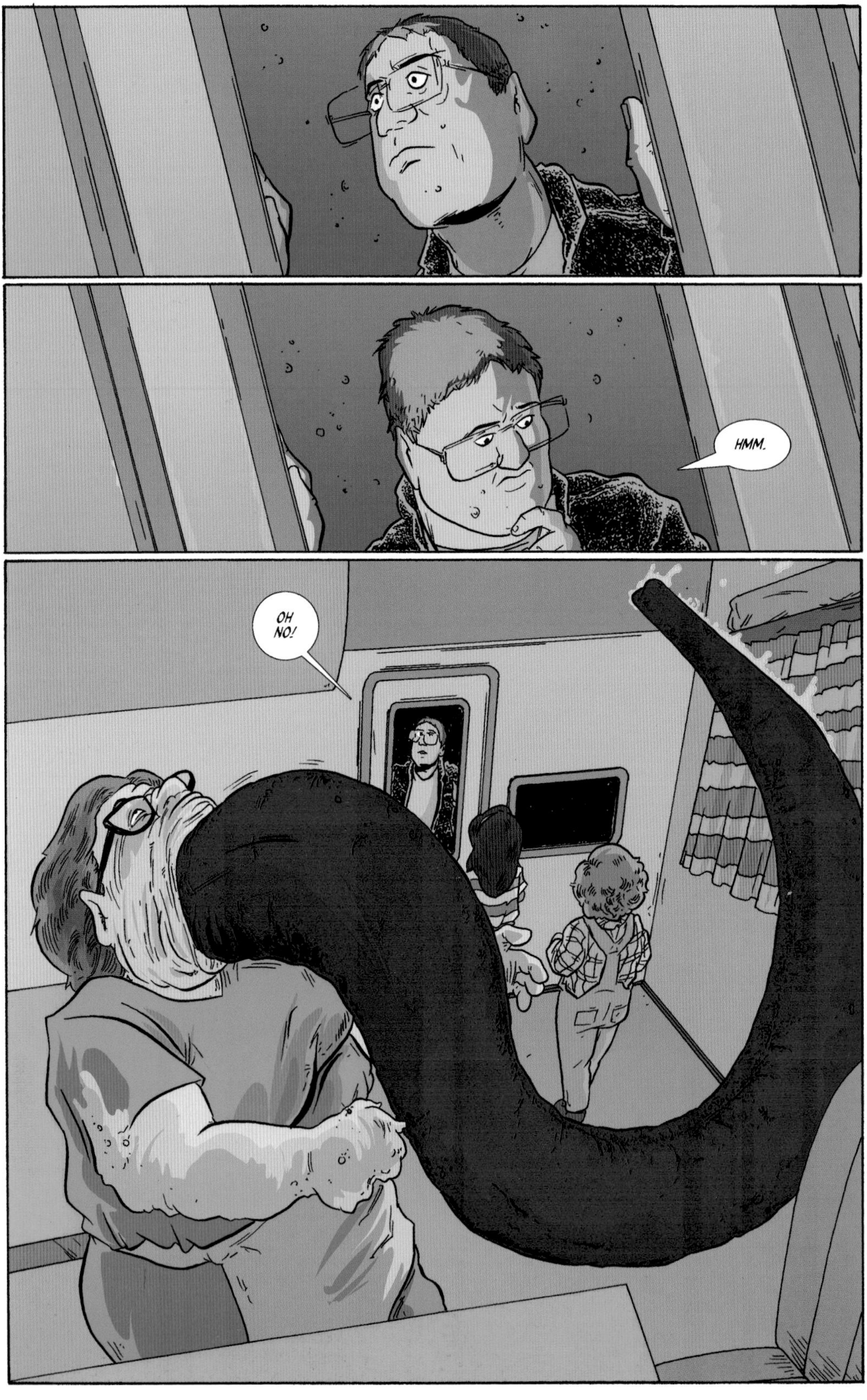
HMM.
OH NO!

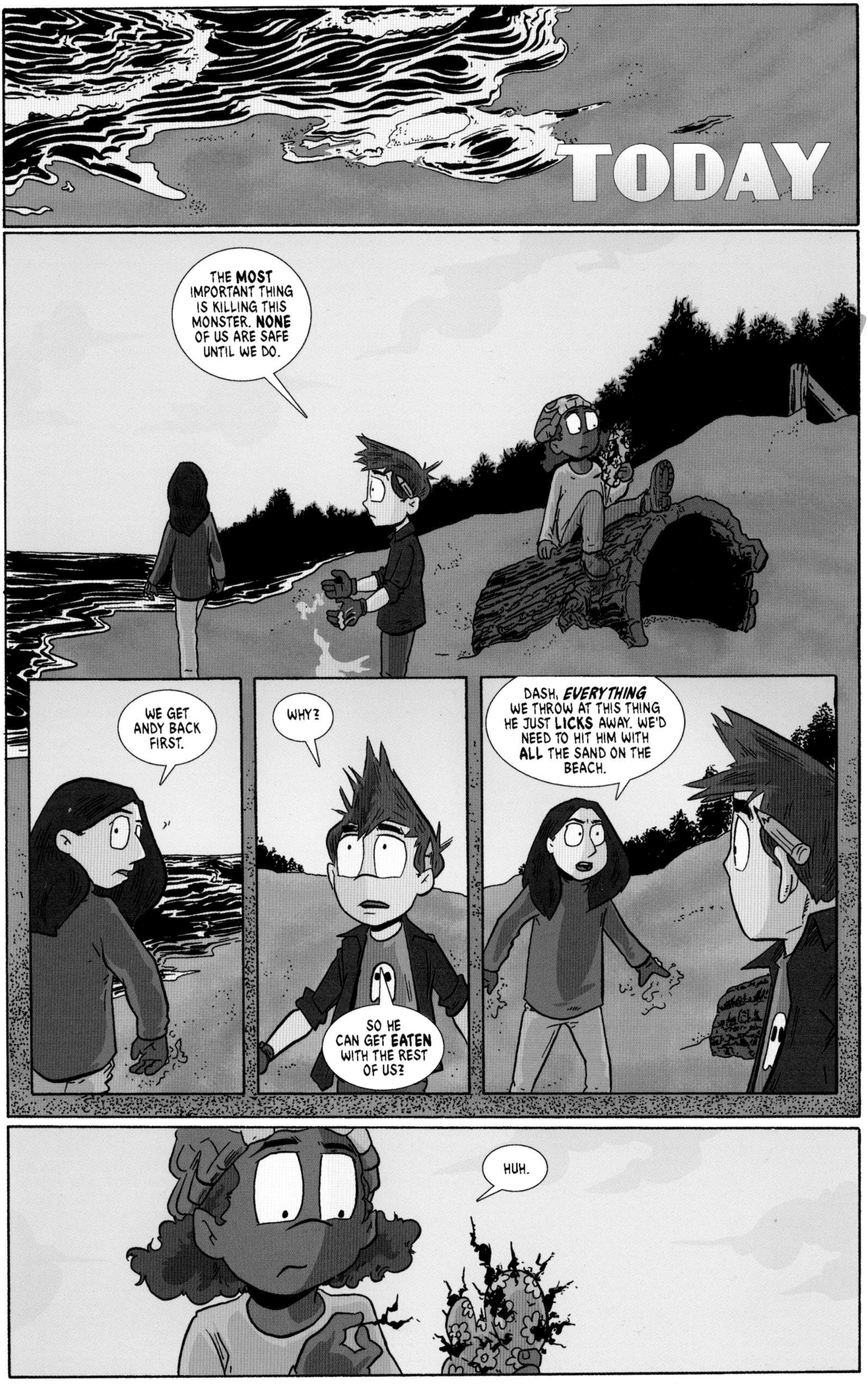
TODAY
THE MOST IMPORTANT THING IS KILLING THIS MONSTER. NONE OF US ARE SAFE UNTIL WE DO.
WE GET ANDY BACK FIRST.
WHY?
SO HE CAN GET EATEN WITH THE REST OF US?
DASH, EVERYTHING WE THROW AT THIS THING HE JUST LICKS AWAY. WE'D NEED TO HIT HIM WITH ALL THE SAND ON THE BEACH.
HUH.

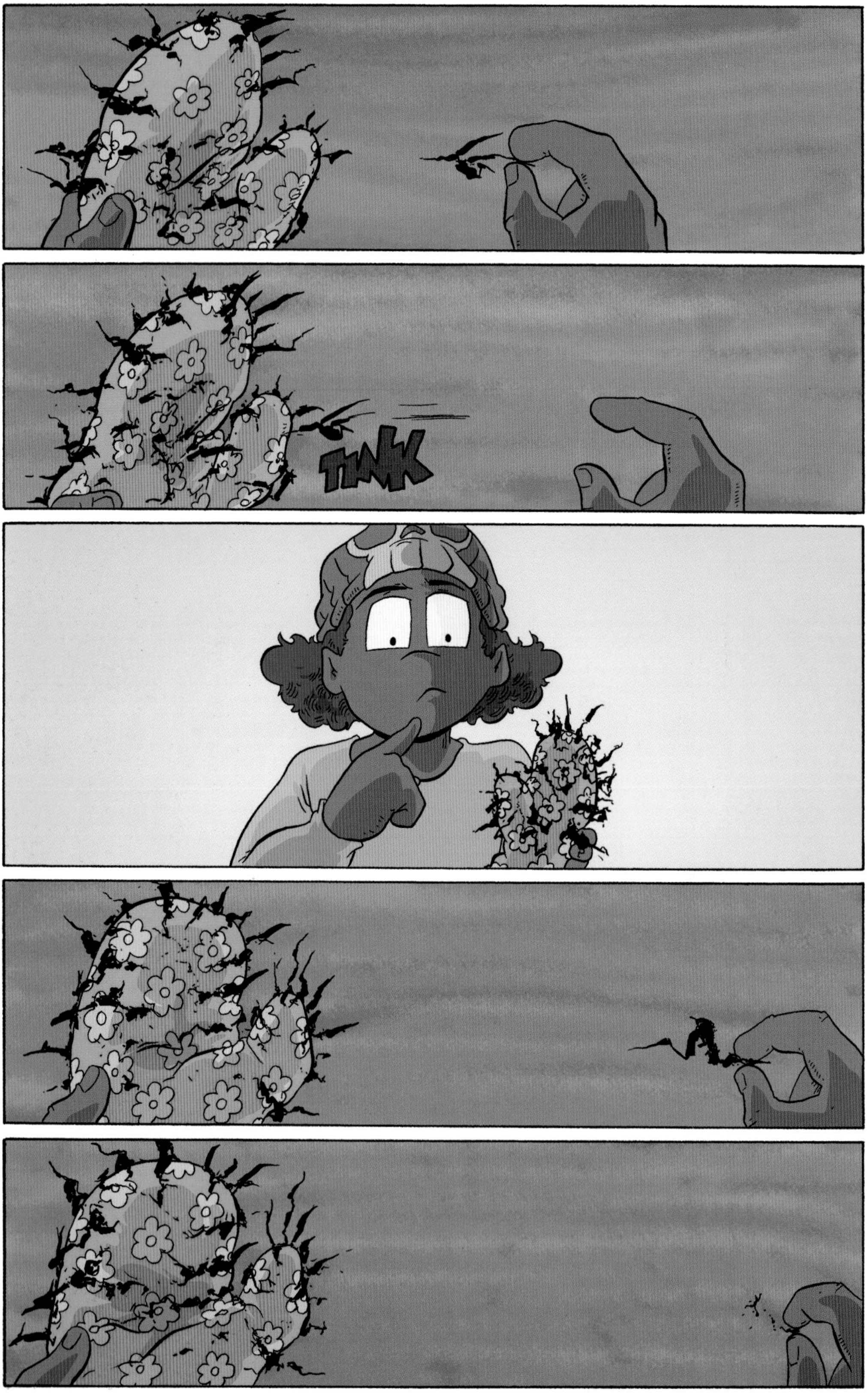
TINK

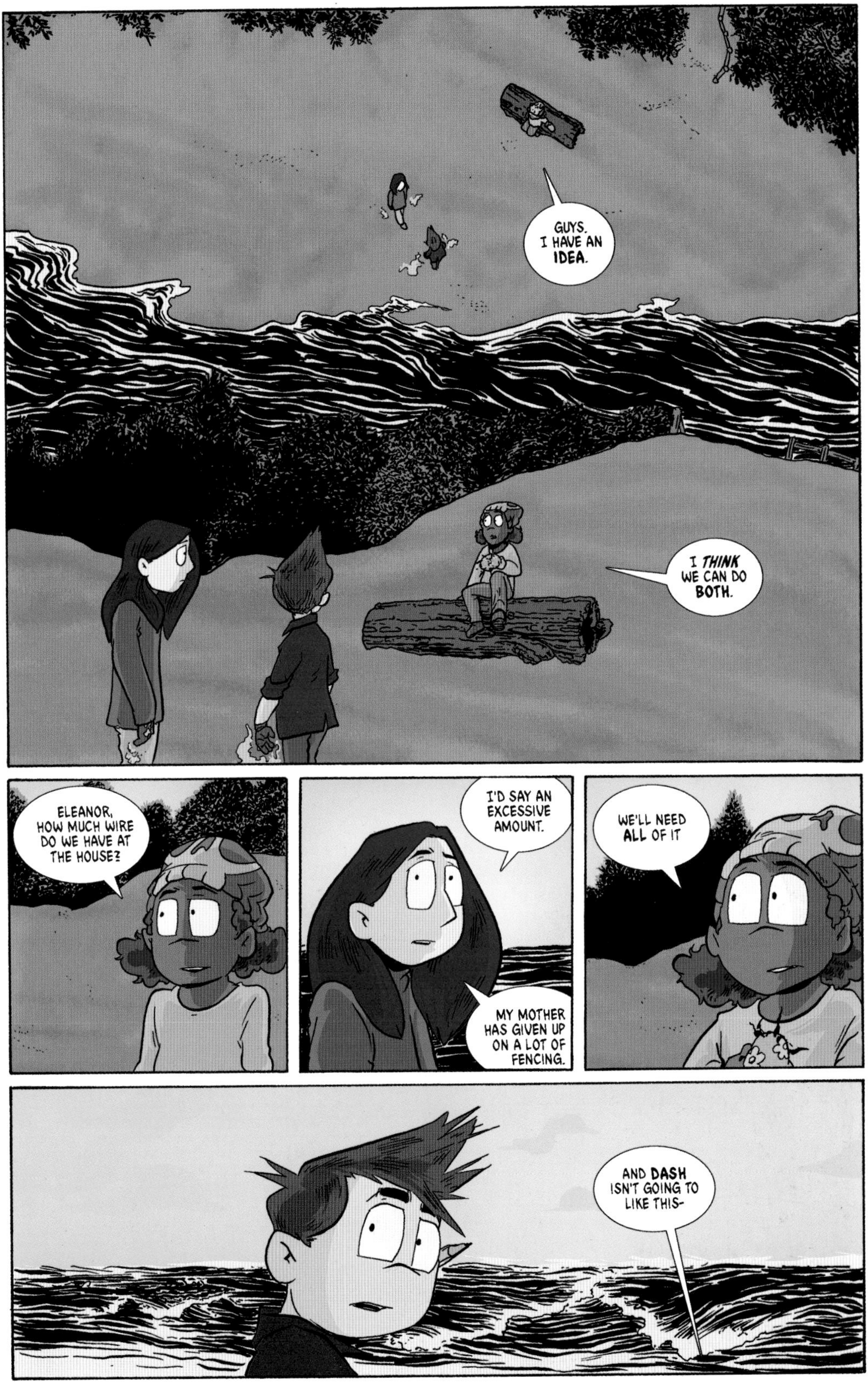
GUYS. I HAVE AN IDEA.
I THINK WE CAN DO BOTH.
ELEANOR, HOW MUCH WIRE DO WE HAVE AT THE HOUSE?
I'D SAY AN EXCESSIVE AMOUNT.
MY MOTHER HAS GIVEN UP ON A LOT OF FENCING.
WE'LL NEED ALL OF IT
AND DASH ISN'T GOING TO LIKE THIS-

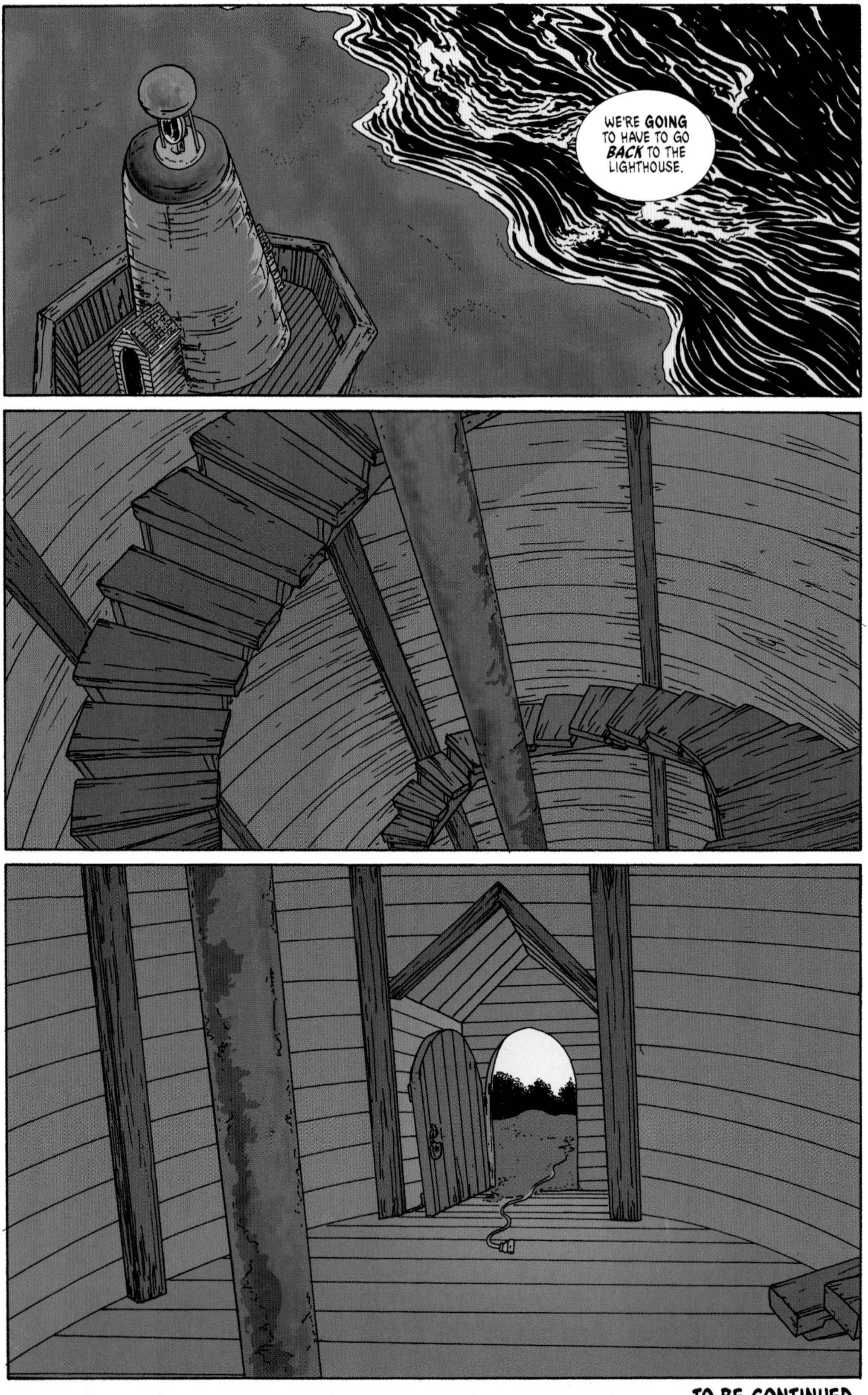
WE'RE GOING TO HAVE TO GO BACK TO THE LIGHTHOUSE.

TO BE CONTINUED.

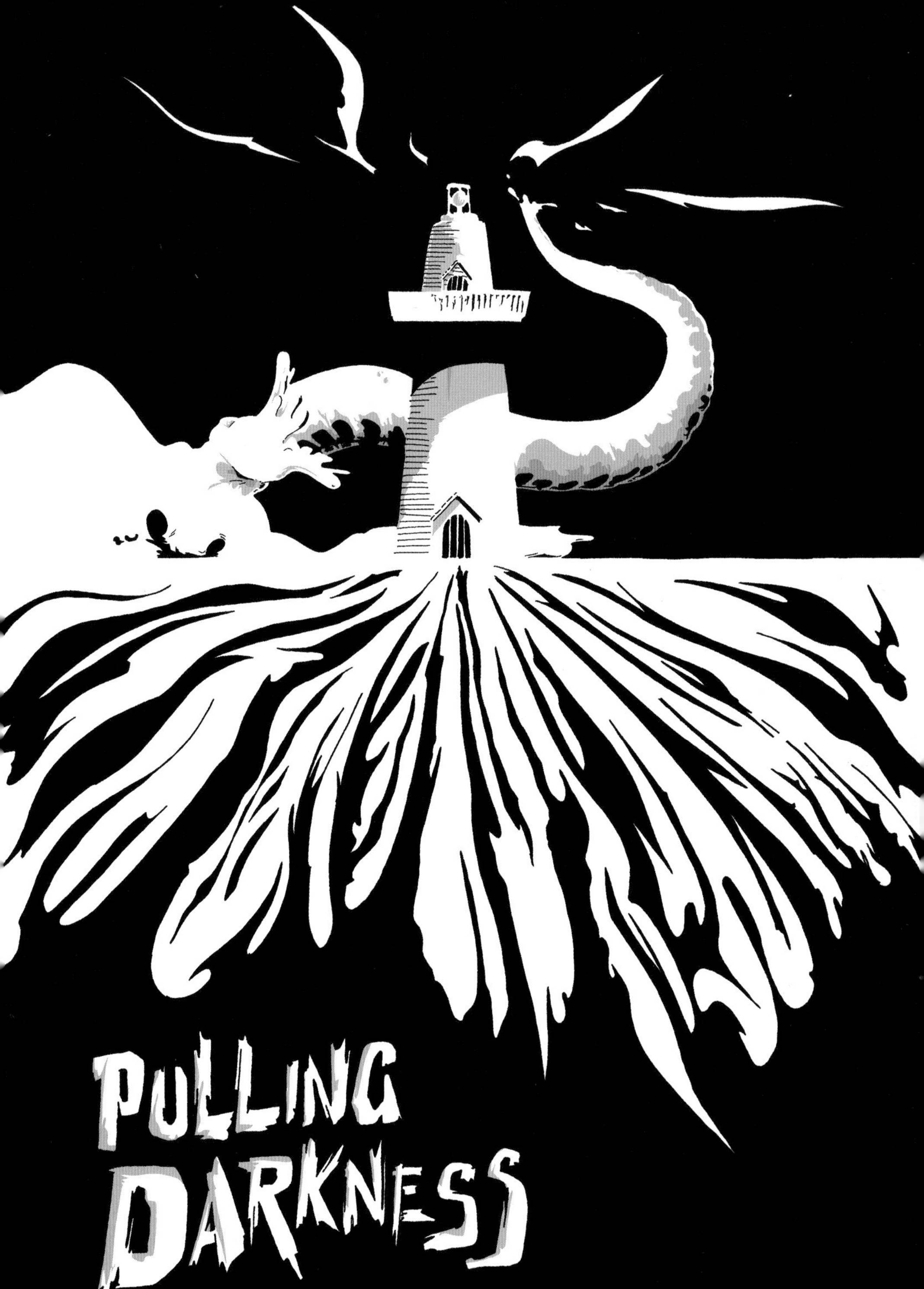
PULLING
DARKNESS

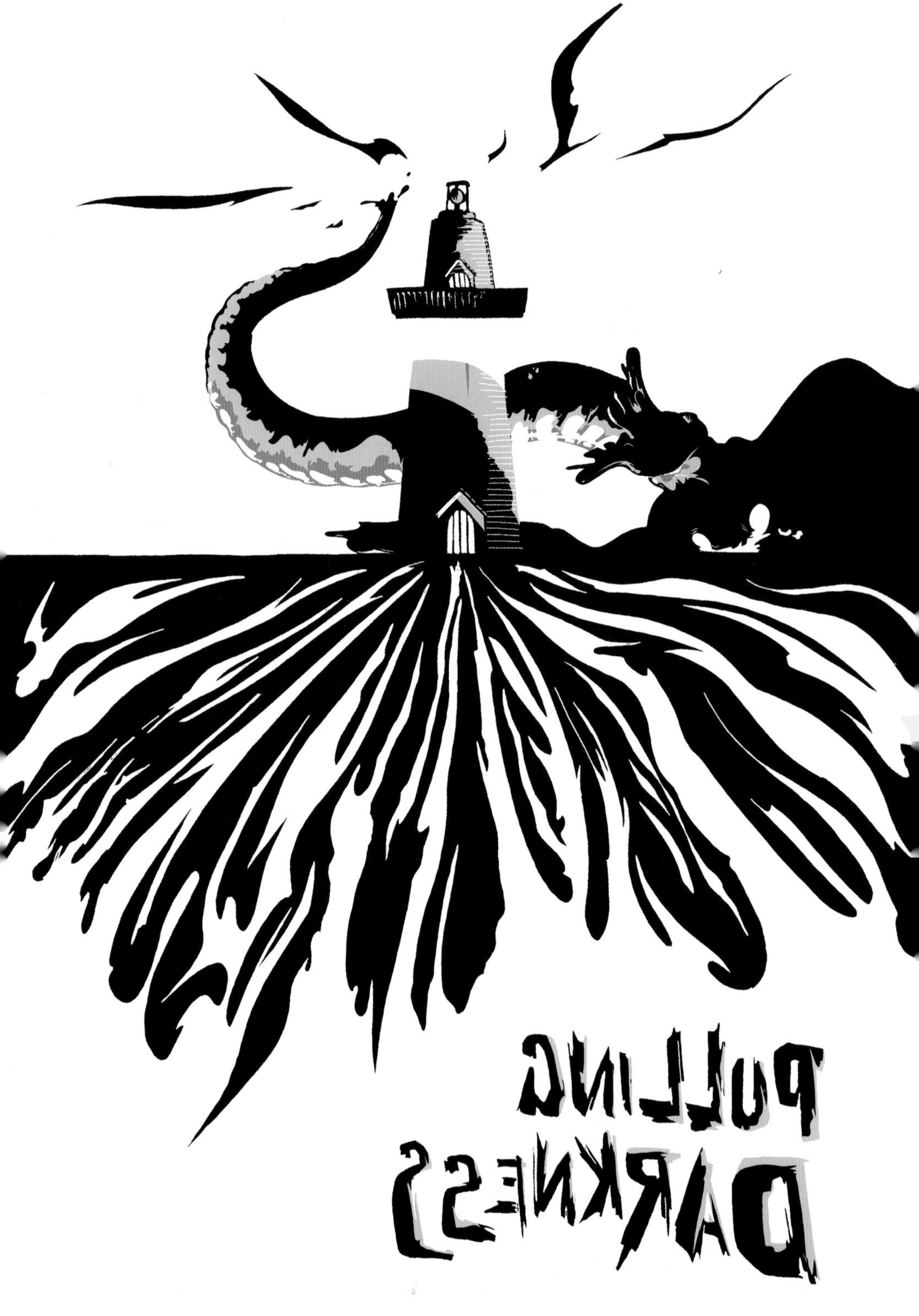
PULLING
DARKNESS

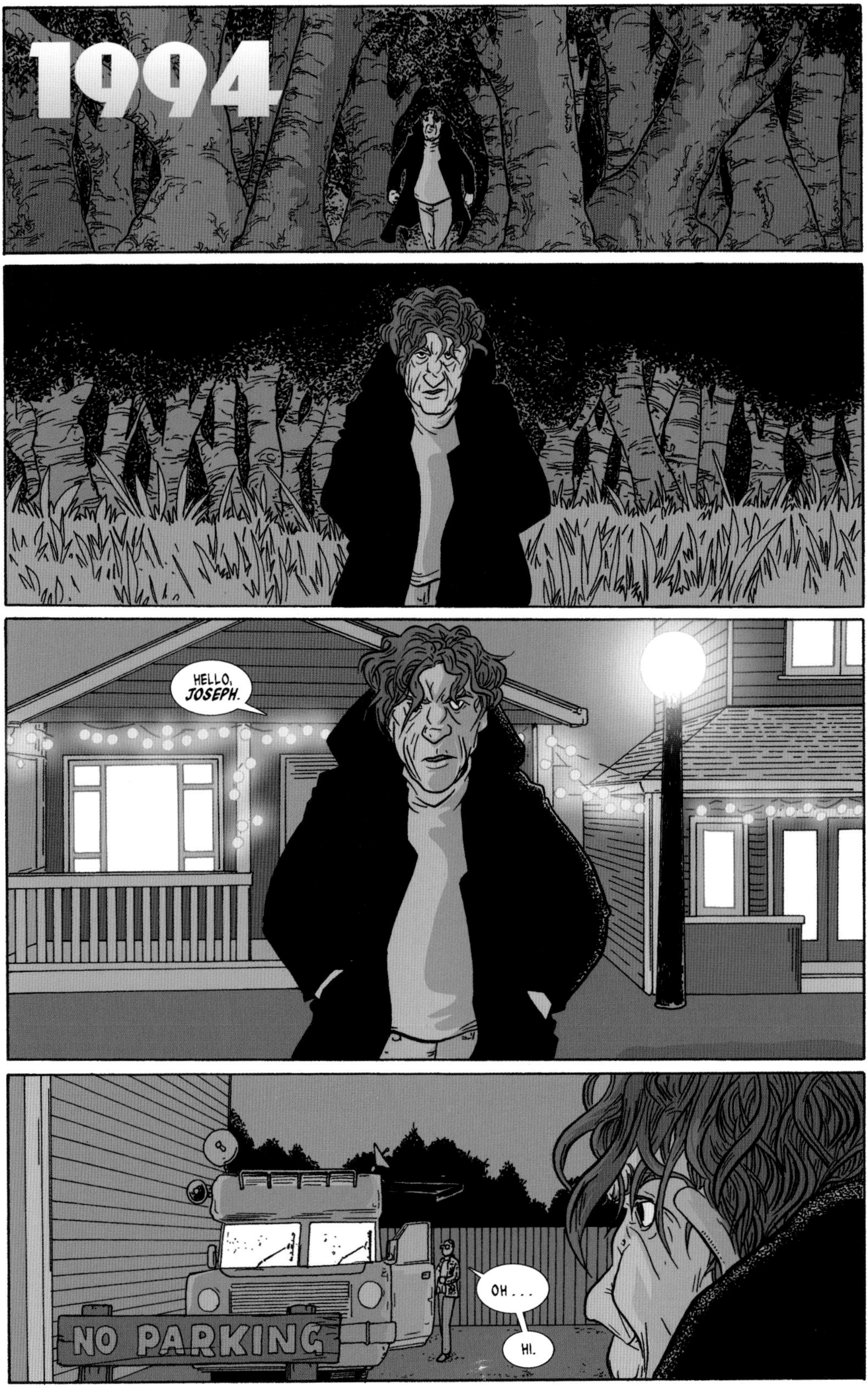
1994
HELLO, JOSEPH.
NO PARKING
OH . . .
HI.

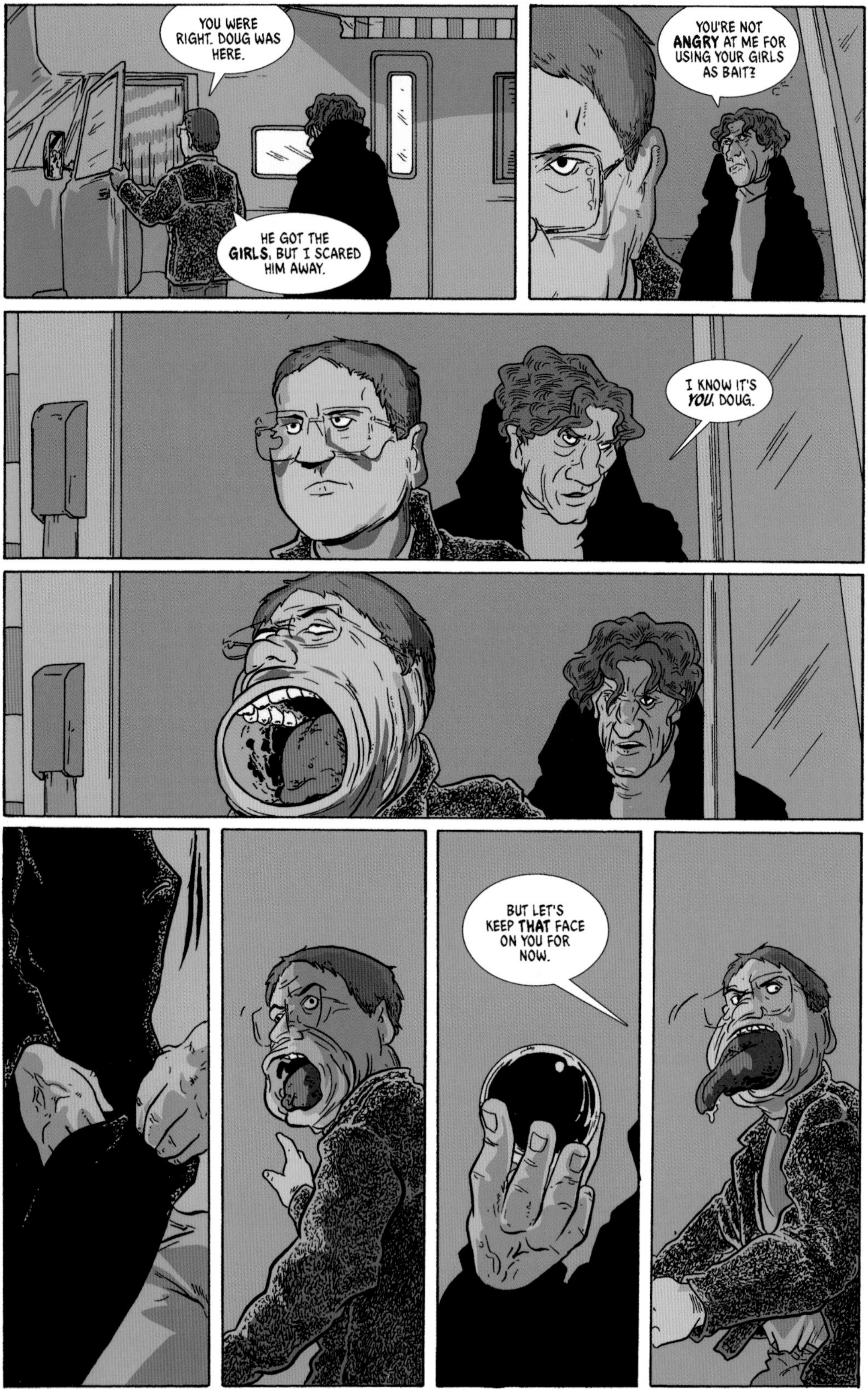

YOU WERE RIGHT. DOUG WAS HERE.
HE GOT THE **GIRLS**, BUT I SCARED HIM AWAY.
YOU'RE NOT **ANGRY** AT ME FOR USING YOUR GIRLS AS BAIT?
I KNOW IT'S ***YOU***, DOUG.
BUT LET'S KEEP **THAT** FACE ON YOU FOR NOW.

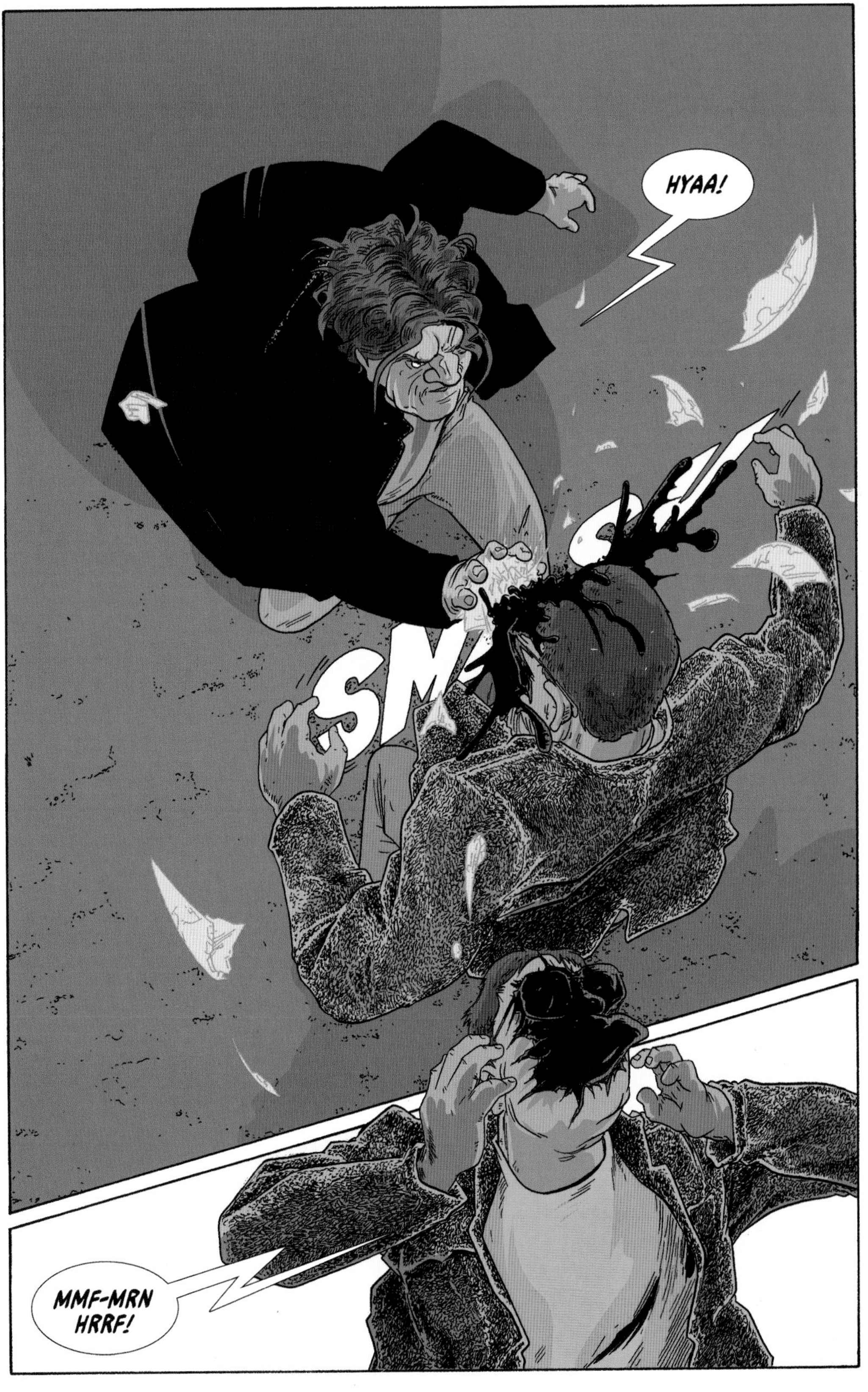
HYAA!
MMF-MRN HRRF!

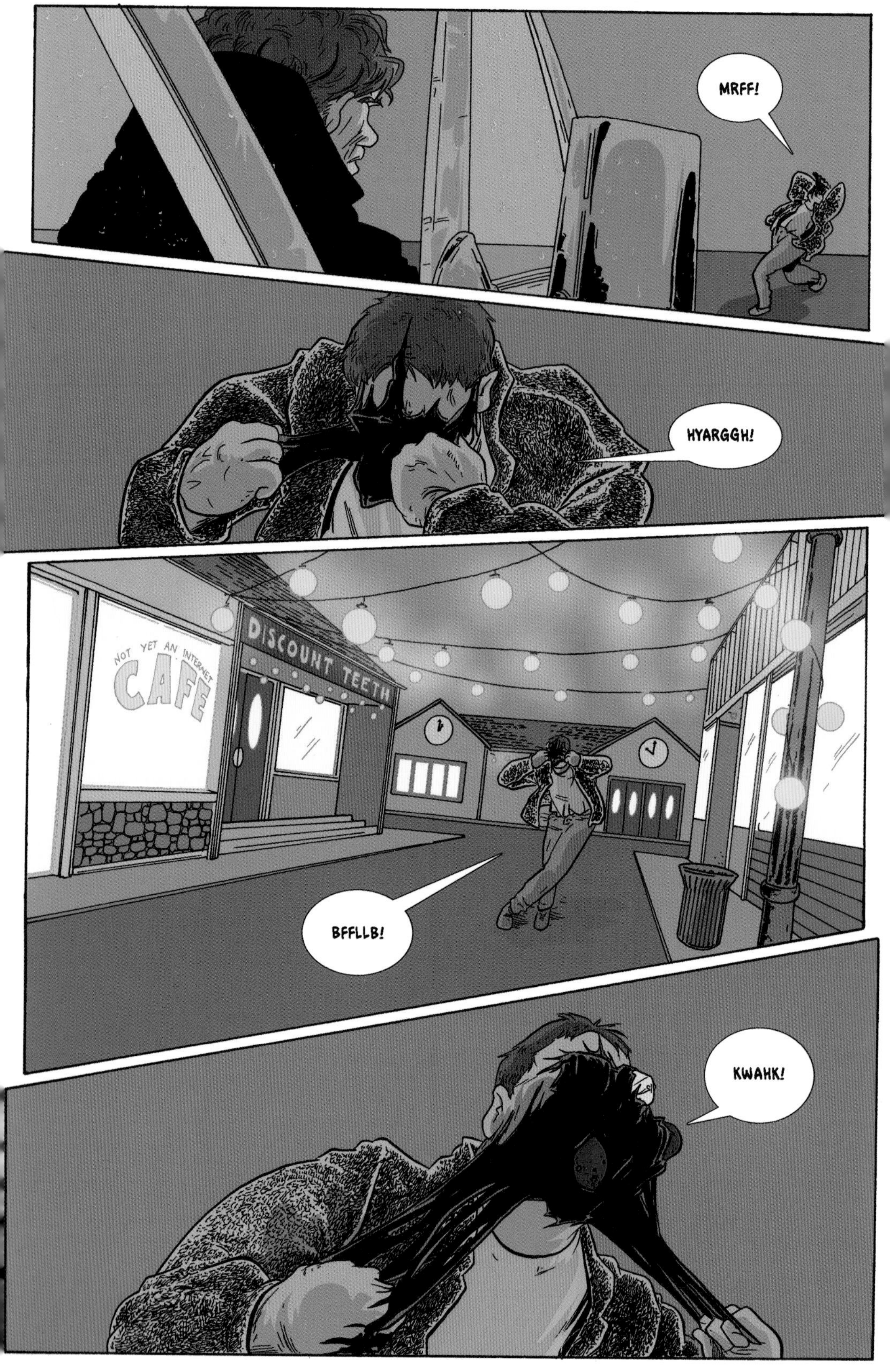
MRFF!
HYARGGH!
NOT YET AN INTERNET
CAFE
DISCOUNT TEETH
BFFLLB!
KWAHK!

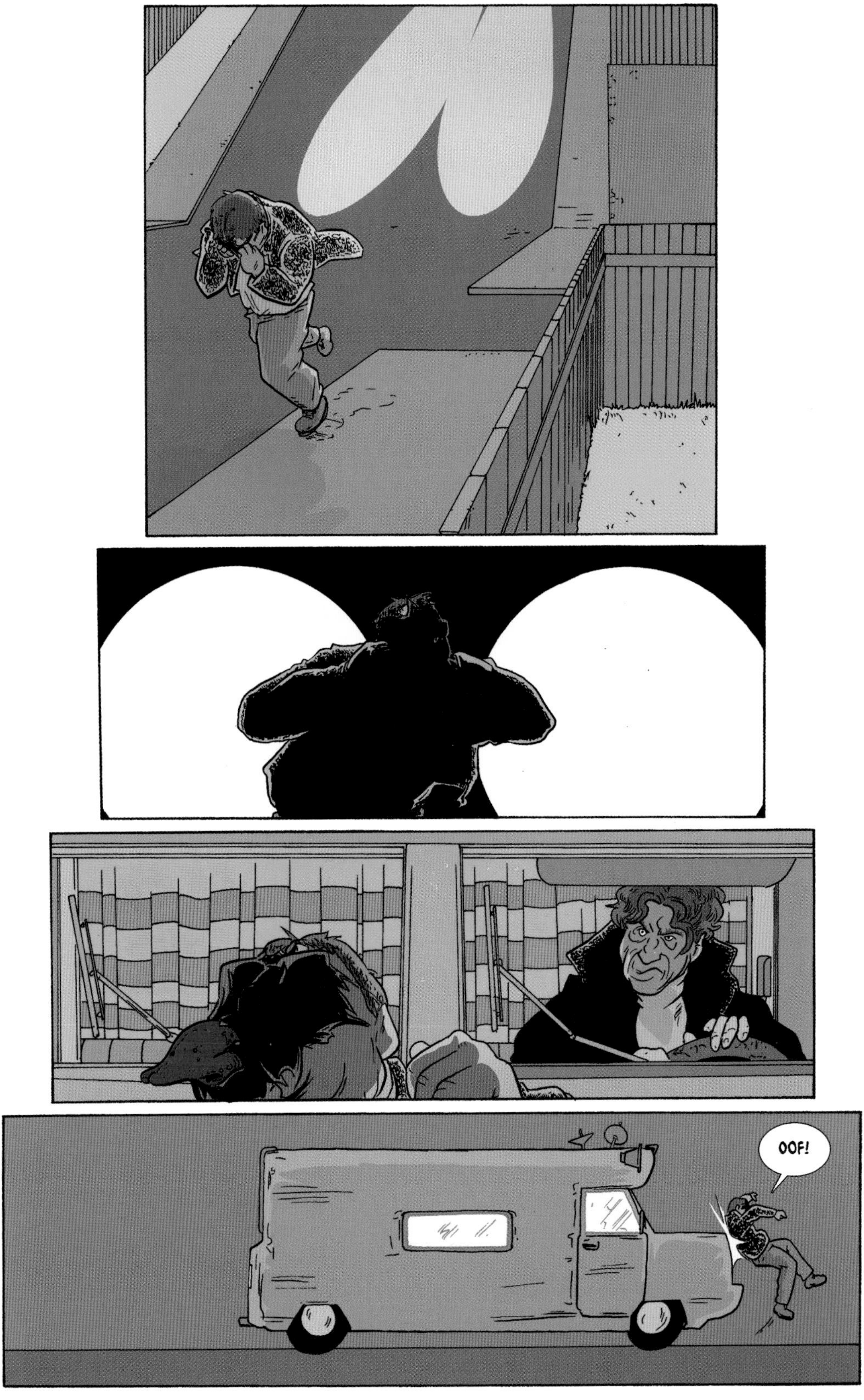
OOF!

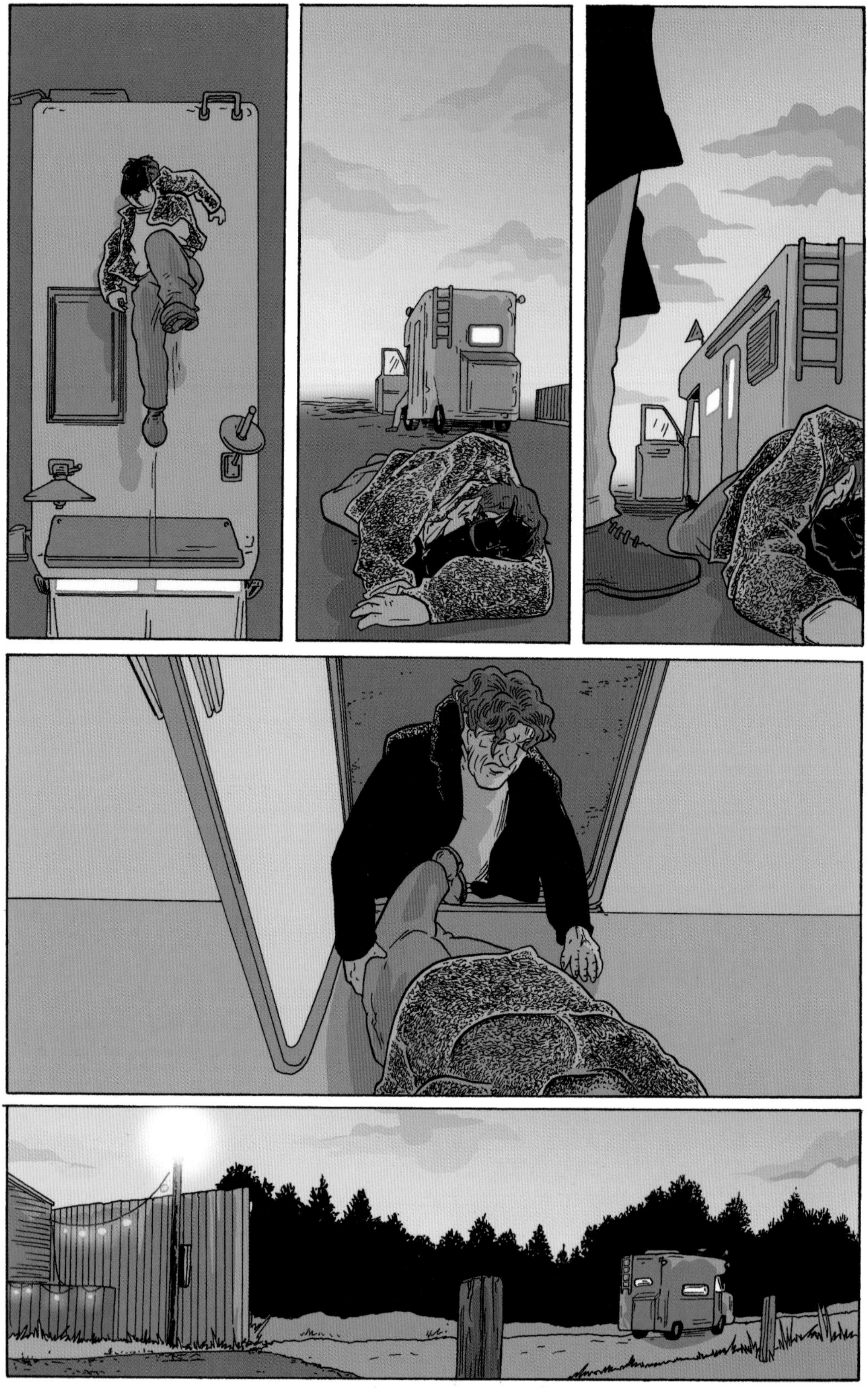

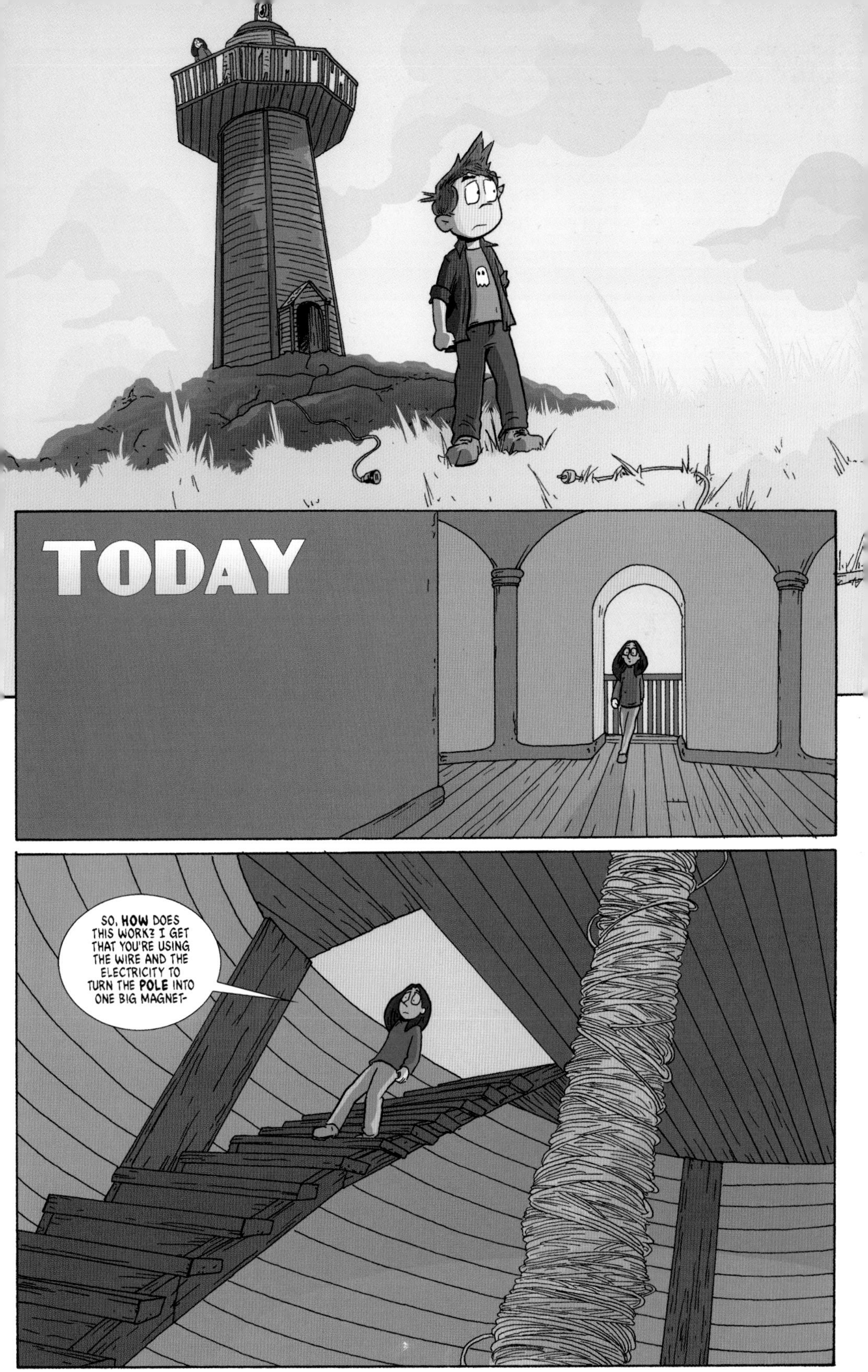
TODAY
SO, HOW DOES THIS WORK? I GET THAT YOU'RE USING THE WIRE AND THE ELECTRICITY TO TURN THE POLE INTO ONE BIG MAGNET-

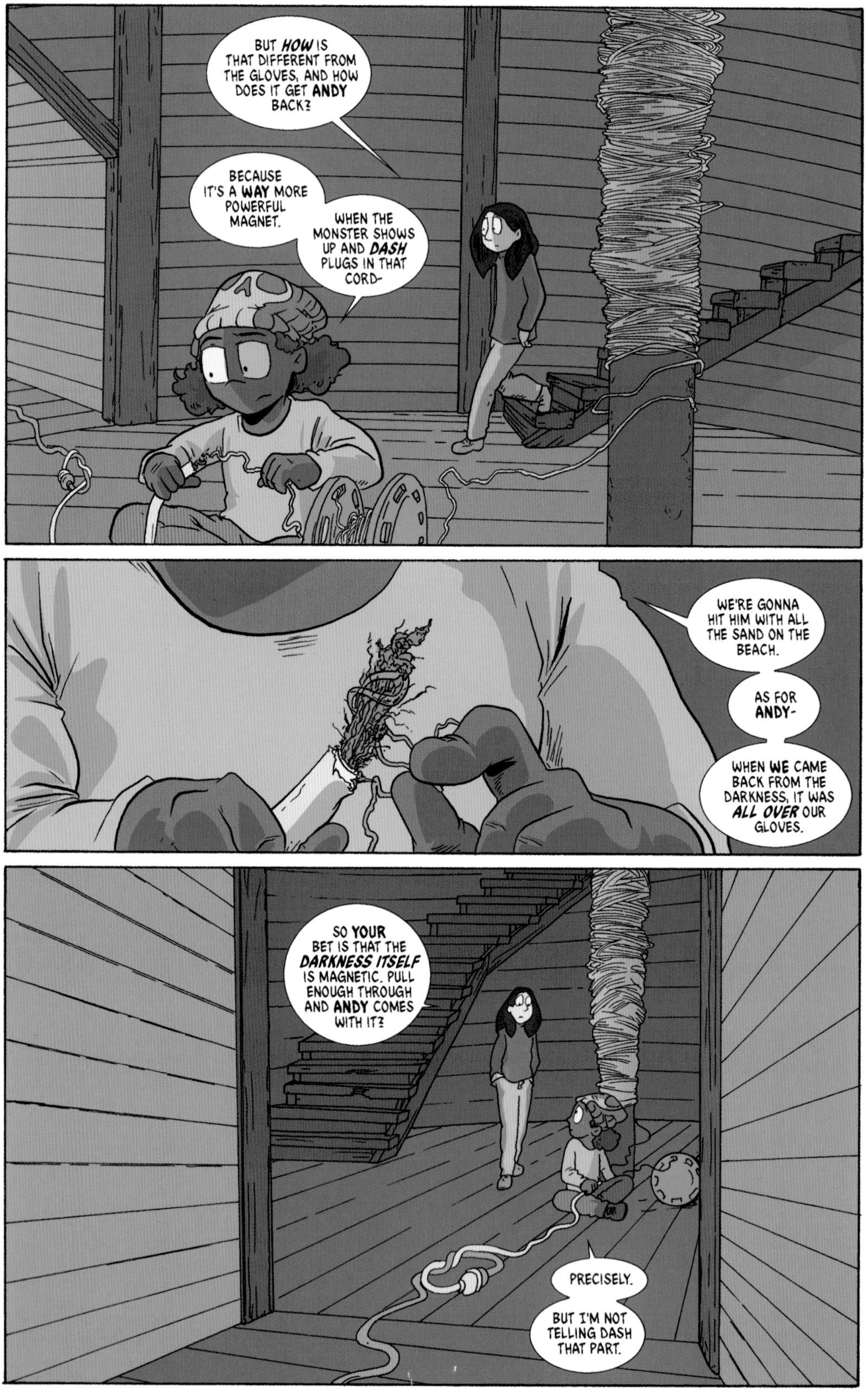

BUT HOW IS THAT DIFFERENT FROM THE GLOVES, AND HOW DOES IT GET ANDY BACK?
BECAUSE IT'S A WAY MORE POWERFUL MAGNET.
WHEN THE MONSTER SHOWS UP AND DASH PLUGS IN THAT CORD-
WE'RE GONNA HIT HIM WITH ALL THE SAND ON THE BEACH.
AS FOR ANDY-
WHEN WE CAME BACK FROM THE DARKNESS, IT WAS ALL OVER OUR GLOVES.
SO YOUR BET IS THAT THE DARKNESS ITSELF IS MAGNETIC. PULL ENOUGH THROUGH AND ANDY COMES WITH IT?
PRECISELY.
BUT I'M NOT TELLING DASH THAT PART.

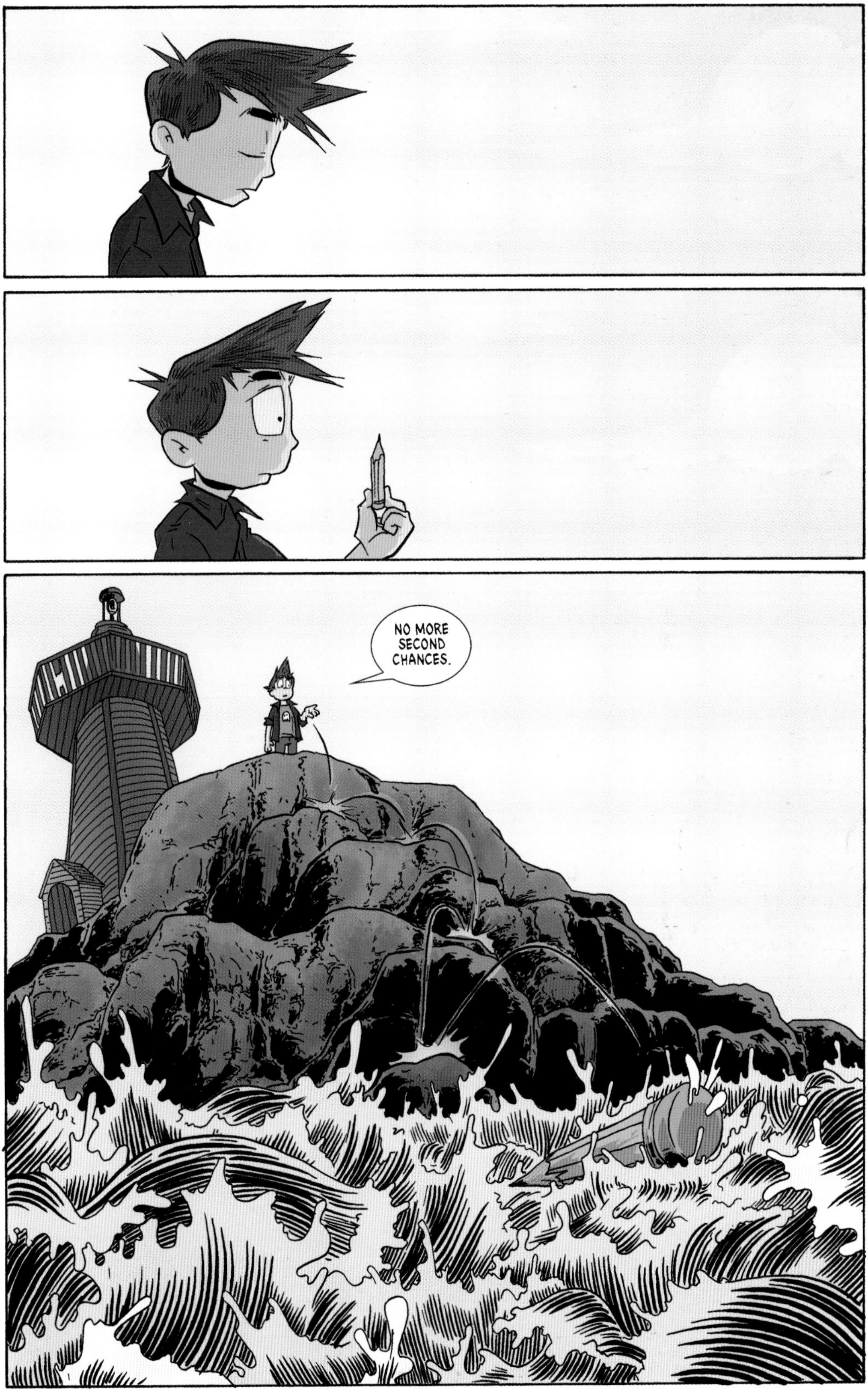
NO MORE SECOND CHANCES.

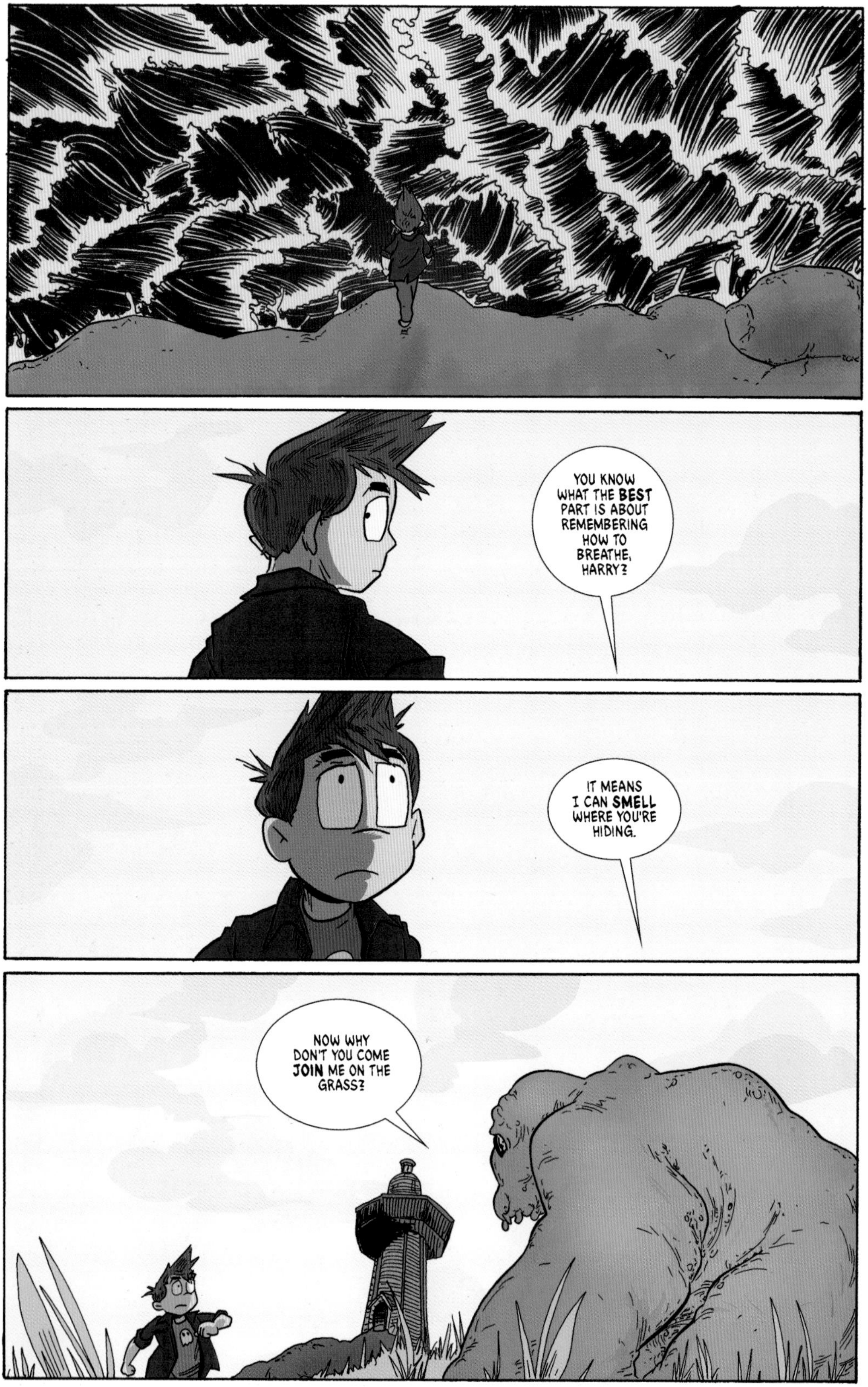
YOU KNOW WHAT THE BEST PART IS ABOUT REMEMBERING HOW TO BREATHE, HARRY?
IT MEANS I CAN SMELL WHERE YOU'RE HIDING.
NOW WHY DON'T YOU COME JOIN ME ON THE GRASS?

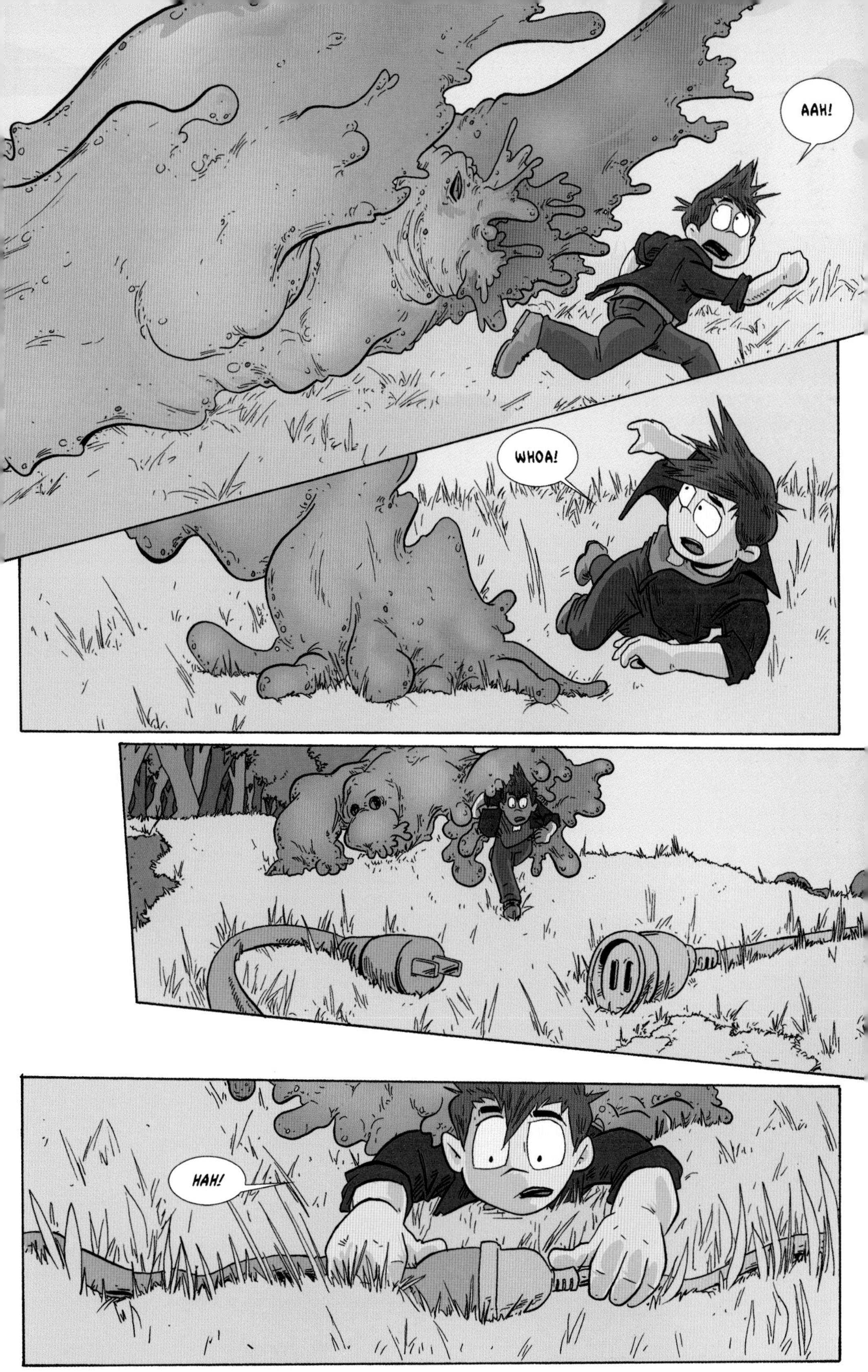
AAH!
WHOA!
HAH!

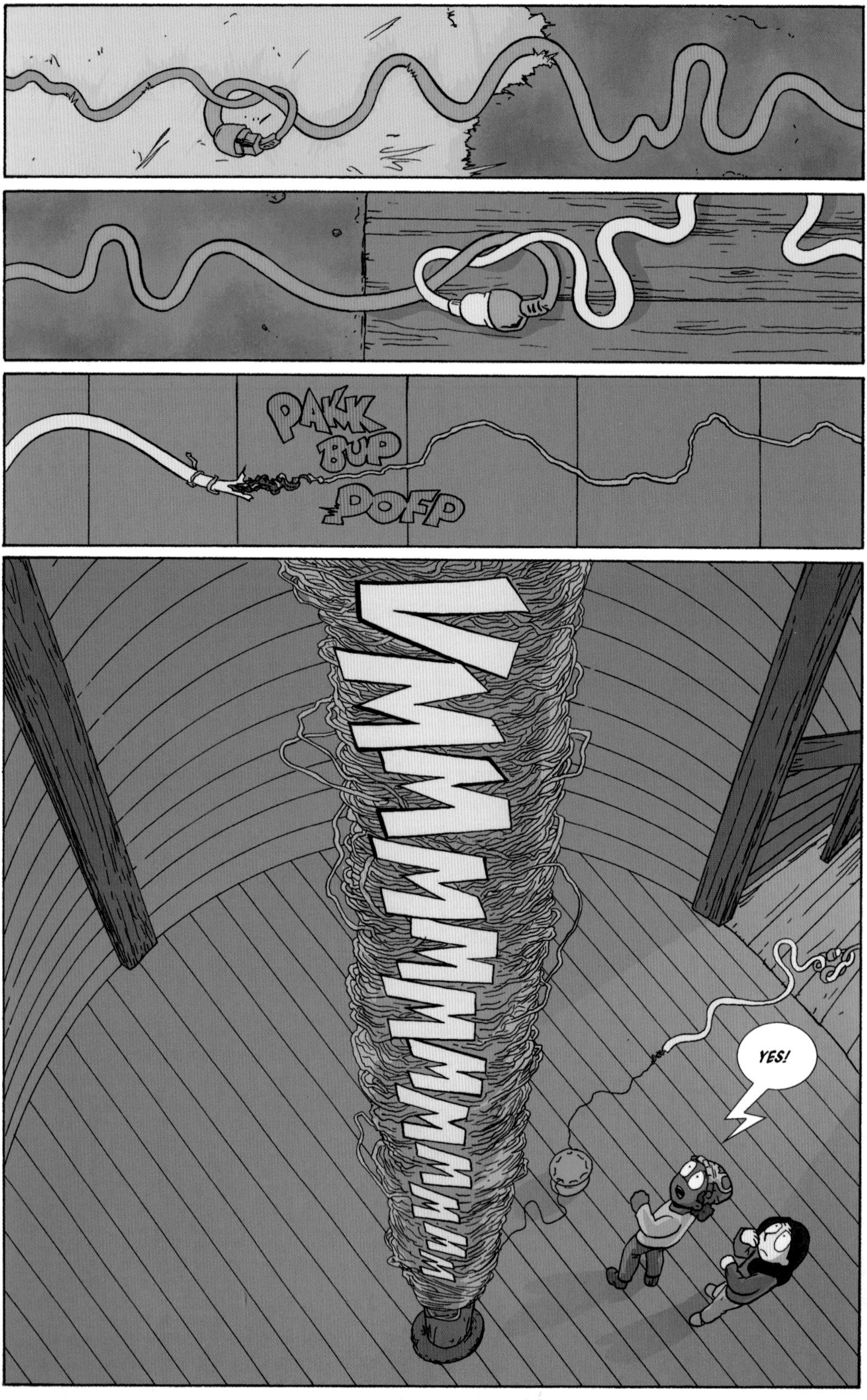
PAKK
BUP
POFP
VMMMMMMMMMM
YES!

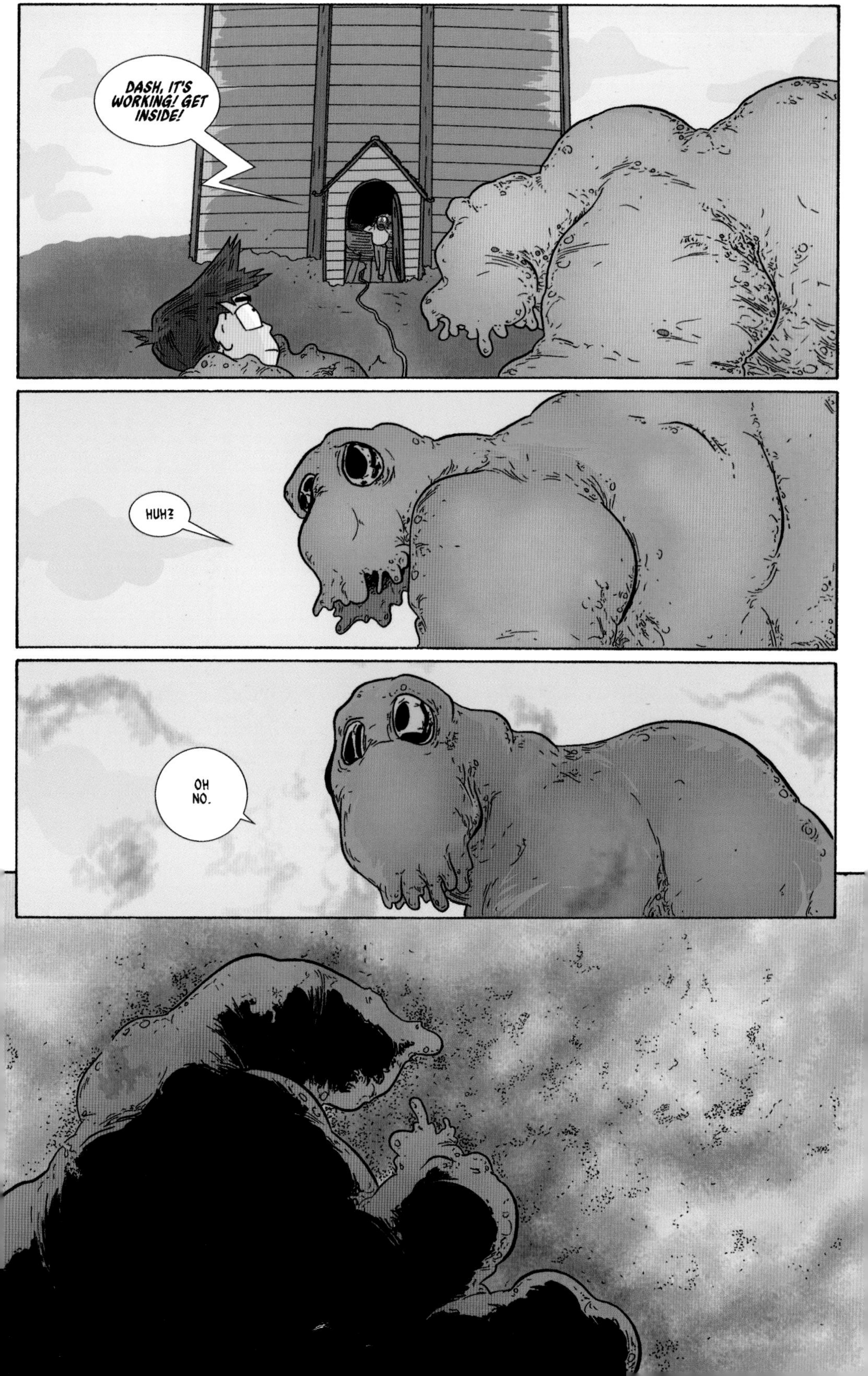
DASH, IT'S WORKING! GET INSIDE!
HUH?
OH NO.

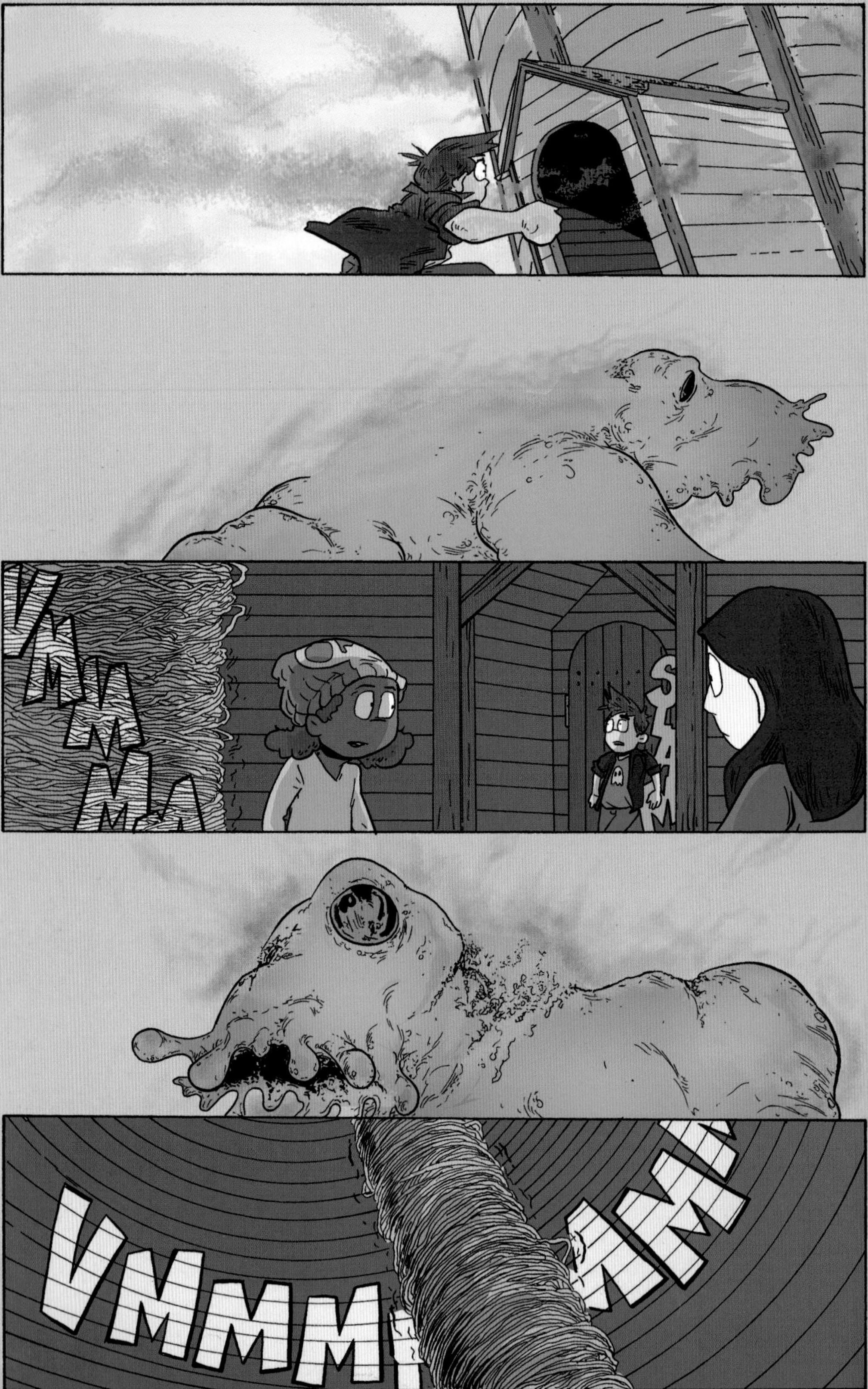
VMMMA
VMMMM
MMM

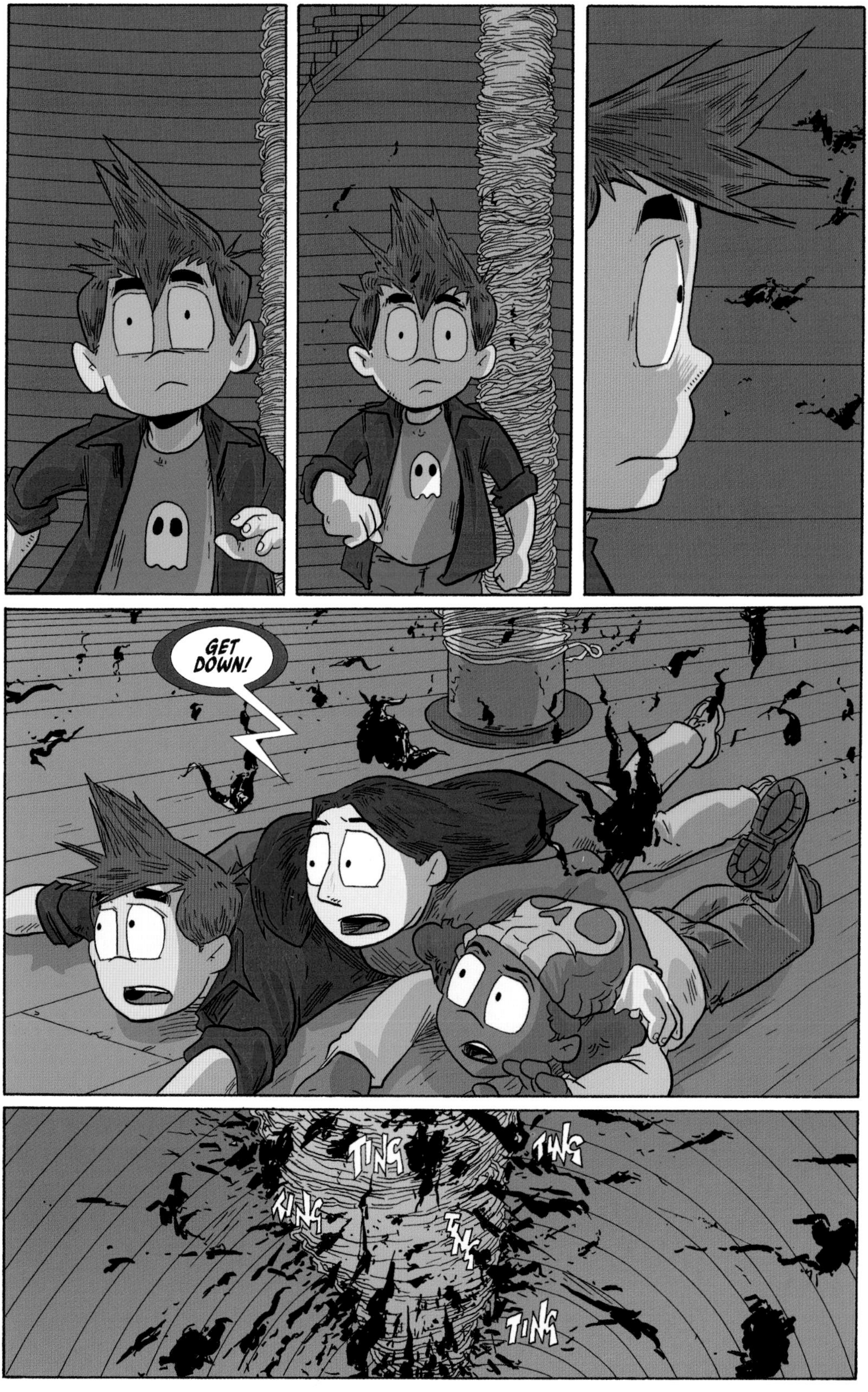
GET DOWN!
TING
TING
TING
TING
TING

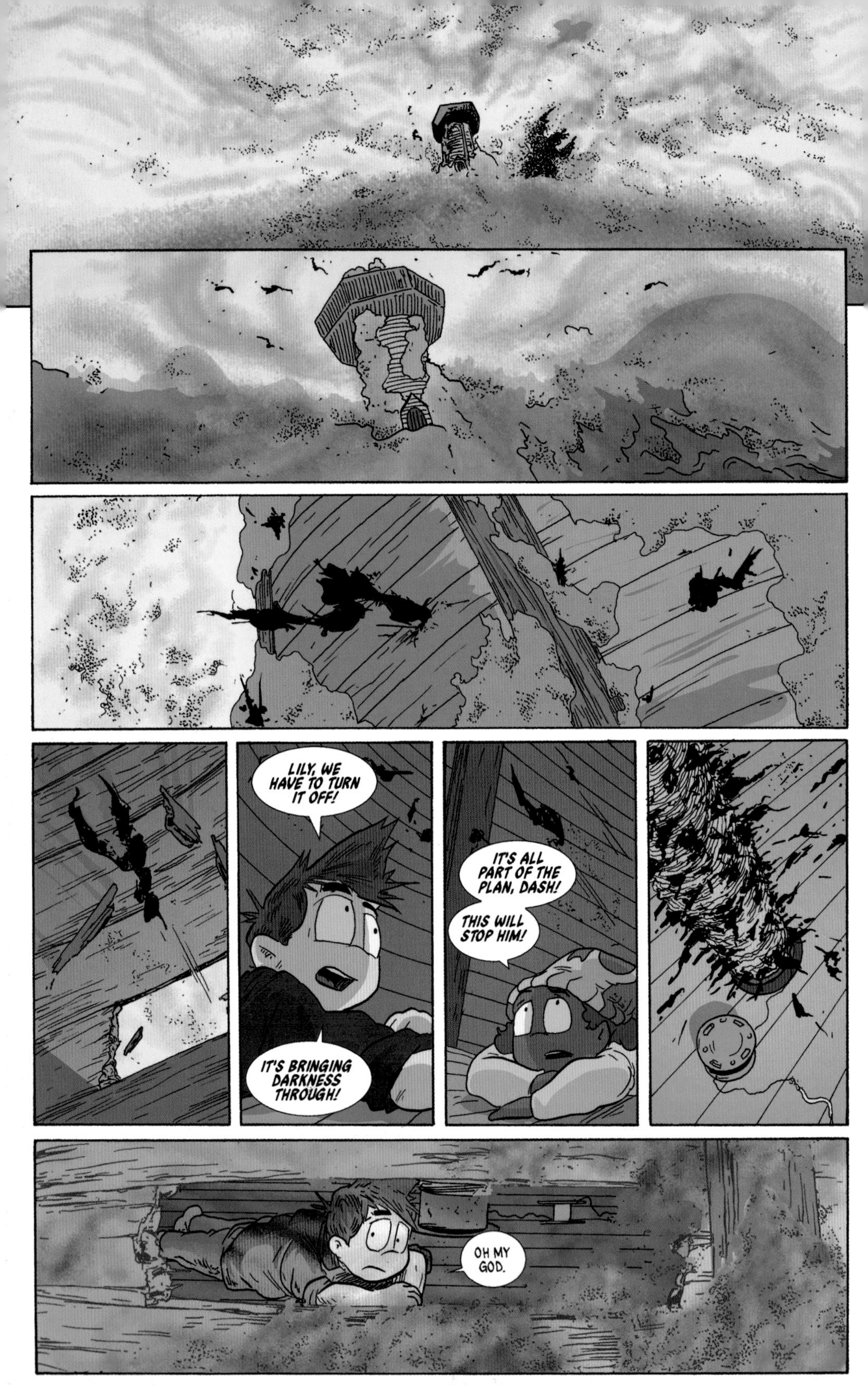
LILY, WE HAVE TO TURN IT OFF!
IT'S BRINGING DARKNESS THROUGH!
IT'S ALL PART OF THE PLAN, DASH!
THIS WILL STOP HIM!
OH MY GOD.

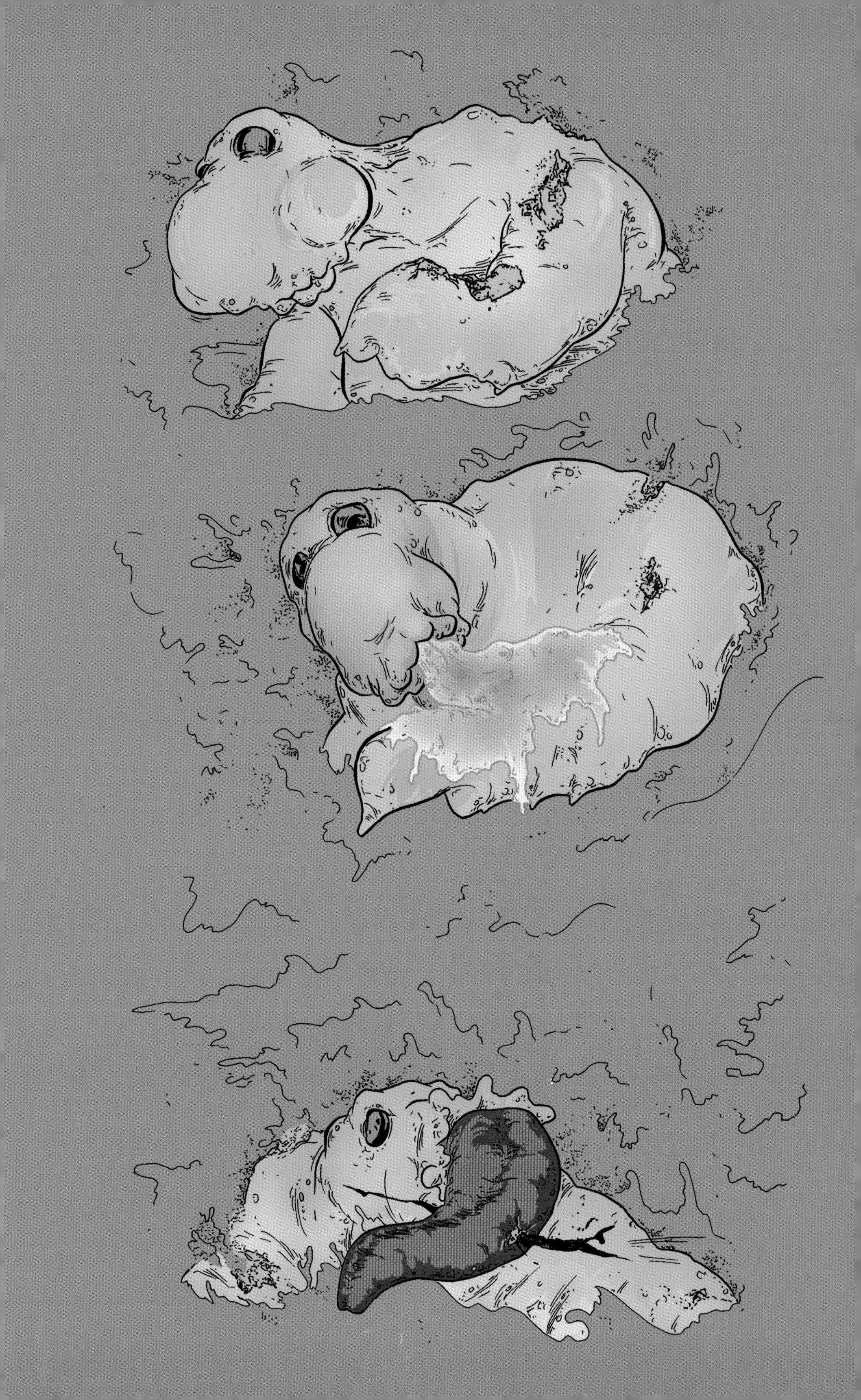

THIS WHOLE PLACE IS GONNA COME DOWN!

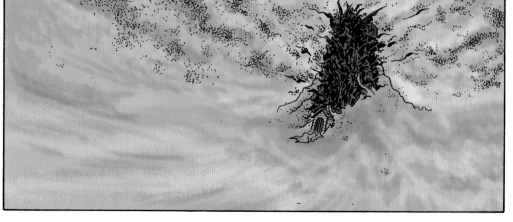

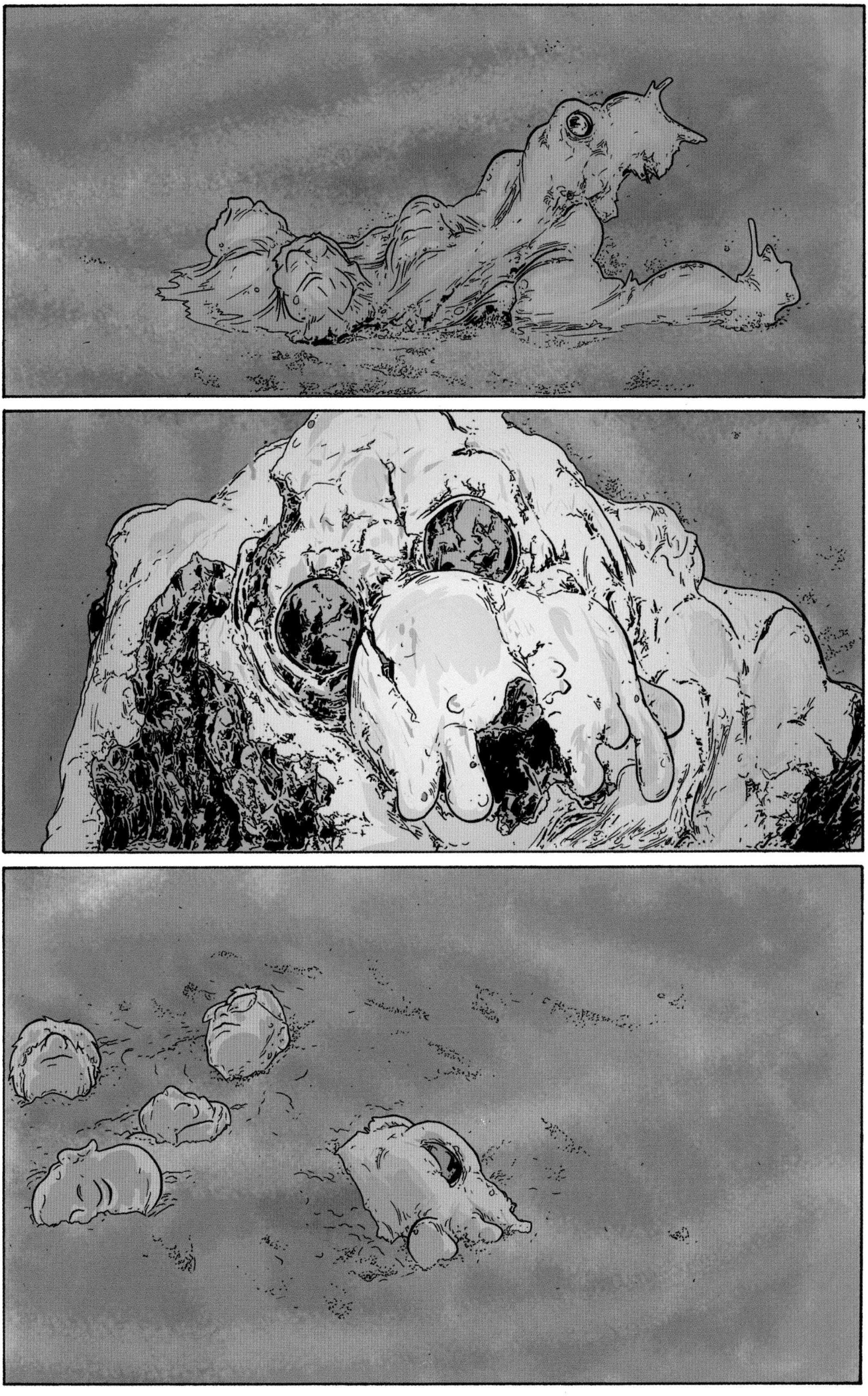

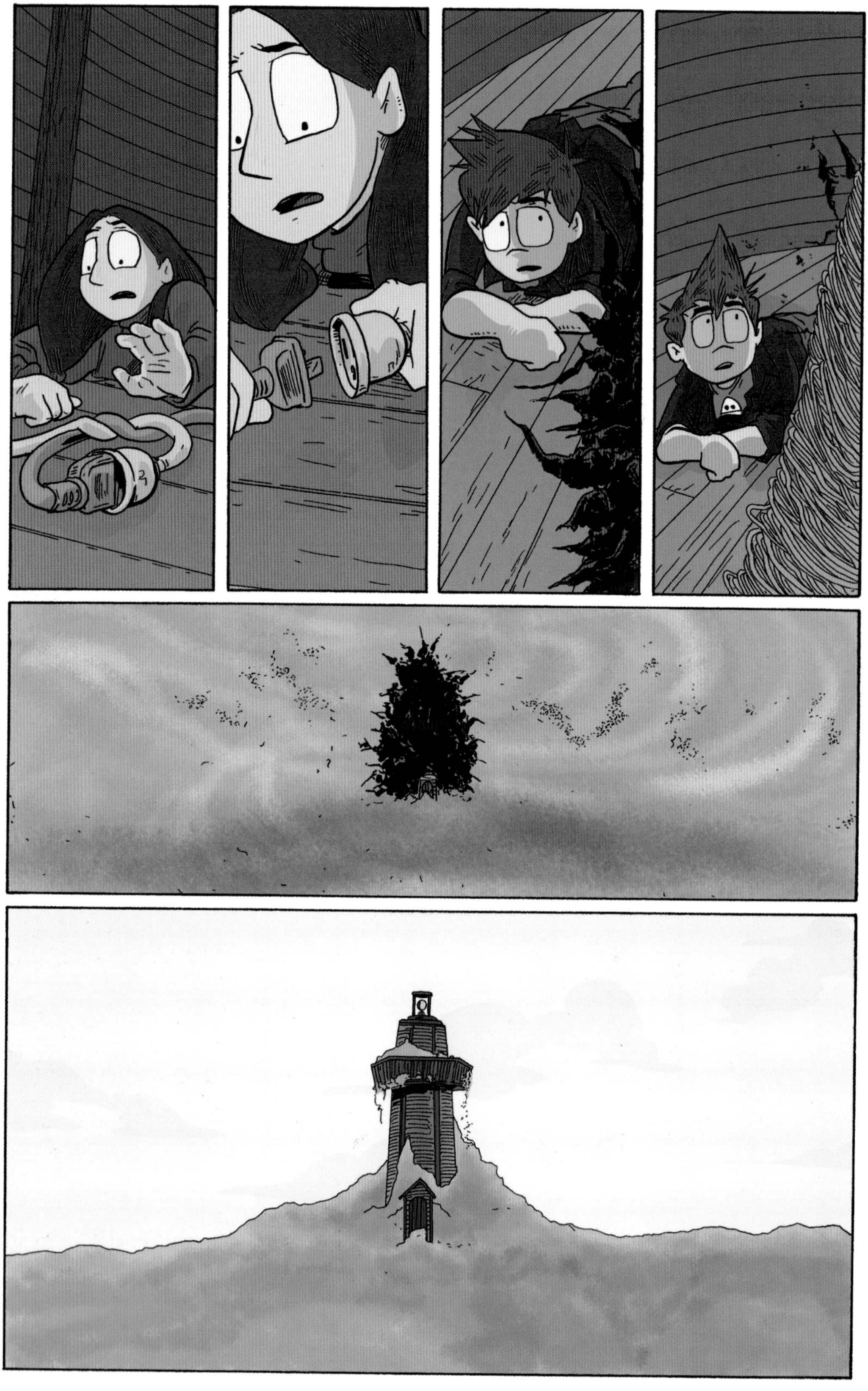

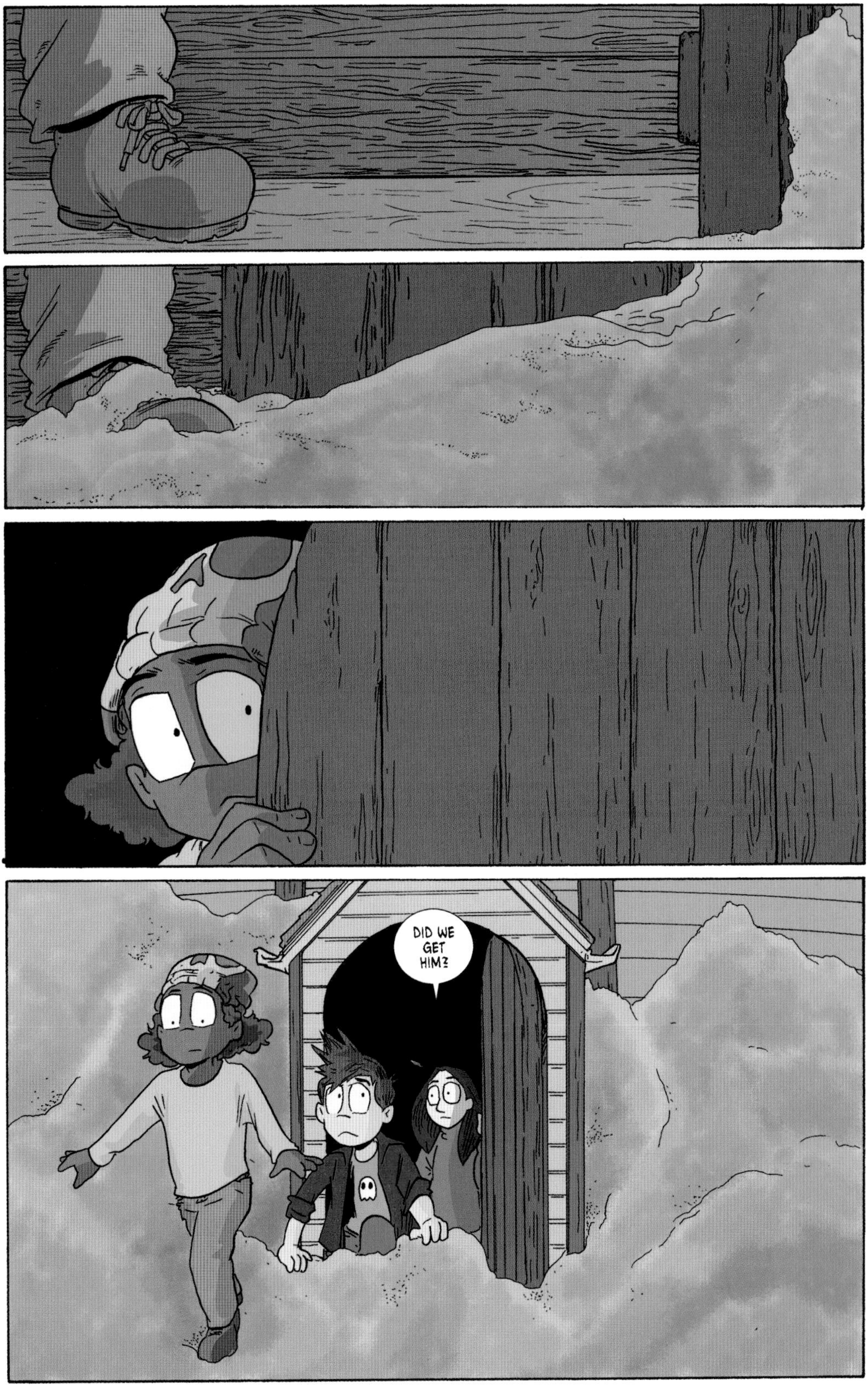
DID WE GET HIM?

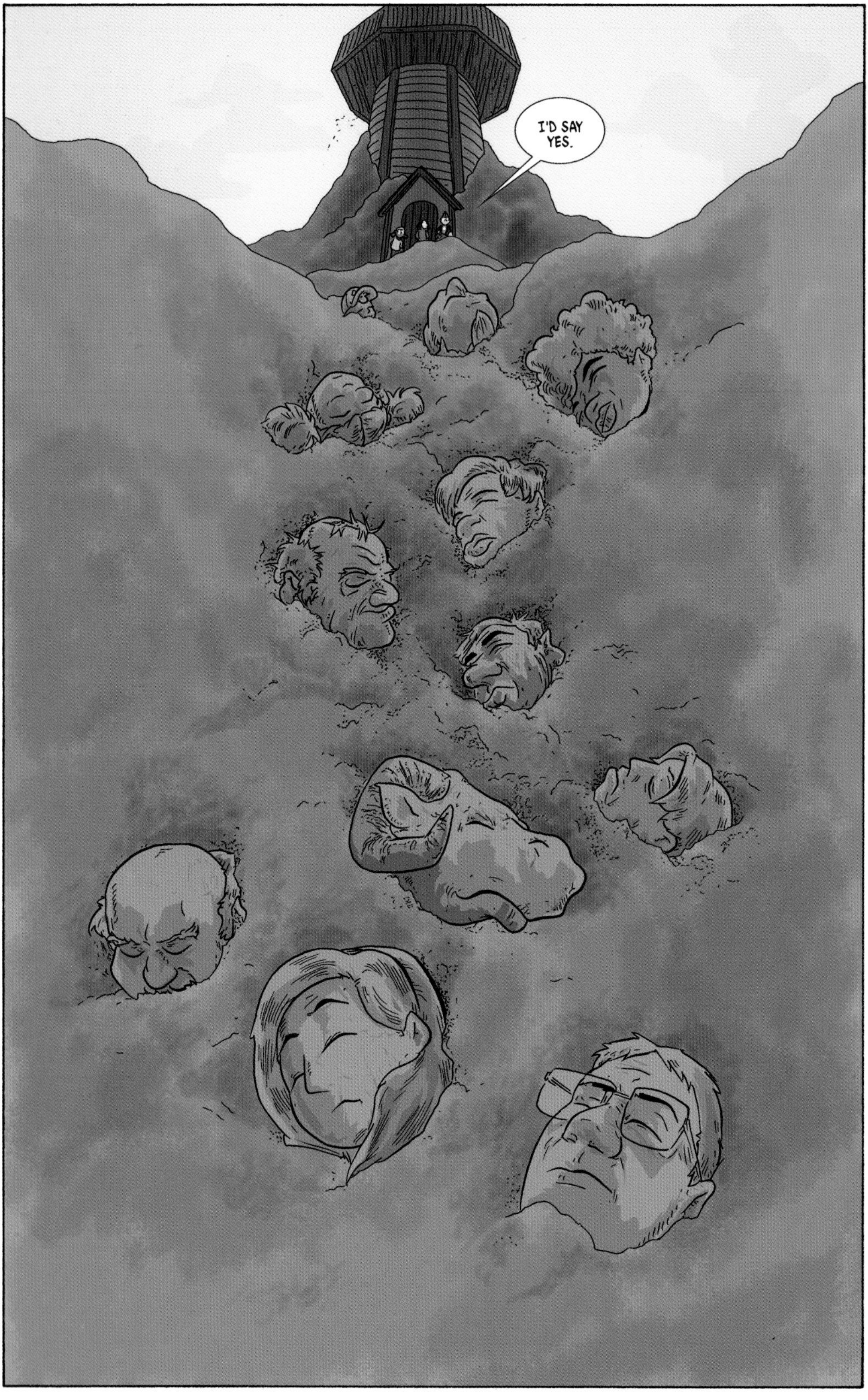
I'D SAY YES.

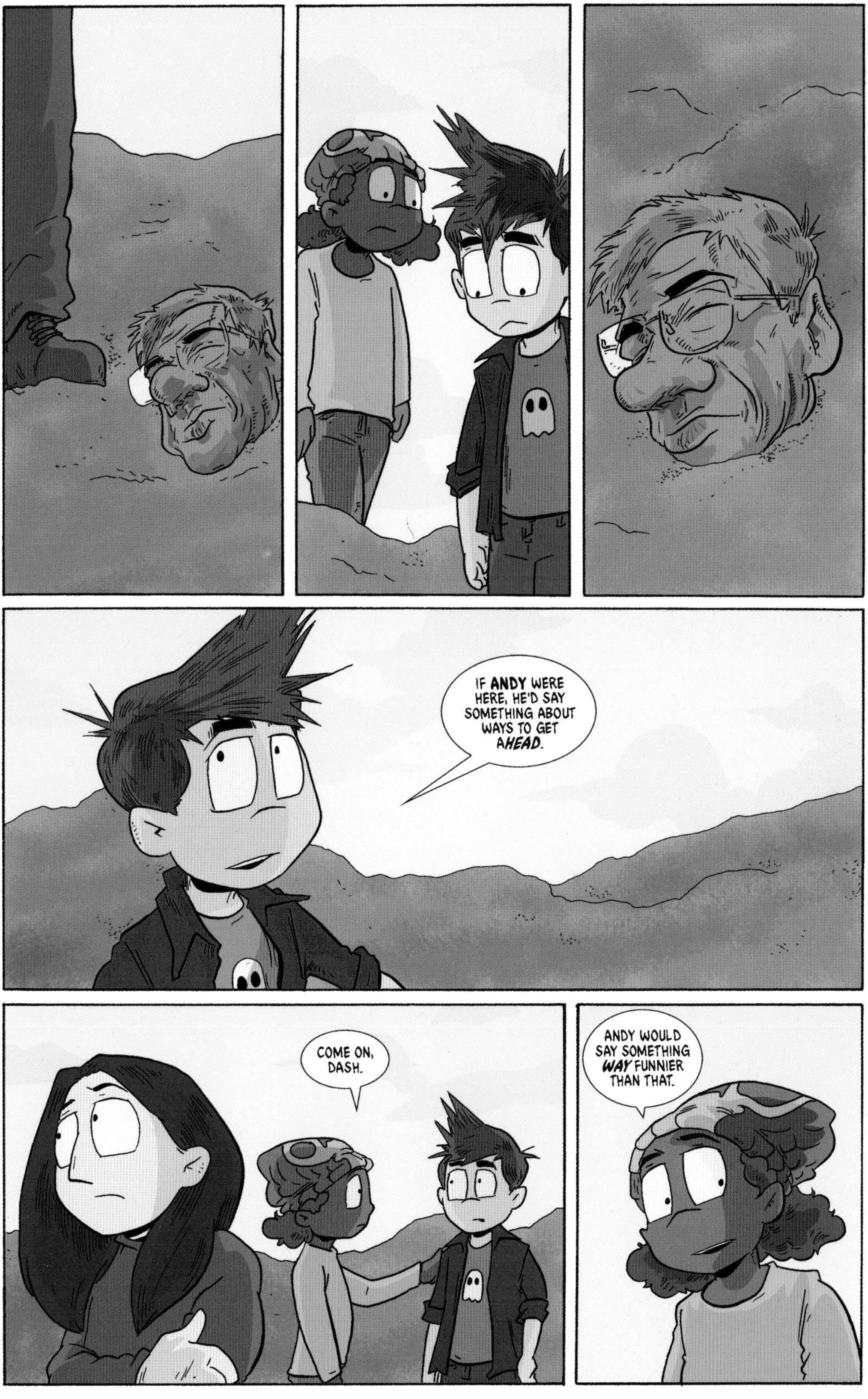
IF ANDY WERE HERE, HE'D SAY SOMETHING ABOUT WAYS TO GET AHEAD.
COME ON, DASH.
ANDY WOULD SAY SOMETHING WAY FUNNIER THAN THAT.

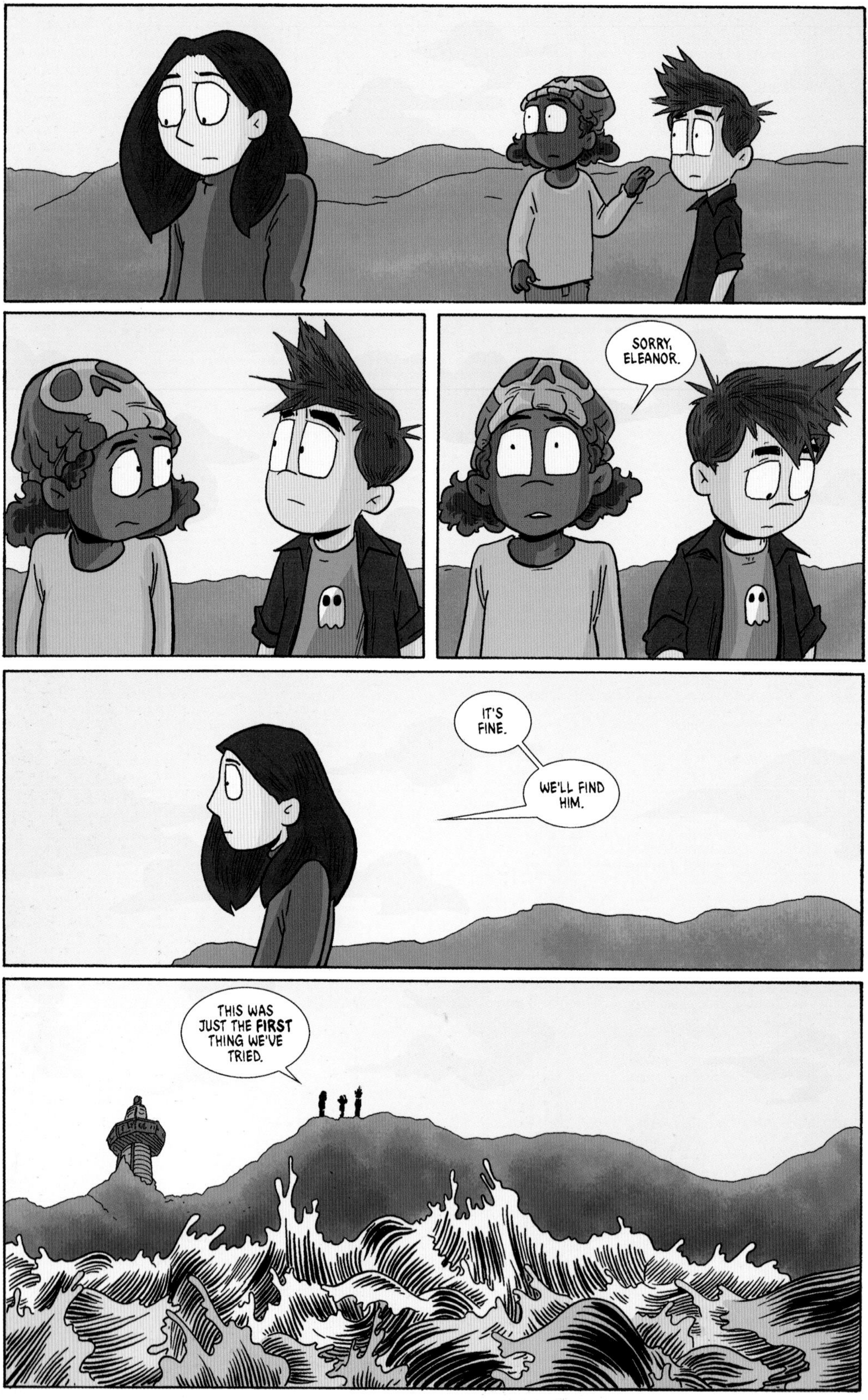
SORRY, ELEANOR.
IT'S FINE.
WE'LL FIND HIM.
THIS WAS JUST THE **FIRST** THING WE'VE TRIED.

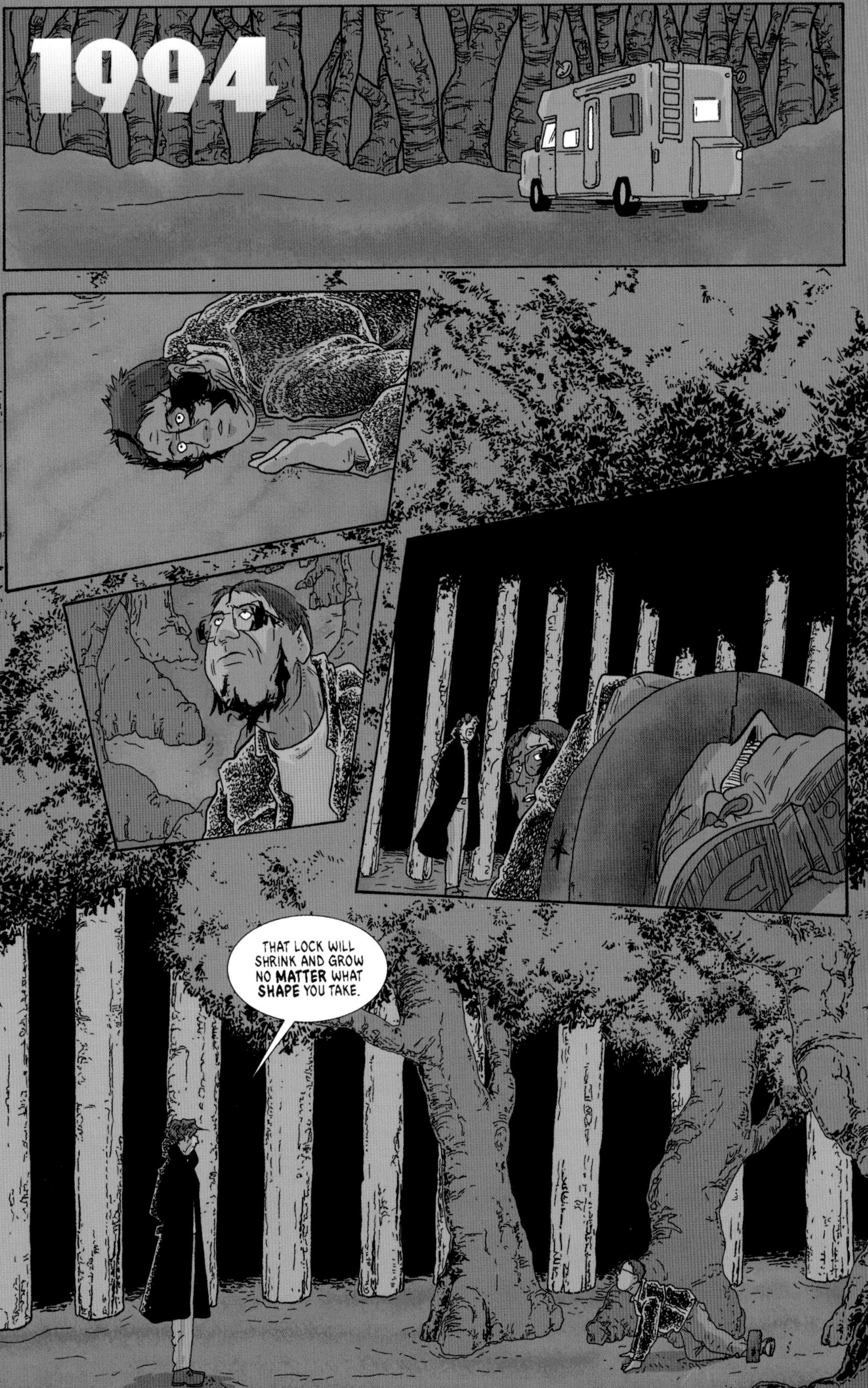
1994
THAT LOCK WILL SHRINK AND GROW NO MATTER WHAT SHAPE YOU TAKE.

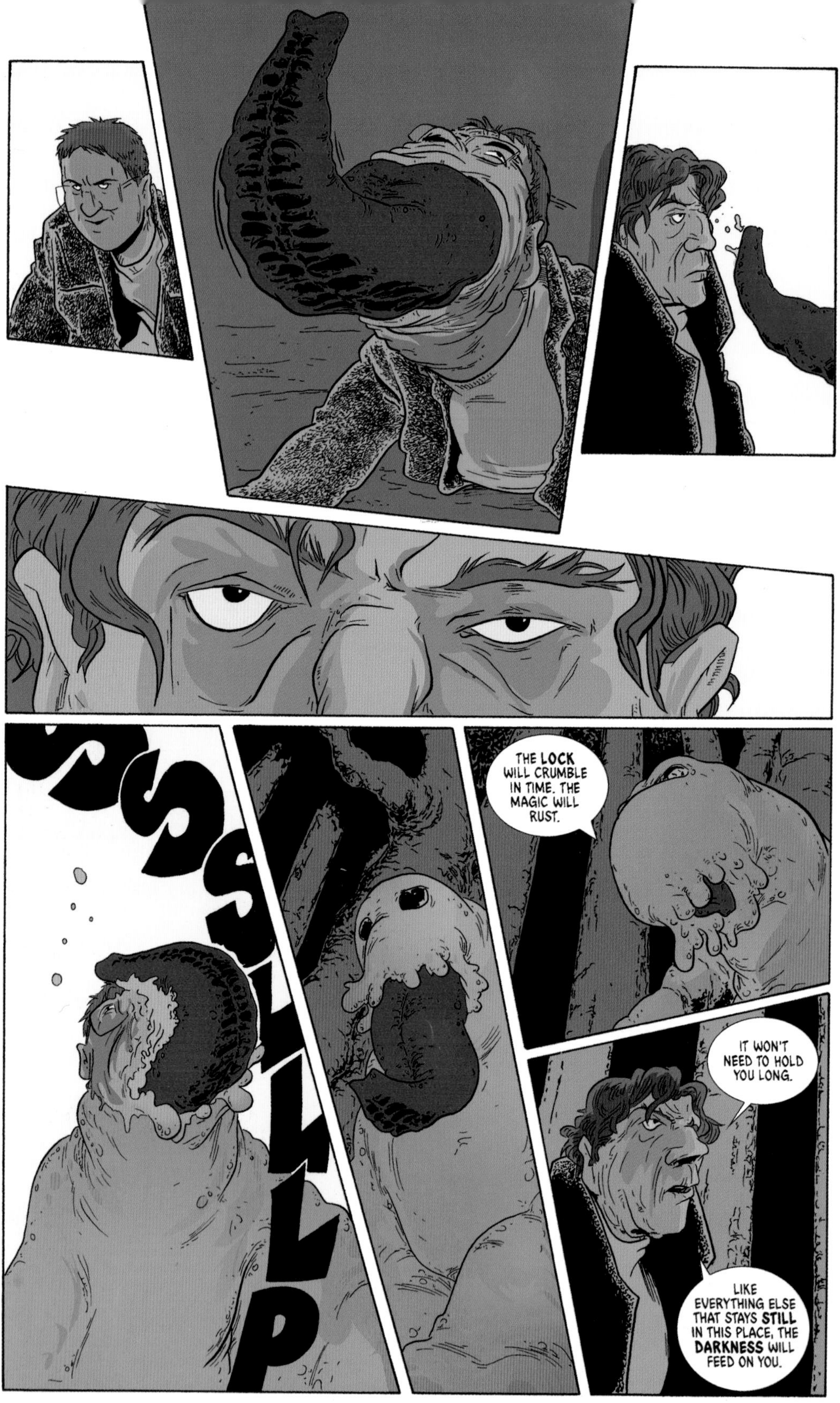
SSSSHLLP
THE LOCK WILL CRUMBLE IN TIME. THE MAGIC WILL RUST.
IT WON'T NEED TO HOLD YOU LONG.
LIKE EVERYTHING ELSE THAT STAYS STILL IN THIS PLACE, THE DARKNESS WILL FEED ON YOU.

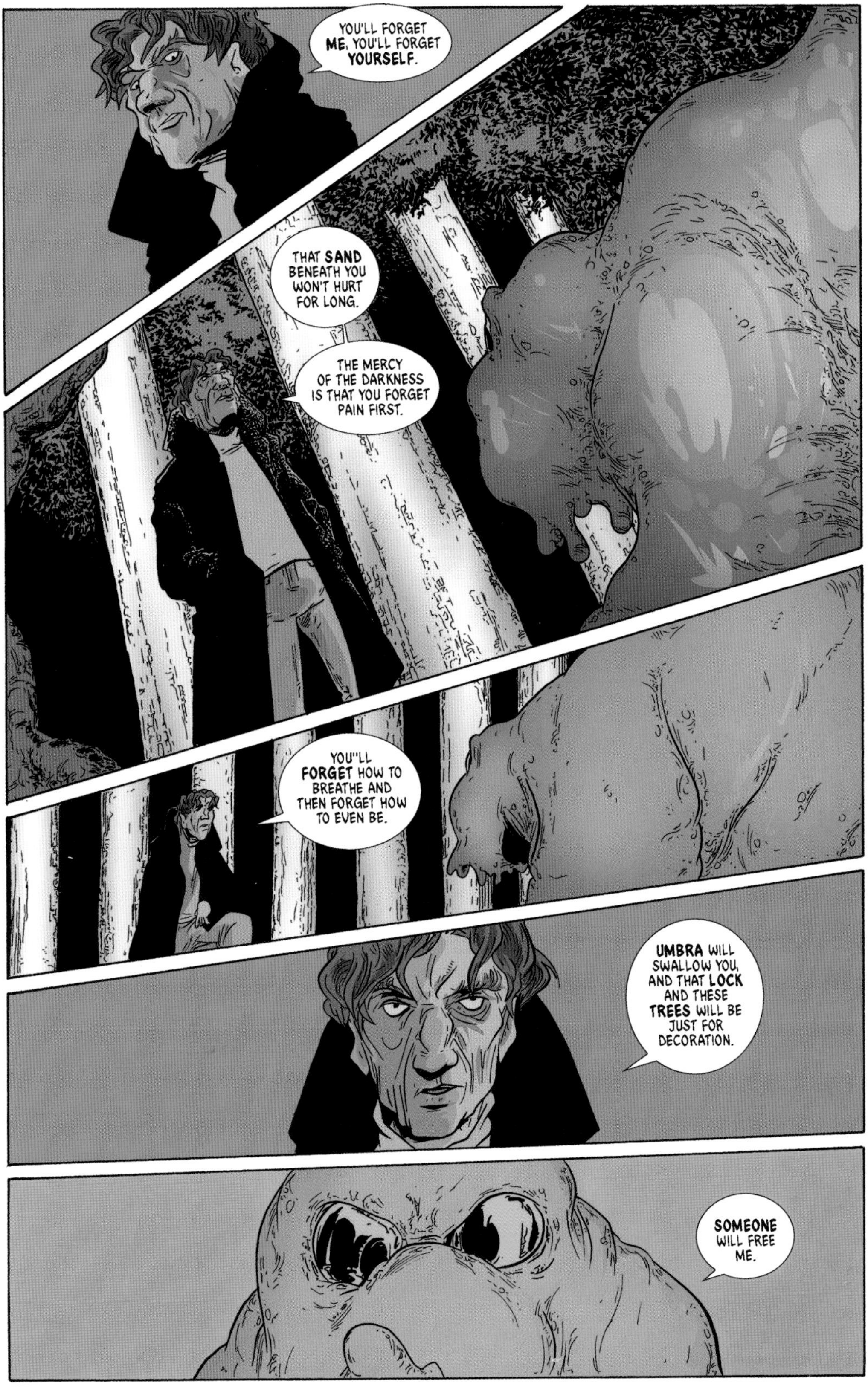
YOU'LL FORGET ME, YOU'LL FORGET YOURSELF.
THAT SAND BENEATH YOU WON'T HURT FOR LONG.
THE MERCY OF THE DARKNESS IS THAT YOU FORGET PAIN FIRST.
YOU''LL FORGET HOW TO BREATHE AND THEN FORGET HOW TO EVEN BE.
UMBRA WILL SWALLOW YOU, AND THAT LOCK AND THESE TREES WILL BE JUST FOR DECORATION.
SOMEONE WILL FREE ME.

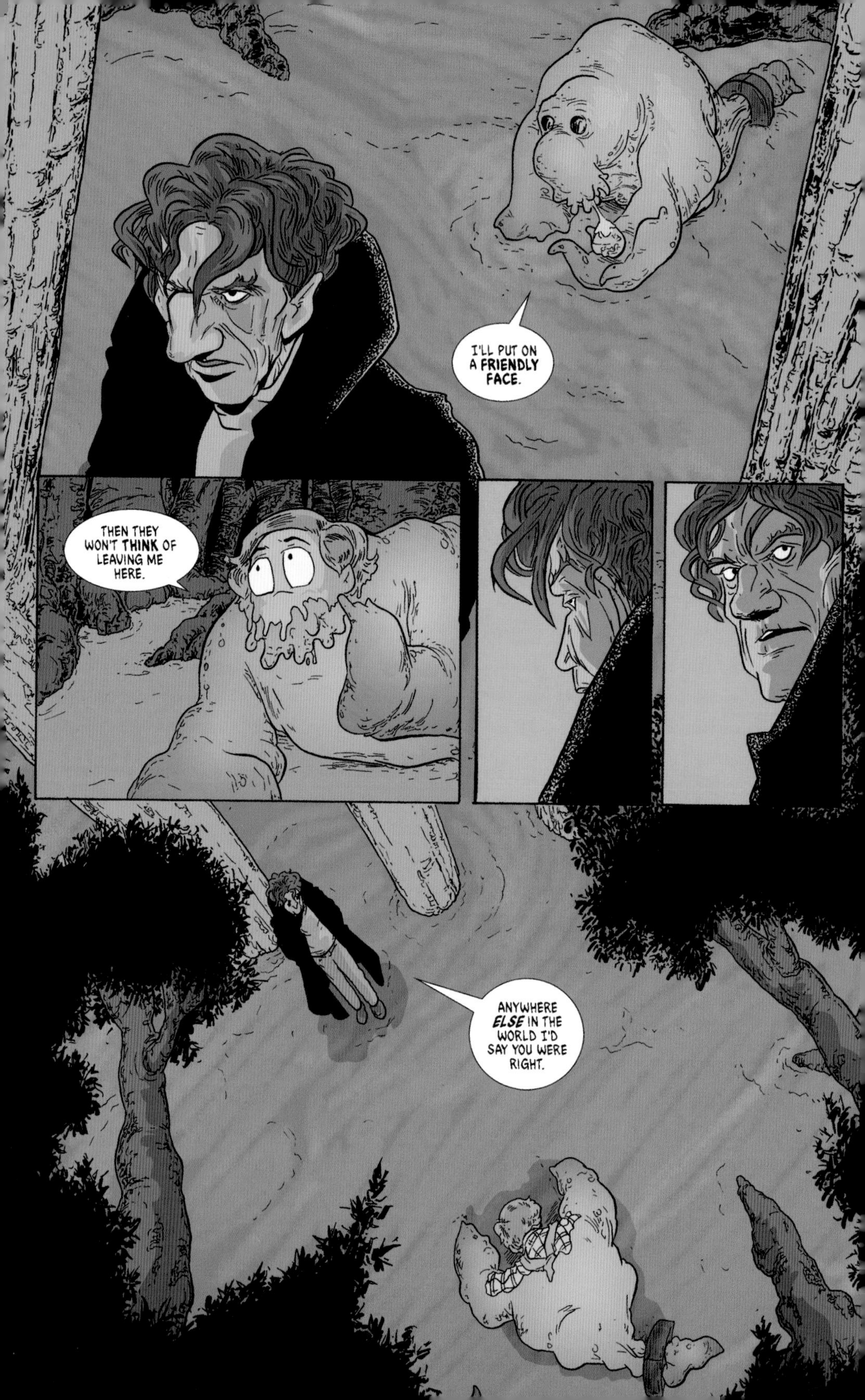
I'LL PUT ON A **FRIENDLY FACE**.
THEN THEY WON'T **THINK** OF LEAVING ME HERE.
ANYWHERE *ELSE* IN THE WORLD I'D SAY YOU WERE RIGHT.

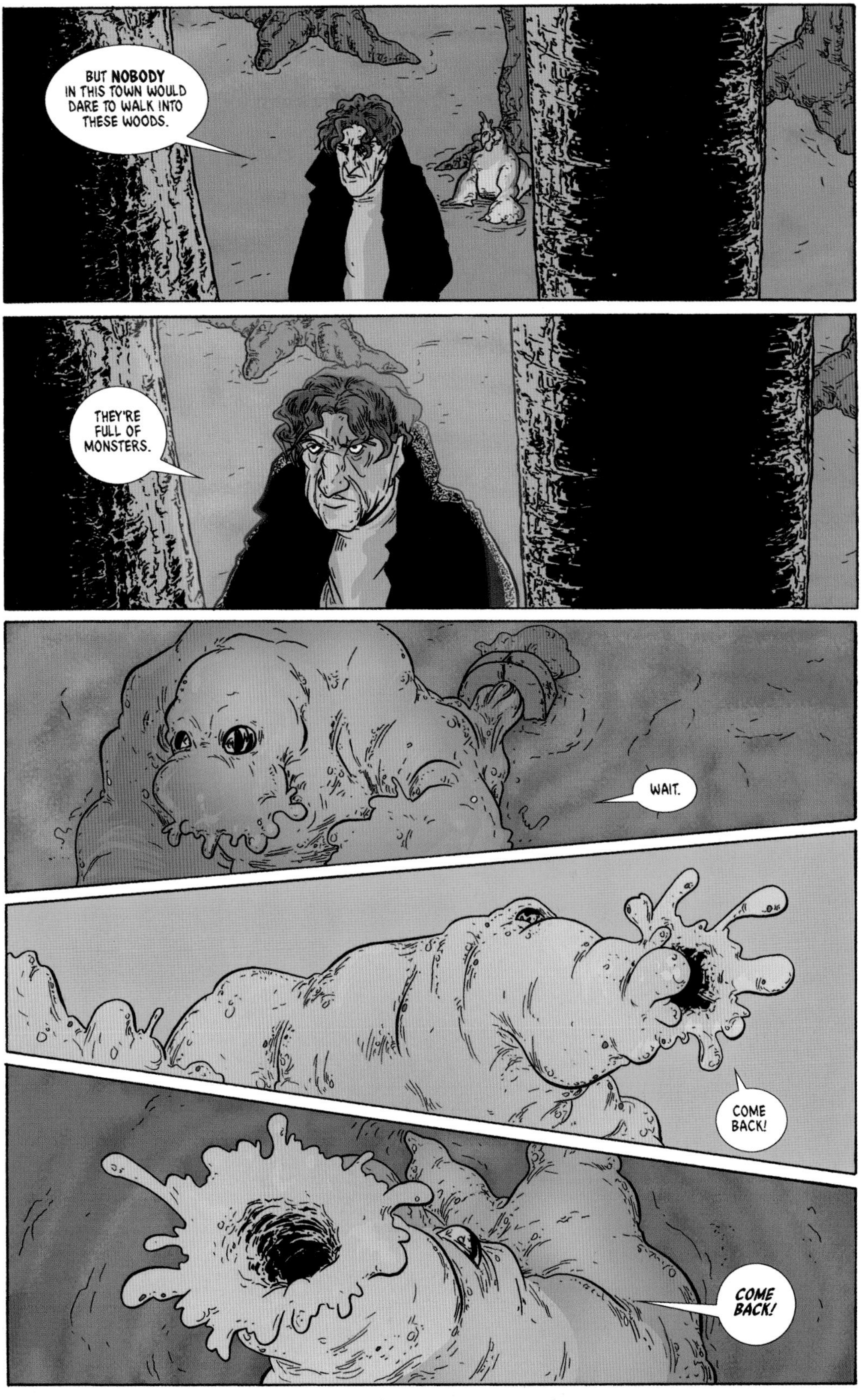
BUT NOBODY IN THIS TOWN WOULD DARE TO WALK INTO THESE WOODS.
THEY'RE FULL OF MONSTERS.
WAIT.
COME BACK!
COME BACK!

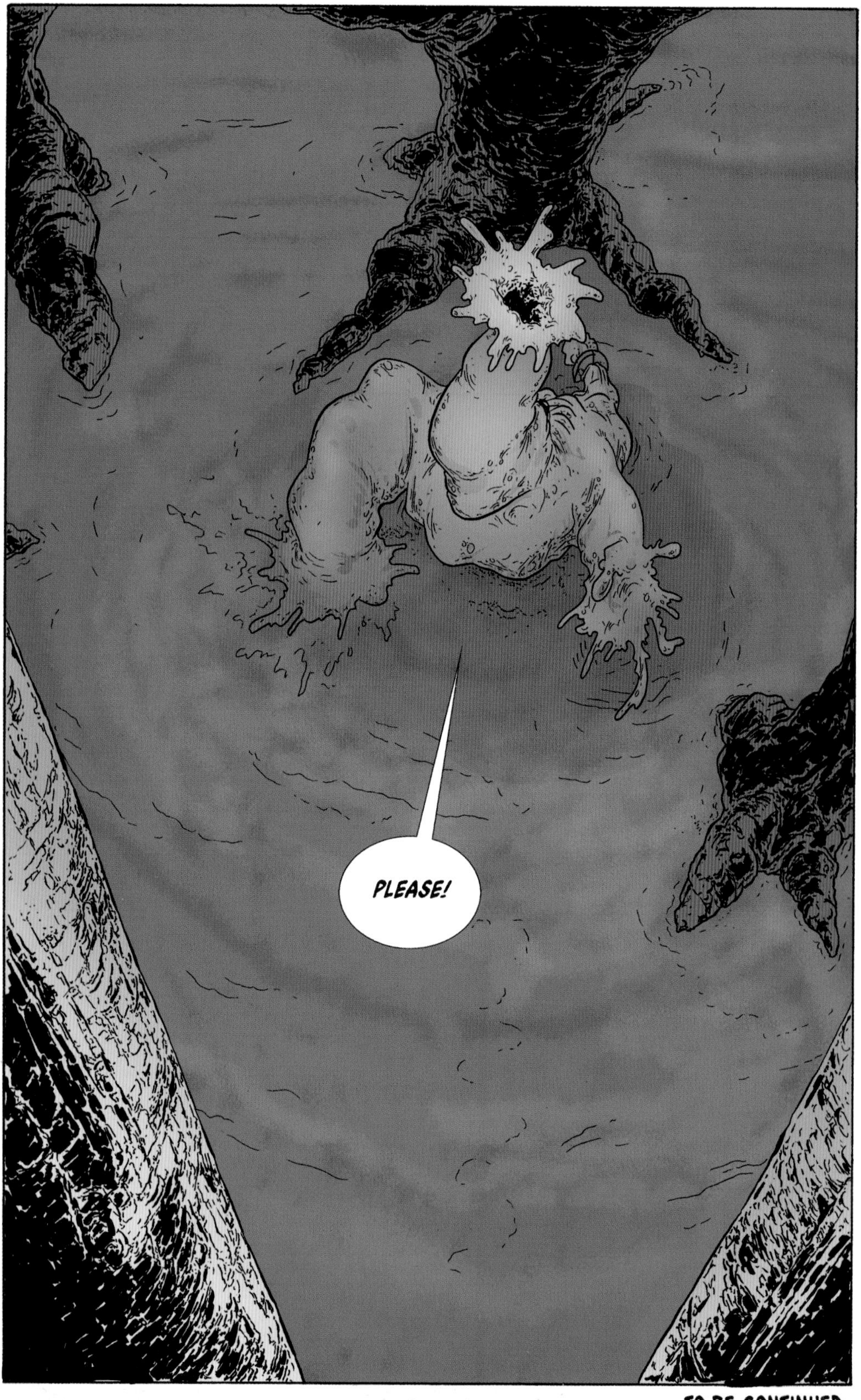
PLEASE!

TO BE CONTINUED.

NOT ALONE IN THE DARK

NOT ALONE IN THE DARK

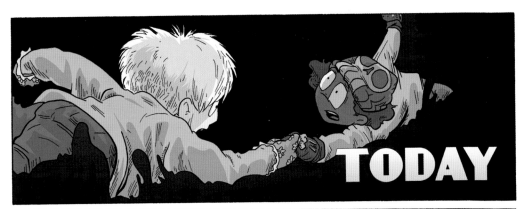

TODAY

ANDY!

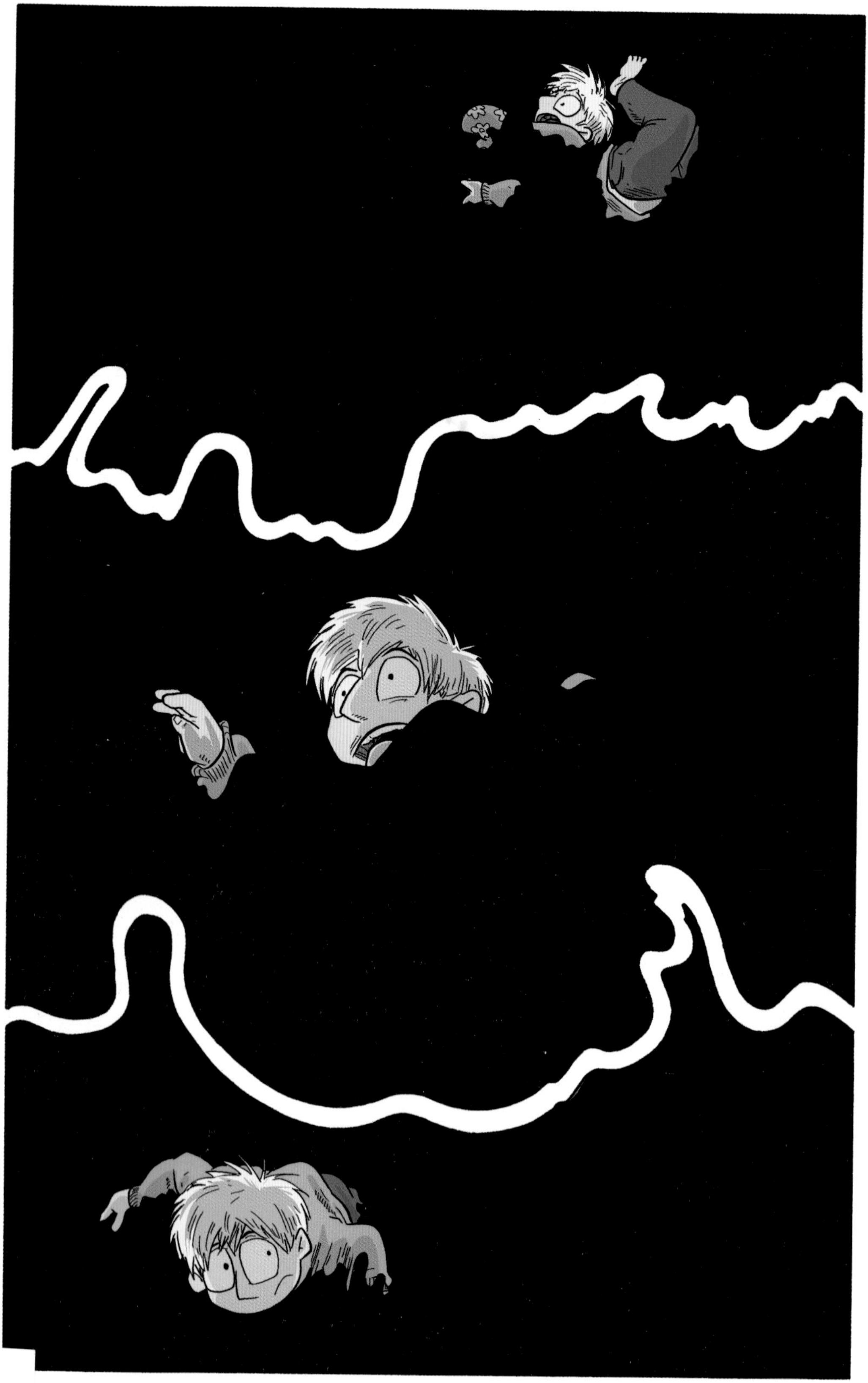

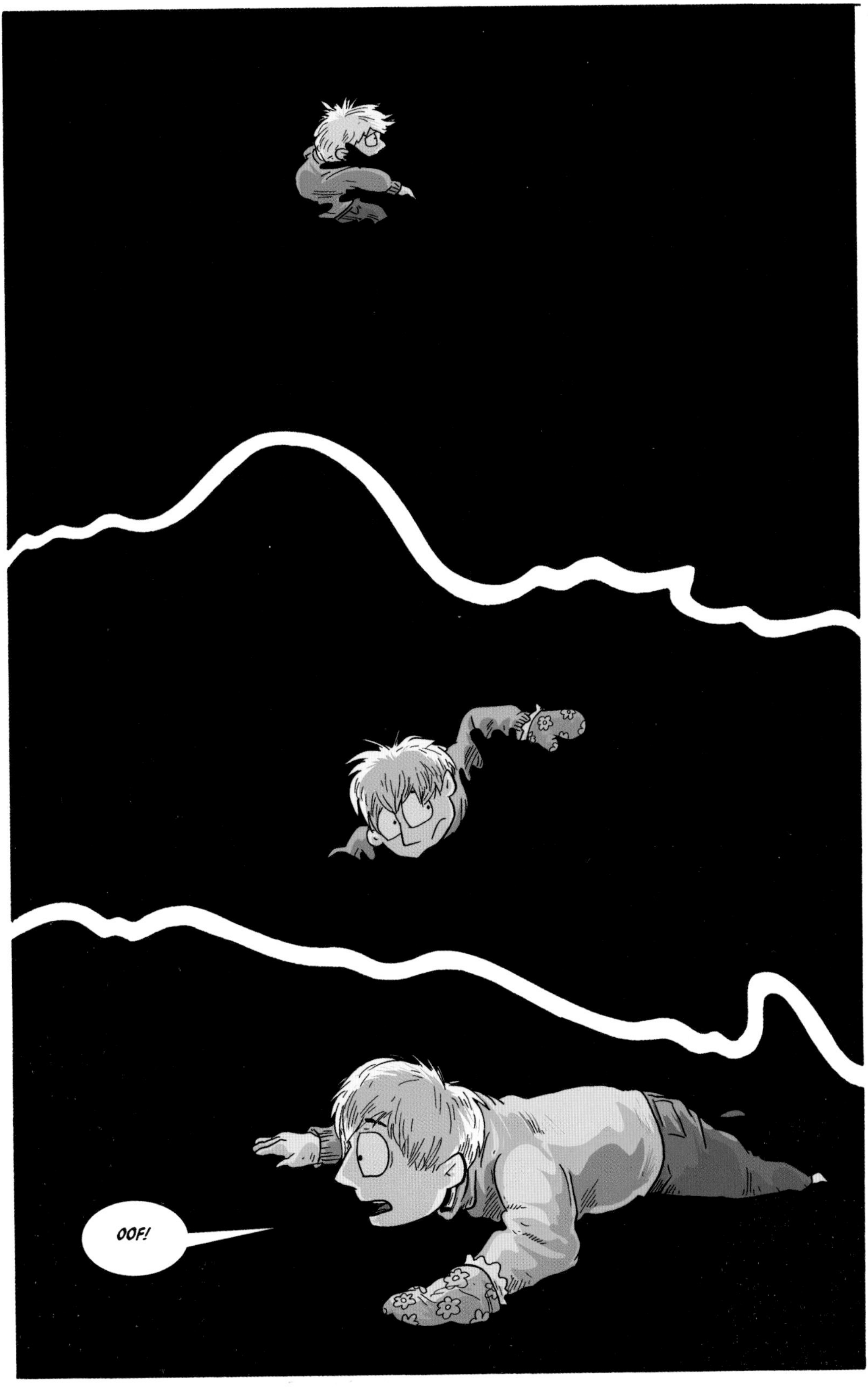
OOF!

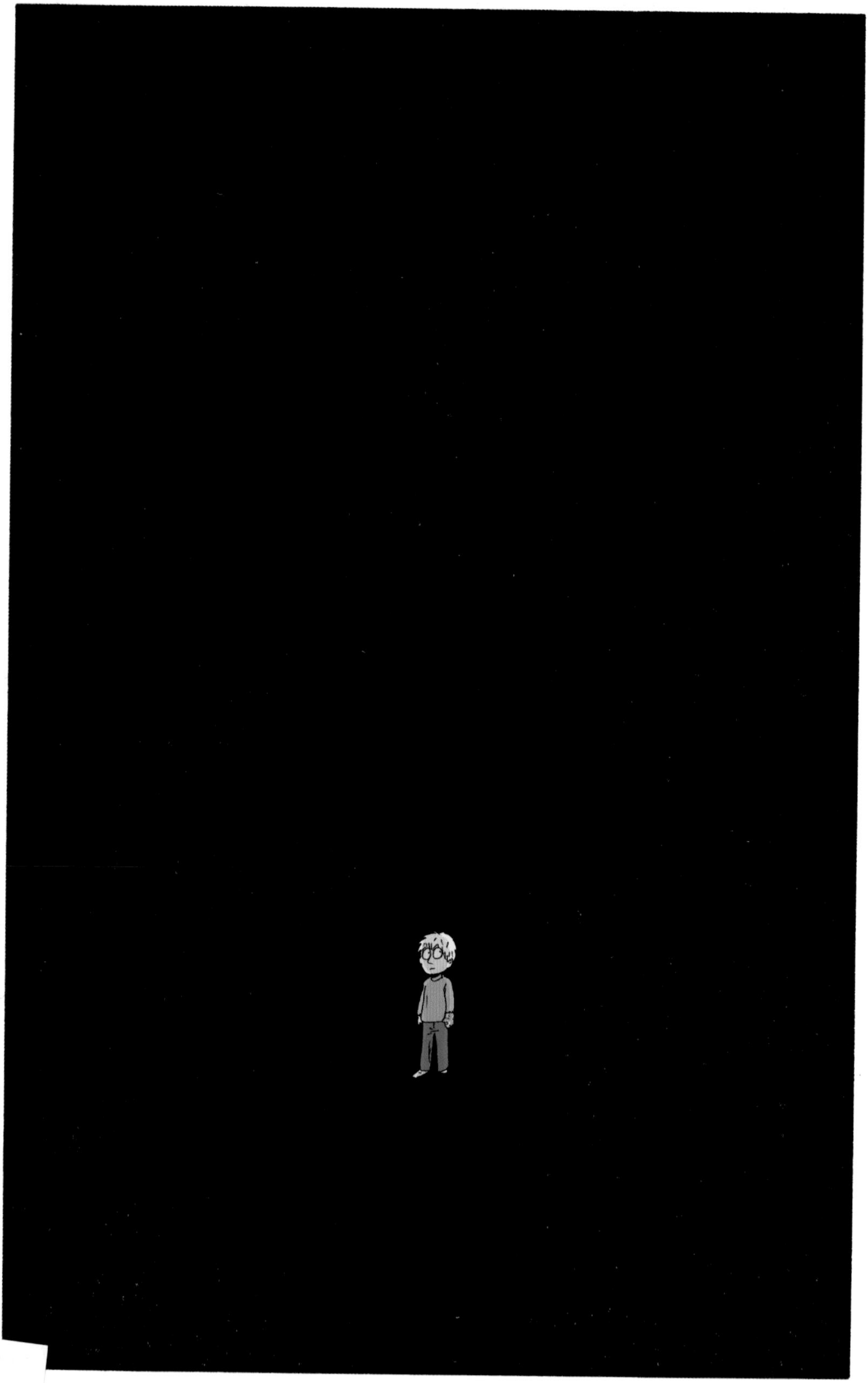

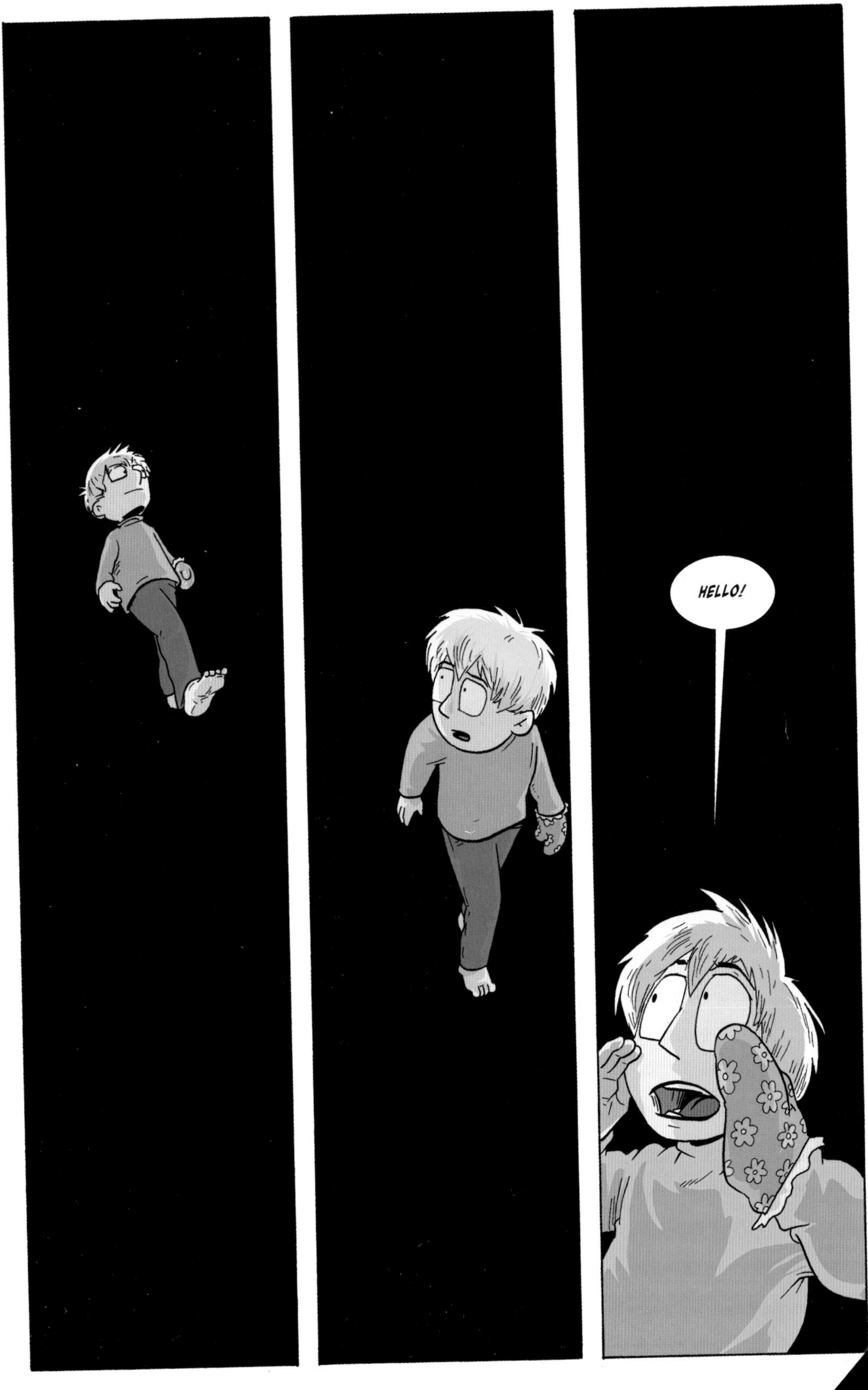
HELLO!

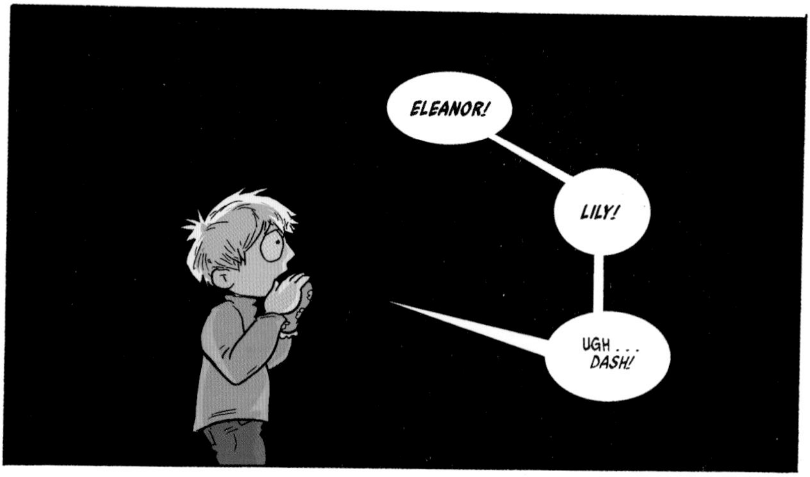
ELEANOR!
LILY!
UGH . . . DASH!

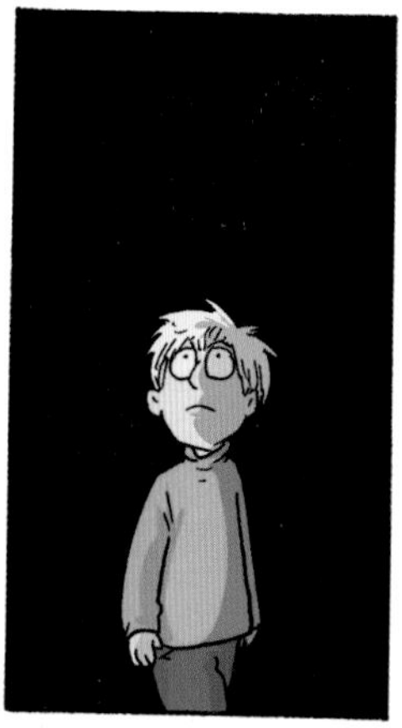

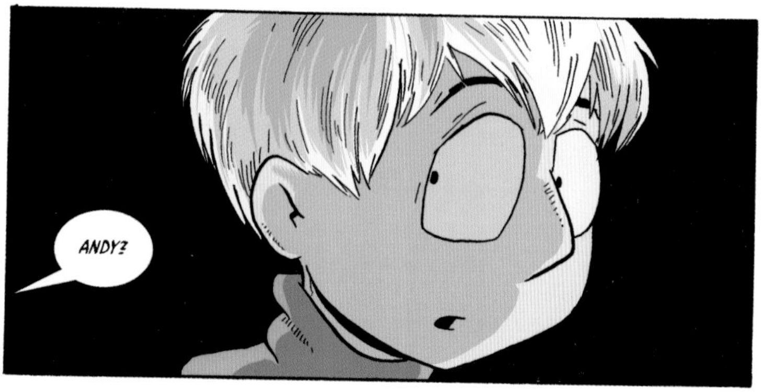
ANDY?

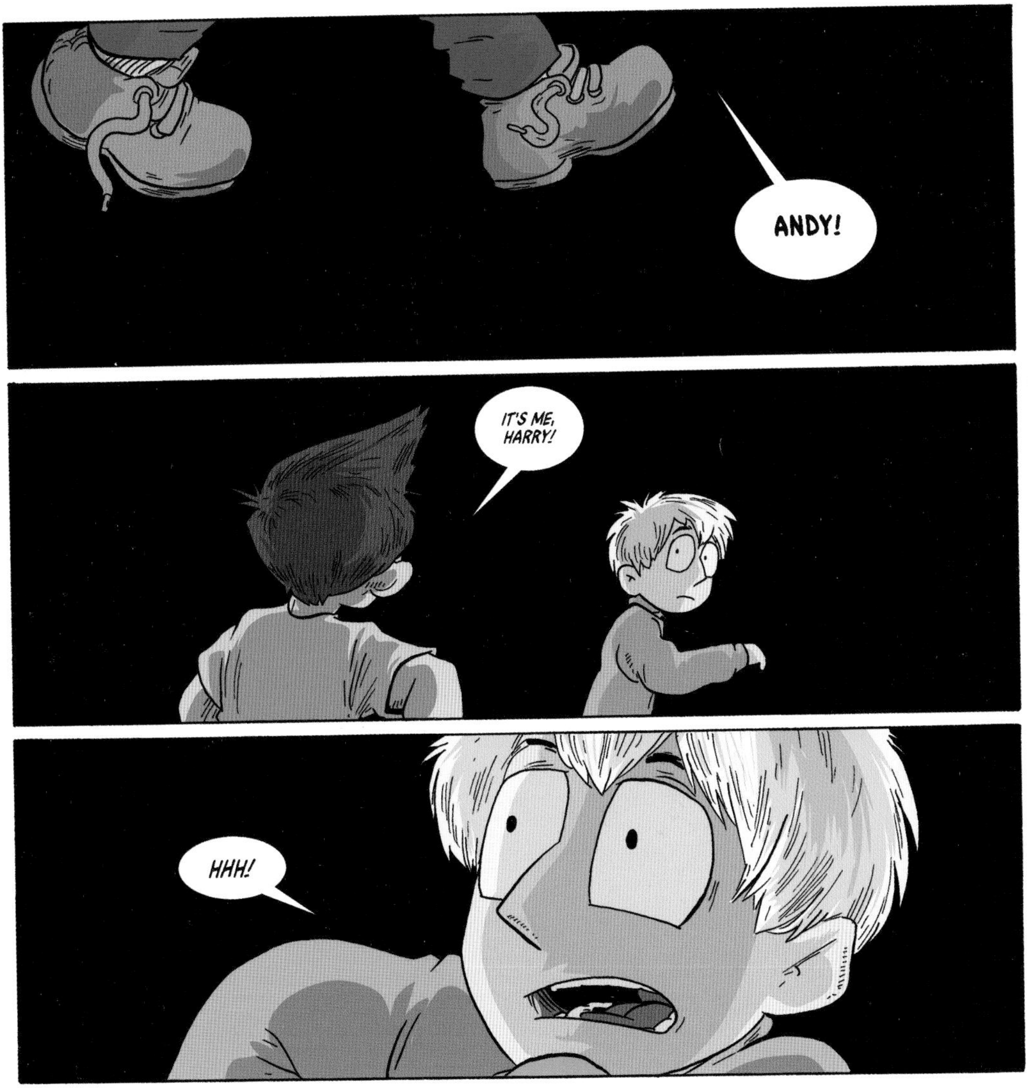
ANDY!
IT'S ME, HARRY!
HHH!

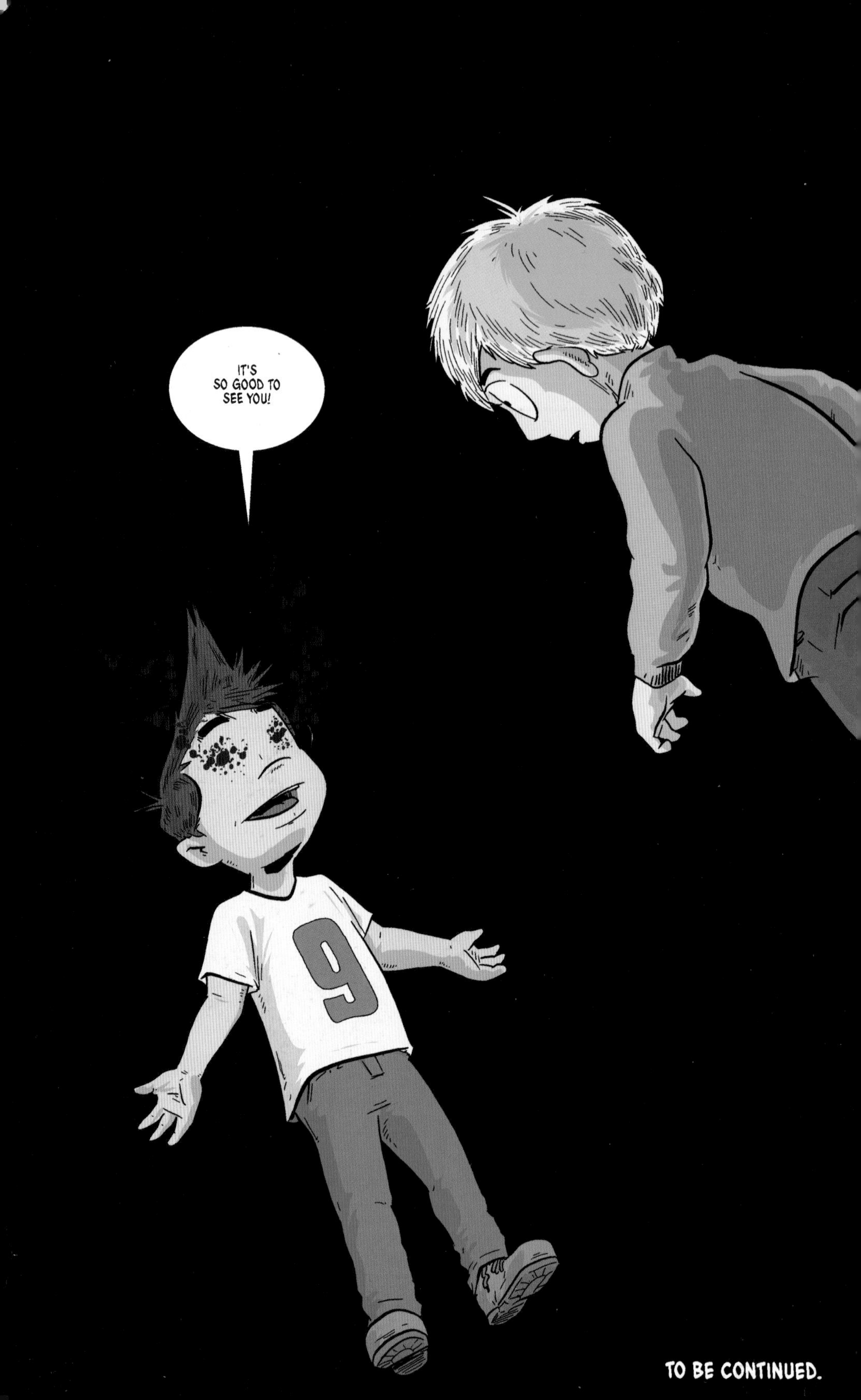
IT'S SO GOOD TO SEE YOU!
TO BE CONTINUED.

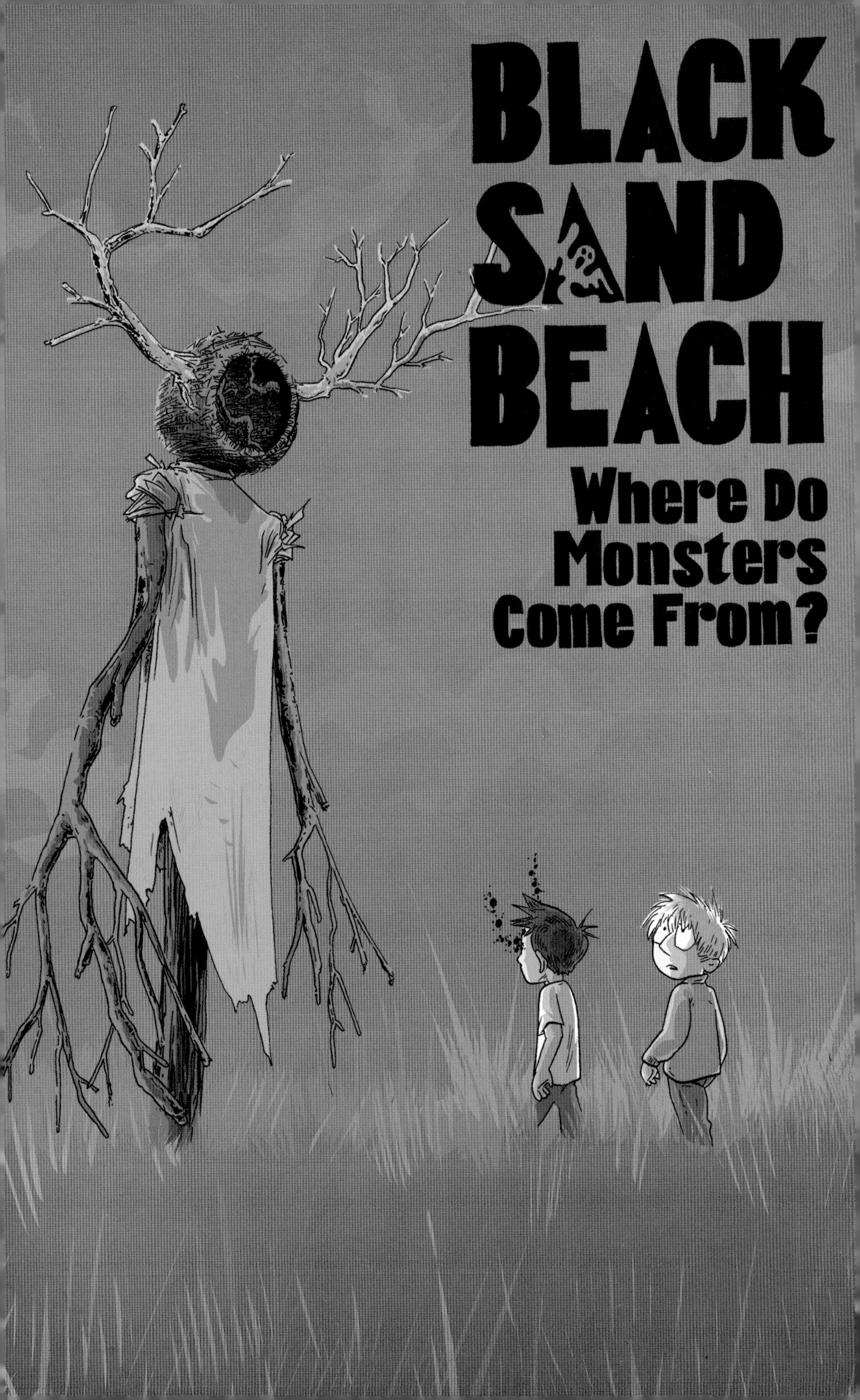
BLACK SAND BEACH
Where Do Monsters Come From?

RICHARD FAIRGRAY

Somewhere in the frozen depths of Canada sits Richard Fairgray. He hunches over his table scribbling trees and sand and monsters as his mind races to come up with new stories. Pink noise crackles through speakers on either side to drown out the world. His home is filled with skeletons and teeth and dogs of varying sizes.

Each night he stops for five hours to sleep and refuel. His dreams are filled with octopuses and ghosts and a low rumbling sound that he is sure is going to start telling him things any day.

His back hurts and his hand is cramping, but he has no choice but to get these stories onto paper.

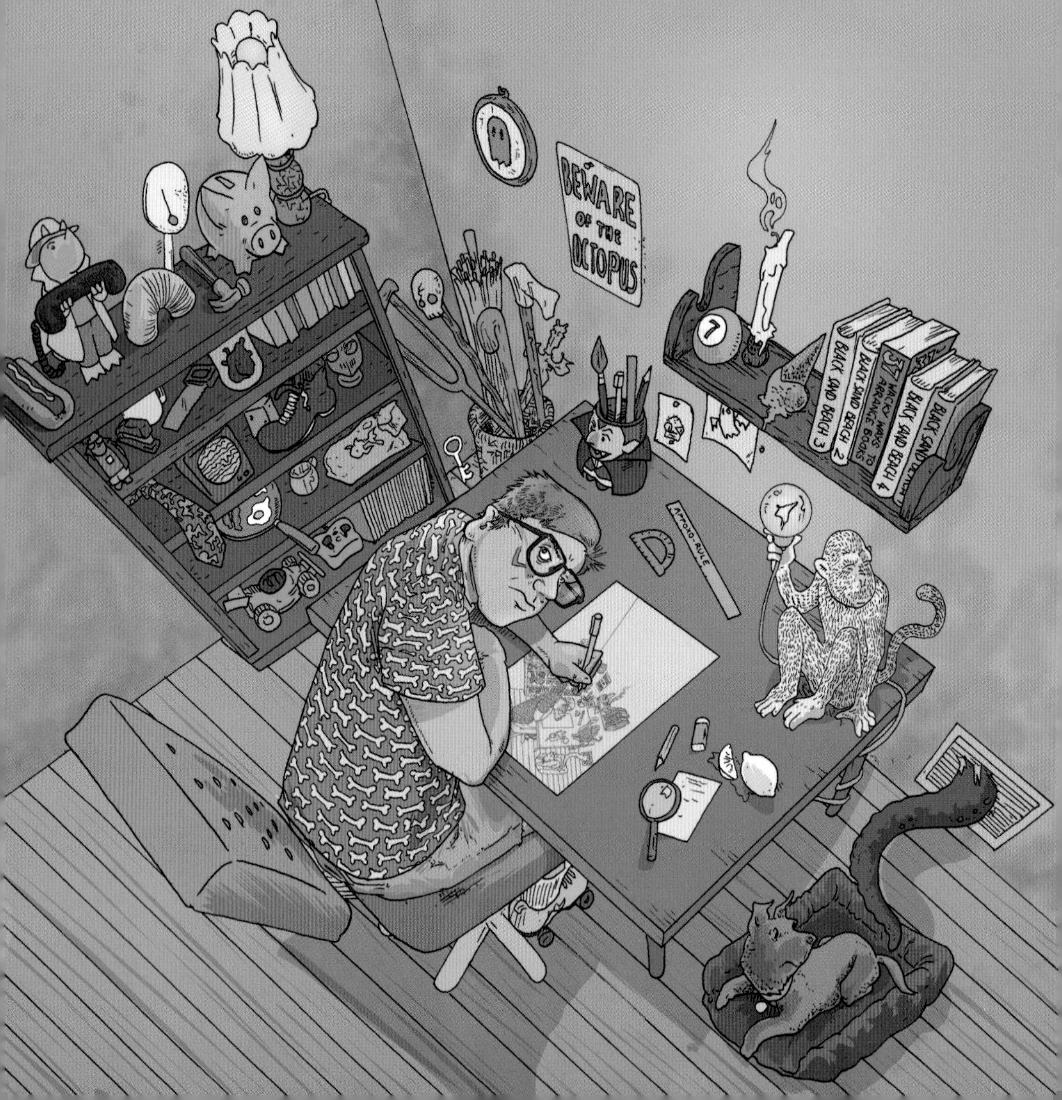
BEWARE OF THE OCTOPUS
BLACK SAND BEACH 3
57 WACKY WAYS TO ARRANGE BOOKS
BLACK SAND BEACH 2
BLACK SAND BEACH 4

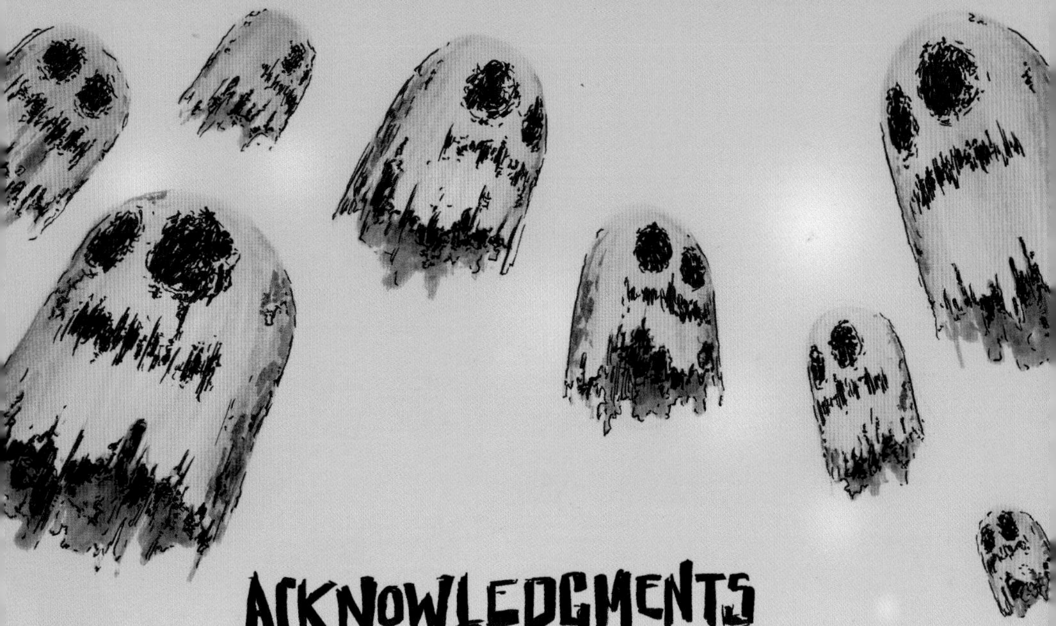

ACKNOWLEDGMENTS

This book was made during a very difficult year, not just for me, but for the whole world. Our ability to reach out to friends and family was tested and limited, and those of us who got through it relied on small handfuls of people.

Hierarchies of distance were wiped out and unexpected connections were made across continents. For me, those people were a lifeline.

This book also helped. This story kept me focused (obsessed, perhaps) and the world of Black Sand Beach became my refuge within my own house.

Tony, RE, Charlie, Lucy, Indira, Alex, Barbra, Bryant, Tilly, Susan, David, and the rest of the Saturday morning Zoom calls, and (of course) my husband, Raymond - this book could easily have been discarded with so many other things if it hadn't been for your presence in my life.

The support of Vicki and Bethany was as invaluable as ever.

The engineering genius of Paul Wolff cannot and will not be understated.

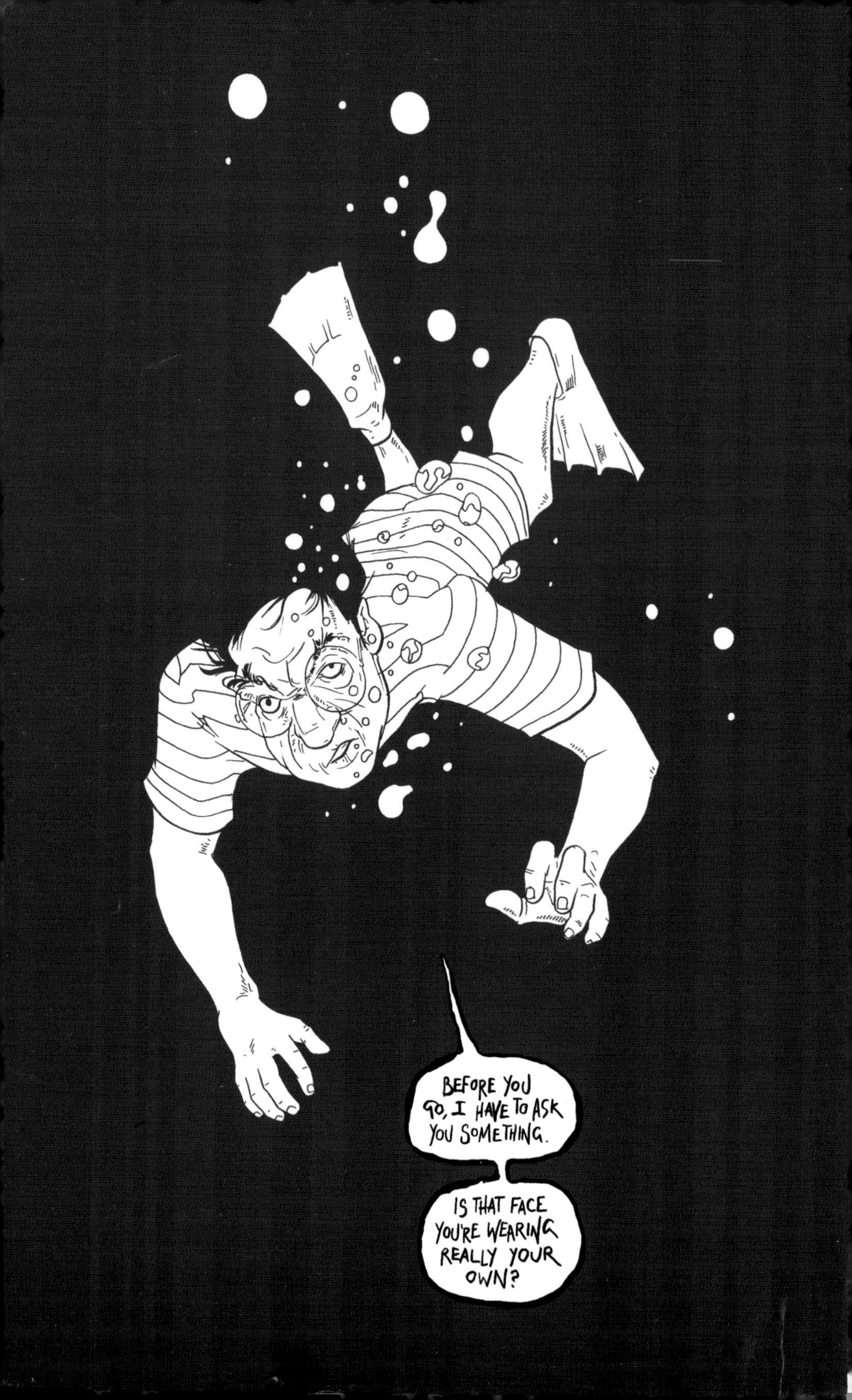
BEFORE YOU GO, I HAVE TO ASK YOU SOMETHING.
IS THAT FACE YOU'RE WEARING REALLY YOUR OWN?